worcestershire
countycouncil
Libraries & Learning

D0227307

Malcolm Walker

WALKER
BOOKS

This is a work of fiction. Names, characters, places and incidents are either the product of the author's imagination or, if real, are used fictitiously. All statements, activities, stunts, descriptions, information and material of any other kind contained herein are included for entertainment purposes only and should not be relied on for accuracy or replicated as they may result in injury.

First published in Great Britain 2009 by Walker Books Ltd
87 Vauxhall Walk, London SE11 5HJ

2 4 6 8 10 9 7 5 3 1

This book has been typeset in Garamond

Printed and bound in Great Britain by Clays Ltd, St Ives plc

British Library Cataloguing in Publication Data:
a catalogue record for this book is available
from the British Library

ISBN 978-1-4063-2151-7

www.walker.co.uk

In memory of my parents,

Rene and Howard

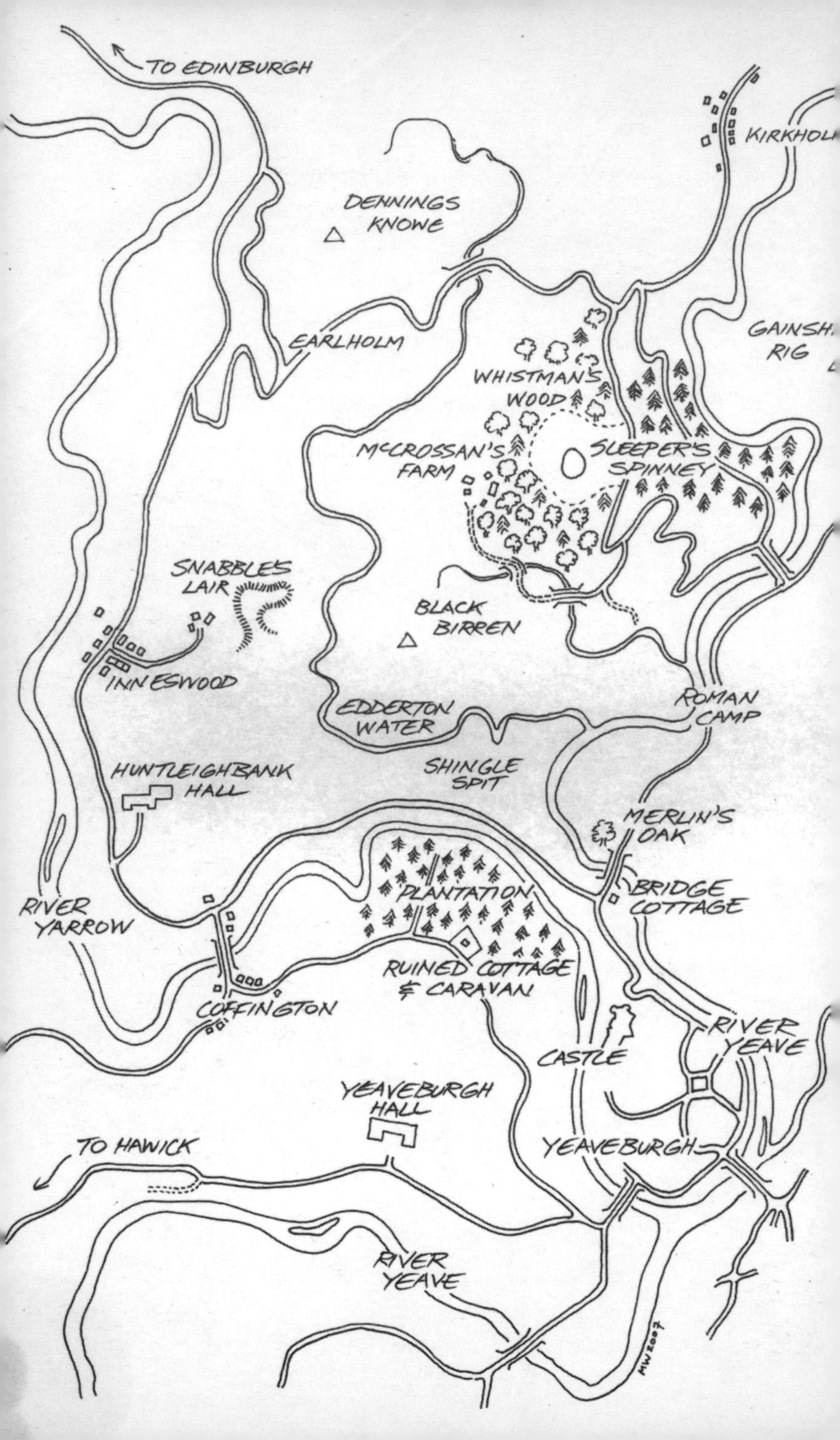
TO EDINBURGH
KIRKHOL
DENNINGS KNOWE
GAINSH RIG
EARLHOLM
WHISTMAN'S WOOD
McCROSSAN'S FARM
SLEEPER'S SPINNEY
SNABBLE'S LAIR
BLACK BIRREN
INNESWOOD
EDDERTON WATER
ROMAN CAMP
SHINGLE SPIT
HUNTLEIGHBANK HALL
MERLIN'S OAK
BRIDGE COTTAGE
PLANTATION
RIVER YARROW
RUINED COTTAGE & CARAVAN
COFFINGTON
RIVER YEAVE
CASTLE
YEAVEBURGH HALL
TO HAWICK
YEAVEBURGH
RIVER YEAVE
MW 2007

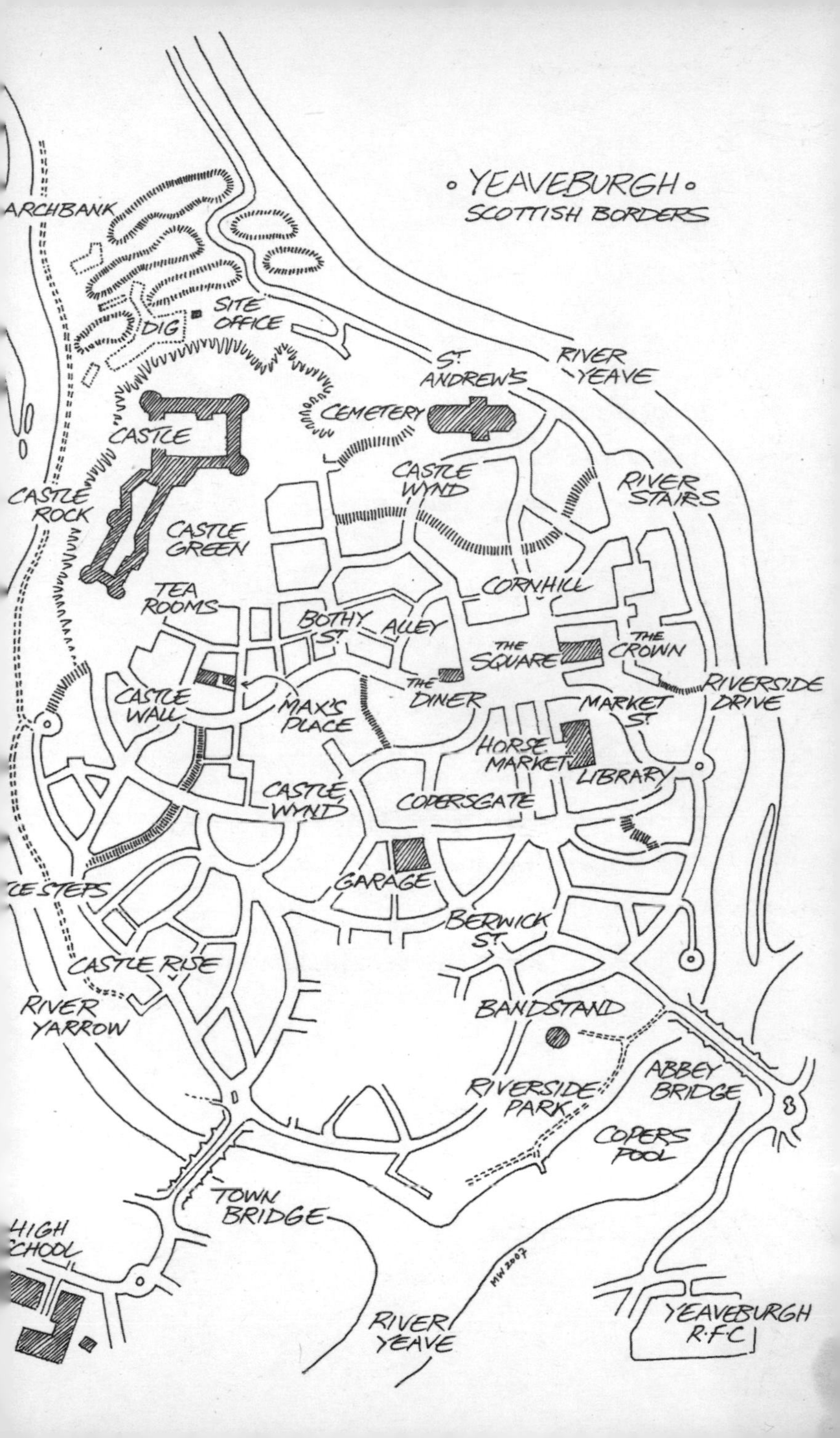
YEAVEBURGH
SCOTTISH BORDERS
ARCHBANK
DIG
SITE OFFICE
ST. ANDREW'S
RIVER YEAVE
CEMETERY
CASTLE
CASTLE ROCK
CASTLE WYND
RIVER STAIRS
CASTLE GREEN
TEA ROOMS
CORNHILL
BOTHY ST.
ALLEY
THE SQUARE
THE CROWN
THE DINER
RIVERSIDE DRIVE
CASTLE WALL
MAX'S PLACE
MARKET ST.
HORSE MARKET
LIBRARY
CASTLE WYND
COPERSGATE
GARAGE
CE STEPS
BERWICK ST.
CASTLE RISE
RIVER YARROW
BANDSTAND
ABBEY BRIDGE
RIVERSIDE PARK
COPERS POOL
TOWN BRIDGE
HIGH SCHOOL
MW 2007
RIVER YEAVE
YEAVEBURGH R·F·C

Foreigners shall return among them
And breech the singing walls;
The long line dreads their coming.

Trapping time with his crystal eye
The cloaked one comes from the South.
His search is for one who is lost.

The raven girl gathers all to her.
Black arms take the mighty to the flame
And their madness falls upon the earth.

QUATRAIN V, VI AND VII
THE PROPHECIES OF THE LADY VIVIENNE

PROLOGUE

A ragged circle of armed horsemen, we shift uneasily in our saddles as our mounts stand patiently in the snow. We are waiting on Arthur. He kicks his mare forward a few paces and the girl feels the point of his lance prick her shoulder. Blood trickles over skin. She shudders and looks about wildly.

It is then, in her confusion and fear, she sees us.

Her eye moves out beyond the tight ring of spears, away from the dying fire, into the trees and the darkness crowding in on all sides. Merlin's oft-repeated words come back to me. Death, he would say, is a fey companion and will drink from any well.

Two others, a man and boy, stumble into the clearing. The man stands a moment and then begins to chant. The lad staggers forward, sinking to his knees near the fire. In a single leap the girl clears the flames and Arthur's lance finds air instead of flesh.

The man is on his hands and knees in the snow. He sings on in defiance. But this is Arthur's hour and, tossing his lance to me, he dismounts and draws his sword. The bitter touch of the blade is beneath the girl's jaw; the cold breath of iron rises in her nostrils.

Arthur's eyes are on her and she knows his cold desire.

MONDAY

1

'You're a complete tosser, Hugh McCrossan, you know that?'

The rising wind carried the girl's voice over the fields to where Emlyn was wedged high in an oak at the edge of Whistman's Wood. Pushing aside the heaving foliage, he trained his binoculars towards Sleeper's Spinney. The low dry-stone wall filled his view, its neat stonework separating the island of Scots pine, beech and ash trees from the surrounding pasture as it curved out of sight around the edge of the spinney. Emlyn adjusted the focus. The two figures stood on the uphill slope, arguing, but the wind, which seemed set on pushing a bank of thunderclouds up behind the hill, carried away their voices and Emlyn caught only the odd word as the girl jabbed the air with her finger.

He pushed the binoculars around behind his back and levelled his camera. With its powerful telephoto lens, their faces leapt at him, every detail sharply in focus. The girl was dressed completely in black: a short clingy dress or skirt, a cheap nylon jacket, black tights and Doc Martens. Yeah, I recognise you now, even without the uniform, he thought. He searched for a name. Martine? No – Maxine. Max: that was it. He'd seen her go ballistic when someone had called her Maxine. She'd come up recently from Newcastle to live with her grandmother. Another newcomer just like me, thought Emlyn.

The burly youth turned away and headed uphill towards the woods. Emlyn had recognised him immediately: there was little love lost between him and Hugh McCrossan. This was McCrossan land; they owned half the valley. And where there was one McCrossan there could easily be others. Instinctively, Emlyn checked for movement, his eye running from the road, up across the horseshoe of arable land, with its patchwork of fields and low dry-stone walls, back to where Sleeper's Spinney sat crown-like atop a grassy hummock. Nothing. Just the girl, who was still alongside the wall, watching Hugh's receding figure until he disappeared among the trees.

'You're game, Max, I'll give you that,' muttered Emlyn, 'hanging around that place on your own.'

Only once had Emlyn been up alongside the brooding knot of trees and then the urge to run had been overpowering. Instead, he had steeled himself to pace out the distance around the wall. At several thousand strides he lost count and gave up, disturbed by the heavy sensation of electrical discharge in the air and a feeling that he was being watched. Since then he'd given the spinney a wide berth; the place gave him the willies, so much so he'd gone a considerable distance out of his way, lugging his camera gear up through the woods rather than taking the shorter route straight across the fields.

'Enough,' he muttered. He could forget the shots he'd come for. The wind had shifted and neither the vixen nor the cubs would show themselves now. Time to go. But Max was heading straight for the bottom gate. His bike was hidden nearby. He couldn't follow her across the fields without taking the chance of being seen and he had no intention of letting her know he'd been spying on her.

'Smartest move'll be down through the wood, boyo, and then she'll never know you were here.' He started down through the branches, one hand cradling his precious telephoto lens. His feet found the branches automatically as he eased himself groundward, the image of her pale face in his lens niggling at him.

A clatter of falling rock made him glance across. Capstones, and then smaller rocks, tumbled into the spinney. Bracing himself in a fork of the tree, Emlyn watched as Max kicked at the dyke with her foot. She was really going at it, demolishing a short section of wall – but why?

She slowed and then stopped, breathing hard. Then, without warning, she hopped through the gap into the spinney, placed her boot against the stonework and pushed. A section of the wall bulged, teetered and crashed into the field. A heavy, lichen-encrusted capstone refused to follow. Crouching, she leant into it, pushing jerkily until, with a grating noise, it toppled onto the turf. Stepping through into the field, Max spat at the rubble and strode away towards the road.

Emlyn stared after the hurrying figure and shivered. With the girl's retreat came a shadowy darkness, as if her diminishing form could bleed the light from everything. A feeling of dread swept over him. He no longer wanted to be in the woods alone. In his haste to reach the ground, he slipped and slithered down the trunk, skinning his wrist as he tried to protect the lens. He caught a low branch and swung out, searching blindly for the top of the paddock wall with his foot, his neck still craned in Max's direction.

Cold thrills prickled his skin.

A horseman materialised in mid-leap through the breach in the spinney wall. Emlyn heard the thud of hooves as the animal landed; through his field glasses he could see the knotted veins on the man's arms as he turned his mount, the jutting red beard, the grizzled hair wild beneath his steel cap. For a moment the rider faced Emlyn and a voice filled his head.

Twice we have been freed, boy, only to be caught again. This time it shall be different.

He watched, open-mouthed, as the rider twitched aside the patched and tattered cloak, and urged his mount to a canter. A sword gleamed in the evening light.

A thin skein of madness seemed to bind Emlyn, paralysing him. It was what he feared most: that the same madness that had consumed his father – hospitalised him only weeks before they'd arrived in Yeaveburgh – ran in his blood.

Further down the field Max hurried on, oblivious.

In his confusion, a loose capstone turned beneath Emlyn's boot and he crashed backwards into the field, his half-cry, half-warning loose before he could stop himself. For several seconds he lay sprawled in front of the wall, the wind knocked from him, struggling to catch his breath amid the pungent odour of sheep droppings. Groaning, he scrambled up, checking his precious camera.

The horseman flashed into his head and he glanced up just as the cloaked rider disappeared. The only movement was Max, working her way back up the slope towards him.

Desperately, he struggled to hold the image – the tattered cloak and leggings, the embossed shield, the chain-mail surcoat – tried to make sense of what he had seen. He *had* glimpsed the horse – seen the divots flying from its hooves. He reached out, steadying himself on the wall, the stones rough under his hand. They were real enough. But so was Max. She had stopped a short distance away and was staring at him.

'I've seen you before – school.' She spoke with a mixed accent: Geordie-Scots or Scots-Geordie – he couldn't really tell. 'You're the new'n. Normally sit in trees and snoop on people, do you?'

'Nah, course not.'

'What then?' She cocked her head slightly. 'This some pathetic attempt to pick me up?'

'*Nah!*'

'You want to be careful dropping out of trees like that; people might think you're overripe.' She snorted at the joke and then scanned the field quickly, jerking her head in the direction of the spinney. 'Say anything about *that* and you're dead, like.'

'Hey, you want to go round knocking holes in walls–'

'Dykes. They're called dykes in Scotland.'

'Dykes – walls – it's no skin off my nose.' But he knew he didn't sound convincing: he was too rattled. In his mind he could hear the hooves still; see the sword cleave the evening air. It was there, he thought, the rider; it was bloody well there. It had to be one of the locals, some weirdo ... but it had disappeared. Nah, he must be mistaken, trick of the evening light or something. But what? 'Look–' he said, waving in the direction of the spinney. 'Really. I'm not interested.'

'Mebbe, mebbe not.' The girl screwed up her face and shrugged. 'But ... new school, make an impression, all that guff.'

'Hey,' said Emlyn, 'we're both new.'

'There's new and there's new.'

The girl's cockiness made him feel awkward.

'Why'd'yer yell like that anyway?' she said. 'Scared me witless.'

'A horseman jumped through that hole you … I thought it was coming after you.'

'What horseman?' she said.

'Come on, you must've seen it. You'd turned around – you were walking back. Had a cloak and a …' She was looking at him strangely and he trailed off. 'Anyway, I fell – thought I'd hurt myself, didn't I.'

'You're having me on, right,' said Max, 'about the rider, 'cause sure as hell I'd have heard a friggin' horse thundering up behind me.'

Somewhere in the valley a woodpecker drilled into the dusk. It was getting chilly now that the sun had sunk behind the hills. He looked around, trying to shrug off his uneasiness and the girl's relentless stare. He felt split, confused. He'd blurted out about the rider but she hadn't seen it – she was sure to think he was some sort of deadset loony. School was tough enough already, without any more labels.

'Maybe you're just overripe,' she chuckled, 'in more ways than one. Mind, you don't look bruised.' She stifled another laugh and looked him up and down. 'Well, not the sort to hurt hisself too easy, like. Saw you in the school cross-country. Everyone were going bananas. You could'a won easy, man, but you came second. How come?'

'I was county champion back home.' He bit his lip: he'd revealed too much. 'Dunno. Didn't feel like it, I s'pose.'

'Anyway, remember,' she said, turning down towards the road, 'if anyone hears about this, you're dead.'

Emlyn studied Max's retreating back for a second time. She was as tall as he was, but slender and with an unruly shock of spiky black hair. He shifted his gaze across to the ragged tear in the wall. The spinney held him. Time seemed to collapse, its usual broad river diminished to a trickle. He shook his head, breaking free of the spell, and checked his camera quickly. Damn it, the lens cap was missing. By the time he found it, Max was almost to the road.

'Wait up,' Emlyn yelled.

He rushed down the hill, his boots sucking at the sodden pasture. The wooded slopes he'd circled up through earlier in the day now seemed to harbour an unseen presence. Thunder rumbled in the hills and below him the autumn evening hung like a heavy curtain across the valley. The girl's steady retreat was contagious.

He ran on, scanning the horizon, the woods and dykes, slipping and regaining his balance as he did so. Nothing – no sign of the rider, no movement, just the girl, who was already over the gate and astride her bike. The last dry-stone wall stood between him and the road. Vaulting it, he tried to talk himself down.

'Steady, *steady*. You're overreacting as usual!'

But despite his rationalisations, he found himself down at the gate, breathing hard. His pushbike was on the other side, hidden in the drainage culvert. He always stashed it there: this was McCrossan land and nobody wanted to be caught up here.

Max was already well down the hill, pedalling furiously, but he'd catch her, no trouble. He glanced over his shoulder. The fields were empty. What the hell had he seen? Jumping from the gate, he hauled his bike from the culvert.

2

Who is this that speaks, I hear you say?

Cei, son of Cynyr, Arthur's sergeant-at-arms – and it is my words that trouble the boy as I turn my horse to face him. Could this be he, I ask myself? Could this be the boy spoken of in the prophecies? Can there be hope after so long?

And the raven girl, as she walks away, what of her?

I urge my mount to a canter. I would give chase but it is hopeless. The stone ring and the Lady's song bind us here and cannot be broken and the girl, she would not see me anyway, would not hear my words even if I caught her.

No, he is our one chance.

He sees me well enough, hears my words.

To break free of the Lady's prison, that is all we crave, and to put an end to this living hell.

How I yearn for the dark waters of death to fold over me.

3

Max pumped the pedals, and the bike, old and rusting though it was, flew down the hill.

First Hugh, dragging her up into the middle of nowhere, only to turn up late and then dump her, and then that jerk, the new kid, 'Binocular Boy', in a tree spying on her. For sure he'd seen her kick the spinney wall over. And all that camera gear! If he'd taken a photo … that was all she needed: a damage to private property report lodged at the local nick and on McCrossan land too – she was in enough strife as it was.

She let the bike coast, allowing her thoughts to unravel with the road.

The ride up from the town had taken longer than she had allowed for, and then there was the walk up through the fields. She'd had to clamber over two dykes on her way up; her precious Doc Martens were caked in muck. Who the hell did Hugh think he was? He could have given her the kiss-off in town, but no, he had to drag her out there and leave her standing around in the middle of a field looking like an idiot, like some sodding farm animal alongside a wall. And what was all that shite about waiting on the side away from the road? Kicking that dyke over had tasted sweet. Yeah, let the bloody McCrossans rebuild it. They were always fiddling with it anyway.

The bike coasted into a bend and she let the wind shred her anger.

'Wait up!'

An expensive-looking mountain bike shot in alongside Max. She was so startled, her front wheel wobbled and she nearly lost control.

'What's your hurry?'

'You might like getting soaked' – Max jerked her head back in the direction of the hills, where thunderheads loomed dark and forbidding – 'but I dinna, see.'

'Where'd you get the antique?'

'It's m'gran's, if you must know.'

Bloody Binocular Boy! The cheeky sod meant her bike. What the hell was his name? Some lads had been giving him a hard time outside the school gates.

Yeah, Emlyn, that was it. Daft bloody name anyway. What was it, Welsh or something? She upped the pace, setting her mouth in a hard line, but her bike had languished in her gran's garage for years and he kept up easily. Then came the questions. The usual crap lads came up with: where was she from; did she like living in the Borders; what sort of things was she into? She grunted yes or no or not much accordingly, until finally they lapsed into an awkward silence, their front wheels passing and re-passing as they dropped down the valley towards the river.

Letting him inch ahead, Max studied him, trying to work him out. He was tall and angular, a feature accentuated by the bicycle, which was too small for him. His dark hair was tied back in a short ponytail over a long, white scarf and an army-surplus greatcoat flapped in his wake; a khaki box, held by a webbing strap, slipped for the umpteenth time and he wedged it around to his back. Wiry, but athletic, she mused. He'd gone great guns in the school cross-country, cruising home ahead of Hugh, who'd come third instead of his usual second – something he'd been dead narked about. She was smiling to herself, enjoying the thought of Hugh's defeat, when Emlyn grinned at her over his shoulder. Max scowled and leant over the handlebars in an attempt to pass him.

Down on the river flats near the town her bicycle slowed considerably. Taking it easy, she watched as he reached the point where the road narrowed to a single lane and passed over the River Yeave. At the top of the stone bridge he stopped and leant over the parapet wall, staring down at the water without dismounting. She'd seen him before – when she'd come past with her gran on the bus to Hawick – doing that, staring at the river.

Moments later, the bridge lifted Max and sent her coursing down the far side, the water murmuring against the cutwaters as she passed. Ahead, the town sign loomed in the dusk.

WELCOME TO
ROYAL BURGH OF
YEAVEBURGH
SCOTLAND IN BLOOM
AWARD WINNER

Flowers, fields and fishing: prison more like, she thought. God, I miss Tyneside: crowds, the city. Well, if you hadn'a gone and got yourself caught, you silly cow, you'd still be there.

'Wait up!' came the cry.

Max clenched her teeth, gripping the handlebars tighter. If he said that one more time …

4

Emlyn listened to the sound of the stream parting against the cutwaters. The bridge was a favourite place of his. He often leant on the parapet wall and watched the river slide past. Now he simply wanted the green, rolling water to wash away the voice he'd heard up at the spinney. He hung his head. What had it meant '*freed twice, only to be caught again*' and what would '*be different*'? Max rode up and coasted past him down the town side of the bridge. He'd tried to talk to her on the way back, get the image of the horseman out of his head, but she wasn't having any of it. She'd kicked down the wall, the dyke, and then he'd seen … No, he mustn't let it get a grip. He squeezed the words away, shutting them out.

'Wait up,' he yelled. Pushing off from the parapet,

he chased her down and slewed to a halt in front of her. Brake blocks squealed on wheel rims as her bike shuddered to a halt.

'What the hell do you think you're doing? Get outta ma road, like.'

'So – why'd you kick it over?'

'D'ya ever let up, or what? I mean, what is this, twenty questions? Besides, why the hell were you up a tree, spying on me?'

'I take photographs: birds, animals – nature stuff.'

'Oh my God, *a twitcher*!'

'Rack off,' said Emlyn, thinking she meant he had a tic.

'A birdwatcher, dopey.' The smile disappeared. 'You take any photos of me up there?'

'*No-oh!*'

'Bit old for that kinda thing, aren't you?'

'What–?'

'For crawling around in the bushes taking pictures?'

'What's that supposed to mean?'

'We're in the same year, so, you gotta be fifteen, mebbe sixteen. You could try acting it, like?'

'It's an interest of mine,' he said. 'Okay.'

'An interest. A man with a *hobby*, eh?'

'You always meet your boyfriends in the middle of a field?'

'Let's get one thing clear: he's no' ma boyfriend,' said Max. 'He picked something up for me, if you must know. Something for ma bike.' Emlyn looked askance at the battered frame and rusting wheels. 'Not this bike, stupid,' she added.

'So-rry.' Emlyn let the singsong tone register. Max opened her mouth to say something caustic but he kept going: 'Hey, look, the thing up at the spinney – yelling like that, scaring you–'

'Scaring yourself more like.'

'That's not what … Look, why don't we just try starting again.' He pointed at a two-storey cottage set back from the road, the only dwelling between the edge of town and the bridge. Light seeped from behind the curtains. 'Bridge Cottage, we're renting it.'

'From the McCrossans; yeah, I know.'

A brilliant flash lit up the darkening fields as the storm broke with unexpected viciousness over the valley. The strike was so close they both jumped. A creaking wail came from down near the river. Lightning had struck an oak; a huge bough separated from the main trunk and came to rest against one of the lower branches, leaving a fresh white scar in the gloom.

'You see that?'

'Aye,' she said, frowning. 'Problem is you're moments away from parking your arse in your cosy little holiday cottage, and I've a mind not to get soaked on the way home, remember. So move your bike – you're in my road.'

'My mum's working here.'

'Yeah, well, you've the cushy end of the McCrossans. We rent off those bastards, an' all, 'cept ma gran's place is a shite-hole in comparison.' She jiggled her front wheel clear and cocked her pedal. 'Remember, mention *anything* – you're a goner.'

'I've got the message, don't worry.'

'The McCrossans give me the creeps but that spinney's creepier.'

'Meaning?' said Emlyn.

'Buggered if I know. Look, pal, I've lived around here off and on – well, more off than on – for most of ma life, an' I'm telling you something weird goes on up there. You've seen the state of the dykes. The McCrossans don't give a toss. If they fall over, they string a bit of wire across and leave it to rust. But not the spinney. If they spent as much time on ma gran's place, she'd be living in a palace.'

The first fat drops of rain hit the road.

'It's coming on,' said Max, 'an' I'm outta here.' As she set off towards the Marchbank, the ancient tree-covered earthworks at the foot of Castle Rock, the wind whipped her voice back at Emlyn. 'And don't worry yourself; them stones'll be back all nice and neat again tomorrow.'

'What?' he shouted. 'Hey! What d'you mean *back again*? Hey, wait up!'

5

Soaked from the storm, Hugh McCrossan left the wood and crossed the pasture onto the dirt track. Ahead, he could see the lights and the ramshackle spread of farm buildings. Hunching against the wind, he trudged up the valley, his thoughts on Max and how he'd given her the flick. People saw him as tough because he was big and didn't say much. Max had liked that. Hah! Not any more, boy; not after that little performance.

* * *

She'd been down by the spinney as he had stepped clear of the trees. He'd hesitated at the edge of the wood, wondering why he had chosen to meet her out here. The place left him feeling edgy, always had done, but it was too late to turn back – she was already waving.

He started down the hill. It was as if he was being reeled in, like one of the big salmon taken down at the pool – no fight left. He really didn't want to do this. He hated arguments, conflict. And then he was standing in front of her. She had smiled and reached out her hand but he kept his in his pockets.

Her face had changed then. 'So … what's all the secrecy, like?'

'Won't be seeing you. On Wednesday night.'

'You haven'a dragged me out here to tell me that. Besides, you said you'd a surprise for me.'

He fished in his coat pocket, pulled out a greasy plastic bag and handed it to Max. 'Carburettor. Wreckers over at Innerleithen. Should fit. It's the same model.'

Max took the package and stared at him.

'Canna see you any more,' he said. There, it was out. Simple, really: in the end, you just said it.

'What you on about?'

'Me dad, and ma grandad, they've said, you know … we canna hang around together.'

'An' you're gonna let them tell you who you can and canna see?'

'It's not like that.'

'What's it like, then?'

He looked everywhere but at her. 'I'm not really ... interested ... any more.'

She was steaming now, he could tell. 'You're a complete tosser, Hugh McCrossan, you know that? A total *dead loss,* man!'

'You've your bits. Quit your complaining. All the bloody same, you girls.'

She squinted at him. 'An' the Beezer?'

'What is it with you and motorbikes?' he said. 'What about it, anyway?'

'I can't get it running without your help, not the carburettor, anyway.'

'I'll see if I can get over.'

'Don't do me any favours.'

'I've to get back,' he had said. 'Help with the pigs.'

He had waited for a response, but Max just stared through him until he turned away up the field.

* * *

Hugh was so deep in thought he nearly walked into the rusting hulk of the tractor that had stood for decades just inside the gate. The farm buildings loomed through the rain and mist as he crossed the yard. He lifted the latch and the wind ripped the back door from his fingers, slamming it against the side of the dresser.

'Shut it, pronto! It's cold enough in here without you making it worse.' His grandfather eyed him from his chair, warming his hands on the Aga. Several empty stout bottles were lined up on the kitchen table. 'Where'd you take yourself off to, boy?'

Hugh stared back at the old man. Ol'man McCrossan was how everybody referred to his grandfather – the whole valley, further afield even. His small neat frame and well-groomed appearance belied the ugly reputation. But it was the face that always threw Hugh – the thin scar of a mouth, the beady eyes – that and the high reedy voice that cut everybody short. It was because of his grandfather and his dad – because of the two of them he'd had to chuck Max.

'Well? Or are you too high'n'mighty these days to answer your elders and betters, eh?'

'Been out in the workshop.'

'I didn'a hear you out there.'

'Wasn'a doing much – just thinking.'

His grandfather snorted. 'Too much time spent out in that shed, thinking on that engineering guff.

You can forget about that, you hear? Your place is here, boy.' His grandfather sucked his stout and dabbed his mouth with a tea towel. 'The pigs? You fed 'em?'

'Not yet.'

'Well, you better get on it then, eh?'

Stepping outside, Hugh wrestled the door shut. He should have told the silly old sod to get stuffed. 'You'll never get this engineering apprenticeship if you just give in to them like that,' he muttered and headed up across the muddy yard towards the piggery. Inside, his father was bent over, treating one of the sows. Rain lashed the tin roof. Looking up, his father shouted above the roar: 'That Fraser lass – you gave her the push?'

'Who I see is ma business,' said Hugh.

'Say something, did you?' Hugh shook his head. 'So – you gave her the flick like we said, because I'll no' have you hanging around with her. You understand, boy?'

Hugh nodded and got on with the job. A warm, earthy smell rose from the pens. He liked the pigs – uncomplicated, they were. Soon he was whistling. He'd shown Max who was boss. He didn'a need her. He didn'a need any of 'em. He was his own man.

6

How I long for death, for the sickle man to finish his work.

And I would be long dead, an honest warrior's death, but for the treachery of Vivienne, the Lady of the Lake – and likewise Merlin's deceit! It is because of them that our spirits lie imprisoned in the wood: Owein, Bedwyr, Gwalchmei, Peredur – all of Arthur's guard.

Twice we have been freed, only to be caught again.

This time it shall be different.

But what of Arthur, I hear you say, for he is renowned through all the lands?

Forget what you have heard of Arthur. He was never a king, although it was in his power to become one; nor was he crowned, except perhaps in death, a ragged crown of stones marking his burial place. His tale, like all stories, will reveal itself soon enough. It is the manner of the telling that matters, for we are nothing if we are not stories in the minds of others.

TUESDAY

7

The surface of the water danced above him as he sank between the massive stone piers of the bridge. The cord around his neck jerked tight and his body swung out into the current. Freezing water filled his lungs and he stopped struggling.

Shocked awake, Emlyn fumbled for the bedside lamp. It was the dream again. He sat up, letting the light push the terror away. The taste of river water was still in his mouth. The digital clock blinked off the minutes. It would be light soon. He rose, pulled on his clothes and crept downstairs into the kitchen. Easing the bolt on the door, he stepped out into the garden. The pre-dawn air held the scent of new-mown grass and roses. A pale tinge was appearing in the eastern sky as Emlyn crossed the bridge on his bike. He did not pause to stare over the parapet at the swirling water as he usually did: not this morning – the dream was still too real.

Forty minutes of hard uphill pedalling, and he was standing on the road, listening. Out of sight down the valley, someone whistled up a sheepdog. A faint bleating drifted up with the mist. No-one was about. He clambered over the gate.

Instead of skirting up through the woods as he had the previous day, he cut straight across the fields. Two dykes lay behind him; the third drew closer, the last between him and the spinney. He hesitated, letting his eye wander along the stonework. Max had been right; on McCrossan land most of the dry-stone walls were poorly maintained. To his right was a large break. A rusting length of barbed wire had been strung between a couple of droppers. Hardly enough to keep in livestock, he thought, eyeing another collapsed section nearby.

The first rays of the sun shouldered the hills along the valley, casting his shadow across the cropped grass: a giant finger reaching towards Sleeper's Spinney. He gazed at the close-packed trees. Unable to shake the feelings of the previous evening, he decided against the direct route across the field. Instead, he followed the wall until it ran up against the dyke that bordered Whistman's Wood. Once he was in among the trees, he worked his way steadily up to where he had first seen the horseman, running its appearance and sudden disappearance through his mind, wondering if he'd imagined it.

If the gap Max had made was to be repaired, it was yet to happen.

He stood at the edge of Whistman's Wood, close to where he had fallen into the field the previous evening. He had intended to jump the wall and cross to the spinney, but something held him back. Come on, he urged silently, get a grip: over the wall, across the field, and you're there. A scattering of sheep eyed him curiously and he measured the distance across the field yet again.

Just get on with it, boyo.

He'd already found a toehold when a stocky figure rounded the northern end of the spinney. Ducking instinctively, he put his eye to a chink in the wall. It was Lawrence McCrossan.

He had picked up bits and pieces about the McCrossans around the town: the grandfather, Ol'man McCrossan, had been the Marquess of Yeaveburgh's head gamekeeper, but was now retired. Lawrence McCrossan and his father ran a large farm, but their main business was renting moorland and woodland from the estate or local farmers and running shoots; they also had a big set-up rearing pheasant poults in one of the more isolated valleys.

Raising his head warily, he peered out through a notch where some larger stones had once sat. Yeah, it was Lawrence McCrossan all right. Emlyn had bumped into him once on rent day when he'd come instead of the grandfather. Trailing some distance behind, peeling bark from a hazel switch with a pocketknife, was Hugh McCrossan. Sodding Hugh, eh – champion toerag and crap distance-runner. Don't you just fancy you can handle yourself?

* * *

Hugh McCrossan studied his father – the frayed wax jacket, the mud-stained trousers and polished boots – hating everything he stood for. Why'd he drag me up here, anyway? What's he thinking? I've got better things to do than stand around here. He stared at the break in the dyke. Had to be Max, he thought. The hot pleasure of yesterday's meeting washed over him. She wouldn'a be feeling so cocky today.

He spat, pitched the stick into the spinney, and watched his father sort through the rubble that spilt onto the sheep-cropped turf. The daft old bugger was always down here checking the dyke around the spinney. Jeezus, I should just shoot off home while he's not looking.

But Hugh remained where he was. He had learnt early on to be wary of the polished stick his father carried – his shillelagh, as he called it. His father's quick tongue and even quicker temper was common knowledge, although it was his grandfather people really feared. Pity they'd left the dogs in the Land Rover, he thought; could've lobbed the stick for them.

The first stone clocked in place. A low tuneless song was on his father's lips. Hugh felt himself swallowed by it. It was like déjà vu, as the slow chanting washed over him. Memories spun silk-like in the bright morning and not all the memories were his. Pale shadows moved around him; faces flickered down through the years. How many times had he accompanied his father or grandfather to the spinney and stood watching as the wall was inspected and maintained? How many times had he been made to sing the old songs? How many generations of McCrossans had sung the songs and held the terror back? Why then could he not remember any of this when he was at school, or feeding the pigs or working on his bike? Why was it that he could only remember when he was here, watching his father or grandfather fixing the spinney wall?

You're in a dream, he thought. A dream within a dream and you need to wake up out of it. He struggled with the feeling, looking down at his hands and the pocketknife he was holding. A few minutes before he'd been doing something with it, but he couldn't remember what.

He turned his back on his father and stared out across the pasture to Whistman's Wood. But for all his mental effort he knew he wouldn't wake from whatever was happening to him, nor would he recall it once they walked back up through the woods to the farm. He knew that he would only remember it when he was back here again with his father singing the stones in place.

You're to be the next keeper.

The knowledge sat in him like a tiny flint, hard and immovable. He was tied to the valley and the ancient stones; tied to the songs that had been handed down through generations; tied to his twenty-first birthday when they would initiate him as the next in line, readying him until the time when his dad would stand aside as his grandfather had done. Until that time, they sung his memories from him, or sung them deep – so deep within his mind that he could not retrieve them.

But this time he would. This time he would make himself remember. Slowly he turned the knife and drew the blade across his hand and watched the blood well up.

He stared at the fleshy base of his thumb.

You've cut yourself. Remember why. Remember where.

Blood dripped onto the grass, his lips moved in silent unison with his father's, and all around the bright air seemed to hold a shadowy threat.

* * *

A tuneless singing drifted across the field. Whatever the language was, thought Emlyn, it wasn't English. He watched as Hugh McCrossan turned away from his father and drew a knife across his palm.

Behind Hugh, Emlyn saw the red-bearded horseman appear just inside the spinney wall. The man looked battered and bloodied, with one eye bruised and swollen. Lawrence McCrossan straightened and his singing increased in strength. Horse and rider stood immobile and then disappeared.

An unexplained sadness welled inside Emlyn and he turned from his spy-hole. He was being pulled up a long tunnel where everything got smaller and smaller and the sounds of the world grew fainter until only the echo of McCrossan's voice remained.

He shook his head violently in an attempt to clear the feeling. The sounds of the natural world crept back around him. Shifting his cramped leg, he pressed his eye against the crack again.

Lawrence McCrossan had almost completed the repairs. The last of the heavy capstones lay where it had tumbled into the field. It was as if no time had passed. Emlyn watched, puzzled, as McCrossan propped the slab on the wall, pulled something from his pocket and drew his hand several times across the underside of the stone before easing it into place. Emlyn felt for the binoculars that usually hung around his neck and remembered he'd left them under his bed.

Hugh was already walking back the way they had come. Lawrence McCrossan looked across the field in Emlyn's direction for several minutes and then followed his son up the slope.

Emlyn sat back against the wall. He felt shaky, nauseous. Why was he creeping around after strangers: first Max and now the McCrossans? The gamekeeper was nothing to him; Hugh even less. Everything felt out of kilter, as if he were rushing towards a far distant point. He rested his head against the cool stone.

Max had been right: the wall was back up.

Emlyn poked his head up. The gap was plugged with stonework so craftily laid that the mend was undetectable – at least from this distance, he thought. Time for a closer look. He clambered into the field and loped towards the spinney. Midway between his hiding place and the neatly repaired stonework he stuttered to a halt. The image of the rider shimmered in his mind. Things, people, didn't just disappear like that. The laws of science told him so. But he'd seen it: twice now. Was it still there, invisible to him, just beyond the dyke? The lichen-covered stones curved away on either side.

'Come on,' he breathed, 'it's just a pile of rocks.'

He put his head down, a trick he used in cross-country races when a gap seemed too great to close or the finish line was beyond reach, and walked on, stopping only when the wall, with its precariously balanced capstones, brought him to a standstill. Glancing up, he half expected the horseman to loom in his vision, but the spinney was empty. He moved closer and pulled at a stone, testing the work, pushing his fingers into a gap in order to get a better purchase. A capstone shifted slightly, trapping his hand. He pulled it free. His fingers were smudged with black. Charcoal: he'd used it last year in art.

He hauled the stone free and turned it over. Chiselled on the underside, and gone over several times, was a strange mark.

The crudely drawn shape seemed oddly familiar. He stared at it, but it was like a dream he couldn't recall, and he pushed the stone back into place. Bending down, he found two more loose stones and pulled them free. Nothing.

A little to the left was another, larger capstone flanked by several smaller wedges. He levered it to the edge and ducked down. The same distinctive design – a crude trident – blackened his fingers. He pushed the stone back into place. Blood pounded in his ears; or was it a dull echo of McCrossan's chanting? Around him the woods and fields were strangely silent. The voice echoed in his head again–

How I yearn for the dark waters of death to fold over me.

He twisted this way and that, the wall at his back, as he tried to find the source of the voice, but there was no-one in sight. He screwed his eyes shut and clamped his hands over his ears. 'No,' he said. 'Not this … not this … *please.*' The staff up at Huntleighbank said that his father heard voices. He willed the words away, and then, as if to escape them, he leapt the wall.

A watery silence descended around him.

The eerie stillness continued as he picked his way through the trees. The bracken-covered slope rose gently until he emerged in a small clearing, where the ground, a mixture of turf and ferns, rose again in a slight hump.

The grass was cropped short but he saw no sign of the rabbit or sheep droppings that littered the fields beyond. For a moment or two, he had an overwhelming sense that time had stopped, that he was trapped in a dream of someone else's making. He could no longer hear the birdsong that had been all around him earlier and he could see no movement among the branches. He cast about, looking for a sign of anything living: a spider's web amid the bracken, a bird's nest in the branches, anything.

Nothing.

It wasn't natural. His eye stopped at a faint line in the turf. It would have been unnoticeable but for the weak autumn sunlight slanting between the trees. There, another shadow running at right angles to the first. He knew what they were immediately: sods. He had helped his father lay turf at their old house. It had been one of the last things they'd done together.

Something was under those carefully placed pieces of grass. He knew it – but what? What would anyone hide out here? He was about to crouch down to inspect the grass when an image of Lawrence McCrossan flashed into his mind. He took off down the slope through the trees, and scrambled over the wall into the field.

He stopped, dead, where he landed. To his right a black labrador, stiff-legged, its lips curled back over its teeth, was walking towards him along the curve of the wall. Frantically, he tried to remember everything he had heard about dealing with dogs: no sudden movements; do not, under any circumstances, run; avoid eye contact. The muscles in his legs liquefied as an answering growl came from his left.

'I'd keep perfectly still, laddie.'

The gamekeeper was striding along the spinney wall towards him, swinging his polished stick.

8

Emlyn swept into the driveway and skidded to a halt on the gravel at the back of the cottage. He was breathing hard from his ride and still rattled from his encounter with Lawrence McCrossan and his dogs. The gamekeeper had made him promise never to set foot there again. Most disconcerting was the fact that it was now nearly midday. He could have sworn that he'd watched the McCrossans for less than an hour. But, when he had prised himself up from where he had been huddled behind the dyke, both the sun and his watch told another story.

The sun was gone now, devoured by black thunderheads, and the rain was just starting as he rolled his bike into the dilapidated iron shed at the end of the drive. The roar of the squall built around him as it lashed the tin roof. Bridget must either be over at the dig or in Edinburgh, he thought. Good thing too, he decided, as he ducked from the shed and sprinted to the back door. Another grilling from his half-sister was the last thing he wanted; he'd be glad when his mum got back from whatever conference or focus group she'd disappeared to.

There was a flurry of nails over slate as Emlyn opened the back door. Digger, his tail a blur, shot from his basket beneath the ancient porcelain sink and launched himself at Emlyn's chest.

'Hey, the winged wonder?' he said, catching the terrier. Scratching the pup's ears and nuzzling the wiry head with his chin, he walked from the gloom of the kitchen into the front room and stared out of the window. Outside, ragged clouds dumped rain on the hills.

'What's the go then, matey?' The Jack Russell leapt from his arms and into an armchair, where he stood defiantly laying claim to his territory. 'Hardly go for a you-know-what in this weather, now can we?'

Emlyn snapped his fingers and the terrier jumped to the floor.

'Good dog,' Emlyn said, grabbing a copy of the magazine *Telephoto* from the coffee table and slumping in an armchair.

School was no problem: his class were all off on some museum trip to Edinburgh that his mother had forgotten to sign for.

* * *

He was startled awake by Digger leaping onto his lap.

'Get down, you little bugger,' he said, dropping the terrier onto the carpet. He chuckled as Digger raced into the hall. 'You scared the crap outta me,' he called. 'And look at the state of my magazine.'

He glanced at his watch. He'd slept away a good portion of the afternoon. The rain had eased but the clouds still loomed ominously. It was on days like this, when the weather swept in from nowhere, that he missed his father. His mother did her best but it always felt as if they were calling to one another from different rooms, even when she hugged him. Not that he saw much of her lately, with her new appointment as head of Archaeology at Edinburgh; not that he wanted much in the way of hugs any more. It was the looming presence of his father that he missed most.

Shaking himself free of his mood, Emlyn glanced down. Digger was lying, leash in mouth, eyes pleading, at his feet.

He chuckled. 'Fancy a trot up the town, do we?'

He needed space to mull over what had happened at the spinney, somewhere high and airy where he could make sense of it all.

'Never mind the rain,' he said, grabbing an umbrella from the coat stand. 'We'll take another look at the castle. What do you reckon, eh?'

* * *

With Digger tucked under his arm, Emlyn paused in the gloom where the arch ran out beneath the twin towers of the barbican. He put him down and the terrier raced away across Castle Green, scattering a straggle of seagulls huddled miserably on the grass. He and Digger had just spent the last part of the afternoon on the windswept upper levels of the keep, huddled in a window embrasure.

Down here the narrow streets and old buildings seemed cluttered and claustrophobic. Up on the battlements he had been able, when the cloud lifted, to let his eye range out across the rooftops that ran from Castle Green down towards the town Square. From the Square, a tangle of streets led down to the Town Bridge and a glimpse of the Yarrow sliding away grey and menacing beneath its curtain of rain.

His sister had told him that packhorses had once used the narrow bridge. On the flats, a little downstream, was Copers Pool, where the Yeave changed course yet again as it looped back and joined its sister stream to form the elongated horseshoe of land on which the Old Town was built.

Staring out at the rain-shrouded Green, he remembered what Bridget had said – that the town was almost an island: it was only an accident of geology, the looming crag of Castle Rock, which separated the rivers. Behind him, beyond the Marchbank, stood Bridge Cottage and the narrow waist of land that separated the two rivers. Out of sight up the valley was Sleeper's Spinney. He slapped the thought away. Would he ever get used to this place? He missed the South. He thought back to the day they had arrived. It had been raining, same as today. There had been an argument, he couldn't recall what about, and he had left his mother and sister amid an avalanche of boxes and crumpled newspaper. The castle, on its windy height, had seemed another world.

A car droned up the hill. Its tyres made a bladdering sound on the cobbles, pulling Emlyn back into the present. The driver stopped outside The Castle Tea Rooms, got out and scurried inside. The building, crouching beneath the castle walls, beckoned to Emlyn, the cheery light of its mullioned windows a beacon against the lowering clouds. He whistled Digger and pulled a handful of change from his pocket. 'Just about enough.'

A bell jangled as he went in. A backpacker was flicking through the postcard display and an older couple sat staring disconsolately across the Green. Behind the counter the manager, a stubby middle-aged woman with ratty hair and chipped nail varnish, was wrapping cutlery.

'Would it be all right to bring my dog inside?' asked Emlyn.

'Look like a kennel, do we?' the woman said curtly, not looking up from her task.

'No, but he's only a Jack–'

'Dog-grooming parlour, then? Veterinary surgery?'

'No, I know this is a teashop–'

'No animals on the premises. Health reasons.'

'How much are the scones?' said Emlyn.

'Prices are on the board.'

'The scones then.'

The woman took his money, checked it and dropped it in the till, then went back to wrapping cutlery.

'Max–*ine*! Devonshire. No tea. When you're ready!'

The swing doors into the kitchen thumped and Max emerged. She glared at Emlyn, pulled a plate from the dresser and disappeared. Choosing a table near a window, Emlyn stared out at the Green. Max reappeared and came across to his table.

'What's your game, eh?' she whispered, tossing his order in front of him.

'Nothing! I was up at the castle.'

She stared pointedly out of the window at the curtain of rain and then squinted at him.

'Look, I came in out of that lot.'

Emlyn watched her walk away. The rain rattled against the windows and his thoughts drifted.

* * *

The other customers had long gone and the manager was clearing the things from his table when Max came through from the back, pulling on a black bomber jacket.

'Will you be needin' me tomorrow?' she asked stiffly.

'You'll get a call if I do.'

'Not too late, mind.'

'Huh, don't overvalue yourself, girlie. There's plenty where you came from.'

Max shot the manager a vicious glance and headed for the door. Emlyn hurried after her, only to find her crouched in the porch. Digger was up on his hind legs, dancing, his tail wagging furiously at the attention.

'Down, boy,' said Emlyn.

'Oh – he's yours.' A battered green Renault pulled into the tea room's car park. Max pushed Digger away and marched out into the rain. Thinking it was a game, the terrier ran alongside her, jumping at her legs. Emlyn followed, fumbling with the umbrella.

'Your dog's muddying ma tights.'

Emlyn snapped his fingers and Digger fell into heel.

'God, that Murcutt woman's got a gob on her like a ten-tonner,' Max said, increasing her pace. 'I've half a mind to tell her to shove it.'

The umbrella opened with a whump. Edging closer, Emlyn thrust it in front of them.

'What you playing at?'

'Keeping the rain off.'

'Bit of water never hurt anyone.' Emlyn moved the umbrella a little to one side. 'She's never a good word to say about anyone. Hey, I can't see where I'm going. You know what she said to me last week?

Lazy, she called me. Lazy! I'm the only one who does any work in that place. She just stands around giving orders, the stupid cow! Hold it down a bit,' she said, grabbing the shaft of the umbrella and lowering it, 'the rain's coming round the side. Got a name, has he?'

'Digger.'

'Tricks? Can he do any?'

'Yeah, he can do a couple of things.' Emlyn snapped his fingers and the dog ran ahead. 'Digger! Dance.' The terrier went up on two legs, waddling in front of them until he got tired of it and resorted to four again.

'Anything else?'

'Sits – stays, for ages, even if I'm not in sight. He's pretty smart. Aren't you, feller?'

With the pup no longer the focus, the conversation faltered. They were off the Green and down among the houses.

'You were right, the spinney wall was rebuilt – first thing this morning,' said Emlyn. 'Hugh was up there too.' Max shot him a look and increased the pace. Emlyn halted. One last try, he thought. 'Something's hidden up there.'

Max stopped to face him, and he found himself relating his early morning visit to the spinney, the recently disturbed turf, and his encounter with the gamekeeper, Lawrence McCrossan.

She snorted, shaking her head. 'Darghh, that doesn't mean anything. It's his land – his job.'

'That's not what you said yesterday,' said Emlyn.

'Dead narky I was yesterday. Real rattled.'

'You don't like them, do you?'

She stopped in front of a terraced cottage – number twenty-eight, the eight dangling upside down from a rusting screw – and pulled out a key.

'We rent off 'em too, like I said. Look at the paintwork. Out the back, away from the street, the frames are rotten. The toilet doesn't flush properly half the time.'

'He comes for our rent as regular as clockwork,' said Emlyn. 'Mum wanted to pay through the bank but–'

'Smartly dressed, likes cash. Right?'

Emlyn nodded.

'Think they own the valley, they do,' said Max. 'Anyhow, he's the knob-head ma gran has to deal with. Spends half her life worrying about the rent, the other half worrying when he's gonna come hammering on the door. Down here the day before yesterday, he was, shouting and carrying on, with half the street watching. Last week he comes into

The Crown – she works at The Crown, right – and starts badmouthing her. It's personal as far as I'm concerned. That were him – Ol'man McCrossan – that pulled up in the green Renault just before at the tea room.'

'Well, I saw what I saw – up there.'

Max rolled her eyes.

'My mother's an archaeologist, and my sister – well, a wannabe archaeologist.'

'And what – that makes you Indiana Jones, I suppose. You're not even local.'

'Neither are you – not with that accent.'

'I was born here, pal. Spent a lotta time up here with Gran when me mum couldn'a – wasn'a herself, like.'

'Some of those stones had marks on them,' Emlyn said pointedly. He wanted to add that his father had been raised in the town; that he'd been born in Yeaveburgh, too. Max stared at him, waiting. 'I don't know. Like, strange marks. Runes or something. Anyway, I was thinking of taking another look.'

'Rightio,' said Max. 'Tonight, like.'

McCrossan's tuneless singing echoed in Emlyn's head and a cold chill swept around him; suddenly he wasn't so sure.

'Tonight?'

'What's the matter? You look like you've nowt better to do.'

It was his turn to shrug.

'Don't panic,' she said, her key half-turned in the lock. 'Just testing. But it's like I thought. When it comes to the McCrossans, you've no more bottle than the rest of 'em around here.'

With a withering look, Max disappeared inside.

9

Arthur's tale starts when he was a boy, just twelve years old, and I, at twenty, a seasoned veteran. We were from the same settlement, Ynys Avallach, where the two rivers meet, but I barely knew him for I had been in the saddle, fighting the Saxon boat-people since I was strong enough to hold a lance.

The rumours – I had heard well enough: a boy chosen for some greater good, it was said.

It was common knowledge a bargain had been made between Merlin and Arthur's uncle – for Arthur's parents had been slain in a raid – that Merlin would take the lad for his own.

To be chosen by the Green One, as Merlin was often called, was not a mark I would wish upon anyone. The druids are a thorny lot, with their signs and their singing, and Merlin the thorniest of all. But I will not waste my breath on Merlin as yet, for Arthur's tale must come first.

10

Down towards the town centre the sun squeezed between the clouds, turning the pavements slick with light and water, and Emlyn thought that perhaps the place wasn't so bad after all. In the Square he strolled to The Diner, an American-style eatery that was a popular hang-out after dark. Digger collapsed in the doorway. Emlyn scratched his ear, wagged his finger at him and told him to 'stay'. Inside, he ordered a Coke.

He wanted to think about Max's proposal. He found the prospect of a night expedition daunting. He was turning the idea over in his mind, pretty sure that he was going to let it go, when Hugh McCrossan walked into the Square flanked by Terry Murcutt and another lad with greasy, ginger hair. What was his name? – Eddie Maxwell, that was it, but everyone called him Ginger.

Emlyn slipped lower in his seat, hoping the trio wasn't headed for The Diner, when he remembered Digger was parked outside on the pavement. The Murcutt kid had a loathing for dogs. Emlyn had caught him lobbing stones at Digger one day in Riverside Park and they'd nearly come to blows. If they spotted the terrier he was a goner. Outside, someone whistled. Emlyn moved to where he could get a better view and sighed; they'd turned off down one of the side streets.

With their constant harassment – the threats and the smart-arsed asides yelled across the press of pupils at home time – Hugh McCrossan and his crew had been making school more painful than it already was. Most of Emlyn's year were wary of Hugh and kept away from him.

Sod him, thought Emlyn. He'd had enough of his rubbish comments and sarcasm. He'd beaten him easily in the cross-country. No, Max's idea was okay. Yeah, stick it up 'em on their own turf. Suddenly the night trip to the spinney seemed plausible. Opening the ammunition box that he used for his camera gear, he pulled out his field notebook.

Meet laneway, back
of St Andrews Church.
8pm. Emlyn. Bring a torch.

Ripping out the page, he folded it, wrote 'Max' boldly across it and with Digger nestled inside his jacket, headed up towards Castle Green.

11

'You're late!' Max's voice came at him out of the darkness. 'I nearly went without you.'

'You've no idea what to look for,' he said, propping his bike against the telephone box.

'Is that right?'

'Hey, I had to go back for my coat. What's a few minutes?'

'Fifteen. And listen,' said Max, 'next time you shove something under ma door, stick it in an envelope. I don't want Gran getting the wrong idea.'

Emlyn had suggested they meet at the church for a reason. His intention was to follow the Kirkholm road as he had done on previous visits to Whistman's Wood. As he moved off, Max grabbed his sleeve.

'Chain's broke on ma bike. We'll have to hoof it.'

Emlyn groaned, padlocked the bike to the railings and started up the road. She grabbed his sleeve again. 'We can cut across country.'

'What about Edderton Water?'

'There's a bend, a spot where the stream narrows. Sort of shingly spit. We can jump it.'

Emlyn grunted and climbed after her into the churchyard.

* * *

As they approached Edderton Water, Emlyn began to have doubts. The darkness magnified sound and in his mind the tranquil murmur of water over gravel became a rushing torrent. He switched on his torch and shone it out over the stream. Max lunged at it, fumbling for the switch.

'Are you mad or what? You want to advertise or something: "Two losers looking for a kick up the arse".'

The torch twisted from his grip, bounced on the bank and, as they both made to grab it, rolled into the water.

'It's one of those waterproof, floating torches,' Emlyn said, dropping to his stomach and reaching for it before the current caught it. As his fingers brushed the handle, the torch sank, cutting a brilliant green halo through the water, and then it settled on the bottom and went out.

'Champion!' said Max. 'What now, like?'

'It had "indestructible" in big letters on the packaging.'

'Really? An' you'll be telling me that a stork dropped you down the chimney, right? Aarghh, the power of advertising.'

'Anyway, you've brought a torch – haven't you?' She stared back at him and he growled. 'I said bring a torch.'

'Gran doesn'a have one. Leastways, that's working. And I wasn't about to go off and buy one.' Holding onto an alder branch, Max leant out over the stream. 'We can reach it, mebbe?'

'It'll have shorted out.' Emlyn strained his eyes in the darkness. 'We can't see to jump now.'

'The moon's nearly up.'

Across the stream, the sky above the hills held a milky incandescence. Emlyn straddled a low tree trunk that hung out over the water. Max squatted in the long grass. They waited in silence as the moon crept above the hills.

'You can see the spit now,' said Max.

She moved away from the bank, her footprints cutting a dark trail in the wet grass. Emlyn was still staring into blackness when she hurtled across the moon-dappled water and landed with a grunt on the shingle. A hoarse whisper carried across the stream. 'Come on!'

As soon as he jumped, Emlyn knew he had taken off short. He landed shin deep, almost losing his footing, and splashed out beside her, water dripping from the bottoms of his jeans. The hem of his greatcoat was soaked.

'Long jump not your strong point then?' she tittered.

'Very funny.'

They clambered up the stream bank between the trees. Emlyn, his shoes waterlogged, slipped twice, nearly falling over. Max was grinning, when a sudden flurry of wings beat the air above her head.

'What the friggin' hell was that?'

'Pheasant,' he said. 'Nocturnal habits of birds not a strong point then?'

'Smart-arse!' Max mouthed at the darkness.

12

The young Arthur and his uncle leave Ynys Avallach, passing out along the serpentine track that winds between the high defensive ditches. It is an early evening in summer as they trudge towards the river. The boy carries a few morsels bound tight in a chequered cloth. Splashing through the shallows at the ford, they start up towards the hills.

Short and dark, and with strength beyond his years, Arthur has shown great promise with the blade. His first, of metal and not a plaything made from sticks, was placed in his hand when he was three. He is quick and has a keen eye. With a bow, he is second-to-none and can pin a hare to the earth from the saddle.

Lagging behind, his features dark with confusion and hurt, Arthur looks back longingly at the settlement far below in the valley. His uncle calls down to him and he toils wearily up the slope, his eyes downcast.

Merlin stands at the edge of the forest to meet them.

To ease their parting the uncle sits on a rocky outcrop. He tells a familiar story, one his nephew has heard many times, but never here under the broad sky with the valley laid out below and the wood at their back.

Our forefathers came with the legions; he says this proudly. They were defeated in a great battle. And, in defeat, they chose to become part of the Empire, to leave their women, their children, and come here with nothing but their weapons and their warhorses. These hills became their home. His uncle takes in the moorland with a sweep of his arm and Arthur squints out across the airy space of the valley and imagines a line of horsemen fording the river. Their blood, and that of the legions, is in you, Arthur. You carry our hope. You must go with Master Merlin into the Great Wood.

Arthur is hesitant. He would appear brave for his uncle, but in truth he is terrified. The sun is setting and, like many of the youngsters of his settlement, he has never passed under the trees in darkness.

But Merlin's patience is renowned. He has not trained twenty long years, endured the pain and the cold and the beatings that is a druid's education, learnt the lore and song, each bough and leaf in the Great Wood, to let the boy slip from his grasp through haste.

The westerly wind is driving dark clouds up the valley, blotting out the sunset. It will rain before nightfall. Only now, with his uncle a speck at the valley bottom, does Arthur follow Merlin willingly in among the trees.

13

Clambering over the stone dyke, they were in the spinney, the sound of their feet on the leaf litter pricking at the darkness. A branch snapped under Emlyn's heel and he halted. Lawrence McCrossan's singing echoed faintly in his head.

'Come on.' Max grabbed Emlyn's arm and pulled him deeper into the wood.

'We're making too much noise.'

'In case you didn'a notice,' said Max, 'I left ma cape and hover jet-pack in the phone box opposite the church.'

'If the McCrossans are about we'll be–'

'Lawrence McCrossan's at The Crown, sucking on a pint,' said Max. 'I checked on the way over. And the old man – he'll be at home, parked in front of the telly.'

Pausing every twenty or so paces to listen, they worked their way between the trees to the grass mound, where Emlyn cast about in the moonlight. After a few minutes he pointed at the ground.

'There – see?'

'Not really,' said Max.

'A torch'd be real handy now.'

'Look, buster, it wasn'a me that dropped the bloody thing.'

'You knocked it out of my hand.'

'An' you switched it on.'

'McCrossan's down the pub,' said Emlyn. 'What's your problem?'

Max started down the hillock.

'Wait up! Just wait up – okay?'

Emlyn strode to a hazel brake at the edge of the clearing. Snapping one of the slender branches at the base, he pulled out a small jackknife, flicked it open and hacked at the wood. Once it was free, he sharpened the thick end to a rough point, walked back, and plunged it into the turf. The stick vibrated, jarring his arms.

'See!' He was almost shouting.

'Shusshh! Keep your voice down. See what?'

'Shove it into the ground,' he said, handing Max the stick. 'No, here!'

Max's hand vibrated. 'What is it?'

'There – that line – and there! The turves have been cut – laid.'

Max leant closer. A shadowy patchwork of lines and indents crisscrossed the mound under the slanting moonlight. Dropping to her knees, she began pulling at the turf.

'Hang on!' said Emlyn. 'They'll know we've been here.'

Max sat back on her haunches, while Emlyn carefully lifted a section of turf and laid it gently to one side. 'Seems like … stone,' he said, feeling around in the void.

Max ferreted in her pack. Emlyn heard the rasp of a match and for a moment they were staring at a patch of damp slate.

'Matches? Great!'

'An' a candle,' she said, lighting it.

Emlyn lifted three more sods, placing them gently alongside the first. The wavering flame showed a brass ring, green with age and verdigris. Emlyn heaved on it. The slate grated, rising slowly until he tipped it to one side.

A deeper darkness stared up at the night sky. He reached for the candle and then lay on his stomach, his head and shoulders in the opening. Pushing himself up off the grass, he gave a backward nod. 'Looks as if the passage runs in that direction.'

'What is this place?' said Max. 'What was it used for?'

'Probably a Bronze Age tumulus,' said Emlyn casually. She stared at him. 'A tomb. An ancient burial mound.'

'Get outta here.'

'No, really.'

'Right. Who's going in then?' said Max. Emlyn hesitated and shook his head. 'Gi's it here,' she sighed. 'And the matches.'

She lowered herself into the hole, ducked and was gone.

* * *

Max stooped to avoid banging her head. Using her left hand, she groped her way along the passage wall. A joint in the stonework snagged her fingernail, tearing it, and she cursed under her breath. Above and all around her, the massive stone slabs compressed the darkness until she could taste it. Several paces on, the wall curved away to the left and she stumbled to a halt, inching the candle higher. The flame revealed a chamber no more than five or six paces across. Ahead, the passage ran on into blackness. On either side were two smaller openings, inky holes in the darkness.

Max tried to visualise what it would look like if the roof were lifted off – a cross imposed over a circle came to mind – but the image made her think of the tons of earth above and she cowered down, her back against the wall. Her foot knocked something hollow-sounding, sending it clattering across the slate floor. Just as she leant forward and her fingers closed over wood, Emlyn's harsh whisper echoed along the passage.

'Someone's coming. I'll get you out later.'

Swinging around, her hand knocked the wall, sending the candle spinning to the ground, where it flared briefly and guttered. The last thing she heard as she groped for the waxy stub was the dull scrape of slate being dragged across the entrance.

* * *

The sound of an engine drifted across the fields. Emlyn assumed the vehicle was down on the road, but as the sound grew louder he realised it was coming from the woods further up the valley. Whoever it was drove slowly and without lights. Suddenly, he realised he could no longer hear the motor. A persistent swishing noise came through the trees. At first he thought it was the wind, until he realised it was the sound of tyres rolling over waterlogged turf. The faint snick of a car door opening drifted across.

They would be on him any minute.

Emlyn ducked his head into the hole and rasped, 'Somebody's coming. I'll get you out later.'

Working quickly, he replaced the slate and then the turf. Looks disturbed, he thought, but it'll have to do. He pushed at some of the lumpier bits with his foot. Damn! There was no way they wouldn't spot it. He gave a final prod at a raised edge, then dropped to a crouch and hurried across to the other side of the clearing, pausing briefly to listen before he stepped into the trees. Dead twigs crackled underfoot. He would be heard crashing about before he could hide.

A shallow ditch filled with last winter's leaves ran in a crescent shape at the foot of the mound. It would have to do. He lay down on his back, tucked the whiteness of his scarf away, and covered himself with leaves. He blinked up at the stars, wondering how Max was faring underground.

Close by someone hissed, 'Damn you, man, there's no-one here.'

'Your hearing's no' what it used to be,' came the answer. 'I definitely heard someone, I tell you.'

The McCrossans, thought Emlyn, as he listened to the two men move around to the far side of the mound. A torch beam flicked on. Now we're *really* screwed.

'What did I tell you?' The voice was reedy, bird-like. 'Somebody's been fossicking.'

Ol'man McCrossan.

Minutes passed and Emlyn heard the familiar grate of slate on rock. Jeezus, he thought, they're opening the mound. Now we're well and truly bollocksed.

'I'll take a look around – while you're down below.'

'Who said I was going down? You've years on me.'

'You know how I feel about going in there,' said the younger man.

'Achh, yer great jessie, gi's the bloody torch.'

There was a clatter as something heavy hit stone and Emlyn jumped. On the far side of the mound someone cursed.

'You trying to vex me on purpose? Gi's your lighter – if you can pass that without dropping it?'

They've dropped their torch, thought Emlyn. Please God, let it be broken. Two torches in one night; the chances weren't good. He strained his ears, listening. A frantic clicking carried over the mound to where he lay.

'Globe's gone.'

'Whoever it was, they could still be around. I'll take a look.'

'Aye, you do that, eh.'

Before Emlyn knew it, Lawrence McCrossan was towering above the ditch, stock-still, staring off into the trees. Emlyn felt he would suffocate as he tried to push his breathing a notch lower. His cheek was pressed into the leaf mould, inches away from the gamekeeper's boot. The glassy surface of the toecap held a reflection: the tiny silver coin of the moon. Emlyn stared into its depths aware that at any moment a violent shiver would give him away.

Without warning, the gleaming toecap disappeared as the gamekeeper grunted and stepped over the ditch, missing the leaf-strewn form by a stride. A branch cracked in the distance, and, as a bout of shivering passed through Emlyn and he sucked the dank night air deep into his lungs, rustling his leafy covering, the thought came to him how remarkably quiet McCrossan was for such a bulky man.

* * *

Max's instinct was to scramble from the chamber and run, but the heavy slate blocked her escape. The wooden carving she had grabbed seconds before was still in her hand. She tried to make out its shape, feeling the texture, trying to calm herself, trying to push away the fear, but she couldn't concentrate on what she held. Shoving it into her coat, she said, 'I'll light the candle.' In her other pocket was the book of matches. But her hands were too shaky. She gave up and settled against the wall to wait. Minutes passed; time became fluid, an extension of the blackness around her.

A cold draught eddied around her face.

It was several seconds before she realised that someone was pulling back the slate. Relief surged through her: Emlyn was getting her out. She shuffled forward on her hands and knees. Near the entrance something heavy clattered onto stone. Max froze. Someone had dropped down into the passage.

'Globe's gone.' Ol'man McCrossan's voice echoed in the darkness.

Logic told her that she was separated from the speaker by the distance of the passage, but kneeling there she felt that if she reached out she would be able to touch him. She shuddered. There was the insect-like sound of a lighter being struck several times.

Max felt her way down the side passage until she could go no further. A slab of stone was blocking her way. She ran her fingers over it and felt it disappear downwards beyond her reach, a cold slash across the passage. One of the great roof stones must have caved in, she thought. Squatting down, she waved her arm blindly into the triangular void beneath the stone and crawled into the space. Squashed beneath the fallen lintel, the damp rock pressed her face sideways, forcing her to look back the way she had come.

A wavering light licked at the walls. Huge shadows swallowed the roof. Ol'man McCrossan's silhouette blocked the chamber as he squatted with his back to her. A sharp, strangled breath sucked at the darkness, making Max jump. Sensing the urgency in his voice, she shrank deeper into her hiding place as the lighter flame swung wildly, this way and that.

'Damn and blast!' he croaked and spun on his heels. 'One's gone.'

Somewhere out in the spinney a gun went off. Max gasped. They were shooting at Emlyn!

'What the–' Ol'man McCrossan launched himself upright. Bone cracked on rock and he sank down again, rubbing his head, until, cursing, he fumbled his way back to the entrance.

Max took a breath and let it out slowly. It was hard to believe what she had seen arranged in a circle on the heavy flagstones, hard to trust her memory and the flickering light of the candle. But seen it, she had. Ol'man McCrossan's reaction confirmed that. Her hand went instinctively to her pocket and she felt the small lumpy shape against her thigh.

In the pitch black the image wavered in front of her eyes. Twenty or so squat, crudely carved wooden horsemen. No more than palm high, they had been arranged neatly in a circle like toy soldiers in some four-year-old's nursery game.

14

Emlyn jumped as the report echoed amongst the trees. What the hell was Lawrence McCrossan shooting at? Moments later a muffled outbreak of cursing came from inside the mound followed by a crashing through the undergrowth. The gamekeeper arrived at the opening, rifle in hand, as his father emerged in the moonlight, rubbing his head.

'You spotted someone, then?' said Ol'man McCrossan. 'Got a shot off?'

'Nope. No sign of anyone.'

'Then what in God's name were you shootin' at, man?'

'Dog fox,' said Lawrence McCrossan. 'Snared himself good and proper. He won't be causing any more problems.'

'No problems, eh? No sign of anyone?'

'No, I told you. Now what's up?'

'Never mind your bloody dog fox,' spat Ol'man McCrossan. 'One's missing – that's what's up.'

'You're certain of that?'

'Dammit, man, I can count. Somebody's taken what's not theirs to take. You've no' been at your job.'

'I canna be everywhere at once.'

'I'm beginning to think I should never've retired.'

'I've said it before and I'll say it again: the wee figures should never've been set out in this dammed wood in the first place.'

'They've stood a long time,' said Ol'man McCrossan quietly. 'Your grandfather, he knew the power of this place. Sleeper's Stones. Called that for a reason.'

Sleeper's Stones? Emlyn mouthed the name. The walled wood was marked as 'Sleeper's Spinney' on the ordnance survey.

'Give me a hand up,' the older man grunted. Lawrence McCrossan helped as his father prised himself awkwardly out of the hole and heaved the slate into place.

'Mebbe it was the Sylvesterson lad. He was sniffing around up here this morning.'

'Bird Boy?' said the old man. 'You didn'a tell me.'

'I canna tell you everything that happens. Besides, I warned him off.'

'You think so, eh? Well, it wouldn'a surprise me if he's been back.'

'It's possible,' said Lawrence McCrossan. 'Seems like the nosey type.'

'Aye, well I've had about enough of him and that dog of his. Reckon it's mebbe been worrying the sheep. What's that? There on the ground?'

They've found something, thought Emlyn.

'Anything?' said Ol'man McCrossan.

'Nothing much. *Wait on–*'

'What?'

'Pass the lighter,' said Lawrence McCrossan. There was a shuffling noise and the sound of a zip being drawn. 'That were none too smart. There, on the lining … no, inside … the name on the inside. See?'

Max's bag, thought Emlyn. She'd tossed it to one side when they'd found the entrance. He hadn't thought to pick it up; hadn't seen it in the darkness. Dammit!

'Maxine Fraser!' snapped Ol'man McCrossan. 'Smart-mouthed little cow, is that one. What's a townie like her doing poking around out here? Mind you, I saw her with Bird Boy this afternoon. Aye, thick as thieves, they were. An' they were probably both up here just now.'

'We should have a good look around.'

'Nah, they'll have legged it,' said Ol'man McCrossan, 'but they came prepared – came looking, for sure. Probably heard us. I'll no' be giving them any such warning next time.'

Emlyn lay shivering as the voices receded. Time moved slower than the stars. He had to be sure they were well away before he got Max out. The smell of the wood was all around him as he rolled from the ditch. He sat up, trying to listen over his shaking. Nothing. The spinney was quiet again.

15

'You took your time,' said Max, grabbing Emlyn's hand as he helped her from the opening.

'I had to make sure they'd gone.'

'I thought they were shooting at you.'

'Nah. But it gave me a fright. I heard Lawrence McCrossan say something about a snare – something about a fox.'

'Come on,' said Max, 'I wanna show you something. Besides, this place is giving me the heebie-jeebies.'

'Hang on. We need to put everything back as it was.' Kneeling to replace the turves, he said, 'Max … they found your bag.'

'Ma bag! *Shite!* Oh, champion. It's got ma name scrawled all over it.'

'Yep. It didn't take 'em long to discover that.'

'Could you not have grabbed it?'

'I was trying to put everything back in place. And then find somewhere to hide.'

Max stared into the trees. Mouthing off about the McCrossans was one thing but messing with them was another. The sooner she was back in Yeaveburgh the better; she'd had enough poxy nature in the last two days to tide her over till Christmas.

* * *

Heavy cloud had obscured the moon and they could barely see each other as they climbed over the dyke into the pasture and started down the hill.

'Well,' said Emlyn, glancing uneasily behind them, 'what is it? What did you want to show me?'

'Wait till the moon's out.'

Emlyn walked backwards, squinting across at the spinney. He could hear the steady breathing of a large animal and the jingle of something that sounded like a harness. Although he couldn't see it, he knew the rider was up near the wall, hidden in the blackness under the trees.

'Run,' he yelled, taking off at a sprint. 'No, not downhill! This way.'

'What is it!' rasped Max, pelting after him towards Whistman's Wood. 'What's up? The McCrossans?'

Emlyn could hear the drumming echo of hooves on turf. He pulled Max towards a spot where the trees were crowded hard against the stonework. The rider would be unable to clear the wall easily. He tumbled over the dyke. Max followed, almost landing on top of him. Scrambling to his feet, he grabbed her arm, towing her deep into the wood.

'What the hell's going–?'

'Shut up! I'm listening.' He stood for a moment, his whole body tensed, his hand still gripping her wrist. 'Come on!'

Emlyn towed Max downhill as they stumbled and slid on the wet ground, branches whipping at them as they crashed through the undergrowth.

'Hey,' she hissed. 'What the hell do you think you're playing at?' A fallen branch snagged her skirt, tearing the hem. 'And watch the clothing, buster.' But Emlyn's grip on her wrist didn't loosen and they were almost down to the road before Max got her answer.

'Something's following,' he said, 'out in the pasture. It's keeping pace with us along the wall. We've got to get across the road without–'

'Without what?' said Max. 'Stop all this cloak and dagger rubbish. What's in the field?'

'A horseman: a rider.'

'Who's gonna be out ridin' at this time o'night?'

'Look, we've got to get across the road without this–' He paused, unable to define what he was feeling.

'This *what*, for chrissakes? Because you're starting to spook me.'

'There's a forestry plantation that runs right down to the river – just across the road.'

'If you think I'm tramping through any more woods–'

'Listen,' he said, grabbing her wrist again, 'yesterday I saw something – something I can't explain – in the field by the spinney, when I yelled and fell, and whatever it is – and I don't know if you can see it or hear it but it's out there – it means business. So if you want to go for a nice stroll back down the Kirkholm road, be my guest, but I'm going down through the woods and then I'm going to figure out the next move.'

He turned down towards the roadside dyke and, finding a gap, climbed through. A fine drizzle was falling now, and the moon, freed for a moment from the drifting clouds, turned the road into a slick ribbon. Max stared at his dark shape for a second and then raced after him.

* * *

They were well in among the densely packed conifers when Emlyn pulled up sharply and Max, who was following closely in the darkness so as not to lose him, slammed into his back. Moonlight filtered down through a gap in the trees and she could see he was listening.

'What?'

'Hooves,' he said. 'Up on the road.'

'I canna hear anything.'

With the thick pine needles cushioning their tread, they worked their way soundlessly downhill, dashed across the Kirkholm road, and then blundered through the narrow band of conifers that separated them from the Yeave.

'What now, Sherlock?' said Max, staring at the river.

She watched as Emlyn glanced up and down the bank. A strip of grassy land and a fire track ran in either direction between the edge of the plantation and the Yeave.

'Yep, I thought so. There,' he said, pointing at a dinghy moored downstream. 'Tied to that willow. Magic.'

'Great! Just dinna expect me to row.'

'We'll be in Yeaveburgh in no time.'

* * *

Out in mid-stream, his back straining at the oars, Emlyn studied Max, who was seated quietly in the stern and staring at the bank they had just left. 'You want to show me what you found then?' he asked.

'There's barely enough light.'

'You've the matches still, haven't you?'

'Hey, pal,' said Max, 'I feel like I've just been dragged backwards through a car wash, so dinna push your luck. Anyway, I want a proper look at it, like. So, you gonna have to be patient, leastways until we get back to ma gran's.'

16

Emlyn hesitated in the doorway of Max's bedroom.

His thoughts were still down in the maze of streets below the castle. Leaving the dinghy tied to a small jetty at Riverside Park in the hope that one of the locals would know who was the owner, they had hurried up through the town. At every corner Emlyn had expected to hear hoof-falls on the cobbles; in each street or alleyway he was sure he'd sense the sudden, looming presence of the rider.

Even now, his ear was tuned to the street outside.

Steady, he thought. Calm down. There's got to be an explanation. There's an explanation for everything. But his mind offered up nothing – a big fat zero. And Max, who seemed unable, or unwilling, to hear what he had quite definitely–

He stopped. Craziness lay that way. Focus, you need to focus, he thought, and he dropped into what he called his 'observation mode', a way of looking that he employed when he was watching wildlife, noting the details, patterns, markings of fur or feather.

He let his eyes flicker around Max's room. The mirrored door of the wardrobe hung ajar: something was scrawled in lipstick across the glass. Inside, he could see a few clothes, mostly black, and a row of empty hangers. Several bottles of perfume sat on a chest of drawers. Otherwise, the room was neat and tidy. Below, in the hall, he heard a door close and Max came rattling up the stairs.

'Shut the door.' She pushed past him and slipped her shoes off, shoved a pillow behind her and sat hunched at the head of the bed, shivering. He left the door ajar and perched on the opposite end of the bed.

'You all right?' he said.

'Apart from being buried alive, like? You should try being shut in there: see how you like it. An' let's not forget you raving on about an invisible friggin' horseman.'

'What else was I supposed to do?'

'You could've got me out, that's what.'

'Like I said, they were coming. There wasn't time. We've been through all that.'

'Yeah, well – mebbe.'

Emlyn shrugged. 'You gonna give us another look at what we found, then?'

'What *who* found?'

'You were in such a rush and those streetlights–'

'Hey, it wasn't me who was cold, like?' Max started groaning, her trembling overtaken by laughter as she tried to force the sentence out. 'Man, your teeth ... they sounded like something ... out ... outta Riverdance.'

'Yeah, well I did land in the river – well, Edderton Water anyway. And I was lying in that ditch up at the spinney for ages.'

'You think that seemed like an age, try below ground.'

The bedroom door opened and Emlyn looked up. A buxom, middle-aged woman stood looking him over.

'I wondered when I was going to meet your new beau?'

'You could knock,' said Max, 'before barging in, like.'

'In the first place, young lady, I'll press you to remember why your Auntie Doreen and your Uncle

Jack sent you back up here.' There was a brief struggle of wills until Max looked away. 'Maxine's mother's no longer with us, God rest her soul.' The woman seemed to be speaking to no-one in particular. 'Still, the past's the past, and canna be undone.' Reaching for the doorhandle, Mrs Fraser turned to Emlyn. 'Would you like some tea?' Like Max's, the eyes that held his were of the deepest yellowy-green. 'Kettle's on. It's nae bother.'

Emlyn glanced at Max but her chin was on her chest, her face immobile.

'That would be nice,' said Emlyn. 'Thank you.'

'Nae bother, like I said. It's good to see *some* youngsters with manners.' Mrs Fraser gave Max a sideways look and then retreated, closing the door quietly.

'I'm sorry about your mum,' said Emlyn.

'Dinna be. She were hopeless.'

'Most oldies are.'

'No, I mean she were *hopeless*. A no-hoper, smack addict. She overdosed one day when I were at school.'

As if to change the subject, Max felt in her pocket and placed a small wooden horseman on the counterpane between them. Emlyn looked at it in silence for a few minutes, his attention caught between her blunt comments about her mother and the curiously wrought figure. Cautiously, he reached for the squat, crudely shaped form. The wood was riven with age, with deep cracks following the grain, and its surface, smooth under his fingers, still carried the tool marks of its shaping. Whoever had carved it had put their soul into it, he thought. Their flight from the spinney – and the rider – came flooding back. Max's well-lit bedroom, with its few colourful knick-knacks, had seemed for an instant a haven against the pressing darkness that had threatened to engulf them. He placed the figure on the bed, stood quickly and walked to the window, where he twitched aside the curtain and searched the empty street. Letting the curtain fall, he began to pace the room.

Max took the carving in her hand and turned it slowly. 'How old do you think it is?'

'Bridget, my sister, she'd know,' said Emlyn, 'for sure. I mean, Romano-British artefacts, they're her specialty.' Max frowned. 'Romano-British,' he continued, 'it's like the time when the Roman Empire collapsed and they pulled out of Britain.'

'It would have rotted – surely?'

'And there were more of them?' said Emlyn, still pacing.

Max shuddered. 'Couple-a-dozen arranged in a circle. It had the smell of something; I dunno, something weird, creepy, like.'

Emlyn stopped and stared at the horseman. His phone rang and he dragged it from his pocket. It was his sister. He switched it off.

'You had that on up at the spinney,' said Max, 'didn'ya?'

'No-oh.'

'Liar. If that had gone off when McCrossan was standing over you, we'd've been history.'

'Well it didn't, did it?'

'Down in that hole, that was something else,' said Max, changing the subject. 'I kept thinking of ma dad. He shot through before I were born, but m'gran, she always said he were terrified of confined spaces. Terrified of being buried alive, an' all. Wanted to be cremated at all cost. Down there I just kept thinking on that; I couldn't shift it outta ma head.'

They looked at one another.

'The place gives me the willies too. I couldn't show you in the dark, but there's no sign of life up there, no birds' nests, no rabbit scats – nothing.'

'Scats?'

'Rabbit droppings.'

'Droppings another area of expertise, are they?'

'I photograph animals, remember?'

The stairs creaked, and Max covered the horseman with her thigh as her grandmother entered with a tea tray.

'Are you no' going to introduce me properly, Maxine?'

'Emlyn, this is m'gran.'

'Well, serve the young man his tea, then.'

Max scooped the figure away behind her as she shifted to the edge of the bed.

'What have you there? You're not hiding anything from me by any chance, m'lady?'

'It's Emlyn's.'

Mrs Fraser held out her hand and Max passed the figure across.

'Is that so.'

'Yes. Well, actually … it's my mother's.' Emlyn stumbled on. 'She's an archaeologist.'

'Aye, and digging up half the town from what I've heard.'

'I thought Max might be interested.'

Max poured the tea as casually as she could manage. Her grandmother placed the horseman on the bed and walked to the door. 'The wee man on his pony – it's not a child's thing. Och, I know you're not bairns any more,' she said, seeing Max's raised eyebrows. 'But there's a glamour on it, that I can all but touch. It's best put back wherever it came from. Back in the ground.' She half closed the door and then popped her head back. 'Your jeans are dry, young man, but that coat of yours is another matter.'

The door closed and they heard her tread on the stairs as she went down.

'Why d'ya wear that humping great thing, anyway? And the scarf?'

'Why d'you wear black?' said Emlyn. 'Besides,' he fingered the silk scarf hanging over the foot of the bed, 'my great-great-grandfather swapped this with a German fighter ace for a packet of fags. He drowned in the trenches – in mud.'

They sat in silence on the bed.

'What did she mean by *glamour*?' asked Emlyn.

'Superstition: ladders, salt, black cats – you name it. It's an old Scottish word for magic.'

Emlyn prised himself up off the bed. Max sat hunched against her pillows, staring at the carving.

'I best head off. My sister'll be having a hernia. Thanks for the loan.' Emlyn flung his scarf theatrically around his neck and made to curtsy in the dressing-gown Max had lent him. Clamping her hand across her mouth, she cut short a raucous laugh. 'My jeans … where are–?'

‘Front room. She’ll have ’em ironed by now.’ The smile became a scowl.

‘What’s up?’

‘My bag,’ said Max in a low voice. ‘I shouldn’a have taken it up there.’

As Max descended the stairs, Emlyn stood poised at the top, thinking through the ramifications of that lost bag.

17

Emlyn stood in the small front parlour with its upright piano and old-fashioned sofa and armchairs. He buckled his belt and crossed to the oak sideboard. Silver-framed photos stood on doilies. The unfamiliar faces gazed back at him.

'Admiring my display, eh.' Mrs Fraser stood in thc doorway.

'This is you.' He pointed to a black-and-white photograph of a woman standing next to a motor scooter.

'When I was younger. Will you look at that get-up?'

'Who's this?' He indicated a small, badly taken photograph of a stocky, dark-haired man, wearing a sweater and heavy sea boots.

'That's my Douglas,' she said, collapsing the ironing board. 'Maxine's grandfather.'

Emlyn studied the grainy photo. The man was staring straight back at the camera. His eyes were dark and intense and he was smiling. Light glinted off the frame and Emlyn felt himself slipping away into another place. He thought of the spinney and McCrossan's singing. Fractured voices pulled him down a dark tunnel. He struggled, but there was nothing to hold on to. Tight-pressed bodies moved to a deep pulse of music. The dark-haired man was dancing with the scooter-woman from the other photograph. Lights flashed and he could smell beer and sweat and cigarettes.

'He really liked dancing, didn't he?' Emlyn heard his voice drift over the crowd. 'You both did. But he really loved it.'

Slowly he came back into the dimly lit parlour. It was like sliding down a tunnel away from the dancers and the flashing lights. Max's grandmother was staring at him.

'Gran? You okay?' Max stood in the open doorway, a puzzled look on her face. She moved to her grandmother's side and squeezed her arm. 'You look like you've seen a ghost.'

'Pop the kettle on, there's a dear.'

The door closed behind Max.

'Oh, he was real keen on dancing. Have you been asking around town about me, or Max, for that matter?' Mrs Fraser stared at him and Emlyn shook his head. 'Are you sure? Don't lie to me, laddie.'

'Why would I … be asking about you?'

'You tell me.'

Emlyn picked up the man's grainy photograph from the sideboard and ran his finger over the frame.

'I'd be obliged if you'd put that back,' said Mrs Fraser.

Gingerly, Emlyn replaced it. The man's weathered face stared back at him: the crooked smile, the cigarette dangling from his lip, the piercing eyes. There was a hissing around Emlyn's head and he was enveloped in cold. Another vision. He *was* going mad. Dark water roared around him. His ears ached and his eyes stung. He reached for the sideboard to steady himself: the solid timber was the only contact now. A huge wave came out of the gloom, towering above a drilling platform, and he was swept over the side into the sea. The waves picked him up and smashed him down. For a second his hand closed over a strut and he felt the barnacle-encrusted steel beneath his fingers, until that too was ripped from his grasp. He fought for breath. He was going to die

– nothing was more certain. The drowning dream had come when he was awake, but this time salt water, not fresh, filled his throat.

'Steady!' Max's grandmother thrust her arm under his. He could feel her strength as she pushed herself between him and the sideboard.

'He drowned.' Emlyn forced the words up from somewhere cold and heavy. His fingers slipped from the polished timber. A deep silence settled around him; hair drifted seaweed-like across his face, salt water stung his lacerated hands. 'He drowned, didn't he?'

'Aye, the rigs.' Mrs Fraser's voice filtered down through the dark water. 'He was swept off in a storm. They never found his body.'

'I'm losing it, aren't I … going mad?'

'Did Maxine tell you about the accident?'

'No.' The waters ebbed away and Emlyn felt confused. 'What accident?'

'The night my Douglas was swept into the North Sea.'

'No. No … I don't think so … no.'

'Somebody in the town then? Mentioned it?'

'No. I don't know anything about any accident.'

'Well, you must've heard it from someone, laddie.'

'I could see you, too,' said Emlyn, 'before, like, as I looked at the photo. It was like watching a movie. You were in some kind of hall. There was a band.'

'See me?' said Mrs Fraser.

'You were dancing. Then there was the water.'

'You're saying that you could see me dancing … and see Douglas on the rig?'

Emlyn nodded. 'You don't understand,' he said, trying to focus on the door. 'My father's in Huntleighbank. It's a mental asylum.'

'Ah, Huntleighbank, is it.' She touched his arm momentarily, as if to bring him back. 'It'll be fine, laddie. I'm beginning to see what's happening here. And you're not going mad.'

Emlyn didn't have the heart to tell Mrs Fraser about the rushing water and her husband's struggle to cling to the rig before the black waters of the North Sea pulled him under. He felt sick in the pit of his stomach. Where had he been in those few minutes? Why was he talking to this woman about things he couldn't possibly know? Again, he felt himself slipping away into the place his father had left them for.

'I've got to go!' He pulled away towards the door.

'Whoa! Steady on.' Emlyn found himself briefly pressed into the comforting softness of Mrs Fraser's embrace before she pushed him away and, grabbing his shoulders, held his eyes intently. 'You've the gift, that's all. Blessing and curse.'

'The gift?'

'The sight. You can see things from the past or maybe even the future. There's one or two around these parts as have it. Come into the kitchen and have some tea now and we'll settle you down before you head off.'

He found himself half-cuddled, half-steered into the bright kitchen, where Max was clattering around with the crockery and singing quietly.

'She's a proper sweet voice, this one.'

'Stop embarrassing me, Gran.'

'There's no shame in a fine voice.'

'What happened?' Max asked, glancing at Emlyn as she poured the tea. 'He's as white as a sheet.'

'Nothing,' said her grandmother. 'Just a wee misunderstanding.'

'For a moment there, you both looked a bit off with the fairies.'

Emlyn sipped the steaming sugary brew, grateful that Max's grandmother said nothing about his father's illness or his strange glimpse into her past.

18

The light from Mrs Fraser's doorway cut a yellow rectangle across the street. Emlyn and Max stood nearby in the shadows.

'Here,' she said, handing him the wooden horseman.

Reluctant to take it, he said, 'My sister can't keep her nose out of my stuff. Can't you keep it?'

'Gran already thinks I lifted it from some antique shop. She'll not believe that story about your mum. So – what you gonna do with it?'

'Don't know,' he said, pocketing the figure. 'Put it in a tin or something, I suppose.'

'Hang on.' Max ducked back into the house.

Emlyn registered the faint clatter of hooves somewhere down in the town. The hoof-falls grew louder, coming at a steady trot up the narrow streets.

Max reappeared with a tin. 'Just the right size,' she said, thrusting it at him. 'What's up?'

'Down town. Can't you hear anything?'

She cocked her head. 'Nah. Hey, look, I've gotta go.'

The yellow block of light shrank to pencil thinness and vanished. Emlyn opened the tin and the faint smell of butterscotch wafted up at him. He grinned, popped the figure inside, pressed the lid on and slipped it in his pocket.

Sensing movement down at the corner, he squinted along the street. Shadows folded over shadows. The unmistakable sound of a horse shifting its weight carried across the cobbles.

'Anybody there?' he called.

A light went off in the house opposite and an eyeless window stared back at him. Whatever was down at the corner stood between him and home. He would have to take the long way around by Castle Wall. Turning quickly, he walked up the street. The hair prickled on the back of his neck. This wasn't right. Something ancient, something chill and foreboding, was stalking him.

Quickly, he tried to assess the situation. On Max's side of the street there was a line of parked cars. Too narrow for a horse, he thought, and broke into a run, dodging between two vehicles and onto the pavement. The hooves came at a clip. He glanced over his shoulder. The bulk of a rider appeared, swerved through a gap and clattered onto the pavement, tearing several wing mirrors from their vehicles. Broken glass tinkled in the gutter. A door opened and someone shouted. Rounding the corner, he pelted downhill. The street was wider and better lit. He knew where he was. There were a couple of bends as the road snaked down towards the Square, and then a row of disused shops. Behind them was an alley. It was his best chance.

He heard the horse round the corner at speed and turned to see it almost lose its legs on the cobbled surface. The rider steadied his mount and came at a canter. Emlyn turned on the juice. His lungs burnt as he fought down the panic.

Emlyn reached the first corner but the rider was gaining. More cars. He leapt between them and careered along the pavement. Thank God it was no more than a strip. Second corner. He could see the shops. The horse and rider had drawn level. He willed himself not to look. Now the horseman was in front and he was running out of pavement. Vaulting between two cars, he shot out behind the horse and ran across the street. 'Jeezus, it's got a sodding great lance,' he said and realised it was his voice he could hear. None of this is possible, he thought. This is the twenty-first century; stuff like this just doesn't happen.

He could feel the vibrations on the cobbles as the horseman wheeled his mount. He cast his thoughts aside, and mustering one last, frantic burst of speed, sprinted past the shops. At his back he could hear the animal's laboured breathing as the rider strove to close the distance. As he shot into the alleyway, he glanced back, trying to judge his chance of escape. The rubbish skip leapt at him, slamming into his shoulder, one of the lugs catching his ear and mashing it against his skull. He dropped to the cobbles. It felt like he had broken a rib or something. You stupid twat! *Idiot!* Did you have to choose that moment to look over your shoulder? Holding his ear, he crawled into the darkness.

The rider reined in his mount and entered the laneway at a walk. Emlyn scrabbled sideways, backing away along the wall, the spear tip quivering in front of his chest. Blood dripped from his ear inside his collar. He couldn't take his eyes off the shimmering point.

19

Max yanked open the front door and peered along the street. At the corner a car rocked gently as if something large had bumped it. 'Get a grip, girl,' she mumbled, stepping onto the pavement. 'You're catching Emlyn's disease.' Broken glass crunched underfoot and she looked down. Curtains were tweaked aside, lighting the street haphazardly, and a neighbour's door opened.

'If I catch the little bastard responsible, I'll brain him.' The man was gawping at his broken wing mirror as Max brushed past. 'Hey, you see anybody?' he asked, but Max was already at the corner.

'You don't have to worry about braining him,' she muttered, 'because, if it's our wee mate, I'll do that myself.'

A running figure disappeared from view down near the old shops. The flapping coat was unmistakable. She loped down the hill and stopped at the corner of Bothy Street. There was no-one in sight. She drew level with the lane at the rear of the shops. Squinting into the shadows, she took a few steps forward. There was only one streetlight and that had been broken months ago. 'Sodding kids,' she muttered. Her eyes were adjusting now. A delivery truck was parked, blocking the lane. She edged in a bit further and paused. A feeling of unease swam past in the darkness; somebody was nearby, she could sense it. She waved her hand in front of her and inched forward.

'Emlyn! Stop messin' around and get out here.'

Moving further in, the fingers of her other hand trailing along the brickwork, she called: 'I know you're there.' She shuffled towards the truck, keeping close to the wall, and stopped. Something hair-like brushed her arm and then her face. Stifling a squeal, she slid into the gap between the wall and the truck and emerged on the far side.

A figure was slumped against the opposite wall.

20

Someone was calling him.

'Emlyn!'

He shook his head, trying to clear it. He must have passed out. The image of the lance exploded in his head; a mewing noise escaped from him and he pressed against the wall, making himself small. He'd thought he was going to die. But the lance hadn't skewered his flesh. There had been a delivery truck, blocking off the lane, and he'd squeezed into the gap alongside the cab.

'Emlyn!' Max was crouched in front of him. 'What the hell did you go and do that for?'

'What?' he said, hauling himself up and cradling his side. 'Aarghhh, my ribs.'

'Never mind your ribs. What did you go and wreck them cars for? 'Cause I canna be doing with tossers, me.'

He stood, listening intently. A tail swished and the steady breathing of a horse came from the far side of the truck.

'Hello, are we on the same planet, or what?'

Cupping his hand to his ear, he said, 'Can't you hear that?'

'Don't start with the hearing stuff again.'

'You came past the truck. Didn't you see it?'

'What?' said Max. 'See what?'

'You're telling me you saw nothing?'

'Should I have? Some clues would be nice.'

'Never mind.' Something slimy was on his fingers. He looked at his hand. It was sticky. He felt his ear. Blood was dripping from his ear lobe onto his shoulder.

'I've cut my head,' he said.

'Look, you've obviously hurt yourself. You were running, right? Well – what happened?'

'I ran into that skip on the corner.'

'An' the broken wing mirrors on our street – how'd'yer explain that?'

'That wasn't me.'

'Gran's bound to think it was you. It happened

minutes after you left. Don't mess me around, Emlyn.'

'It wasn't me – *all right*!'

'Look – whatever,' she said gently. 'Just come back to Gran's and we'll have a look at your ear.'

'No way I'm going back through there.' He jerked his head at the van and, holding his side, limped away.

'Hey, where you going? We've to explain to Gran – tell her it wasn'a you.'

But he was already jogging towards the end of the lane, grunting every second step.

* * *

Two streets away a drunk rolled out of a taxi. Emlyn banged on the door as the driver was pulling away. The cabbie rolled down his window.

'Got any cash, son?' Emlyn pulled a couple of notes from his pocket. The driver took them and nodded for him to get in. 'You get the change when we get where you're going. And try an' not bleed all over ma upholstery.'

As the taxi rolled down the hill, Emlyn heard the sound of hooves turn into the top of the street.

21

A dull thumping entered his consciousness and then someone was shaking him. He grunted and opened one eye. Bridget loomed over him, silhouetted by the landing light.

'I'm sleeping. Leave me be.'

'Where the hell were you this evening? Can't trust you to stick around for two seconds, can I?'

'Sleeping,' he grunted.

'I phoned but you wouldn't pick up. Then you were switched off for the rest of the evening.'

'Go away, Bridge.'

'Sure, I'm going. Thought you might have wanted to hear about your dog though.'

'What?' He rolled over, away from the thick taste of sleep.

'Digger's at the vet,' she said, moving to the doorway. 'But, given your complete lack of interest, I guess that little bit of information can wait until the morning.' The door closed.

Stumbling out of bed, he rummaged blindly for his jeans, pulled them on and bumped onto the landing. The lights were off and Bridget was nowhere to be seen. He slapped at a switch, hurried down the passage to her room and tapped on her door.

'I'm in bed, Emlyn.'

He tried the handle. Locked.

'What's with Digger?' His voice echoed down the empty passage. 'Bridge? Open up.'

'He took a bait,' came the muffled reply.

'Poison?' The lock clicked, the door opened and he stepped back. 'He's all right, isn't he?'

'Emlyn, I needed you to hold Digger while I drove. I mean, you're always going on about animals and then you're not there for your own dog.'

'But he's going to be okay, right?'

'Yes, he's okay. But no thanks to you.' Then she saw his ear. 'What the hell's that? Have you been fighting?'

'I haven't been fighting. I came off my bike ... into a skip.'

'Let me have a look.' She reached for his arm but he shrugged her off.

'I've cleaned it up already, okay.'

'Suit yourself. Just trying to do the sister-thing.'

'You're not going to tell Mum about Digger, are you?'

'What do you think? Who's going to stump up the cash for the vet's bill?'

Emlyn shook his head. 'When's she back?'

'Another week, probably. Now if you don't mind, I've been sitting in the vet's surgery for an hour-and-a-half while they treated the poor little mite. I'm a tad frazzled, so if you've no objection, I'm going back to bed. We'll talk in the morning.'

22

At the foot of a cliff is a dark slash in the rock face. Before the cave, Arthur sits on a low boulder, warming his back in the sun and idly tossing a stone from hand to hand.

Tonight, Merlin says. The time is right. He'll come when the moon rises. I will call him.

Arthur blinks at first and then grunts; he is relieved. His eye is on the small bird that is hopping in the dust near Merlin's feet. The old man squats and holds out his hand. The chaffinch flutters onto his finger, chirruping and turning its eye beadily into his.

It isn't possible, says the boy, to die three times. He watches the bird intently. He could kill it with the stone without doing any injury to the hand that holds it, his eye is that good.

Merlin says, You've heard the stories of the three-fold death. What point is there in my repeating them?

Arthur looks puzzled; the man is a druid and his teacher.

Merlin holds the bird aloft and it becomes a flashing line among the trees. Sometimes a truth is only as solid as its speaker, he says cautiously. If you had killed the bird, would you have been any wiser? Arthur shakes his head. Truth then is rather like the bird, is it not? It seeks air and light: its capture is no easy task.

Arthur is told to ready himself: to collect and prepare certain plants that grow on the hillside. When the lad returns the sacred fire is ready and Merlin is crouched, staring into the flames, waiting for the call. The fire is like river water as it eddies and swirls; a gateway through which Merlin slips. He is calling the Oak God.

Later, the full moon snaring their shadows, they stand near the fire, naked except for the blue markings that cover their bodies. Merlin chants and calls out and stamps his feet. Arthur shivers in the moonlight. His feet drum half-heartedly in the dust, as much from cold and boredom as from what he has been instructed to do. Acrid smokes rises from the plants that have been tossed on the fire.

Merlin stops and Arthur shuffles on for a few moments. The wind rises in the trees. He is here, says Merlin. There is a great rushing through the forest that is not the wind.

Arthur senses it moments before the Oak God tears into his body. Jerking twice, he falls to the dirt, twitching and slobbering. The whites of his eyes gleam wolf-like in the firelight. Merlin squats, and passing his hands repeatedly over the thrashing body, sings quietly. The flailing subsides into tremors, and the tremors into tics and twitches. Arthur lies still and the dust settles softly over the two of them.

Merlin continues to sing, rocking slowly on his haunches.

The treetops mark the passage of the stars.

Then, wild-eyed, Arthur is on his feet and into the forest. He weaves between the trees, leaping fallen trunks, ducking under branches as the moonlight picks out the gleam of sweat across his muscles. He runs on. He is the hunter and the hunted. The forest god governs his body now.

Night shifts around to night. Stars and sun hold the forest pinned in a dream.

Fear and a great loneliness fill Arthur.

23

Merlin crouches beside the sacred fire. His task is almost done.

Three things are possible. The first two Merlin pitches from his mind: that the boy will be lost to the forest and perish among the wild creatures; or he will return, his senses stripped, his mind taken flight. A choice here for Master Merlin – to return him to the settlement, where he'll be left drooling in some dark corner; or to put the boy from his misery, an offering to the forest.

But it is the third way that Merlin hopes for.

It was the same for him when he was sent alone into the forest at a younger age than this, part of his initiation as a druid. He does not foresee Arthur's death. The lad is young and strong, but Merlin knows only too well that nothing is certain and an occasional prophecy of his has gone astray before now.

He has spent years waiting, watching over the growing Arthur, planting ideas in his uncle's mind, readying the tribes and families for this moment when the boy will emerge as their leader. All his herb-lore, all the long years of training have sent the chant spinning like a silvery web around the two of them.

Merlin sings on.

His patience will be tested.

A part of his mind, not taken up with the endless chant, clings to the belief that he has read the omens right – the signs that say it is this twelve-year-old orphan, and no other, who will unite the tribes and drive the boat-people back into the sea. Yet another part of Merlin's mind, his inner sight, watches over Arthur where the boy crouches, shivering against an oak. Silence becomes a beast creeping between the trees. All the colour and movement of the forest are swept together in a single note that fills Arthur's head.

Merlin tenses: this is the moment he has waited on. A she-bear, her cubs killed by a large male, ambles into the clearing where Arthur lies. She could tear the boy apart with her claws but she grunts, rolls on her side and lets him suckle. Merlin allows himself a smile. A year before, did he not see this in a dream?

For that is the meaning of Arthur's name: bear.

Suckling at the bear's teat is the one thing the lad remembers. And it will be used to great effect by Merlin.

24

Arthur returns: bruised, cut, famished, barely able to stand. Three nights he has been alone in the forest. Merlin tends his wounds and spoons a broth of wild nettles into him. He watches carefully, for the boy has dreams in which he calls out, roaring and bellowing. Twice he tries to leave the cave but the old man wrestles him back onto the skins and presses crushed leaves to his nose. The struggles diminish and he falls into a fitful sleep.

On a pale, dew-soaked morning several weeks later, Merlin returns to find Arthur sitting on the boulder at the mouth of the cave. He looks much the same as when his uncle first brought him up from the settlement.

It is time to go down again.

* * *

It was Merlin who took Arthur and made him what he became and it was in this shaping that we all came undone. But there were things the Green One could not see, paths he would not tread in his spirit journeys – paths which would place us all in peril.

WEDNESDAY

25

Emlyn shuffled around the kitchen, bleary-eyed. Sleep had tossed him through a series of uneasy dreams, punctuated by the thunder of hooves, in which he was searching for something. He'd woken to the sound of his sister's car pulling out of the drive. With Digger on his mind, and his body still sore from the previous night, he sat stiffly at the table, waiting for her to get back.

Tyres crunched on gravel and a car door slammed. He had the back door open as Bridget stalked towards him, head down, face set.

'Digger? How is he, Bridge? What happened?'

Bridget pushed past, put the cartons in the fridge and faced Emlyn. 'Mum rang me while I was out getting the milk. She'd just had an interview about some more consulting. Short notice – some Dark Ages film, advising them on costuming. She's going to ring back in a while. She wants to talk to you.'

'And you said what? You didn't tell her about Digger?'

'No, not yet. Emlyn, listen, matey. She's got a lot on her plate at the moment. She doesn't always let on but she stresses about stuff. You know when she rings most evenings and talks, well after, later, when you've gone to bed or you're upstairs tinkering, she rings me again. She's worried, what with this sleepwalking thing starting up again. I mean, we all thought you were well over that.'

'I am, Bridge.'

'Well, she's not convinced and she doesn't need anything else to worry her. Like you nicking off early yesterday morning and then gallivanting round town all hours.'

Emlyn grabbed the cereal, pulled a bowl gingerly from the overhead cupboard – his side was throbbing – and sat at the table.

'I'm all ears, Em?'

'Wait up, Bridge, you haven't filled me in about Digger yet.'

'We'll get to Digger in a minute. I called the vet first thing and he's fine. So ... where were you?

Because it was yesterday morning that Ol'man McCrossan paid us a visit and hinted that a dog had been at his sheep. "Vermin" was the word he used. "I'll not have vermin bothering my animals".'

'The old plonker's always on about something or other.'

'Answer my question,' said Bridget.

'Calm down. I was trying for some shots, if you must know,' he said. 'Fox cubs.' Bridget stared at him and for some reason he couldn't explain he found himself lying about the exact spot. 'Up by the old Roman camp.'

'Your camera was on the hall table. All day.'

'Recce trip,' he replied. 'Just took the binoculars. Now, what about Digger?'

'I told you. He's fine. Some bastard tried to poison him. I found him out under the wall at the bottom of the garden, shivering, unable to stand. He'd taken some sort of bait according to the vet. Something totally unpronounceable that's used on fruit trees: reduces the core temperature – animal dies of hypothermia.'

'Who'd do something like that?'

'Hell-ooh?' said Bridget. 'My money's on yesterday's visitor. "Vermin" is pretty strong language.'

'Ol'man McCrossan,' said Emlyn, pushing up from the table. 'The prick!'

'I didn't say he did it. But …'

The phone rang and Bridget scooted into the hall. It was their mother. He could tell by Bridget's tone, a sort of thick-as-thieves conspiratorial voice that she reserved for such moments. There was a squeal and then Bridget was in the doorway, waving the phone at him. 'She's got it! Mum's got the gig with the film people. Here, she wants to speak to you.'

The line was bad. A sound shadow dogged his mother's words. 'How's tricks, Em?'

'All right.'

'You're all right?'

'Fine.'

'Any more episodes … you know, with the dreams … and the sleepwalking?'

'Not lately.' Why was he lying? The dreams were getting worse. 'Can we talk about something else?'

'Good news about this film thing, because you know what production companies are like – they throw money around like it's going out of style.' There was an awkward silence at Emlyn's end. 'Aren't you going to ask me what it's about?' said his mother.

'What's the go then?'

'It's about King Arthur. It's called *The Thirteenth Battle.* Well, anyway, that's the working title. You know what these arty film-types are like. Look, Emlyn, I've got to go. Just checking in. Be good for your sister, eh? I've put her in charge down at the dig, basically. She's got a lot on at the moment, what with finishing off her Doctorate.'

'Archaeology, holes in the ground, bits of rubbish – that's all you two think about. You've already been away a week. What about Dad?'

'We're doing the best we can. He's in good hands. We'll talk about it when I get back.'

'You are coming back then?'

There was a sigh and a pause. He expected her to comment on his sarcasm but she let it go.

'Week: ten days … tops. Emlyn, I can't just drop it. All this was booked ages ago.'

'Not the film stuff.'

'No, not the filming stuff, as you say. Anyway, help Bridget out when you can, matey. Got to run. Going into an important meeting any minute. Big kiss, sweetheart, and huge one when I get back.'

The line went dead and he cradled the phone. He didn't want a kiss; he just didn't want two weeks of his half-sister bossing him about – that and her awful cooking. And now he could add the Bridget guilt factor to the list; she wasn't about to let last night's crisis slide.

Emlyn wandered into the kitchen and sat down at his breakfast again.

'You need any more milk on those?' Bridget opened the fridge a crack. Emlyn shook his head and pushed the unfinished cereal away. 'God, it's chaos up town,' she said, nudging the fridge door closed. 'Police everywhere.'

'Police?' Somehow he knew what she was going to say next.

'Some drunk got stabbed or something. He's on the critical list.' His sister leant against the sink, staring at him intently. 'What *were* you doing last night?'

'Friend's place.' The image of the drunk paying the cabbie and reeling up the hill lodged in his head and wouldn't shift.

'Your bike – where is it? I didn't see it in the shed.'

'Like I said, me friend's place.' Damn, he'd forgotten about the bike. It was still chained where he'd met Max.

'If you're going to take up lying to your big sister, you're going to have to do a more convincing job – practise more, you know. I saw your bike on the way back, chained to the railings in front of St Andrew's. So, anyone I know?'

'What?'

'Do I know the person you were out with?'

Emlyn shrugged. 'And this drunk, he's on the critical list?'

'Apparently. Which is what you'll be on if you don't stop jerking me around and answer my questions.' Bridget pulled Max's tin from her bag, removed the lid and stood the wooden figurine on the table beside the sugar bowl.

For all its stillness, the thing leapt at Emlyn like a plunging horse. Had Bridget crept into his room, gone through his pockets? He stared at it, his mind a groggy blank, struggling to recall his movements the night before.

The last few days – from Max's breaching of the wall, to the photographs in her grandmother's parlour, and then last night's episode with the horseman, the frantic chase through Yeaveburgh's cobbled streets – the whole thing had taken on a nightmarish quality. It was hard to work out where he was, even now, standing in the kitchen. The wall clock ticked on faintly, a reassurance that the world was moving.

Focus: *focus*! He'd felt exhausted when he'd got home ... and he'd thrown his coat on the chair in the hall. His sister had bloody well gone through his pockets. He lunged for the carving but Bridget was too quick. The sugar spread in a wave across the table. He just caught the cereal packet before it toppled.

Stupid – *stupid*!

'Uh-uh,' said Bridget. 'Explanation time.'

'What about going through my pockets? How about explaining *that*!'

'I didn't.' His sister raised her eyebrows. 'You chucked your coat on the chair. I went to hang it up. That fell out.' She continued to stare at him. 'So, what's the story?'

'Okay – look – her dad's a dealer. He's got an antique shop. She borrowed it to show me.' Emlyn put the cereal box back in the cupboard. 'I'm giving it back, today, at school, okay?'

'It looks old: valuable. Your friend ought never to have *borrowed* it in the first place.'

'Yeah, yeah.'

'You can always *yeah-yeah* Mum.' Bridget picked up her mobile.

'Great,' said Emlyn, backing down, 'Mum's not content with Edinburgh – I mean, what, she's a professor isn't she – and now she's off moonlighting as a film consultant?'

'Two weeks, she reckoned. Then everything'll be back to normal.'

'Haven't we got family around here? Somebody I could go and stay with. Give you a break, like.'

'Thinking of your sister. Very noble.' Bridget held up her fingers. 'Two weeks. Think we can make peace for that long?'

Emlyn grinned. 'I was thinking about my stomach.'

'There's always takeaway. Mum left some emergency dosh.'

'Now you tell me. After a week of your culinary experiments.'

'Got to have someone to experiment on. I mean, I don't want to go poisoning any future husbands.'

'Excellent,' said Emlyn. 'But seriously, don't we have relatives up here? Mum said we did.'

'Aunt, I think, on your dad's side. Bit of a busybody, apparently.' She gave him a measured look. 'Anyway, you've got me.'

As Emlyn reached for the horseman and picked it up, Bridget's hand closed over his wrist.

'It goes back. Right?' Gravel crunched out in the driveway and Emlyn's gaze strayed to the kitchen window. His sister was staring at him. 'What's up?'

The window was small and low; he had to stoop to see the hills. The kitchen had once been a dairy, according to his mother. The flank of a horse and a rider's knee passed close to the glass. The leggings showed clearly through the net curtains. Something matted and bloody hung from the harness. Bridget turned to follow his gaze.

'Visitors!' said Bridget moving to the back door. 'That's all I need.'

She'd seen something? But how? Wasn't he the only one who could see the rider? Max had seen nothing. The taxi driver had definitely checked his mirrors before he'd pulled away.

Bridget wandered back in from outside. 'Could have sworn … never mind. By the way, the gravel's all scuffed up. You been kicking that ball around again? Ol'man McCrossan'll have a fit.'

'You can't pin that on me. The ball's in my locker at school.' Emlyn's hands were shaking as he closed the lid on the tin. 'Any chance of visiting Dad?' He needed to get away from the rider, as far away as possible, and just sit with the big man: sit and watch his father's face, sit and think this through.

'I've got to go,' said Bridget. 'Talk to Mum.'

'I was thinking of going today,' he said shakily. 'She never agrees to anything over the phone. Besides, she's in a meeting. She'll have it switched off. You know what she's like.'

'Emlyn, Dad's not my problem. Meantime you've got school. And I'm into Edinburgh this morning.'

'Dad's on the way. Couldn't you drop me off?'

'Emlyn. Look, I know it's difficult with Dad. But you've got to see Mum's side of it. She can't just drop everything. I realise it's hard, you know, at your age, but she hasn't forgotten him or anything.'

Hooves crunched on gravel. Emlyn positioned himself between his sister and the kitchen window. What the hell was he going to do? Last night he'd nearly got pinned to a wall … and the drunk? He grimaced and, patting his stomach, said: 'I'm feeling a bit … off-colour, actually.'

'Nice try, Em. But you're not missing any classes on my watch,' said Bridget. 'I'll give you a lift up town.'

His sister disappeared to her room to collect her stuff. A panicky weakness had latched onto Emlyn and wouldn't let go. *Think!* Her car was up near the road. He was calculating his chances of getting Bridget out of the front door and into the car without her seeing … but she hadn't seen anything, leastways not when she'd gone outside. How the hell were they going to get past it? No, with that thing tromping around in the drive, the back way was out of the question.

Bridget came into the kitchen.

'Bridge, your car's up on the road. The front's quicker.'

'Front door's deadlocked,' said Bridget, raising her eyebrows and opening the back door. 'Two minutes. You're not in the car – I'm ringing Mum.'

Emlyn grabbed his coat, expecting any second to hear a scream, shoved the tin in his pocket, and raced outside. Steeling himself, he stepped into the driveway. His sister had passed the horseman, who sat passively, watching the road.

She couldn't see the damn thing. What the hell was going on?

Then she was at the car, beckoning him to hurry. The rider swivelled slowly in his saddle; goose bumps marched across Emlyn's scalp. The man turned his mount and lowered his lance.

26

'Wait up … two ticks,' Emlyn shouted. 'Forgot my bag.'

He raced inside and stood in the kitchen. How the hell was he going to get past the sharp end of that lance? He was thinking about the previous evening in the alley, how the truck had saved him, when the idea materialised: what if the horseman was after the wooden figure? With Bridget waiting in the car there was a chance to hide it. Yeah, he'd stash it. It'd buy him some time, surely?

Upstairs, he yanked free the bottom drawer of his desk, and slid the tin into the hollow space of the pedestal. He was about to replace the drawer when he stopped.

'No! Think. *Thi-iink!*'

Bridget was nothing if not predictable. Grabbing the tin again, he removed the horseman and slipped it back into the void. The drawer was tight and he had to struggle to get it back in. Bridget would be on the phone if he didn't hurry. He looked around. There was an athletics trophy, one of half-a-dozen on the dresser. He picked it up. The base was too big. He snapped off the figure of the runner and put it in the tin. It rattled a bit but it would have to do. Shoving the tin in his pocket, he scurried downstairs and slammed the back door. The horseman was at the corner of the cottage. Emlyn darted around the other side of the house, across the front lawn, and leapt in the car.

'Come on, let's go.'

The horseman was still there, watching the back garden, but made no move to follow.

'Stomach ache gone then?'

His sister had mumbled something but he wasn't listening. It's whoever's got the figure, he thought. That had to be it. It explained everything. It's after whoever's got–

'Not the quickest way to make new friends,' said Bridget, twisting to look out the rear window. 'Talking to yourself.'

He stopped. He'd been speaking softly, but aloud.

His sister ground into reverse and backed out. 'Where's your uniform?'

'Casual day,' said Emlyn, lying. 'Didn't I tell you?'

'No, you didn't. And our little wooden friend?'

He shoved his hand in his greatcoat and a muffled rattle came from the pocket. 'You're nothing if not predictable, Bridge.'

'I am so *not* predictable, I'll have you know. And go easy with that. It's probably worth a bucket load. And make sure it goes back. *Today*.'

As they approached the Marchbank, Emlyn lowered the passenger visor to check in the vanity mirror. A flash of khaki appeared in the glass. Turning around, he glanced out of the rear window. Lawrence McCrossan's Land Rover was powering down the straight behind them.

'Bridge, do us a favour and drop me at the River Stairs.'

'Hardly the quickest route to school, is it?'

'I lent a book to a kid. His place is just off there.' Virus-like, his lies were replicating.

The Land Rover came chugging into Riverside Drive as he took the first steps. He was almost at the top when he remembered his phone. In his hurry he'd left it on his bed.

27

Emlyn crossed the Square and turned down Horse Market. He'd wanted to pop into the vet, get a minute with Digger, but he couldn't chance it with his sister still cruising around. She'd had several unspecified errands to attend to before she headed for Edinburgh. He decided to check the ordnance survey maps at the library. What he'd heard last night up at the spinney – Ol'man McCrossan's reference to the 'Sleeper's Stones' – had been bothering him. Besides, with the Land Rover following them into town, he had a niggling feeling that Lawrence McCrossan might be looking for him.

In a short close off Horse Market stood a dilapidated Victorian building called The Institute, its steps and classical portico marking a dead end. The town library was housed in its cavernous interior. Turning into the street, he saw that the huge doors were closed. He was way too early. What had he been thinking? Besides, the librarian, a stylishly dressed woman in her late thirties, never seemed to stick to the official opening hours. He sat on the steps to wait, hoping it would be one of the volunteers who unlocked this morning. He'd made the mistake of showing the librarian his folio of photos, and a joint exhibition with the local Natural History Society had been suggested. She'd bailed him up in the street twice already. He wasn't in the mood for her buzz-words and overly cheerful encouragement; he had other things on his mind.

He'd come to a decision: he'd skip school and visit his father. London this wasn't: the odds on being spotted before he got on the bus were not in his favour. Even without the uniform he'd be lucky if no-one saw him. You'll just have to chance it, sunshine, he decided.

A group of schoolies passed along Horse Market, skylarking and fooling around. Damn! Hugh McCrossan and his crew were at the centre of the group. Eddie Maxwell glanced over, nudged Terry Murcutt and spoke quickly to Hugh. The three of them peeled away, heading for the library. Emlyn forced himself to remain sitting.

* * *

'Can I help you?'

Max turned away from the newsagent's window. She had been searching the Square, thinking about Lawrence McCrossan, about how he'd kerb-crawled her on the way down. His Land Rover had chugged by twice already. She'd watched him rubbernecking, looking for her, but the magazine rack hid her. Where the hell was he now? She hated this cat-and-mouse stuff. And then there was bloody Emlyn. Her gran was still going on about it. She had sent two text messages but he hadn't answered either. The sales girl was staring at her. 'Sorry?'

'I wondered if you needed any help?'

'Just the paper,' she said.

She turned to the horoscope page; her gran hated missing her daily stars. Glancing up, she scanned the pedestrians, her eye catching Emlyn as he disappeared down Horse Market.

'The little sod!' she muttered.

* * *

Hugh McCrossan had been at the centre of the crowd, laughing and kidding, but he moved away now and sauntered across to the library with Ginger and Terry.

'What,' said Ginger, sitting on the steps next to Emlyn, 'no school uniform today?'

'Somebody's stuck one on 'im,' said Terry, gesturing at Emlyn's blood-encrusted ear. He leant back against the wall and tossed a stone from hand to hand. 'That sister of yours, maybe – very tasty. Been smacking yer around, 'as she? 'Bout time someone paid you some attention, you little faggot.'

Hugh lounged to the side, one foot casually propped against one of a pair of low pedestals at the bottom of the library steps.

'Yeah, about time,' echoed Ginger.

'What's he call himself again, orni … orni–?'

Hugh looked at Terry Murcutt. What was it with Londoners? Never knew when to shut up.

'Come on, fellers, help us out here, eh?' chided Terry.

'Orny bastard?' said Ginger. 'Orni – mental? Well, aye, definitely mental.'

'Ornithologist,' said Emlyn, getting up and moving towards Horse Market. 'So rack off, why don't you?'

Giggling, Ginger muscled Emlyn into the wall. He had hold of that white scarf the kid always wore, tugging on it. And Terry, well, he was winding himself up as usual.

'A poxy birdwatcher: a friggin' twitcher. That all you do, Sylvesterson – *watch*?'

Enough of being a bystander, thought Hugh; time for some action. He moved up alongside Ginger. A woman with a toddler hurried by down Horse Market, sensing trouble.

'What's with all this nancy boy stuff?' said Hugh, winding the silk tight around his knuckles and pulling Emlyn towards him. 'And that stupid coat you've always got on?'

'Terry Murcutt, well, well.' From Horse Market a voice interrupted, its tone baiting, sarcastic. 'And Eddie Maxwell. Up to our usual, are we? Not man enough to go one-on-one?'

28

'Oh, brilliant!' said Terry. 'If it ain't Maxi the Taxi. Taken anyone for a ride lately, 'ave we, darling?'

'Not at liberty to say, Terry,' she said, grinning broadly, 'but, while we're on the subject of transport, how's your flat tyre, like?'

'Why don't you shut it,' said Terry, letting fly with the stone. Emlyn flinched as bits of mortar spattered down his collar from where it smacked into the wall above his head.

'You can stop that right now.' An attractive woman in her late thirties had rounded the corner and was walking towards the group, a bunch of keys in her hand.

Hugh sneered, clamped a hand to the back of Ginger's neck, and shoved him towards Horse

Market. Terry Murcutt brooded sullenly for a few seconds, gave the librarian the finger, and then hurried after his mates.

'God save me from redheaded Celts. The last stoning around these parts ended up in tears. Are you all right?' added the librarian, looking at Emlyn. He nodded and glanced at Max. The librarian was on the steps, an ancient-looking key poised before the lock. 'I know we're not supposed to be open for another half-hour but you may as well come in. Thought any more about that exhibition proposal? Those photos – they're pretty much professional quality.'

'Sort of,' said Emlyn.

Max mouthed, 'What proposal?'

'What did you mean about the last stoning?' he said, ignoring the comment and following the woman inside. Max hesitated, grimaced, and trudged up the steps.

'Merlin.' The librarian was behind the counter. 'Shepherds stoned him and he fell into the Yeave, straight onto a fish trap – nasty, pointy, wooden things: pierced his side. Not satisfied with that, they think he got himself caught in some cords, strangled, sank beneath the water and drowned. Anyway, he predicted his own death: predicted that he'd die three times. Not that you can, of course.'

'I thought Merlin was supposed to be Welsh or something?' said Emlyn.

'Welsh was spoken right here. A variation, anyway. Some accounts say that he went mad and wandered the forest after he witnessed a battle.'

'We need to talk,' said Max, digging him in the back. '*Now.*'

Emlyn pointed to the rear of the library. 'Map section.'

Max followed him between the stacks to a rack full of ordnance survey maps. She watched as he flicked through them, found what he wanted and unfolded it across an empty table. He followed the river up the valley with his finger, spotted McCrossan's farm and Whistman's Wood and found the spinney. Max slapped her palm over the spinney and he looked up.

'I said, we need to talk. Ma gran, she went ballistic when she heard about them cars.'

'Hey, wait up, okay.' He peeled her fingers off the map and stared at the spinney. There was no name next to it. Most, if not all, of the features marked had names, even the smallest. It didn't make sense: he was sure he'd seen the name – Sleeper's Spinney – on the map when he had first looked at it.

'What was all that last night?' said Max. 'In the laneway?'

'Will you just shut up for a minute? This is important.'

'Oh, an' I'm not, I suppose.'

He returned to the contour lines, poring over the roads and the unfamiliar names: Dennings Knowe, Gainshaw Rig, Snabble's Lair, Black Birren.

The voices echoed in his head.

Three ravens up at Black Birren.

Only three?

– picking – at the carcass of a she-bear.

He shook his head to clear it. He knew Max was watching him closely, her fingers drumming on the table. This was ridiculous. Not only was he hearing things, now he was imagining map entries. How the hell did he know the name of the place, though? Pushing past Max, he walked to the service desk.

'The Sleeper's Stones?' he said tentatively. 'Do you have any information–'

The librarian shook her head. 'There's the catalogue.'

'Interested in the Sleeper's Stones, are you?'

Emlyn turned. A tall, grey-haired woman in tweeds was standing behind him. 'That's "stanes", spelt with an "a" not an "o". There's not many know of that name these days. Where did you hear it?'

Fuming, Max flopped into an easy chair near the magazines.

'Oh' – the woman was watching him intently – 'school project,' Emlyn said quickly. 'Anyway, what's the story with them?'

'Legend has it there was a ring of standing stones, about twenty-odd, small ones by all account, that had the habit of moving in the dead of night. Hence the name, presumably. Not that they've ever been located. A quaint local superstition, no doubt.'

'I've never heard that story, all the time I've lived here,' said the librarian, beaming at the grey-haired woman. 'Oh, and Florence, I finally remembered to bring it in with me.' She pulled a book from her bag and passed it across the counter. Emlyn glanced at the title: *Thirteen Battles: The Search for the Scottish Arthur.*

'I thought King Arthur was English or Cornish. I didn't know he was from around here,' said Emlyn.

'He was no king,' said the grey-haired woman. 'He was the *Dux Bellorum*. You're looking at our local authority on all things Arthurian.' She nodded at the librarian. 'This is her book. What I'm meaning to say is, that she wrote it.'

'You're not so dusty on the subject yourself,' said the librarian, beaming at the older woman. 'Florence, here, knows more than she's letting on.'

'Dux … Bellorum?' said Emlyn.

'*Dux Bellorum*: the leader of battles, a kind of warlord.'

'Jousting and feasting,' said Emlyn.

'Forget the Round Table,' the librarian continued. 'Norman invention, that. It backed up their dynastic claims to the throne. If you want to know what Arthur was really like,' she said, 'go watch the local lads in a game of rugby.'

'Rugby?'

'I'm not explaining myself very well,' said the librarian. She began loading books onto a trolley and seemed to have regained enthusiasm for her topic. 'Polo – ever seen it played?'

'On the telly once,' said Emlyn. 'I thought you were talking about rugby?'

Max let go a noisy sigh, pulled a bored face and stared at the crossword page for the umpteenth time.

'Like I said, I'm not explaining this correctly. Okay, well you take the lads from the rugby pitch and stick them on horses, give them the riding skills, of course – this is where the polo analogy comes in – put something sharp in their hands and tell them some strangers with foreign-sounding names have kidnapped one of their sisters. I'm making a huge generalisation here, one that my politically correct bosses would have me on unemployment for if it ever got back to them. But politically correct, Arthur was not. A unique combination of the right to lead and a sort of headbanging working-class obsession with tribalism.'

'That'd be right,' chipped in Max from her chair. 'Town full of toerags, this is.'

The tweedy-looking woman was nodding. 'Best description of Arthur I've heard in years.' She was studying Emlyn's face intently again. 'Do we know one another?' He shook his head. 'It's just that you remind me of someone.'

Emlyn glanced up at the wall clock and then at his watch. 'Got to run. The bus – sorry.' He could feel the old woman watching him as he ran down the steps into the narrow street. Max catapulted from her seat. Outside, she grabbed Emlyn and spun him around.

'Is this the point I get to talk or should I make an appointment, like? So, last night – in the laneway? What was all that about?'

'I've a bus to catch.' He caught her look. 'Shortly.'

'You sure you didn'a do them cars last night, because we've some dead agitated neighbours?'

'I don't *do* vandalism. Period. You're the one who does *vandalism*, remember – the spinney wall.' Max continued to stare at him. 'Anyway, there was something up there on the other side of the van. That's what damaged the cars. I know you're going to think I'm loopy but it was a … a …'

'What? Dinna make me squeeze it outta you.'

'A horseman: a rider, dressed like out of some medieval movie or something, and he had a flaming great–'

'What?'

'Spear – lance – I don't know.'

'So this horseman – like the one I didn'a see up at the spinney, was it?'

'Some bloke was hospitalised last night. I saw him. He got out of the taxi – the taxi I took home.'

'You took a taxi?'

'Yeah, I'd just had the crap frightened outta me. I wasn't about to hang around to find out what it was going to do. And I heard it at the top of the street where the drunk got skewered.'

'Don't talk wet, man. You'll have me believing in fairies next. Malcolm McKlintock, he's a piss-head. Owes money all over. Somebody stuck him 'cause of that. You just heard what the library lady said. There's some right hard-nuts in this town.'

'What's the use,' said Emlyn. 'Have it your own way.'

'I'm planning on that, dinna bother yourself.'

'Besides, I've got other things to worry about.'

'Like what?' said Max.

'Like Digger's been taken to the vet. Like some scrote tried to poison him. Like my money's on Ol'man McCrossan, because he said he'd been worrying his sheep.'

'Shite. He'd be capable of something like that, an' all.' Max looked away, her face creased in thought. 'Okay, okay, I believe you – about the cars, like. So, anyway, where you skiving off to?'

'Aren't you late for class?' said Emlyn.

'No later than you.' Max raised her eyebrows as she studied his greatcoat. 'C'mon, you can tell me. Where you going, eh? You want some company, 'cause I've frees all morning?'

'Nowhere – exactly.' He was reluctant to mention his father. 'I've an aunt,' he said quickly; he was getting good at this fabrication business. 'Out past Inneswood.'

Max shrugged. 'Suit y'self.'

He indicated the paper in her hand, open at the crossword section. 'Do the crosswords, do you?'

'Nah, Gran's into Sabina, Star Woman.'

'You've read it?' She nodded. He took the newspaper gently between his fingers. 'Any chance I could–?'

'Get your own paper. This one's ma gran's.' She grabbed his arm again and then let her hand drop. 'Look, McCrossan, he was hanging around when I left for school,' she added, pulling a face, 'an', what with ma bag an' all … well, he's definitely on to us, like.'

'We'll talk,' he said, running backwards. 'Tomorrow. School.'

'Today. It canna wait. The tea rooms,' said Max. 'Five: I'll take a quick break. There's a bench on the Green. Be there, okay.'

Emlyn tore down Horse Market, across the Square and into the newsagent. *The Herald* would give him something to read on the bus. Besides, he'd really wanted Max's copy for his dad; the old feller had been a cryptic crossword buff before his illness.

29

The year has died twice since Arthur ran beneath the moon, although he remembers little now of what happened in the forest. Merlin has come down off the mountain and taken house temporarily behind the palisade to watch over the youngster. The boy comes to the old man in his dreams and many times Merlin wakes to cries others cannot hear. At his bedside he sings away Arthur's night fears and fevers, quieting the god in him, easing the boy's memories of fear and pain and power so raw that it would break a lesser spirit.

Arthur's fevers spin Merlin back into his own dreams and nightmares, back to when he was a child: the knowledge of his parents' death, the faces of the men that he saw long before they came for him, the long training he endured. How strange in old age to still feel like an orphan, while those around him avert their eyes and make the sign from fear or reverence. Merlin's own words, not mine.

But power orphans us in other ways. The boy will know this soon enough.

Has it not already begun? There is a glamour about Arthur that the people sense. In the settlement he is constantly stared at but no-one will meet his eye. Only in the privacy of his bed or alone on the hillsides does he shed their gaze. Merlin, ever the politician, has wrought his work. Magic is not his only tool. Rumour and gossip serve him just as well. Word of Arthur's suckling from the she-bear has spread like floodwater through the valleys.

30

Here and there a leaf tumbled earthwards as Emlyn sauntered along beneath the tunnel of plane trees that marked the drive of Huntleighbank Hall. Soon the branches would be bare, he thought; winter would settle in over the countryside. There'd be snow. He loved those hours before the first fall: the leaden skies; the anticipation they brought. He thought of the spinney and the surrounding wood, the crowded trees dark smudges on a white canvas. An image of Ol'man McCrossan tramping across the whiteness disturbed his reverie. Jeezus, he thought, even in his quietest moments the McCrossans seemed inescapable.

Emerging a short distance from the sprawling Victorian mansion, Emlyn came to a halt, thoughts of winter and the McCrossans momentarily banished. He was still a little awed by the structure; its neo-gothic ornateness. The buildings made him feel oddly self-conscious, somehow embarrassed for his father.

According to his mother, Emlyn's paternal great-grandfather had built the house. The family fortune had been made in shipbuilding during the great days of the Clyde and no expense had been spared. As a child, Emlyn's father had run amok through the grounds and the endless passages until his father – Emlyn's grandfather – had squandered the family fortune on a series of slow horses and ill-timed business deals. The irony of his father's current situation was not lost on him.

Emlyn pushed the memory away – seeing his father again after a break was always difficult – and walked around to the modern annex at the rear of the building. Behind the glass doors, he stood for a moment in the air-conditioned lobby, gathering himself before he rang the buzzer. The walls were a pale lilac; racks full of mental health leaflets lined one side of the room. He pushed the button and waited. Already he felt hot in his greatcoat. He picked out a pamphlet – *A Guide to Electroconvulsive Therapy: The Latest Evidence* – and started reading. A nurse entered the lobby.

'Visiting?'

'My father, Rory Sylvesterson.'

The nurse swiped a card and disappeared through the double doors. Emlyn put the pamphlet back in the rack, sat down and glanced at the crossword on the couch beside him. He had no pen. His thoughts spun back towards the first signs of his father's illness. It had been a month or so before they'd been due to move up to Yeaveburgh and the house had been a chaotic jumble of boxes and packing cases.

His father, a huge avalanche of a man with a greying goatee, had always been obsessive, especially about little things – caps on toothpaste, dripping taps – and was seen as somewhat eccentric by some of his friends and more distant relations. When he'd started collecting pens, mostly ballpoints, a few years previously – bunches of pens bound with elastic bands appeared briefly before vanishing – no-one had taken much notice.

One Saturday morning, when the chipped cup in the kitchen had disgorged only toothless pencil stubs, Emlyn wandered upstairs and paused on the landing. His father had always been territorial about his study: no-one went up there without invitation, not even Emlyn's mother. To look for something as prosaic as a pen – well, his father would've had a fit.

A chaotic raft of colours, shapes and sizes stared back at him as he pulled out the writing drawer of his father's desk. He opened the other drawers. Two were full of pens, the remaining four in various stages of completion.

He mentioned nothing to his mother, who'd taken an important teaching post at Edinburgh the previous year, and who seemed preoccupied with 'departmental politics', as she put it. Emlyn had heard the late-night 'discussions' issuing from beneath their bedroom door. She was tired of commuting at weekends, tired of running two households. Bridget was in Edinburgh. It all made perfect sense. She couldn't fathom why he was so agitated by the prospect of moving back. He'd love it. Might even connect with some old school chums. Beside, she'd found 'just the place', right alongside *the* major archaeological find of the decade, and she had no intention of letting either the cottage, which they could rent indefinitely, or the dig slip from her grasp.

Emlyn had thought his father's edginess about moving back to his hometown of Yeaveburgh was just that – the usual adult twitchiness about change – and the following day, when the big man was doing the crossword, he'd asked hesitantly: 'What's with the pens, Dad?'

'There's never a pen when you need one,' his father had said, his massive frame hunched over the table. 'They'll always take a pen. Pocket it, pick it up off your desk, off the telephone table, and then, when you need it to write down what they're saying, then you don't have one.' Emlyn had assumed the 'what they are saying' component had been his father's colleagues, or the clients who rang, interrupting meal times.

But he had been talking about the voices in his head.

The call came the following Saturday. It was Emlyn who answered the phone. With Bridget in Edinburgh, and sensing the urgency in his mother's staccato responses, he'd felt obliged to accompany her on her dash into the city. 'On a rampage,' his secretary had said, 'smashing computers and bellowing "he was tired of being a prisoner of the cold" and that "when he found out who had switched off the heating he was going to have them hung, drawn and quartered".' The secretary had smiled shakily at them, while his mother's hand had briefly searched out his.

In the police cells, his hair in disarray, spittle flying from his lips, his father had roared at the custody sergeant in a strange language. His mother chivvied Emlyn back to the front desk. Later, he learnt it was Latin.

His father had been moved to the Borders after Emlyn's mother had pulled some strings and arranged a transfer. While smaller and somehow less institutional than the hospital in Berkshire, Emlyn was in two minds about Huntleighbank. His father, far from improving, had retreated more steadily into his shell.

The electronic door buzzed and Emlyn started as a charge-nurse barrelled into the foyer. He was one Emlyn liked from previous visits: a tall, garrulous man with a shock of ginger hair. Emlyn followed him into the older part of the building, down a corridor, through the oak-panelled patients' lounge and out onto the side terrace. Across the lawn, his father sat on a dilapidated wooden bench that circled the trunk of an enormous Cedar of Lebanon.

'Is he–?'

'Your father's pretty subdued today. He's doing okay,' said the charge-nurse, turning back towards the patients' lounge. 'Couple of months, we're hoping that, mebbe, we can get him into a residential care unit.'

His father sat hunched in an old black overcoat. Emlyn had never seen him without it since his illness, even during summer. His carers were always at him to take it off, always saying how his father complained of the bitter cold.

'Hello, Dad, I brought the crossword.' He held out the newspaper, folded to the crossword page. His father stared at the lawn. It was always like this at the beginning of a visit – awkward, imprecise. 'You used to like doing the crossword.' As far as he knew, his father hadn't done one for years; he'd been particularly good at cryptic puzzles.

Emlyn chattered on for a while, eventually running out of things to say. He would just sit: keep his father company. No, he'd try the crossword. He studied the clues. None of them made sense. There was one with a Scottish twist. He'd try that.

'Dad? Nineteen down. "Argyle trawlerman's broken leg helped considerably as boat casts off for fair isles." Eight letters.'

'Knitting.'

How did he do that: sit for days, saying nothing, and then just come up with the answer like that? Emlyn stared. His father hadn't moved. He'd try another one. He scanned the clues.

'Bet you won't get this one. "Loss of ring leads cavalry regiment to adopt mythical creatures as mascots." Seven letters.'

‘Dragons.’

‘Nanoseconds this time,’ said Emlyn. ‘But I don’t get it?’

‘Dragoons: cavalry regiment. Take out an “o”, a ring: dragons.’

‘Blimey! You could break into this professionally–’

A hand shot out and grabbed his wrist. His father’s stubbly face was pressed close to his. ‘The raven girl, she’s breached the wall and the horseman’s loose.’ Emlyn’s arm hurt and he bit his lip.

31

His father stared into the distance and his grip lessened. Emlyn's mind spun. How did he know he'd seen the rider clear the wall that day? He'd told nobody about the horseman, apart from Max, who was hardly likely to blab to anyone. It wasn't possible for his father to know any of this. And the raven girl? Did his father mean Max?

'Know about the horsemen, boyo?' said his father, his face close again. 'Do you? Do you, eh, boyo? You're in it too, with them, aren't you?' His grip tightened again and Emlyn cried out.

'You're hurting me!'

His father was standing now, a fiery stream of Latin drifting across the lawn on the breeze. Dragging Emlyn up off the bench, he began to walk towards the house. A nursing assistant appeared at his father's shoulder. The man was a finger's width shorter than his father, but broader, heavier – and younger.

'It's all right,' he said calmly. 'Mr Sylvesterson? You can let your son go now.'

The nursing assistant's hand closed over Emlyn's father's wrist and the two men slewed to a halt, their bellies touching. His father's hold tightened. Emlyn's eyes watered.

'Almost morning tea time.' The nurse who had escorted Emlyn into the grounds was at their side. 'I'm sure both you and your son would like a cuppa. How's that sound, Emlyn?'

His father's grip relaxed and his arm went limp. The female nurse who he had seen in the foyer stepped onto the terrace and he found himself separated from his father and drawn away up the steps. Outside the French windows stood the tall elderly woman from the library.

'Of course I know why you reminded me of someone,' she said. 'It's Emlyn, isn't it?'

Somewhere in his memory her face bobbed out of reach alongside a bright coloured beach ball blowing out to sea.

'You're my great-aunt–'

'Florence. A beach ball is a precious thing when you're three.'

'How did you know about the ball?'

'That was a lovely holiday. Of course, I only came for a few days. It's funny what you remember as you get older because almost nothing else comes to mind about that holiday except – well, let's say you were simply inconsolable over its loss.' The old lady let her eyes wander as if she were searching for something and then smiled. 'I was thinking of sitting with my nephew – your father, but–'

Emlyn gazed at the figure on the lawn, slumped like a huge child, his back to the steps, surrounded by staff. They were trying to get him to stand but he kept shrugging them off.

'I'm just down the road at Inneswood.' She smiled at Emlyn. 'I was wondering if you'd like to brighten up my parlour for a while? My car's out front. Shall we go through or around?'

'Around,' said Emlyn. He was thinking about the casual line he had fed Max outside the library, the one about having an aunt out near Inneswood.

While his great-aunt rummaged for her keys, Emlyn turned over what his father had said. It was as if he'd been there, seen the rider jump the gap. And Mrs Fraser's photograph and the other times with the horseman. And telling Max about his great-aunt like that, before he'd even met her, even really knew about her. He thought about his father slumped on the lawn. Was that his road too? Cloud shadows ghosted across the surrounding hills and he wished himself up on their flanks, buffeted by the wind, with his binoculars and the silence.

32

Not far short of the size he will be as a man, Arthur has filled out into a stocky youth. The scrag ends of a beard have shown themselves. All autumn the women and girls have laughed and whispered amongst themselves as they passed, often stopping to watch and nudge one another. He has bulked up, muscled out, for his uncle drives him hard, taunting him, saying there's time enough for a wife when you're a man. Practise, he says, until you drop. And Arthur does – horse and lance, sword and knife – but more at Merlin's bidding than his uncle's.

His uncle, seeing the lad's need for comradeship – Merlin being neither talkative, nor handy with a sword – suggests the need for a companion, a mentor skilled in arms.

A message and rich gifts are sent to Feinu, the chieftain at Traprain Law, for Merlin wishes the loan for one year of Cei, the chieftain's bodyguard. Feinu, seeing the generosity of the trade but failing to understand Merlin's cunning, agrees, and I am sent back to my old home at the meeting of the two rivers.

I am a mere eight years Arthur's senior but it is from me that he must learn to hone his skills. But, by degrees, I am less demanding, slower to criticise, quicker to praise than the boy's uncle, and, unlike Master Merlin, I speak with the bluntness of a soldier. We find time for other things: hunting and hawking. At Traprain Law, where Arthur has been sent by Merlin to negotiate certain alliances with my old liege-lord, it is I who introduce him to his first woman.

Slowly the bond of friendship grows between us.

33

Max stood just inside the school's heavy glass doors, craning her head to see if Lawrence McCrossan's battered Land Rover was anywhere in sight. She had a nasty feeling he was waiting for her. Behind her the last of the students clattered down the stairs and out into the afternoon sunshine. Earlier, as the bell had sounded for dismissal, a teacher had told her she was wanted in the Rector's office. She turned away from the door and almost bumped into the school secretary.

'Have you seen the Rector, Maxine?'

'On ma way now, Mrs Dale.'

As the woman disappeared towards the car park, Max thought momentarily about ignoring the request, but decided that her grandmother's wrath wasn't worth the trouble.

* * *

'This won't take long, Maxine,' said the Rector when he finally looked up from his desk. 'You're finding your feet?'

Max nodded.

'No problems fitting in?'

'No.'

'Midmorning, you were seen in town during class time. I know your first period was free. Do you have any reasonable explanation? I know you were down at the library earlier.'

That would've been one of Hugh's little mates, thought Max. Terry Murcutt and Eddie Maxwell were both in her class. Max disguised her hesitation by rummaging in her bag.

'We've a project on that local charity that collapsed and I thought it'd be canny to get a newspaper, like. Check the facts, like – not that you're likely to get the facts from the media but, you know, try and back up what I'm saying.'

'I see.'

'I seem to have left it in class.' She flipped her bag closed. 'Is that it, Mr Lowrie? Can I go now?'

'Secondly, Mrs Beckindale drew my attention to your attire. What do you think might be amiss here?'

Max shrugged. The Rector moved to the window and leant against the sill. He folded his arms and stared at the carpet for a moment. 'Nobody's saying that you can't be an individual, Maxine. But the school has a dress code. Black shirts and blouses are unacceptable.'

'Is that all, Mr Lowrie?'

'A week should be enough time to organise the uniform, don't you think?'

'Yes, Mr Lowrie.'

'There's always a guidance teacher.'

* * *

Guidance teacher, that's all I need, she thought as she hurried down the stairs. She peered out through the glass doors. Lawrence McCrossan's battered Land Rover was across the street from the school. Never mind the guidance teacher – she could run rings around them social worker types – right now she had to deal with the McCrossans.

Ducking through the glass doors, she struck out for the corner gate that fronted Scott Street. She was hardly clear of the wrought-iron arch when she heard the Land Rover start up and chug out of a side street. McCrossan's transport, like his clothes, was crumpled and long suffering. As she walked down towards the bridge, she could hear the vehicle idling as he crawled along some distance behind her. She repressed the desire to look and kept walking. McCrossan's little game, she thought. She knew the rules; they weren't too different from those on the Tyneside estate where she'd lived on and off. Show hesitation or fear and you were a goner; appear too confident, too cocky, and you were a goner. It was like juggling: if you didn't think about it too much you were all right.

Yeaveburgh High School was across from the Old Town, part of the newer developments – this meant anything built after seventeen hundred as far as Max could tell – and she had to get across the river first. The town's two bridges were old, their medieval arches still spanning the turbulent waters, with the Town Bridge, the one she must now cross, the narrowest. Traffic was confined to a single lane controlled by traffic lights on either side.

As she hurried across, the lights turned red and the oncoming traffic pulled onto the bridge. McCrossan's Land Rover was wedged in behind a tractor and trailer. McCrossan would have his work cut out behind that sucker. She would lose him in the narrow streets around Castle Rise, down behind the river where the three-storey terraced houses had narrow passages running between and behind them.

She glanced back to where the Land Rover was still waiting at the lights. She could see McCrossan behind the mud-spattered windscreen, his fingers drumming on the steering wheel. The last few cars were trickling over the bridge and then she heard the crunch of gears as he gunned the vehicle impatiently, tailgating the tractor as it pulled onto the bridge.

She wasn't about to run from Lawrence McCrossan or anybody else.

McCrossan would know that she worked up at the Castle Tea Rooms. Yeaveburgh was that kind of place. But would he know her days? Her shifts were irregular and Mrs Murcutt only let her know the evening, or at worst the morning, before she was needed. Normally she went home to change. Not today. She had a feeling McCrossan's Land Rover would be parked outside her gran's.

She had come to Castle Steps, the narrow flight of stone steps that climbed away from the Yarrow. If she turned up the dark cleft between the houses, she would come out at the rear of the tea rooms. Max trusted her instincts; they rarely let her down. She turned up between the houses, taking the steps two, three at a time. On one side were the backs or sides of houses, on the other a retaining wall, with wild flowers clinging to the cracks. Above stood a row of neat gardens. She slowed down. A vehicle stopped briefly at the base of the steps, but the passage curved and she could no longer see the river. The vehicle continued on its way. It sounded like McCrossan's Land Rover but the steps magnified and distorted sound and it was hard to be sure.

She did not frighten easily, she knew that, but there was something about McCrossan, now that they had taken the figure, which made her uneasy. She glanced up and down the steps, trying to make up her mind whether she should head back the way she had come.

Instinct deserted her; she felt trapped and alone.

It was impossible for McCrossan to be at both the top and the bottom of the steps at the same time, but she couldn't shake the feeling that he was: the sense that whichever direction she chose, he would be waiting. Her eyes closed and a voice echoed in her head. It was her mother's, ugly and strident and full of self-pity. She wanted to yell back.

Opening her eyes, she started back down in the direction she had come. She moaned. Something dark was reaching out. Her feet took the steps in slow motion arcs; gravity and panic had taken over. Boots thudded on the steps behind her. Someone was coming down at speed. It was McCrossan. She knew it.

34

Max was at the bend in the steps where she could see Castle Wynd. She slowed down and stopped. Think, girl! *Think!* She pressed her back up against the cool stone. Above her, footfalls still echoed on granite. Let him come. She hadn'a got the carving. Emlyn had it stashed, safe somewhere. What was Lawrence McCrossan going to do? Kidnap her? Hardly. The footsteps thundered closer and a skinny ten-year-old with a skateboard said something rude as he hurtled past.

She laughed, took a coin from her pocket and flipped it in the air. It rolled to a stop by the wall. Heads she would go down, tails she would go up. She walked to where it had rolled. Tails it was. She took the stairs at a steady lope, leaving the coin below her like a good luck sign.

At the edge of Castle Green, she hung back between the houses. A number of cars were parked in the bays alongside the grass: tourists by the look of it. Up by the castle, a driver was ushering a handful of tardy Asians back onto his coach. Faces stared at her from behind the smoked glass of the coach windows. She swept the Green one final time and strode onto the grass, hoping that Lawrence McCrossan did not go bothering her gran.

The bell jangled as she went in. The tea rooms were busy. She glanced around: several families, a few couples, and a table of Danish or Swedish tourists – she could never tell the difference – talking in their singsong accent.

Mrs Murcutt butted her way through the swing doors with a tray of cakes.

'You're late. And where's your uniform? We've that big do on this evening.'

'I didn'a have time to fetch it.'

'You'll find a spare apron out back.'

A chill stole over her and she glanced around. Sitting at the same window seat as Emlyn had the day he had come in from the rain was Ol'man McCrossan. He winked and waved the menu at her. It seemed impossible that she hadn't seen him immediately. She walked straight to his table and glowered at him.

'What's your game, eh? What youse two up to? Your son – following me around.'

'Smoked salmon sandwich: now, that would go down a treat.'

'You wriggly piece of–'

'Why would my lad Lawrence follow you?'

'Because he's a sicko? I dunno – you tell me.'

'Just a word is all we want, with you, and that wee boyfriend of yours.'

'He's no' ma boyfriend. An' poisoning dogs ... that's ... that's criminal – and an offence.'

'I've no idea what you're on about, lassie,' said Ol'man McCrossan. 'The scones – good, are they?'

'I don't bake 'em, I just serve 'em.'

'I'll take that as a recommendation then. Forget the sandwich.' Ol'man McCrossan reached under the table and produced a small backpack. 'Thought you might like this back. You should be more careful with your things, lassie.'

'You'll be wanting tea with the scones!' said Max, snatching the bag from him. Without waiting for an answer, she marched back to the kitchen and began banging around with the cups and plates.

'Breakages come out of your wages.' Mrs Murcutt

bumped through the doors. 'You fixing those for Ol'man McCrossan?'

'Aye. But I'll not be serving that dog poisoner.'

'What? You should watch your tongue. A smart mouth finds trouble fast.'

'He baits dogs, that one.'

'Rubbish – and you'll do as you're directed!'

'Anybody else, but not him.'

Mrs Murcutt sighed and eased her tray in among the clutter on the counter.

'All right, you do the Germans and–'

'They're Scandinavians.'

'They could be little green men. Just serve them. I'll do himself.'

Two more coaches drew up outside and Max was rushed off her feet. Suddenly, McCrossan Senior was at the till, running his eye up and down her. She looked around for Mrs Murcutt but she was taking an order for a table of six.

'Four-ninety,' she said thinly.

'Mebbe you – or your wee friend perhaps – has something.' He pulled out his wallet and handed her the money. 'Something that doesn'a belong to you. We'd like it back. No fuss. No questions. Am I making sense? No? Shame, I thought mebbe you'd know something about it? You know his father's in that private loony bin out on the Edinburgh road.'

Max pushed his change back at him.

'What's this?' He nodded at the solitary coin. 'I gave you a twenty.'

'Purely no chance. You gave me five, an' you know it, you lying piece of–'

'Maxine!' Mrs Murcutt was at her side. 'Now, what seems to be the trouble?'

'He's saying he gave–'

'I was asking Mr McCrossan.'

'A wee mistake, that's all.'

'Mistake my arse.'

'Maxine! Enough!'

'I gave her a twenty. She seems to think I gave her five.'

'He handed me a fiver.'

McCrossan Senior shrugged.

'Why don't you ask *him* why I'm late? I had to walk around by the river because–' She could hear what she sounded like. Mrs Murcutt was looking at her; customers were staring.

'That's it,' said Mrs Murcutt. 'We'll not be needing you tonight, or any other for that matter. As of now – you can go.'

'And ma wages?' said Max.

'Ha! You can want away. You'll no' be getting any money from me!'

'Keep your brass then,' said Max, throwing her apron at the open till and stuffing her backpack inside her schoolbag. She glared at Ol'man McCrossan. Mrs Murcutt sucked at her teeth and handed him the change from a twenty. Max stormed towards the door. When she was level with the Scandinavians she stopped.

'Where youse from?'

They smiled nervously. 'Copenhagen.'

'That's in Denmark, isn't it?' They nodded. 'You see,' she shouted across the room, 'they're not Germans, they're Denmarkians, you great fat cow.'

'No,' said a dark-haired girl. 'Danes. We're Danes – not Denmarkians.'

'Great! Danes.'

'No, this is a dog, yes, you are speaking of.'

Max shook her head and strode towards the exit. The bell jangled crazily. She stood on Castle Green, shaking with rage. The ruined teeth of the keep gnawed at a brilliant autumn sky. A lace curtain twitched in one of the houses that fronted the Green. Max jabbed her finger in the air and the curtain fell back. An overwhelming feeling of humiliation flooded through her. She was about to stride down the hill when she remembered Emlyn and looked at her watch. He would be another half an hour – if he bothered to come at all.

35

A year has passed and Merlin believes Arthur to be ready. It is Merlin's plan to present him to the Lords and their druid advisers at Woden Law, the great hill fort to the south, during the yearly gathering of the clans, for it is the time of the Beltane fires, when men drive their cattle between the flames to bring them protection over the coming year.

Arguments break out like spot fires in dry summer grass. Drunk, and nursing family grievances, the warriors fight amongst themselves. A jaw is broken and bloody teeth spat onto the turf. Swords are drawn and a man loses an arm in a scuffle, his life leaking away under the night sky.

The dead man is from our settlement. Word spreads across the camp and suddenly Arthur is there in the firelight. I stand deep in the shadows with Merlin, watching.

Enough, Arthur says. You want to fight? Then draw your blades against the boat-people who advance upon your lands each summer.

No beardless stripling speaks for our clan. The man says this quietly, kneeling and cleaning his blade on the turf. His eye never leaves the burly youth standing at the edge of the firelight.

We follow none but our own, says another.

As sheep do, eh, replies Arthur.

The man roars and launches at Arthur, who steps casually aside, his dagger skewering the man beneath the jaw. Arthur frees the point and the body falls to the grass.

Swords are drawn and a man leaps forward into the firelight.

36

'The family moved here,' said Emlyn's great-aunt, 'after the bankruptcy. A lot of your father's things are still here.'

Emlyn nodded and followed her up the wood-panelled stairs with their threadbare carpet. At the end of the landing, she pushed open a door and motioned him into a sunny room filled with bookshelves. Model aeroplanes, their tissue stretched drum-like over balsa wood, hung from the ceiling on dusty cotton. A bright quilt lay on the bed; books lined the shelves; mothballs stained the air; and behind that another smell hovered just out of reach – the smell of cold and winter and creeping ice.

An oak desk squatted before the casement windows; afternoon sun streamed across the blotter.

To one side stood an ornate silver frame. Pen lines and bright colours lay intertwined on heavy paper.

'What does it say?'

His great-aunt's voice drifted across the sunlit room.

'"*Quis custodiet ipsos custodes?*" It's rather beautiful, isn't it? Calligraphy and illumination: one of your father's passing interests. It's Latin and means, "Who will guard the guards?"'

The frame flashed in the sunlight. The room shifted and grew smaller. He was being sucked along a tunnel. He thought of the birds he watched, how they looked down upon the world. Voices called to one another, their timbre curiously muffled. Sick and panicky, he closed his eyes, struggling to shut them out.

Who will guard the guards?

Was that his great-aunt speaking? Voices skittered through the icy air.

How strange – to feel like an orphan, while those around you avert their eyes and make the sign from fear or reverence. But power orphans us in other ways. The boy will know this soon enough.

Snow covered the ground. Cold chewed at his bones. A boy ran through the wood. A Scots pine lay where it had toppled, its dark web of roots and clay thrust towards the sky. A broken bough had punched through the snowy mound and the boy stood looking into the dark opening.

Emlyn knew this place: Sleeper's Spinney.

A sky the colour of lead covered the world. The room was filled with slowly falling snowflakes.

His great-aunt's voice drifted across the silent fields and between the trees. 'I never really knew what to do with the models. It seemed a pity to throw them away.'

He nodded and heard his reply stop in the air in front of him, the sound deadened by the snow. So, this was what insanity felt like. He wasn't going to struggle like his father had: the terror and the ugliness were too much. Give in. Let it slide over you.

The boy in his vision slipped into the opening and disappeared.

Snow fell: huge flakes floating to earth, defeating time.

Scrambling up out of the opening, cradling the wooden horseman, against the brilliant stillness of the snow, the boy seemed cut from paper.

The room breathed Emlyn back into the sunlight and the smell of polish and mothballs.

The boy was his father.

Images and feelings crowded in around him. Emlyn could sense his father at every turn, in every object. Memories peeled from his skin like an old shirt or a pair of shoes: his father teaching him to ride, holding the saddle and shouting encouragement as he let go; a kite, green and yellow against the sky; his father bent low over his cot staring down at him. Emlyn shivered, drifting back towards the whiteness and the silence.

It was easier just to join him. No more struggle.

Easy.

Emlyn jumped. The report of a shotgun cracked the bitter air. The boy was running, but another, older lad, broke from the trees and in a few strides brought him down. A man hopped over the wall and walked towards the figures struggling in the snow. A second shot barked out. Rooks flapped away, black echoes amongst the trees. The man had his father by the collar and was dragging him back towards the spinney. His father's face was ashen as he was forced over the wall and in among the trees.

Slowly the snow and the spinney faded from his vision. Emlyn found himself staring up into an old woman's face. She was bent over him and seemed familiar.

'I thought for a moment you were going to faint.'

He tried to stand up but she pushed him back down into the leather swivel chair. He stared at the huge oak desk and remembered where he was.

'You'll feel better in a minute.'

Emlyn nodded and stood. Something crunched under his feet. The silver frame lay where it had fallen, its glass broken, its calligraphy askew.

'You picked it up,' said his great-aunt. 'Then you went all vague and it slipped. You're sure you don't want to sit for a bit? You still look a little shaky. Your father had episodes like this.'

His father's calligraphy – *"Quis custodiet ipsos custodes?"* – it meant something, but he couldn't remember what. Who was his father? He realised he had never really known him. His father's past, his childhood, and the man he had become, were simply stories handed to him by his mother: somebody else's memories.

How little he remembered – actually remembered. His father was lost to him: a small boy running away in the snow, footprints staring back at an empty sky.

His chest ached and there was a knot in his throat.

His great-aunt stooped slowly, picked up the frame and ushered him onto the landing. The house was old fashioned, full of antiques and wall hangings, but there was a warmth that seemed to come from the old lady.

'Why has the room been left that way?'

'Nostalgia, on my part – for your father's childhood or lack of it. Everything in that room was precious to him. It was how he held the world at bay.'

'Lack of childhood?' said Emlyn. 'I don't–?'

'My brother, your grandfather, was something of a martinet.'

'Sounds like something in the army.' He followed her downstairs and she ushered him into a room at the front of the house.

'You're close.' She sat straight and gathered her skirt around her knees. 'It means a rigid disciplinarian. Your father was allowed no childhood as such, and I for one will call it what it was – cruel. He was an only child. Cruelty for cruelty's sake.'

The silver frame was on the low table between them. She smiled at him. He smiled back. Suddenly he was exhausted.

'What about his mother?'

'A fragile woman: highly strung. The house was run like a regimental headquarters. My brother had been in the Black Watch, you see. A bonnie regiment: bonnie fighters.

'But your father was a dreamer. His mind was on Arthur and Excalibur and the Grail. I sometimes feel more than a little responsible for–' She paused, frowning. 'I *encouraged* him in things Arthurian. He used to scour the countryside, when he was allowed out, that is. Always coming home with something; always a tale woven around it. "Relics," he'd say. But Archie, my brother, had everything laid out for him: a commission in the Black Watch. "Officer material," he'd say. Cannon fodder, more like.

'Barricaded indoors – not here, this was over at that rambling warren of a place, Huntleighbank Hall – when he should have been off across the fields. He hardly ever went out. His favourite hiding place was up in the attic: well, more a loft, really. He'd made some sort of ladder that he kept hidden away, and my brother couldn't reach him up there. No doubt it's all been nailed shut now.'

'Was he sick?' said Emlyn. 'Ill, I mean?'

'Your father had, still has, the constitution of an ox. No, he wasn't sickly – but, if he had a cough, say, then your grandfather expected an essay on the common cold. It was no childhood for a boy. When Theodora, his mother, died ... when she ... when the debtors closed in, my brother tried to hold the place together – started selling things off, bit by bit. Eventually there was nothing left to sell. He and your father were rattling around in that place like dried peas in a bath. My brother hardly went out. Rory, your father, was expected to toe the line. Then, of course, they moved in here with me.'

'I should get this fixed,' said Emlyn, reaching for the frame.

'Don't worry about the frame. Keep it. It's yours by rights. Look, I've an appointment in town shortly. Can I give you a lift?'

'That'd be terrific. I don't suppose you've got room for my bike, have you? I left it chained up down at St Andrew's.'

* * *

His great-aunt swung the car into the driveway of the cottage and slewed to a halt on the gravel. Bridget's car wasn't in its usual spot. Emlyn was relieved she was out; he wouldn't have to explain why he was home early from school. He got out, lifted his bike free and slammed the boot.

'How come,' he said, sticking his head through the passenger window, 'you've never visited us?'

'I've never been what you might call the most tactful of people. Your mother – well, let's just say we never quite saw eye to eye.'

The window slid up and his great-aunt reversed onto the road. Emlyn watched the car disappear between the flanks of the Marchbank and then wheeled the bike down towards the garage. It was then that he spotted the flat back tyre.

37

I step from the shadows and the clansmen hesitate.

You've no quarrel with us, Cei, one of them calls.

Pointing at Arthur, I say, If you've no quarrel with him, I've none with you.

A voice from the back of the ruck: always a voice from the back. What puts you at his side? it says. He's taken one of ours.

I reply, And you one of his: fair enough exchange.

The fire crackles and sheds sparks into the night sky: not a soul moves or speaks. Hearts mark the beating of time as we stand, swords drawn. All have heard of Arthur's reputation – two dead here, four there – and mine is known well enough.

Arthur drops his sword onto the turf, saying: You want my head, then take it. But think on it first. The boat-

people aren't going away. Down south they're taking slaves and building farms. One day they'll be here for your land.

We'll stick 'em all, says the voice from the back.

I relax. He has them now. He has had lessons not just in arms: Merlin has taught him well also. He has the gift of calming men.

And when they come, a great army pouring down from the hills, will you be ready? Will you be trained? Will we fight together? Or will you stand as one clan here, one settlement there? Remember, it was prophesised long ago that a leader would come, one who had been suckled by a she-bear.

The Bear, shouts another.

One by one swords are sheathed. Muttering, the men return to their sheepskins, their pots of mead or beer. Some are already talking around his words.

Cloaked in shadow, Merlin sees what others cannot; sees why men will follow him.

Arthur is a child no longer.

38

Emlyn woke with a start, staring at the ceiling, disoriented and unsure where he was. After he had been dropped off, he had gone up to his room and lain on his bed. Must have dozed off, he thought, rolling over and trying to bring himself awake. The tin pressed into his ribs. Yes – he'd taken it from its hiding place in the desk. He'd been going to find a safer spot to hide it before Bridget got home – she always seemed to be poking around in his room – but he'd come over all strange, the same sort of feeling he had when he'd been standing looking at his father's framed calligraphy. That was the last thing he remembered before waking up.

He swung his legs onto the floor. The door was ajar. He'd been pretty sure that he'd shut it. Safe – oh yeah!

With him asleep and the door wide open. God, he thought, if Bridget had wandered up, you'd be toast.

Reaching for the butterscotch tin, he prised the lid free. His breath hissed between his teeth. The figure lay on its side amid cotton wool. Around the edge some flat river stones had been sandwiched in. He pulled one out and turned it over. A black mark was scrawled on the underside. He pulled the others free; each had the same sign – the same symbol he'd seen scrawled on the stones up at Sleeper's Spinney. When the hell had he done that? Had he done it? The cold prickle of insanity, of being his father's child, beckoned to him.

He stared down at the tin in bewilderment. The stones had been on his windowsill for ages. He had collected them that first week in Yeaveburgh, from the shingle spit downriver from the cottage. He'd loved their colour and the delicate flatness of them.

He removed the figure and stared at it.

Below his window something heavy crunched on the gravel and he stood up quickly. Horse and rider turned impatiently in the driveway below. They had appeared as he had taken the carving from among the stones. He pushed the figure back. The horseman disappeared.

He couldn't remember arranging the cottonwool or the stones like that. When the hell had he put the stones in the tin, made the marks on their backs? Had he been sleepwalking? The faintest trace of a dream niggled at his memory – about the dyke and the markings the McCrossans scrawled beneath its stones. He tried to tether it but the images drifted out of reach.

He glanced at the clock: twenty-five-to-five. Max! Damn! His bike was out in the back shed with a slow puncture. And she was definitely not the waiting kind. You'll never make it up to the castle in time, he thought. Grabbing the tin, he pulled on his coat, tumbled downstairs, and ducked into the study.

'Hello,' said Bridget, leaning back from the keyboard and looking up at Emlyn. 'I had no idea you were home, matey.'

'It wasn't a uniform-free day. I got my dates mixed up. Got sent home early.'

'I'm going to burn that coat. When you eventually remove it, that is.'

'Over my dead body.'

'Specific request, is that? To be buried in an army-surplus greatcoat?'

'Yep.' He smiled to himself. His sister was in one of her lighter moods. 'Is there any chance of a ride to town?'

'I've got to be at the vet's by quarter-to-five. I'll run you wherever after we've picked Digger up.'

39

Digger stood on Emlyn's lap, his paws on the window, eyeing the pedestrians as the car swung up Castle Wynd. He seemed his usual self and had been ecstatic when they'd picked him up from the vet.

Bridget glanced across at her brother. 'You've got tomorrow and Friday off, haven't you? For in-service days?'

'That's right.'

'Turning out to be a pretty easy week school-wise?' He nodded and Bridget continued. 'Tomorrow afternoon then, when it's calmed down a bit, why don't you bring your girlfriend down to the dig? I'll show her around.'

'She's not my girlfriend.'

'Your friend then.'

'So you can report back?'

'Pardon?'

'To Mum. Keep her up to speed.'

'Come on, Em, it's not like that. Your *friend* might enjoy it, you never know.'

'*You* might enjoy it.'

'Tad tetchy today, aren't we?'

'Yeah, with Mum. Is that okay?'

'More likely Dad,' mumbled Bridget.

'And what's that supposed to mean?'

'He's the one who left you in the lurch.'

'You sound like that doctor. The one Mum made me go and see.'

'Sleepwalking's dangerous. It was causing you ... everybody grief. Nobody was getting a decent night's rest. She had to do something.'

They drove on in silence for a while. A delivery truck swung out and Bridget leant on the horn. People stared. As the car turned into the Square, Emlyn sensed a looming question.

'Taken that figure back, have we?'

'Yep.'

'Thought I'd forgotten about it?'

'Nope.'

'Where do you need to be dropped?'

'Castle Green.'

'You're sure it's gone back.'

'Yep.'

'Bring your friend to the dig. I won't mention anything.'

'About the horseman, or my new *friend*? And is that to Mum or Max? *I mean*, being devious, is that supposed to be a natural sisterly trait? Don't answer that – I really don't want to know!'

They were coming up into the high part of the town.

'I don't appreciate you calling me devious. God, you are such an ungrateful little – I mean, some people might actually see it as being protective.'

'I don't need protecting.'

'It would be irresponsible of me not to have–'

'Don't give me that.' He pushed his voice an octave higher, mimicking his sister. 'Bring your friend down to the dig? Show her around?' His anger came in a rush. 'You can drop me here!'

'I'm only trying to talk to you,' she said, slowing down.

'No! Dad used to talk to me. You and Mum – that is, when she's around – you just talk over me!'

He scooped up the terrier and opened the car door.

'For God's sake, Emlyn! The car's still moving!'

Bridget pulled over, hauled the passenger door closed, and watched him weave between a group of tourists and disappear into one of the town's many passages, Digger trotting at his heels.

40

Emlyn leant out over the battlements and looked down on Castle Green. 'What was wrong with the bench?' he said.

Max shrugged and continued stroking Digger, who was perched on the wall, surveying the town. She'd wanted to get away from the tea rooms and was finding it hard to mention Ol'man McCrossan, fearful that she'd start blubbing when she did. The job had provided her with a few little luxuries.

'Bridget asked if you wanted to come down to the dig,' said Emlyn.

'Try something different every week, that's ma motto.'

'What?'

'You'll be there, so what's your problem? Your sister's hardly likely to bite ma head off, is she?'

'But you're not interested in that sort of stuff.'

'How do you know what I'm interested in? You've known me what – all of five minutes?'

They leant on the wall and gazed out over the town. It was Max's turn to bridge the silence.

'I was thinking of having it put on ma coat of arms, like.'

'Beg yours?'

'Ma motto: "Try something different every week." It'd look good in Greek or Latin or whatever. Anyway, I'll come. Even if it's just to annoy this sister of yours.'

'Half-sister – and I've a feeling I'm going to have to apologise to her. God, she's so–'

'Darrgh, there's plenty worse, man. Besides, she's your sister, like.' Max jerked her head in the direction of the teashop. 'There's her down there, for a start. She sacked me, you know – this afternoon.'

'Sacked you?'

'People like them,' said Max, spitting in the direction of the teashop, 'the McCrossans and the Murcutts of the world, they don't keel over at fifty. They live to a hundred and seven and terrorise the nursing home they're shoved in.' She pulled her coat about her, folded her arms and drifted towards the steps. 'Digger's okay then?' she said. 'No ill effects?'

'Seems not.' Emlyn clicked his fingers and the terrier trotted along the wall and jumped into his arms. 'He's a tough little sod.' Emlyn opened his coat and the terrier scrambled into the nest of arms and cloth, his eyes blissfully closed. 'And the biggest sook out.'

They started down the steps and Max said: 'It was Ol'man McCrossan as got me sacked.'

* * *

Down on Castle Green, Max explained the afternoon's events: the gamekeeper following her from school; how she'd lost him in the town; and the uncanny appearance of his father at her work. 'They're not gonna let up,' she said, 'about the horseman. He more or less accused you – well, us – of stealing.'

Digger ran on ahead, sniffing everything in sight and occasionally waiting for them to catch up as they walked in silence for a while, lost in their separate worlds. Max pondered the McCrossans' two-pronged tactics – whatever the wooden figure was, they wanted it back, and in a hurry – but eventually her thoughts slipped into the feud between her grandmother and the McCrossans. She was picking across various conversations she'd heard over the years, things her gran had said, but without making any real connections, when Emlyn broke into her reverie.

'So Ol'man McCrossan lied just to drop you in it?'

Max nodded. 'Remember I told you I'd seen Lawrence McCrossan this morning? I was away getting the paper for Gran and he comes trawling along in his Land Rover. "Tell that lad of yours he doesn'a know what he's meddling with!" In a sense he's right, like. Stole it, didn't we.'

'Maybe …' said Emlyn, 'it's best we put it back.'

'I've something to show you out back.' Max paused outside her front door. 'Let me just check if Gran's home first. You're not exactly man of the month.'

Max opened up; the house was quiet. She motioned Emlyn to follow her. He made a quick hand movement and Digger slumped against the wall.

At the back of the terrace they came out into a tiny walled yard. A narrow passage ran alongside a stone garage to the back lane. Max slipped between the dank, mossy walls where she opened a side door, fumbled in the gloom and pulled on a cord. Two dusty bulbs cast a dim light over a partially stripped Beezer Bantam.

'Can you get it to run?' said Emlyn, motioning at

the ancient motorbike lying on its side on the oil-stained concrete.

'Mebbe. Belonged to ma grandpa. You've your silk scarf: I've this.' She started to shift the clutter of tools, rags and boxes. 'Besides, shit hits the fan – that's ma ticket outta here.'

'Didn't know you had a licence.'

'Basic rule of shite and fans – by that time, the paperwork's irrelevant.'

Max picked up the carburettor and a set of screwdrivers off the bench, and they wandered back into the house. 'Not enough light: kitchen table's the go.'

'It's practically a museum piece. How do you know which bit goes where?'

'There was a lad, back in Newcastle, fancied me. His idea of romance was stripping his bike. I must have a flair for it, 'cause I picked it up right speedy, like. Besides, I've a bit of local expertise on tap.'

'Who's that?'

'Never you mind. So – Dobbin – I take it you stashed him somewhere safe?'

The penny dropped and Emlyn grinned. 'Yeah, he's getting high on butterscotch fumes.'

Max paused, her hand on the kitchen door. 'I want to see if I can fix this. I'll be there, at the dig, tomorrow. Can you see yourself out?'

'Sure.' Smiling back at Max, he opened the front door and nearly fell over Mrs Fraser, who was crouched beside Digger, reading his identity disc. She had her key out and was clutching a newspaper and a bunch of flowers.

'Just the person I wanted to see.' Seeing Max standing in the hall, Mrs Fraser pulled the door closed. 'I thought he was lost but he's yours, isn't he?' Emlyn nodded. 'No doubt you know about the business in the street last night.' He nodded again. 'I'm going to ask you straight, laddie: did you damage those cars?'

'No.'

'Then I'll take you at your word. You dinna strike me as the sort of boy who'd amuse himself in that way – or a liar.'

Ah, lying, well, now you mention it, thought Emlyn, I've just taken it up, more as a sort of hobby thing, 'cause Max seems to like a bloke with an interest. Unable to meet Mrs Fraser's eye, he stared at the flowers.

'They're for ma Douglas. I like to pop some next to his photo once in a while. Well, I must be away inside and put these in some water.' Pointing at Digger, she said, 'You shouldn'a leave him outside; he could get pinched. Next time bring him in.'

41

Arthur – no longer a youth, but an ill-humoured man in his middle years – calls Merlin down to his stronghold on Ynys Avallach, the Isle of Apples. I am woken before dawn, a rough hand shaking my shoulder, and told to take counsel. As Arthur's man I do as I am bid and stumble up to the hall, where my Lord is seated in his chair.

They – he waves his hand to indicate the settlement below hidden by the walls of his court – they need a sign, he says, something to follow. I am no longer enough.

There are signs aplenty, I say, and not all of them good.

Arthur has been awake all night, drinking and rutting with his latest woman, a redheaded slave-girl taken in a raid, and his usual tetchiness has been banished.

Fetch me Merlin, he bawls.

I do as I am bid and Merlin shuffles into the hall, rubbing his eyes and complaining.

A token is needed, Green One. A rallying point that they will follow. Something … what do you suggest? A crown … a coronation, perhaps?

Silver or gold, my Lord? Merlin is in no mood for Arthur's trifling.

Your mouth may be the end of you, Master Merlin, growls Arthur. Do not think that you are indispensable. Perhaps you would like a small plot all to yourself up on that hillside that you are so fond of, a neat coverlet of turf amidst your ring of stones. Arthur guffaws and slaps his thigh. Yes, a stone crown for Master Merlin. A king he will be, rather than a king's adviser: King of the lands of air and darkness.

Below us, in the shadows, the door ward, one of his guard, has fallen asleep, his sword across his knees. His grip loosened, the blade falls to the ground, ringing on the stone threshold. Arthur stares, his eye clearing, and bounds down the hall to where the startled man has awoken and is retrieving his weapon. Terrified, the door ward stares back wide-eyed. Arthur's capricious brutality is known in every valley: men have been garrotted for less. Instead, Arthur slaps the man's thigh and grabs his jaw.

A sign, Arthur bawls, picking up the man's blade. Not a crown but a sword. They shall have a sword. To the smithy, he shouts.

We do as we are bid and I lead Merlin down from the hall to the smithy, where Arthur awaits. I pull the leather curtain aside and the three of us duck into the warmth. I would like to stand there in the darkness, half asleep, guarding the door and watching the bellows turn the charcoal white, listening to the ring of the hammer, but Arthur pulls the smith outside before he has finished tempering the axe head he is working on. Merlin and I follow.

Make me a blade, Arthur says, that will split open the belly of the sky.

Merlin makes to speak, but Arthur holds his palm out and the old man's thoughts remain his own. I can see the displeasure in his hooded eyes and it is not simply from his being pulled from his bed before time. The first pale fingers of dawn settle on the hills as we watch the smith search for the right words.

That is hardly possible, my Lord, he says at length.

You work metal, man, do you not?

The smith looks first to Merlin and then to me for guidance and finding none, nods.

Then make me a blade, says Arthur.

The smith cannot so easily be swayed. One of the new Christian converts, he does not like the notion of a magical blade and his answer is couched carefully, lest it offend his Lord.

My blades are keen and well sought after, yes, he says, but what you ask is beyond my skill. You will need metal blessed by – he falters here, caught between his new belief and Arthur's cold eye – blessed by God. Where such metal is to be found is beyond my knowledge.

The smith shrugs, dips his head in respect and ducks back into the forge. Arthur scowls, spits into the dirt, and walks away. Merlin glances at me and we follow.

* * *

It is but a matter of time before the Isles are in Arthur's hands and as the leader of the battle-host he proves his strength beyond our darkest dreams. As yet he has not met the Lady of the Lake, nor received from her the sacred blade that will become Excalibur.

42

THE SACRED POOL

Iron blessed by God, the smith had said.

It is Merlin's hope that Arthur will forget his dawn visit to the smithy, for he hates the unlooked for, both in word and deed. And in this instance he is less than keen to act upon the whims of his Lord.

But not even Merlin senses the darkness contained within the smith's words.

Iron blessed by God. It will become a rallying cry.

A hunting expedition takes Arthur downriver with his lads.

A morning's ride from the Isle of Apples is a pool: a stretch of crystal water cut off from the river, surrounded by reeds and fed by a sacred spring. Here, time out of mind, people have brought offerings of metal, weapons and jewellery, and cast them away to appease the water gods.

Close by, but out of sight, stands a plain bothy of turf and stone. It is the abode of Vivienne, or the Lady of the Lake as she is known among the valleys. It is said she makes her living selling osier baskets and healing potions at the settlements. She is rumoured to be a wise woman – although barely fifteen – and the guardian of the pool: a living goddess, say some. Others mutter that she has faerie blood. That she has power, none doubt, for Merlin keeps a close ear upon her doings and is wary of meeting her. He has already counselled that the game we are hunting is more plentiful across the valley, but Arthur does not rely on Merlin for hunting knowledge, except when meat is scarce.

And Arthur – dismounted and pulling his spear from the boar kicking its life out beside the pool – well, he has no thought of Vivienne, for she is not to be seen this day and he has barely heard her name in the Great Hall. No, it is the clear, cloud-reflected water and what lies beneath that troubles him. He rides back to Ynys Avallach with the seed of an idea already sprouting in his mind.

A few days later, when Arthur next journeys to the pool, Merlin is bid accompany him on some pretext or other.

Metal blessed by God, Arthur says.

We stand uneasily, listening to the ripples lapping at our feet.

Those were the smith's words. Arthur speaks uncertainly

at first, measuring our reaction. Countless swords lie at the bottom of this pool, Merlin.

We would do well to leave undisturbed what's been placed here, Merlin chimes. There is another world beneath the surface that any man would be loath to enter.

I am not any man. You changed that when you took me into the Great Wood. The Oak God – here he taps his chest – is not to be denied. If I am to do what it is you say I am to do, to fulfil the prophecies and cleanse the land of these usurpers, then I need a blade to match what is in me, a blade that will unite the tribes. I doubt the spirit of the pool will punish me for disturbing her gifts.

With that, he pulls off his boots and wades in, muddying the water as he searches the bottom with his toes. Any argument Merlin might form sits stillborn on his tongue. Arthur will have his way. Advice is shunned these days, or openly scorned, for he treads a different path altogether now. I sense Merlin's unease. He sees more clearly the creature he has shaped, for he no longer controls the wading figure, the dark silhouette against the sparkling water, who calls to us to come and help.

I hold back, shuddering as the breeze sweeps in across the water.

There is movement on the far side of the pool.

Merlin tenses. He has seen it too.

43

How long had Vivienne, the Lady of the Lake, been stood there so quiet, so perfectly still, clad in greens and browns, I cannot say. Something, some inner sense, makes me look. Merlin too, for we see her in the same instant. She has been cutting rushes. The sickle is still in her hand and a bundle of reeds tucked beneath her arm. Squinting, I study her as I would an enemy outpost or a drunk with a knife. I would not call her beautiful, but she is a winsome thing, tall and willowy for her age, with dark hair and a wide sensual mouth. And she radiates peril: the kind of peril that a man can drown in.

That neither Arthur's hunting eye, nor mine, espied her against the curtain of reeds bodes ill. And Merlin? At hearthstones across the breadth of the land tales are woven around the power of Merlin's sight.

Something is amiss.

I could already feel the ripples moving out from that fateful day. It was something I began to understand much later: the sight fails even the wisest at times. There are patterns, pitfalls in the world that cannot be seen no matter how keen the inner eye. In that place where the water gods reigned, where the spirits cavorted beneath the wind-pocked surface, even Master Merlin could not see that far ahead.

But Arthur senses nothing of the Lady, for he is still too preoccupied with his search.

Throwing down her bundle and sickle, Vivienne starts towards us around the pool, and I hear a sharp intake of breath: Merlin's. He makes a sign with his hand and his lips move, although I cannot hear what it is he speaks. Words of power and protection, no doubt, for there is something in the way she moves that both excites and repels.

It is all I can do to stand and watch her approach.

Vivienne circles the lake, watching us as she comes, and then in all her youthful brightness is standing but a few paces away. Her perfume is heady: her charms all the clearer for her closeness. But it is her silence, purposeful and shadow-like beside her on the bank, that roots me to the spot.

Merlin, ever more alert to such subtleties than me, must speak.

His lips are still and he stands, like me, gawping at her loveliness.

Arthur finally senses her presence and looks up. It is he who speaks first. It is a net of such open weave that Merlin shakes his head. By doing so, it is Arthur who is under her spell. She has been taught well. And Merlin sees too late what she has in mind.

44

Now Arthur is gawping. A pretty trio we make, too.

You've no right here, she says.

Like a crystal bowl in which we have been held, the silence shatters around us. Bird calls rush in and a fish leaps on the far side of the pool.

Know who I am, girl? Arthur smiles and flexes his muscles, unable to see that she is no more a girl than Merlin is a witless stripling.

You could be the Green One, Merlin himself, she says, and still have no right to disturb the waters.

Merlin blinks in astonishment.

What brings you to the sacred pool? she asks.

We're searching for a blade, says Arthur. But he is searching no longer; he is gaping like a stricken youth. He does not know it, but she is to become more than a passing interest. He already has two wives and has wooed a third, Gwenhwyfar, who has been his bed-favourite since she came from the South last winter.

This blade, says Vivienne, what is it that you will do with it?

Forge another, stronger blade from it.

The offerings are to be left where they lie, she declares. They have been thrown to the Goddess.

Merlin makes the sign of protection over us. She has invoked the Goddess.

Perhaps, says Arthur, I should make plain who I am.

I know you well enough. She stares at him from beneath her tresses. And you still need my blessing.

Your blessing! I think not.

I am the guardian of the pool. What belongs here is not yours to take. Are you so arrogant that you would risk being swallowed up by her?

Nothing will swallow me, girl.

The dark waters, she says unhurriedly, swallow us all eventually.

I am watching Arthur's face. I see his flickering doubt. He has but one response to doubt: action. And so he stoops again, reaching into the water. His hand comes up dark and sticky with mud, clutching a broken blade.

Vivienne hitches up her gown, and wades out to stand

close beside Arthur. I will find what you seek, she says, and then you'll not be troubled by the Goddess.

The breeze has died and the rippled surface of the lake has become a mirror. She holds out her hand and takes the rotten iron from him, letting it slip back into the water. The ripples move out, and Merlin watches from the shore as she moves away from Arthur into deeper water. Standing waist-deep, she closes her eyes and we three hold our breath.

Suddenly she ducks low, with only her head showing above the surface, her fingers feeling in the ooze. With a clatter of drops, she is standing. Before her she holds a long shape, muddy and covered in waterweed. Every muscle tenses in me. I sense that this is something from the other world – a gift.

But how is it to be used and at what price has it been given?

Vivienne wades slowly towards Arthur and, pulling a sword from the sticky mess, tosses it to him. Catching it by the blade, he lets out a gasp. The edge is still keen. His blood mingles with the dark waters and a cry echoes over their ruffled surface – Arthur's – as he takes the blade by the hilt and holds it aloft. He is ecstatic, grinning. Here is what we came for, he bellows.

I cast a glance at Merlin. His eyes are hooded, his face pale. Are his thoughts on the same path as mine? For, *unlike the other offerings resting in the mud, this sword is unmarred and shows no sign of damage.*

But this is a sacred pool. People journey days to worship here: strips of cloth, the cast-offs of the sick and lame, can be seen tied to the thorn bushes nearby. Gifts are still tossed into the waters but what is given to the Goddess is always marred in some way: blades are snapped, jewellery and goblets dented or flattened. It is no accident that the sword Arthur brandishes is unbroken.

45

As I watch Arthur and Vivienne wade together from the pool, I remember that not long past other darker offerings were made here and in times of hardship still may be. It is not only blades and charms that lie in the ooze. The pool is not guarded by the Goddess alone but by the shades of those sacrificed here.

And still Merlin stands transfixed.

I dare not speak for fear I shall be drawn under the girl's veil as well. Something must be done. I draw my sword a hand's span and slam it back into its scabbard, the metal grating on the base plate. It does the trick.

Glancing at me, Arthur moves to the pool's edge, where the wavelets break over his boots. The water is no longer clear: a muddy stain drifts out towards the further shore. What Arthur holds before Merlin for his inspection, alarms me. The wooden hilt has long rotted away, but the blade, although pitted here and there with rust, was smeared so thick with animal fat at the time of its casting away that in places it still gleams. Curious forms lace their way across its surface: animals, a hunt, and a flying worm.

Merlin's face is a shade paler now. He has caught up with my fears. He is saying to himself, This is no mere offering, it is whole, undamaged. The question forms in Merlin's mind: Whence came this and to what purpose? So busy is he with these dark questions that he does not see the change.

Vivienne is no longer strung tight as a harp. She has what she wants, for handing her the reins of Merlin's horse, Arthur says: You must come to Ynys Avallach and see the new sword born from the old.

She takes them, smiling secretly. And Merlin steps back into the world. Too late has he seen her designs. But the Green One's mind is subtle, jinking and twisting, as quick as a coursed hare. Already he is fitting this new upheaval into his plans; already he is weighing benefits. He knows the power of such a place as the sacred pool. Above all he is a teller of tales and knows the story will spread – once he has embellished it. If Arthur must have his way, then let it be blessed by the Goddess; let the tale build how Vivienne, Lady of the Lake, brought Arthur his sacred sword.

Merlin contemplates her, endeavouring to pierce the veil, and smiling, thinks, Yes, girl, like me, you too have the sight and have known of this sword many a long day, and you have waited for this moment, knowing that it would come.

It is the girl's sight that he is left to ponder as Arthur, his hands around her waist, hoists her up and she rides away from her old life, never to return. Truly, I think that Merlin was half in love himself that day, for the powerful always seek those who are their match.

* * *

And Vivienne, who Merlin comes to understand so late? At that moment her chief desire was straightforward: Arthur would be hers and no other's. She had him under her spell, or so she thought. From that all other things would flow, for Vivienne's sight had granted her a glimpse of her new life. She saw her hands on the reins of power, not weaving osier baskets.

But Arthur will cast her aside, as he does all his women. She has no inkling of this as we ride towards Ynys Avallach, but when the time comes she will hold hard, all her life – a long life, full of power and adversity – to his ruin.

* * *

The rumours spread, as Merlin knew they would: a sword of the dead; a weapon stolen from the gods; a sword brought to Arthur's feet by Vivienne, Lady of the Lake. Arthur cares little for rumour; he is a god and his arrogance grows daily.

But the settlement's smith will not touch the blade.

There is another smith, two days' journey downriver. He is a small, nut-brown man from across the sea, a trader and worker in metal, who has settled with a local woman. His speech is strangely laced with foreign words, his accent unfamiliar, but his face is alight with smiles. He is happy to forge a blade of renown, and for the great Arthur. His reputation is made; his children will want for nothing – well, every warrior north of Woden Law will be beating a path to his door. Nor is he concerned with sacred pools and ancestors. These are not his gods, nor his people. He knows words of power that will keep him safe and ancient marks that will protect him from harm. Just such a mark is hidden in the dust at the foot of his anvil and all his tools bear the same symbol in miniature.

Arthur has his blade before the fulling of the moon.

Excalibur: truly, it was a blade like no other.

THURSDAY

46

The next day was Thursday, an in-service day and no school. Emlyn rang Max but she was working on the Beezer again. She hadn't offered for him to go up and he hadn't asked. 'See you at the dig,' she'd said as they rang off.

Emlyn sat on his bed with the tin beside him. He'd have to find a better hiding place, he thought, but he found it hard to concentrate. His mind drifted. The strange, snowy vision of the spinney that had swallowed him at his great-aunt's place hovered enticingly. He shut his eyes and concentrated on remembering the Latin phrase. The cold numbed everything; the blank whiteness could be written over. He could see his father's calligraphy forming. *Quis custodiet ipsos custodes? Who will guard the guards?* The voice was in his head. 'No,' he grunted, 'not this time.' He yanked himself free and stared at the silver frame propped up on the chest of drawers. His wrist hurt and he could feel his father's fingers tight on his skin.

He reached over and picked the frame up. The back was coming loose. If he left now he might have time to pop into the hardware shop. He fiddled with it, trying to get it to sit neatly but only succeeded in loosening it further. A folded paper dropped to the floor from where it had been sandwiched between the calligraphy and the backing. He reached down. Somewhere a cold wind rattled snow-laden branches.

'*No!*' he said. 'I'm not going there.' And he shook his head, struggling to pull himself back into the room. Instinct told him that what he held in his hand had something to do with his vision of the snow-shrouded spinney. He turned the paper slowly, reluctant to open it. A jagged edge showed where it had been torn from an exercise book of some sort. Carefully he unfolded the sheet. The paper was ruled and yellowing. A child's writing filled the page.

I know I shouldn't have been in the spinney but I just had a feeling there was something up there, treasure or relics or something. You should be allowed to keep treasure because when it's buried like that it doesn't belong to anyone. That's not what McCrossan said though, him with his kid, that tough-nut Lawrence, trailing around after him in the snow. It was Lawrence that caught me. I could've got away but for him.

Emlyn looked up. The kid from the vision – the one who chased his father and wrestled him down – was Lawrence McCrossan? Then it was Ol'man McCrossan with the shotgun? Yes, the elder McCrossan: had to be him.

McCrossan said it belonged to the land, whatever that means. I had something in my hand. I can still feel it sort of, but it's as if I dreamt everything. He said he'd tell my dad. I was scared then. He grabbed my wrist and took whatever I was holding and put it in his pocket. It goes back, he said. Came over all funny, didn't he, with his beady eyes, and pushed Lawrence behind him. You know this place is haunted. Turn around, he said. I didn't want to. He was scaring me. But he made me. There was a dirty great horseman dressed all funny, with a spear and stuff. I started crying. Then McCrossan hauled me round to face him. You've meddled, boy. Then he bent down and I could smell his breath in my face. You've got something on your back now, he said.

It'll follow you. You're going to journey in the dark and lose your way and there won't be no coming back. No way back from that place but one, and that's if someone connected dances with the sickle man. Not dance the once only, though; they got to dance three times.

I didn't understand anything of what he was talking about and I'm pretty hot on riddles. That's why I'm writing it down, so I don't forget what he said.

He started singing, with a low voice, grumbling sort of. I started humming, singing a favourite tune off the radio, but in my head. It all went funny then and I couldn't remember what I'd had in my hand or why I was up there, though I know it's because the big tree went over and I wanted to take a look. I remembered that. And the horseman. I took off and McCrossan let fly with his shotgun. Shouted that he'd shove me down inside that hole and leave me there if he saw me again.

Snow and a running, silhouetted figure. Emlyn pushed the memory aside. He needed to think. The handwriting, with its distinctive ts and gs, was his father's: a childish version, but still his.

A horseman laboured uphill.

We rode forth from Ynys Avallach that fateful day, a snell wind at our back, wolves calling in the woods. Winter had come down early. I should have seen their singing for what it was – an omen.

Emlyn leapt from the bed and punched the wall. His knuckles stung and the voice withered.

'Wait up. Think, boyo – *think*!'

So, one: Ol'man McCrossan and his son Lawrence had been there. Two: Lawrence sounded about the same age as his father. Three: critical, this was – his dad had seen the horseman. It was there written in black and white. But what was all that stuff about dancing three times with, what was it – he glanced down at the note – the sickle man? Who the bloody hell was that? The singing – yeah, the singing made sense. He'd heard that for himself, up at the spinney a few days ago.

He wanted to run after his father; question him.

He needed to talk to someone about this. Bridget? Think again, boyo. That one's all hard data. Max, he decided. I'll talk to her, show her the note. Then he remembered that he'd never told Max the truth about his old man.

He folded the note and pocketed it. Wandering around the cottage, he pondered the problem of the tin, but could come up with nowhere better than its current hidey-hole. He couldn't really carry it with him all the time. Where to put it? Where? Grabbing his coat, he went outside. The garden beds were freshly raked. He could bury it, maybe. Nah, water might get in.

The dig! Bugger! He'd completely forgotten. He needed to hurry.

Digger trotted out from inside and started barking at the driveway. Maybe he could sense the horseman, thought Emlyn. Dogs were supposed to be able to do that, weren't they? He was going to be late if he didn't get going soon. Emlyn whistled and the terrier trotted back into the kitchen. 'On your bed, matey,' he said and pulled the door to.

Out in the drive, he could sense the rider close but couldn't see him. The butterscotch tin, with its stones, was working. He rattled it gently. It's going to have to be the garage, he thought. No way am I taking this up town.

Behind the cottage at the end of the drive stood the garage, a dilapidated and doorless corrugated iron and wood construction that was slowly sinking back into the earth. A jumble of tools, bottles and old furniture was piled at the rear. Two towers of yellowing newspapers beckoned from the gloom. He would hide the tin there. Nobody was going to start searching through this lot, he thought, as he carefully restacked the papers. He looked back as he wheeled his bike onto the road. No, it's much safer under that lot than inside the cottage.

He climbed on and cranked the pedals. The rear tyre made a sinuous, rubbery noise as it slewed under the rim. He'd forgotten it was flat. With no pump, his only choice was to wheel it to the service station.

And now he was really going to be late meeting Max.

47

Arthur's interest in women is his downfall – he hurt too many of them – that, and the bedding of his older half-sister, Morgawse. The issue of that union is his bastard son, Modred.

Knowing Arthur's mood, and worried for the unborn bairn, Morgawse leaves Ynys Avallach long before her time. Twice Arthur plots Modred's death as a child. But Morgawse keeps them on the move, eventually settling in the islands far to the North, where Arthur's reach is limited.

Modred's hatred of his father is legendary.

But Arthur spawns only daughters and Morgawse's acid whisperings about Lordship and titles turns Modred's thoughts to his father's mortality and how that might be advanced. It is Modred who calls the Northern tribes to him: the disaffected clansmen, the Picts, the Irish, anyone who has a grudge or who has been overlooked once too often or who can see an opening for profit or for power.

Arthur has his twelve battles and drives the Saxons back to their boats. The thirteenth and the last could have been avoided if he had listened to me, if he had listened to Merlin's counsel even. But by then he was no longer the pliable youngster on the rock outside the forest cave. He was, as some would whisper, a leech on every household and croft within a week's ride, a liege whose taxes went on weapons and horses and summer campaigns far to the South. Others called him the Butcher of Ynys Avallach, a man – if that was what he was – without thought or care for the havoc he wrought.

48

Max stared across at the small marquee marked 'Site Office'. She'd come along the river, thinking it was a short cut, and was now on the wrong side of the excavation. 'Looks like someone went berko with a spade,' she muttered.

A group – half-a-dozen of what Max took to be students – emerged from the marquee and drifted away towards the castle.

'Hey,' yelled Max, as Bridget emerged from the marquee and turned in her direction. 'You're Emlyn's sister, right? He said to come down and have a look.' Max stepped down into the trench in front of her. 'I'll come across.'

'No! Wait there,' shouted Bridget. 'Don't move. I'll come and get you.'

Max watched as Bridget negotiated the maze of trenches and stepped cuts. Moments later she was alongside her on the grassy bank.

'Hello, I'm Bridget.'

'I guess you were worried I might've damaged some old bit of something or other, like?'

'Probably looks like a mess to the untrained eye.' Bridget smiled fleetingly, her eye flickering over Max. 'But, yeah, it wouldn't be difficult to put a foot in the wrong place. So, you're Maxine?'

'Max, eh. Nobody calls me Maxine, 'cept m'gran.' She nodded at the site. 'Champion. Looks just like on the telly.'

'The television?'

'Aye. Them archaeological programs.'

'Ah, I see where you're coming from now.'

'Because ma gran, phew, she's a demon for them documentaries. Anything to do with bits of old rubbi– pots and things, she'll be there. She'd love all this.'

'Not your sort of thing then – documentaries, on the telly, that is?'

'Aye, well, ma gran only has the one set. An' fightin' ma gran, when she's onto one of her special programs, well, there's not a lot of gain in that.'

'Sounds like a wise move.'

'What, the one telly or not fightin' ma gran?'

'Well, both I suppose.'

Max returned Bridget's gaze until she looked away. You wouldn't last five minutes, she thought, not back where I come from.

'Trust Emlyn not to be here.' Bridget glanced at her watch. 'He's been a bit scattered of late. Oh well. Would you like me to show you around?'

'Aye. Well, that's what I'm here for, I suppose. But I was kinda thinking that Emlyn was–'

'No doubt he'll turn up in his own good time. Really it's his mother, well, our mother I should say – did he tell you we're half-siblings, same mother, different fathers? No. Okay. Well, I suppose that's more information than you need. Anyway, it's Mum that should be showing you around. This is her pet project. She's away doing a film at the moment.'

Max followed Bridget along the grassy slope of the Marchbank and around into the ring ditch. 'I'll show you where we found some Bronze Age swords, and what we think might be part of a ghost fence.'

'Ghost fence,' said Max. 'What's that?'

'Best I show you first, then it'll have a context.'

Bridget led the way along the curve of the Marchbank until they emerged in a more open section where the turf-covered bank was cut by a wide breach, beyond and below which the River Yarrow slid on its sinuous path towards the town and the junction with its sister stream. A large area had been excavated across and to the sides of the opening.

'It's kinda like a maze, really,' said Max, gesturing at the walls of the Marchbank. 'To confuse attackers?'

'Yes. Defensive positions often were. And this one bridges the narrowest point between the two rivers. It's merely a geological accident that we're not standing on an island. The ditches would have been deeper, the embankments steeper, because they've slowly filled with soil over the years, but apart from the road, which has been here for hundreds of years, it's all pretty much as it was.' Bridget pointed to a deep cut that curved away parallel with the embankment. 'We found the skulls over there in trench four. There's evidence suggesting that they were stuck on poles … part of the ghost fences I mentioned. Sacrificed, probably. They used the skulls to try and drive off evil, during the darkness of winter, or their enemies.'

'Ghost fences … made of human heads?'

'Of course it didn't work with the legions … different gods. Different beliefs.'

'So who were the poor sods who,' Max made a throat-slicing gesture, 'you know … provided–?'

'Short answer: we don't know. Volunteers maybe, although that's probably the wrong word, selected from their own people, or maybe slaves – captive warriors. Not a lot's known about the druids.'

'And they really believed that lopping off heads and keeping the skulls would frighten their enemies?' said Max.

'Skulls were potent ritual objects with magical properties,' continued Bridget, warming to her subject. 'They'd be placed strategically, say here at the Marchbank, to ward off an enemy and protect the inhabitants. American Halloween pumpkins – grinning its evil grin, candle-lit – they're a hangover. You have to try and put yourself back in their mindset. The world was alive with their gods. Water – pools, streams, lochs – was sacred to them.'

'You must find all kinda stuff?' Despite herself, Max was finding Bridget's talk engrossing.

'Yes. We also found this,' said Bridget, jumping down into the trench, where she pointed to a large slab of stone. 'See the hole? We think this is where the poles were placed. It's the markings that have us puzzled. We haven't been able to identify them. Can you see it?' She traced a deep-set groove with her finger. 'We think they were some sort of ritual marking … a sort of power booster, if you like, to complement the skulls.'

Max's thoughts drifted back to what Emlyn had mentioned about the marks on the stones up at the spinney: 'strange marks … like runes or something'. Were these the same marks? she wondered.

'Emlyn tells me you've a relative in the antiques trade?' said Bridget, brushing dirt from her hands as she stepped clear of the trench.

Emlyn! For sure he'd be able to say if the marks were the same. Where the hell was he anyway? She glanced at her watch and then scanned the horizon. The pillock was at least twenty minutes late. Catching a movement up near the castle car park, Max raised her hand and squinted into the sun. Beneath the precipitous walls Lawrence McCrossan was leant against his Land Rover, watching them through binoculars. Max dragged her gaze away from the castle, only to find Bridget gazing intently at her. 'Sorry, you asked me something?'

'Emlyn said your dad's in antiques?'

Split between Bridget's question and the castle walls, she hedged. 'Oh … did he?'

'He has a shop … somewhere local?'

Max was struggling to come up with something when a young man appeared at the top of the embankment. He was overweight and looked out of breath.

'Ah, Bridget. I forgot to ask you.' He pulled a form from his pocket. 'Could you sign this?'

'Pen?' said Bridget. The student patted his pockets and gave a wan smile. Bridget turned to Max. 'You wouldn't have a pen on you?'

Max shook her head. 'Sorry.'

As Bridget strode up the bank, displeasure at the student's forgetfulness written across her face, Emlyn came jogging along the sweeping curve between the grassy fortifications of the Marchbank.

'Where the hell have you been?' said Max.

'Flat tyre,' he said, looking sheepish. 'Sorry. I got here as quick as I could.'

'Yeah, well, your sister was just quizzing me about some antique dealer I'm supposed to be related to ... some shop. What the hell are you playing at?'

'She found the figure.'

'She what? How'd she do that?'

'Look, she just found it, all right.'

'No, it's not all right,' countered Max. 'What, you left it on the kitchen table or something?'

'She was moving my coat ... it fell out of the pocket.'

'Oh, champion, like!'

'No, it's not. But it happened.'

'Hey, you could have told me. I was about to be grilled about relatives who were into antiques. And another thing: Lawrence McCrossan is up at the castle.'

'Where?'

'Yeah, you didn'a see him, did you? Too busy falling over your own feet trying to get here. Parked just below the castle, he is – with a pair of binoculars.'

'Well, he's not there now.'

Max rounded in the direction of the castle. 'He was there. I'd know his cruddy Land Rover anywhere,' said Max, gesticulating.

'What,' said Emlyn, 'he just vanished?'

'Look, it's all getting too weird for me,' said Max pointing into the trench. 'Check out that lump of rock there. You remember you said something about some marks on the stones up at the spinney? An' I've got the weirdest feeling you're gonna tell me that's what they looked like. Bridget thinks they're to hold something back. Sort of like a power thing.'

Emlyn jumped into the trench and squatted beside the flat block of granite. He studied the markings, tracing it with his hand in much the same way Bridget had, and then – nothing. He remained crouching, immobile.

'Emlyn, man, what's up? Stop playing funny buggers and talk to me. Right now, I canna be dealing with this, me. ' Slowly he looked up at Max. His face was pale and drawn. 'What is it?' she said.

'This ... it's–'

But Emlyn wouldn't hold Max's gaze and he looked down again. There's something he's not telling me, she thought.

'Something's not right,' he added, lamely.

'Yeah, tell us something that makes us change me mind. C'mon, I wanna see if McCrossan's gone.'

Max turned away up the embankment. Emlyn followed at a lope, catching her by the sleeve as they rounded the top. 'Look,' he said, 'the marking on the rock back there–'

'What?' said Max. No answer was forthcoming. Emlyn's fingers dug into her elbow. Down by the marquee Bridget was talking to Lawrence McCrossan.

'C'mon,' he said, 'I wanna know why he's bailed her up.'

* * *

'Well, Mr McCrossan,' said Bridget, frowning, 'how can I put this ... any artefacts that are surplus will probably be catalogued and stored at the University.'

Max and Emlyn slowed to a saunter as they approached the tent, loitering close enough to hear the conversation but far enough away to feign disinterest.

'I understand that, lassie, all I'm saying is that a few of the choicer pieces, once you've finished with your carbon dating or whatever it is you get up to, could just as easily be placed in the museum up at Yeaveburgh Hall, or in the Town Museum for that matter.'

'I'll speak to my mother. She's the project coordinator.' She caught sight of Emlyn and Max and turned to them. 'Have you met Mr McCrossan? He's interested in some of the pieces we've excavated.'

'I'm always alarmed when anything ancient disappears.' He paused, eyeing the two youngsters. 'When any bits of Scots' heritage cross over the Border to England, that is.'

'Mr McCrossan, this is my brother, Emlyn, and his–'

'Aye, I've seen you taking photographs with that wee camera of yours. But have a care where you wander. There's plenty of farmers around these parts that wouldn'a think twice if you were on their land.'

'Wouldn't think twice about what?' said Emlyn defiantly.

'I'll be on ma way, lassie.' Lawrence McCrossan tipped his cap to Bridget and made towards the castle.

'What was all that about?' said Bridget, once he was out of earshot. 'Have you been trespassing on his land? You didn't take Digger with you, did you?'

'I took a few photos, that's all. And I left Digger at home.'

'Well, don't go back again,' said Bridget. 'Right. Now Lawrence McCrossan's off my back, I need a drink. Who's up for the pub?'

49

Outside The Crown the streetlights were coming on as dusk gathered. Bridget had driven off with Emlyn's bike wedged in the boot, looking for a parking spot in one of the side streets.

'How many apologies do you want?' said Emlyn. 'Flat tyre. Wheel it to the servo. Any pictures forming?'

Max watched Bridget's tail-lights disappear around the corner and then rounded on Emlyn.

'Back at your precious site, I were getting a grilling … about antiques. And now all your sister's gotta do is contact ma gran, an' I'm sunk: no trace.'

'Hey, you're not the only one in a tight spot. Antiquities, that's Bridget's field.'

'I don't *know* any antique dealers, you dozy git. I've a shoplifting record as long as your arm. Did you no' think?'

'I told you she went through my pockets.'

'Aye, well, we've got to put it back. And soon.'

'You're talking rubbish again.'

'I can't be dealing with tossers, me. An' you've been spouting complete bollocks.'

'Bollocks, eh,' said Emlyn hotly. 'That's a laugh, after what you started on about down at the dig. Bridget was only in the tent. She could've heard you easy.'

'Oh yeah, an' I s'pose it's gonna be you laughing all the way to court. I told you about ma shoplifting record … an' I say it should go back in that hole, just like ma gran said.'

'The only reason you were down in that hole in the first place was me – remember? The turf, all that stuff about nothing being up there. Besides, it's not as simple as that any more.'

'Seems pretty simple to me. Jeezus, this is going bloody nowhere. Fast.'

'Because someone,' said Emlyn, 'won't be reasonable.'

'Someone! *Someone!* Start playing them middle-class games with me, an' I'll clout you.'

'Got lucky with a park,' said Bridget rounding

the corner. 'Still arguing, you two. I'd have thought you'd be ensconced in the bar by now.' She pointed at Emlyn. 'Did you feed Digger before you left?'

Emlyn slapped his forehead theatrically.

'You've been neglecting that animal lately.'

'He's ... he'll be fine.'

'Opening a can of dog food,' said Bridget, pushing open the door into the noisy, smoke-filled bar, 'I mean, it's hardly rocket science, Emlyn.'

* * *

Emlyn watched Bridget work her way between the drinkers and around the low stage that jutted belligerently into the crowded bar. The argument with Max had thrown him; he felt dislocated, as if he were sitting in a cinema alone and the noisy crowd around him was just a movie. A young woman climbed up on the scuffed and beer-stained platform, and finding herself isolated above the conversation, stepped back down, barely missing Bridget and her carefully balanced drinks.

'Didn't know if you wanted Worcestershire Sauce,' said Bridget, sliding three glasses onto the table and pulling her chair in opposite Max.

'Spicy's how I like it,' said Max.

'Well – it's in anyway.' Bridget sipped her drink and glanced between the two of them. 'So, what did you think of the dig?'

'Apart from himself being late, like?' said Max.

She gave him a look over the rim of her glass, but he turned away, letting the bar noise drive away his thoughts. He heard her continue but he wasn't listening.

'Yeah – interesting. 'Specially that stuff about warding off evil … and the sacrificial stuff. You didn'a really say much about that.'

'Probably *the* most famous example of what I'm talking about,' said Bridget, pulling a large book from her bag. She opened it, tapped a page with several large colour plates, and passed it across.

'Yuck! Dead gruesome.' Max read the captions cautiously. 'Lindow Man. Looks like he's made of poor quality leather.'

'So would you if you'd lain in a Cheshire bog for two millennia.'

'What happened to him?' said Max.

'Sacrificial victims were strangled, stabbed, clubbed, had their throats cut; sometimes they were drowned. The number three was important: the idea of dying three times.'

'The librarian was going on about it. Merlin, he was stoned, skewered on a stake and drowned, wasn't he?' Tapping the plates with her finger, Max turned to Emlyn. 'That's what she said. Hey, you been listening or what, like?'

'Merlin's a figment of the over-fertile imagination,' said Bridget. 'That bloke, in the photo, he was alive and breathing right up until the moment they led him down to the water's edge.'

Max nudged Emlyn.

'Huh?' he said. 'What's up?'

'Away with the zombies, were we?' Max passed the book across to Emlyn. 'Take a shufty at that.'

Emlyn let his eye wander over the pictures and the text. Several phrases – 'young adult male', 'ruling elite', 'triple death'– niggled at him. He looked at Bridget. 'The triple death,' he said. 'What's that mean?' His father's childhood note was still in his shirt pocket. The phrase 'dance three times' chafed at him.

'You can't die three times,' said Max. 'It's not possible.'

'Nowadays the meaning's symbolic.' Bridget took the book from Emlyn and dropped it in her bag. 'At the time, well, it's impossible to put our heads back in that space. We really can't do it. The hills and forests and streams were peopled with unseen forces that had to be placated at the appropriate times. The Celts were fascinated with death. It's like those old medieval woodcuts of the danse macabre – the dance of death – you know, with the skeleton and the scythe. The old grim reaper bizzo.' Chuckling, Bridget stood. 'Anyone for another?'

As Bridget sidled away to the bar, the crowd thinned and a trio of musicians lugged their gear towards the stage. A channel cleared between the bodies as the band came and went with various items of equipment.

Emlyn nudged Max. 'How long's he been sitting there?'

Lawrence McCrossan was ensconced in a shadowy corner, watching them. Leaning sideways, he wrestled a phone free of his clothes, mouthed a few words, and then returned it to his pocket.

'Dunno. It's pretty crowded tonight. The toerag could've been there since we came in. Mebbe he's calling for reinforcements.'

'I'm going to have a look around,' said Emlyn. 'I want to see if we can slip out without ending up on the Square. I don't want him bailing us up again while Bridget's around.'

'I'll come with you.'

'Toilet break first – sorry. Besides, best if one of us keeps an eye on him.'

'Great,' said Max. 'Leave me all alone with McCrossan and the archaeology police then, why don't you.'

50

Arthur's youth has given way to stiffness in the joints and a grizzled beard. The summer has been wet, the harvest bad. Although the Saxon boats are few now, he hears word of a settlement far to the south and west, well beyond our normal reach, and he rides forth with his men, taking Merlin with him. The moon is full and clear of the hills as we look down on the meagre scattering of huts. A dog barks and a man steps from a doorway, scanning the night. We are hidden below the skyline. The man stretches and returns indoors as Arthur bids his marshal to light the torches and we canter into the valley.

The dogs slink away.

Figures, some bearing arms, emerge from the burning huts and are cut down. Arthur spots a boy, no more than nine, break cover, and he turns his mount. I watch, sickened, wanting to shout a warning, but I hold my tongue.

Escape is the boy's only thought.

Did I not feel that same fear the first time I rode out to battle, a lad of twelve?

Glancing back, his feet slip in the mire between the huts. Arthur's mare rears over him. One scrawny arm raised, the child sees the sword at the last moment, a flashing arc that cuts across the stars.

I know Merlin sees what he has made of Arthur and is sickened too.

As it happens the settlement was not even Saxon. The majority were southerners displaced by some disaster or other. Among the dead is a greater problem. Some of Modred's men, who had been making their way west through the hill country, had quartered there overnight. Thinking themselves safe, they set no guard and drank themselves into a stupor. Modred is incensed. One of the fallen was his marshal. The man was a favourite and will be hard to replace.

Arthur's raid is not the only thing that prompts Modred to move his plans forward. He has heard that all is not well in the Great Hall at Ynys Avallach. Rumour that Vivienne is no longer at Arthur's side has travelled as far as the Northern Isles.

51

The toilets were out in the hotel proper. Another world, thought Emlyn, all polished oak, brass and red carpet. As the bar door sucked shut behind him, he looked around. He could see the women's, but where the hell was the men's? Must be upstairs, he thought. He needed to have a look around anyway – check for an escape route.

Emlyn took the stairs at a run. On the landing, one of a pair of heavy double doors stood ajar and he went in. The room was large and set out with chairs and folding tables, each with a chessboard. A door marked 'Emergency Exit' stood at the far end of the room. He walked across and opened it. A fire escape ran down into the darkened alley.

Starting back, he caught sight of a low coffee table. Situated by the fireplace and flanked by a pair of huge armchairs, the table held a board on which sat a strange-looking chess set. Emlyn wandered over. The figures were squat, bullet-shaped almost, and he was reminded of the wooden horseman.

'Sort of chess on steroids,' he said under his breath.

'Can I be of any assistance?'

Emlyn turned around. A thin, balding man in a regimental blazer was smiling at him as he was unlocking a cupboard.

'You're a bit early, I'm afraid. We don't start for another hour.' The man pulled half-a-dozen largish biscuit tins from the cupboard and, balancing them, squeezed between the tables. 'Admiring the Lewis Chessmen, I see. Not the real ones unfortunately: copies.'

One of the tins slipped from his grasp and crashed to the carpet, where it rolled against the wall, spilling its contents along the skirting.

'Whoops! Butter-fingers.' The man piled the tins on a table and went to retrieve the chessmen. 'Would you care to wait?'

'No, it's okay.'

'On Saturday evening we've a tournament here. You're most welcome to come along.'

'I'd better head off. Whereabouts are the toilets?'

'Skirts or trousers, old chap?'

Extraterrestrials, you stupid tosser. 'Gents.'

'Back of the Saloon Bar.'

Out on the landing, Emlyn charged down the stairs. He could forget the bog: Max would be going spare.

* * *

Max watched Bridget clean the rim of her glass with a tissue before taking a sip. Miss fastidious, she thought, and then silently cursed Emlyn for leaving them alone. The conversation had petered out when she asked Bridget which football team she supported.

A dull ringing came from Bridget's bag. She rummaged around, unzipping several compartments before finding her phone.

'What? Sorry, it's a bit loud.' She paused, listening intently. 'Is that you, Mum? Look, you keep dropping out. Give me five minutes. I'll call you back.'

'Something up?' said Max.

'I'll have to walk down the hill. Keep an eye on my bag, would you?'

As the doors swung shut behind Bridget, Max spotted Emlyn sidling through the crowd.

'Where's Bridget?' he said, indicating the empty seat.

Max held an imaginary phone to her ear. 'Bad reception. She's gone outside.'

'And buggerlugs?'

'Nowt, 'cept eyeballing our table.'

Lawrence McCrossan continued to stare at them for a few moments longer, and then after sinking his pint, he made for the door.

'He's got something planned,' said Emlyn. 'I can sense it. We need to give him the slip, like I said. There's a fire escape. Unfortunately it comes out in the delivery area. The lane's closed off with a bloody great brick wall.'

'Well lit?' she asked. He shook his head. 'Good! 'Cause it's got to be better'n advertising ourselves – parading out the front door, like.'

52

Vivienne is tossed aside by Arthur, as all his women are. She is older now and wiser, and her cunning has increased tenfold. Under Merlin's tutelage she has advanced her knowledge, learning from him many of the old ways. Latching close onto her ageing teacher, she speaks only bright words of Arthur, forgiving him, and blaming herself in not providing him with a boy-child. Barely two seasons pass before she takes Merlin as her lover. Her pace is matched cunningly to Merlin's lust, although his eye does not pierce her web of deceit. Her bitterness and hatred of Arthur she holds close to her, for none must know her true desire – that more than anything she seeks his downfall.

* * *

Vivienne has long known the story of Arthur's time at the cave and his spirit-journey in the forest, but since she has taken Merlin to her bed she has heard the true version from one who was there. In her hatred of her old lover, she tries many spells, many curses and chants alone upon the hillside, but nothing loosens the Oak God's hold and Arthur's power seems undimmed and his reign unlimited.

One sunrise they are down by the river, gathering plants together. Merlin has been grumbling about Arthur's drunken rages and his disastrous raids, how he has lost the people's respect, how there are fewer and fewer of the boat-people to fight and the only real threat is Modred in the north. Straightening from her task, Vivienne spies a great oak downstream and an idea blossoms.

You say Arthur is of the forest, Merlin. That this is the source of his power?

The forest god is housed within him, he answers.

But, she says, you are less than happy now with your creation, are you not?

There is the matter of Modred, says Merlin. In this he will see no sense. He will neither treat with him, nor will he ride out to crush his northern fastness.

Forget Modred. It is Arthur that is the problem. He has grown too …

Arrogant, Merlin says, completing her carefully unfinished musing.

Then use the forest to tame him.

Merlin straightens, some of the flowers he has collected in his robe spilling onto the grass in his surprise. He laughs, mocking her.

You are right to mock me, she says. I know little of the forest gods and there are none above Merlin in such matters, for in this lore you are truly the master. No, I am a foolish girl and you are probably right, but ...?

But what?

Could you not take the wood – an oaken likeness, say – and sing the power from him?

Merlin, who can see clear beyond the borders of this world, is blind to her subtleties and devices. The vain will always believe they are the source of things. And so, hatched in Merlin's vanity, is the notion of once again controlling Arthur.

53

'There he is,' said Max, pointing across the Square to the shadowy figure flattened in the doorway. 'Over at the newsagent's, the canny toerag.'

'T'rrific,' said Emlyn. 'What do we do now?'

'Mebbe he thinks we've the figure on us? You haven't got it, have you?'

'Nah, it's back home.'

'Keep it down,' said Max. 'He might be able to hear us. I don't want to be bailed up by him at the moment. Him and his father are starting to give me the willies.'

'You're not the only one.'

Bridget sauntered into view and stopped in the mouth of the laneway. 'Emlyn? Come on out. I know you're there. I have got ears.'

Emlyn emerged into the glow of the streetlight.

'What are you playing at? Where's Maxi–' Max materialised from the shadows behind Emlyn and Bridget ran her eye over her. 'My bag – where's my bag? You've bloody left it in the pub, haven't you, you little–' Her face set, she hurried off.

'He's onto us now, for sure,' said Max.

As Lawrence McCrossan stepped from the doorway, two cars filled with hooting teenagers turned into the Square. He paused at the kerb to let them pass. The second vehicle stopped and somebody leant from the rear window.

'You take the River Stairs,' said Max. 'I'll do Castle Wynd. Fifty-fifty then, isn't it?'

Emlyn ran to the corner and looked back. Tyres squealed and Lawrence McCrossan started across the Square in his direction. Emlyn's feet drummed on the pavement. It looked like he was it.

The River Stairs showed as a dark maw halfway down Cornhill. He increased his pace until he reached the steps, checking once that McCrossan was still in pursuit, and turned off, taking them two at a time. Further down, the streetlights were sparse and poorly spaced. Emlyn halted in the shadows beyond one of the lights. He would wait; he wanted to make sure he was being followed.

* * *

Lawrence McCrossan's voice echoed between the walls. 'I know you're down there.'

Emlyn could see the gamekeeper silhouetted at the head of the River Stairs. He was speaking quietly, conversationally, but, due to some peculiar acoustic anomaly with the steps, it sounded as if he were standing right next to Emlyn. Up on Cornhill a match flared in the darkness.

'We want it back, laddie, you hear.'

Emlyn stood perfectly still under the shadow of the wall. He was already wishing he'd found the pub toilet.

'Cat got your tongue?'

The protecting darkness vanished as a light spilt from the window of the house opposite.

'Da-daahhnn!' said McCrossan. 'You see, we've friends everywhere. So, what's it to be, laddie, because, y'ken, I've absolutely no intention of chasing you – not down there, anyway. Hand it over and we'll forget the whole episode. What d'you say?'

Emlyn remained silent. The light from the window had spoken for him.

'Is it money you're wanting?'

A phone rang and Emlyn jumped. Lawrence McCrossan reached into his jacket.

'Aye,' said the gamekeeper. 'Okay ... Pity ... No, everything's dandy here.' The silhouette rang off and pocketed the phone. 'Well, this has been a nice little chat. Bit one sided – but there you go.' He paused and for a moment Emlyn thought he was coming down the steps after him. 'So, I take it I'll no' be getting the wee man back tonight?'

The light opposite went off as quickly as it had come on. Darkness and silence engulfed Emlyn. Lawrence McCrossan's question had gone unanswered.

'Suit yourself,' he said. 'You've it hidden somewhere and we'll find it. But remember, that's no toy soldier you're playing with. The horsemen submit to no-one, laddie. Just remember that, eh, when you're up amongst those peat bogs you're so fond of.'

Whistling tunelessly, Lawrence McCrossan disappeared towards the Square.

* * *

Emlyn was breathing hard by the time he reached Max's street. He poked his head around the corner. There were other cars parked in the street, but no Land Rover. Max's place was in darkness. He hung about, waiting, his ear cocked for the sound of an engine, unsure whether she'd already got there and was inside with the lights off, or whether she was wandering around trying to dodge one of the McCrossans. After an hour or so he gave up and ran home.

54

With Merlin's direction, oak is sung and cut under a waxing moon from a sacred grove deep in the Great Wood. He uses many of the same chants with which he trapped the God, but with tiny variations: a word here, a phrase there – sometimes simply a change in intonation.

The timber is brought down and put away to season.

It is Vivienne who carves Arthur's likeness, for such work has never been Merlin's gift. Great care she takes, singing the wood to her will, as her knife brings forth the squat figure.

Merlin, always greedy for new lore, particularly of plants, finds Vivienne willing to part with many of her secrets – but always for a price. She plays upon his vanity and teases from him the words of power aligned to each of the sacred forest trees.

Oak is one. But that is spoken for – oak for the Oak God. Already Arthur's carving lies hidden among Merlin's ritual objects.

And it is this, Merlin's pillow talk of lore and sacred trees, which is the undoing of Arthur's guard, of whom I was the foremost, for the Lady Vivienne is not content with trapping Arthur. She wishes to draw the net tight about us for purposes of her own. With Arthur gone, Modred will seek control of his lands. Vivienne knows well enough that the strength of mortal men is not enough; the power of the dead is needed. She and Merlin have talked this through long into the night, for irrespective of Arthur's fate, they both know that Modred will strike – and soon.

Call up a ghost army, she says. You've done this before, have you not?

The dead are not enough and strike fear into our own. Merlin pauses, nodding quietly. Better than the dead, he says, are living men called back from yesteryear.

She laughs. Surely that cannot be, my Lord?

My teacher worked just such a binding. And I too, once, with one of the Lords of the North. His blade was needed to treat with another tribe but he died as we tried to pull him from a fever. The words were sung and his spirit trapped in a dagger. It is what we will do with Arthur, with the carving – the very same. Only upon his death, and may that be long hence, will the carving call Arthur to it and he will join the God – and be trapped within the wood. It saddens me, my Lady, for there can be no reprieve. Not for the child who sat so long ago, stone in hand, watching as a chaffinch taught him of truth, nor for the man who has beaten back the Saxon horde. If he is released, the Oak God will come with him and that is not so easily swayed. I would have it some other way, that he might die a warrior's death and go into the west, but–

But what? she says.

It took great strength to call the God, to trap and hold him that night when Arthur ran from the cave. It cost me dear. Something of me was spent that day. There is much that is intertwined – the Spirit of the Oak has sunk his roots deep into Arthur's soul. I do not think they can be split the way you cleave the heartwood from the sapwood.

But Vivienne's mind travels another road.

How, she asks, how is the flesh brought–? She stammers to a halt; the notion is too great to take in at once.

With the right words, the proper plants, their trapped spirit calls their body back. But they must be willing. The Northern Lord believed me to be healing him.

And they can be controlled, she says, when they return?

He nods and kisses her hair.

And how do they appear? As they were in life?

Merlin laughs. They do not appear, he says. A few of the wise, those with the gift of sight, they can see them, and those who have taken the right plants, also. And sometimes those who've drunk too much mead – but no other.

They are invisible?

You could say that. They see us. They are solid and can skewer a man, as our Northern Lord did at my behest. Time is a gateway through which they do not fully step. Our world merges with theirs, merges with the past.

That such a thing can be, says Vivienne. That you, Merlin, have power over time – over death?

Like many things beneath the sun it cannot be explained. Of more importance is how such things can be used by those who would shape the world.

And so she teases from him the sacred words.

Teases from him each tree's sacred word: the ancient signs.

This is not so difficult for the Lady. She has him in her palm now like a smitten youth. And Merlin? He knows well enough the difficulties of singing the Oak God from Arthur; he understands the power of two and has already enlisted her help in this task, teaching her all she needs in this respect.

Her plot to trap us, to call us back when she sees fit, is hatched. In so doing, she believes she can control each, individually, or all at a time if her need is great. For each man in Arthur's guard, Vivienne will carve a horseman. Each will be made from the wood of a sacred tree.

She tramps deep into the Great Wood, to the groves of ash and beech, to the alder and the willow with their legs astride the stream, and the solitary yew and holly. Here, she places offerings amid their roots and sings to the spirit dwelling in each. Her spells are traceries of holding and procurement. She croons over her axe, for there must be no mistakes. Climbing into the larger trees, she hews her chosen bough from the trunk, letting it fall to the forest floor. The smaller kinds – birch, alder, rowan – she fells at their base. In all this her voice never wavers, nor does she cease her singing until she arrives back at the abandoned bothy. None come there now – they seek their healing and basket ware elsewhere – and she can work undisturbed. She likes the circular notion of return, of her old home by the sacred pool: here she snared Arthur in love, and here a darker purpose will see him trapped yet again.

Merlin knows nothing of all this.

* * *

But before Vivienne sets knife to wood she needs surety that the signs are right. A dog is taken and slaughtered. Meat is cut from its haunch, and chewing upon the flesh she summons the animal's spirit. The sight reveals the omens are good. All winter she works in secret, carving Arthur's guard from the seasoned timber.

55

Emlyn wandered into the cottage driveway. The curtains were drawn back and all the lights were on, washing the lawn and garden with an eerie light. Bridget stood, hose in hand, watering the flowerbeds along the fence.

'Where the hell did you disappear to?' The words were flung at him. 'My bag! She left my bag! Dammit, it had a marked-up chapter of my thesis in it. All the annotations from my supervisor. One copy – d'you understand – *one copy*! And what were you doing? Having a quick pash out in the alley with that bloody girl.'

'I've been at Max's. And we weren't *doing anything* in the alley.'

Emlyn, hands in his pockets, watched as his sister moved along the fence, hosing each shrub in turn.

Her hands were shaking, sending the water in a fractured arc across the plants.

'Why are you doing that in the dark?' he said. 'What's going on? You're shaking.'

'Take a bloody look inside the bloody cottage.' Bridget threw the hose down and followed her brother to the open front door. Books and papers spilt from the living room onto the hall carpet. His sister pushed past, gesticulating at the mess underfoot, and he followed her through to the kitchen.

'We've been burgled?'

'No. They were collecting for charity. What's it look like?' Bridget slumped onto the bench by the phone and put her face in her hands. Emlyn couldn't be certain, but he thought she might be crying.

'Did they take much?'

From between her fingers came a muffled, 'What?'

'Did they take anything much?'

Bridget sucked in a wad of air and stood, brushing her hair back and tidying her clothes. 'No – it seems not. The police sergeant thought that was strange. He said it might've been kids – got disturbed. There were some cars damaged in town last night.' She started reaching for various objects on the floor. 'Anyway, we better get this cleaned up.'

He stared at her, nonplussed.

'Tidied, Emlyn – hello? I'm sorry I went at you outside but I … I didn't want to be in the cottage on my own. It felt like they were still here when I arrived, still in the cottage … and then … like somebody was watching, looking in through the windows. I need a hand now.'

He drifted around the house, screwing down his fears, picking things up and putting them back in their old spots. He gave it ten minutes and went into the kitchen. Bridget was mopping the floor.

'Did you check the garage?'

'Just junk out there.' Bridget squeezed out the mop and attacked the floor again. 'Oh, yes, your bike. I put it in the shed. Go check, though. I guess they could have taken it when I went inside … and it cost Mum an arm and a leg.'

Grabbing the torch from the cupboard, he walked out to the garage and felt under the pile of newspapers. The tin was where he had left it.

'Bike's still there,' he said, entering the kitchen. 'I'll check my room.'

'I checked. It's fine. Untouched.'

He took the stairs two at a time. He stared at his bed and a chill went over him. Three of his running trophies – which had been getting progressively bigger and grander as he got older – had been set out on the covers. To the front was the smallest of the three, while behind and in close order were the two larger trophies. He felt sick. On his pillow, as if watching the runners, was Bonzo, the chipped china dog he had been given as a child.

Emlyn ricocheted down the stairs.

'Where's Digger?'

'I haven't seen him since this morning.' Bridget looked up from her mopping. 'He can't be – not again.'

'They … they wouldn't have taken Digger. He'd have gone ballistic,' he added, trying to sound normal. His heart sank. This was payback, he thought. They hadn't found the figure and in their desperation they'd taken him. That was why Lawrence McCrossan had been at the pub, and at the bloody dig – watching, keeping check. And that's who he was talking to on the phone: his father. His father, that's who it must have been: used his key, made a mess and smashed a window to make it look good. Ol'man McCrossan was the sort to take a dog just for sheer, bloody-minded retribution. Emlyn tried to steady his thoughts but he couldn't get his sister's description of a shivering Digger lying alongside the garden wall out of his head.

'I'm going to look for him.'

'Wait,' said Bridget. 'Let me finish this and we'll go together. In the pub tonight, you looked a bit ... off with the fairies. Mum's worried about you and I'm not exactly keen on you roaming–'

'Great. What've you said?'

'I had to tell her about Maxine and about the antique dealer. She said to keep an eye on you. It was suggested ... that, perhaps, you need to see somebody again?'

They both knew exactly what 'somebody' meant, and it wasn't the family doctor.

'I'm *all right*. What's the matter with everyone? Why can't any of you believe me?'

'How about *you* taking some responsibility for a change? What about this wooden horse thingummy for a start.'

'Oh, right – responsibility. That'd be something Mum would know all about. Her husband' – Emlyn spat the word at Bridget, refusing to use 'father' or 'dad' – 'is rotting in a glorified loony bin and she's gallivanting around the country: conferences, book launches, and now film gigs. She is still married to him, you know.'

'She's entitled to a life–'

'Yeah, well what about Dad? Has he gotta live some sort of half-life? Because it's rubbish for him up at Huntleighbank. How about Mum taking some responsibility for that?'

'Oh, responsibility. Shall I give you a little lesson? Where's your dog?'

56

CAMLANN EVE

Sensing some change in Merlin, Arthur keeps the Green One near at hand, busying him with various demands, not the least of which is the preparation of a second ring of earthworks across the narrow neck of land that has held off countless raids. Rituals are observed as the ditch takes shape. Sacrifices are made: offerings proffered. Bloodied heads are sat atop poles. Any enemy who wins through to the inner ditch will have more than steel and mortal men at their throats. On the heights above, Arthur looks down upon the work and ponders what is bothering his old adviser.

But Merlin's distraction and apparent reticence is just a ploy. He directs the earthworks and baits his brief conversations with Arthur, watching and waiting until he rises, like the fish that hang lazily above the gravel shoals, to take the fly. If treachery is your aim – and Vivienne's aim was nothing if not true – then it is best that the hand that seals another's fate is trusted and not your own. She plays Merlin, who in turn plays Arthur.

Merlin's belief is that with the Oak God sung into the carving, Arthur will once again be reliant on his old adviser. Unlike Vivienne, it is not Arthur's death that Merlin seeks; it is control, moderation, parley – above all, his concern is to buy time until Modred can be dealt with swiftly and for good. But the sight, his ability to see the future, was either diminishing or was more fallible than legend would have it. Perhaps much that was attributed to his sight was merely a remarkable intelligence at work. Maybe he was blinded in love, for he had not lain with a woman for many years. Whatever the cause, his betrayal of Arthur stung us all.

* * *

Like me, Merlin has a river of time in which to contemplate his deception, for once the Lady binds us tight our fates run parallel.

It is my only consolation in the blackness.

57

All summer Arthur tries to draw Modred forth, to tempt him down from the high country. But his bastard son – his nephew, as many now openly whisper – is not forthcoming, not in force at least, making only cattle raids and sending lightning skirmishes that prick at Arthur's pride.

Word comes that Modred is planning a large raid to the south.

And in this, Vivienne's hand is at work, although none as yet understand how deep her plotting runs. She has met in secret with Modred: promises have been made.

It is time, says Merlin.

All that remains then, says Vivienne, handing him the solitary carving, is for the Oak God to be sung from him, and that is your task, Master Merlin.

No, he says, it is ours. And she takes his proffered hand. In this, great care is needed, he says.

And it is true: Arthur can smell a trap like a bear noses the wind for carrion. Merlin has laid the groundwork over many months, speaking of omens and visions. The signs are many and real enough: the red fever holds three settlements in its maw; there's news from the south of renewed raids; the crops fail; but feared most is the omen in the night sky – a tailed star, where no star should hang. A harbinger of death, some say.

A sense of foreboding settles about Arthur's shoulders like summer thunder upon the hills. Few dare approach him. It is my task to break the news of Modred's forthcoming southern raid.

58

On the eve of the battle at Camlann, Merlin looks into Arthur's eyes and lies. The signs are ill, he says.

Ill? How so?

Three ravens up at Black Birren is the reply.

Arthur shrugs and laughs. Only three?

Picking at the carcass of a she-bear, Merlin says.

Arthur turns pale, then flushes, clutching at the jet amulet that hangs about his neck. The leather thong is threaded with a rearing bear no bigger than a child's thumb: a gift from Master Merlin many long years past.

You think it is time? he asks. You think that the sickle man stalks me. Say it, man! But I have you to protect me. Surely it cannot–

I've been wrong in the past, says Merlin. The Green One has already turned his face from Arthur's.

You are wrong, says Arthur. I feel no such doubts. But doubt is writ large across his face. He walks to the doorway and pauses. You could strengthen us, he continues. Your singing spells have worked before.

Yes, Merlin says, but this time it should not be you alone that is sung. Bring your guard. They must see this done. It will lend them strength … but not here at Ynys Avallach, not in the Great Hall. No, we must prepare a place of power.

On Camlann Eve, as Arthur and his guard ride into the hills, each man bearing a torch, some with the shrunken heads of their enemies slung from their saddles, Merlin is already waiting up among the standing stones.

59

Arthur stands beside the sacred fire, his head bowed, listening to Merlin's whisperings as his guard, dressed only in their breeches and carrying their weapons, sit astride their mounts. Some are the worse for drink, some laughing and swaggering, charged with the moment and the coming fight.

We are ranged in a circle, calling and joking quietly to one another, the air thick with aromatic smoke from Merlin's fire. Arthur stands upon the tomb of our forefathers, while the Green One weaves among us, chanting and calling out for the power he needs. In time we fall to silence; bored, perhaps, or each in his own thoughts.

Merlin has placed the oaken horseman in a bearskin pouch, telling Arthur that it is a talisman of power. Crouched within the rock-bound tomb is Vivienne, the other carvings arranged around her in a circle. For each man that sits patiently upon his horse there is a wooden figure.

It is said that Merlin's power is in his voice. He has Vivienne's help this night, for they need every bit of strength to pull the Oak God forth from Arthur's breast. Later, Merlin, in his pride, will say to her that they made a powerful duet. The Lady only smiles, for hers was a different song, whispering the lines that he leaves out, and her verses are patterned, both in word and sound, to trap man and horse upon their death, for these men are nothing without their steeds. Little did any of us know how soon fate would throw us to the pack.

60

It is our loyalty to Arthur that sees us ride out from Ynys Avallach that fateful day, a snell wind at our back, myself and his guard, at the head of a long line of men. That and the Lady's tokens, stowed from sight, for each believes he is favoured and that to tell another will break the power bestowed upon them. Merlin and the Lady Vivienne ride with us also, further back among the men. Arthur is alongside them, feeling uncannily himself as he sits astride Llamrei, his battle-mare. He reads this as the protection that he sought from Merlin. He is not to know the real reason he feels so.

It will be a full day's journey before we reach the River Cam. Winter has come down early. Wolves call in the woods. I should have seen their singing for what it was – an omen. By nightfall they would be snarling and snapping over our jerking carcasses and the waters of Camlann ford, that cursed valley, would run red with blood that should never have been spilt.

Do not speak to me of favour or of power.

It is power that drives Vivienne. Her brief time at Arthur's side has taught her much. She knows that with his guard roaming the countryside after his demise nothing is certain and it is for this reason the figures have been carved and sung. But, between when the Lady Vivienne hid us away in her bothy by the pool and when we rode out to face Modred at the fords of Camlann with the figures in our saddlebags, there is a precarious time. Arthur is yet to be cowed. And Vivienne, still fearful of discovery, has no sure knowledge of when Arthur will ride out to face Modred and until that day the wooden horsemen need to be held in check. So she continues singing the figures to render them safe and to hold the power within them.

For this she has need of a special place.

Even in our time the sprawling ring of stones, said by many to become men and to walk at night, was as ancient as the hills. And within these stony, broken teeth, the sacred tomb fashioned by our forefathers, the workers of bronze – perhaps older still. It is to this place she moves the figures and weaves her magic. It is there that we are sung into submission. It is here I lie trapped in ash wood waiting for those who will free me at last.

* * *

But there is another figure Vivienne carves over the winter. No horseman this, no warrior, but a cloaked figure with a staff – Merlin.

Her treachery runs deeper than he can guess.

She has carved his likeness also, for, beyond Arthur's death, she seeks his too. She has no use for him. She has his store of wisdom and lore. With the figures to command, what need has she of a doddering old man. Her alliances are already made and his death, the three-fold death he has prophesied, has seen so often in his night dreams, will fall into step and rush upon him like a falcon from the summer sky.

Our fates, Merlin's and mine, are not dissimilar. Upon his death she traps his spirit in an oak.

Truly, from that moment when Merlin took her to his bed, his sight deserted him.

FRIDAY

61

The next morning, Emlyn headed up through the town. Things were happening too fast and he needed to talk to Max. After the argument with Bridget, she'd been good to her word and driven them around the places where Digger might have wandered off to, but the terrier had not shown himself. Later she had cajoled him into making some posters with the dog's picture to put up in the town. Listlessly he had knocked some up on the computer and printed them off. It all seemed so futile – he was sure the McCrossans had taken Digger – but he went through the motions anyway; at the very least it'd keep Bridget off his back.

As if to add to his despondency, Max's front door remained unanswered and sat mutely warming itself in the sunshine. Turning down towards the town centre, he passed the laneway at the rear of the terrace. The front wheel of the Beezer caught his eye. She must be working in the shed, he thought. He wandered down. The doors were folded back and the bike stood propped in the sunlight. The smell of grease and warm metal rose around him and Max's voice came from the dim depths of the garage.

'Look, just get the carburettor working and I'll be out of your hair.'

'It's not a five minute job.' Hugh grabbed Max's waist and pulled her close. At the base of his thumb Emlyn could clearly see a plaster covering the cut he'd made up at Sleeper's Spinney.

'I canna be dealing with this, me, at the moment,' said Max, smiling sweetly and pushing him away. 'Besides *you* gave *me* the flick, remember?'

'The old man's not going to know.' He lunged at her again but she slipped out of reach. So, Hugh was her *bit* of local expertise, thought Emlyn. What the hell did she see in the jerk? An ugly chorus sung in his head. Maxi the Taxi. Jealousy raised its horns and bellowed, and he bit into his lip.

'You always sneak up on people like that?'

Max was glaring at Emlyn. Hugh scowled and folded his arms, but made no move towards him.

Not so friggin' tough now, are we, McCrossan, thought Emlyn. Not without your mates, anyway?

'Cut your hand?' he said, staring pointedly at Hugh's thumb.

'Dangerous places, farm workshops.' Hugh stared coldly as if trying to remember something.

'Finished discussing your medical problems?' said Max. 'Because I've a motorbike to fix.'

Hugh shrugged and began hanging spanners on the shadow board.

'Workshop, my arse,' said Emlyn, edging into the shed. 'That's self-inflicted.'

Hugh moved away from the bench until they were standing face to face. He grabbed Emlyn's collar and twisted it. 'I cut it on the lathe, see. Or are you asking for a smack in the face?'

'Bollocks!' hissed Emlyn, grabbing his wrist. 'You did *that* up at the spinney.'

Mrs Fraser appeared outside the doors, rummaging in her bag. 'Forgot the blasted front door key.' She looked up and saw Hugh. 'What the hell are you doing here? Go on, take yourself off and tell that father of yours that I dinna want to see you hanging around here again. You be sure to tell him that from me, eh?'

'Gran!' But Max's protest was ignored and Hugh,

grinning moodily, slipped past Emlyn into the laneway. '*Gran!* There was only the carbie to do and I'd've had it running.'

'If I'd known that rusting heap of junk was going to bring *him* around here.' Lindsay Fraser jabbed her finger at Hugh's receding back. 'I see you with him again and–'

'He were just helping with the bike.'

'Test me, why don't you?' said Mrs Fraser, disappearing through the back gate.

'*Daa-rrgh!*' Max growled. 'I'm never gonna get the carbie fixed now.'

'Something'll turn up – surely.'

'Purely no chance. Hugh was it on the carbie front.' She kicked an orange crate full of rags and thrust her hands in her pockets. Looking up, she said: 'What was all that with Hugh and his hand?'

'He cut it deliberately – that day at the spinney.'

'And?'

'I dunno,' said Emlyn, 'it was like he was trying to wake himself up or something. But then I wasn't that close and I was peering through a crack in the dyke.' He trailed off and Max looked at him.

'Something's up, isn't it?'

'Digger's missing,' said Emlyn. 'I think Ol'man McCrossan's got him.'

'What?' Max stared blankly at him.

'Ol'man McCrossan – he's taken him.'

'Taking Digger, that's not his style. Is it? Mebbe the wee feller's just gone off somewhere.'

'He follows me around like a shadow, you know that.'

Max's face was creased in thought. A couple of fifties stools, their vinyl tops split and cracked, their legs dull with rust, were stacked in the corner of the shed. Grabbing them, she set them across the laneway and they sat with their backs against the sun-soaked stone.

Max sucked in a breath and sighed. 'You definitely think he has him?'

Emlyn sat hunched over, staring at the cobbles.

'Right then, all the more reason to put Dobbin back. Whatever them little wooden fellers are for, they hardly want it publicised. If he's got Digger, then he'll give him back. I mean, he'd have no reason to keep him then, would he? We say nothing – 'cept mebbe a note under his windscreen wiper.'

Emlyn sighed and slid off the stool. 'I suppose.'

'Can you gi's a hand with the bike?' said Max. 'Just wheel it inside for me, eh.'

Emlyn moved the Beezer, while Max wiped her hands on a rag, grabbed the stools and shut the doors.

She took the machine and propped it against the wall. 'Stand's broken.'

They moved into the passage and she closed the side door. In the yard the television squawked at them through the open kitchen window. Inside, Mrs Fraser was ironing and looking up now and again at the screen. Max shepherded Emlyn through the gate and into the back lane, where he stood staring at the brick wall opposite. Max stepped in front of him.

'Hey, snap out of it. You're freakin' me out. I canna be doing with all this zombie-land-of-the-dead stuff, me.'

'Those markings … on the granite slabs in the trench, I didn't tell you everything. McCrossan … seeing him talking to Bridge; well, it threw me.' Max was watching him closely and he stumbled on. 'It's just that, yeah, they're like the markings up at the spinney … but I'd seen them somewhere else as well.'

'Where?' said Max.

'I drew them.'

'You drew 'em?'

'Yeah, on some river stones. Small bits of shingle.' He drew his thumb and forefinger into a tight circle. 'I drew them and put them in with Dobbin, but I don't remember doing it. I don't remember drawing them.'

'What do you mean, you don't remember?'

'I opened the tin and they were there. That's it.'

'Sort of like you did it in your sleep … kinda like in a trance or something?'

Max was so near the mark, Emlyn said nothing, only nodded. 'It's probably nothing,' he said finally. 'Forget it.'

'No, wait. Bridget said they were kinda magical, some sort of sign to keep out evil. Maybe the signs up at the spinney are to keep something in. You follow my drift?'

'I don't really know what I'm thinking. Bridget, my mum, they think there's something wrong with me. Do you think I'm – you know – odd or anything?'

'If you mean are you like all those pillocks at school, then no.'

'Sometimes, when I see things, I think I'm going–'

'Hey, ma gran said she thought you had the sight. You should celebrate the difference, not worry about it so much. Buy a few lottery tickets mebbe?'

'Max? Can I say something … about your gran?'

She studied his face. 'At the moment you can say what you bloody well like about her.'

'It's just that I don't want you to take it the wrong way. I like her.'

'You gonna tell me what it is or are you putting yourself up for adoption, like?'

'There's something – I don't know – a darkness around her. When she saw Hugh off, it was like I could see her, when she was younger. Not a lot younger. Lots of images: little flashes. There was a baby. She was holding it, cradling it. She was really sad about something.'

'If you've the sight you'd be able to tell things like that. And that'd be ma mum. She lost a baby – 'fore she had me. Cot death.'

'Your mum, when did she–?'

'She died when I were thirteen.'

'Oh,' said Emlyn.

'Dobbin? When d'you want to whack him back in his hole?'

62

Emlyn sat propped on his bike, staring down at the water and fingering the tin in his greatcoat pocket. He was beginning to doubt Max's plan to replace the carving. No matter how hard he tried to push them away, the faces of Lawrence and Ol'man McCrossan reared in front of him. He very nearly hadn't turned up to meet her.

'You've a thing about this bridge,' said Max, cycling up. 'The times I've seen you hanging over this wall.'

'Who's doing the spying now?'

'Three times – on the bus to Hawick: hardly surveillance. What you looking at, like?'

Max parked her bike and leant over. Their elbows touched.

'Phew, you pong a bit. Bit like Bridget when her boyfriend's up from Durham.'

'You wanna be careful with your compliments; you'll find yourself writing sonnets next. And it's *Pleasure* by L'Antonne, if you must know. One of Gran's little luxuries. Me an' countryside aromas have fallen out a bit since our last expedition spinney-side.'

The water slid by under their silence. Three olive shapes hung in the shallows, their tails flicking gently against the current.

'Down there,' said Emlyn, 'between the weed.'

'What are they?'

'Fish.'

'I know that!' snorted Max. 'What sort?'

He smiled. 'Grayling.'

She winked, climbed on her bike and patted the frame. 'Gran's thrown nothing out since Grandad went in the water. Let's hope the chain holds out. Anyway, I shouldn'a grumble – I've ma wheels for today's outing. Have some motorised ones soon, if I play ma cards right.'

Emlyn frowned at her.

'Fingers crossed, carbie problem's fixed. I phoned Hugh before heading off.'

'What about your gran? Didn't she say to keep away–?'

'M'gran says a lotta things. Anyhow, there's no harm in stringing him along. Silly plonker still wants to take me to the seniors' dance, so I thought, he can do up the carbie at work an' mebbe I'll go to the dance with him. Anyway, Gran'll know nowt either way.'

'And the dance?' said Emlyn.

'You've got a lot to learn about girls, pal. Like I said: mebbe. 'Cause, I canna be dealing with tossers, me.'

* * *

Putting on a final spurt, Emlyn and Max laboured up the straight stretch below Whitman's Wood until they were alongside the pasture that ran up to Sleeper's Spinney. Down in the valley, where the road doubled back on itself, Lawrence McCrossan's Land Rover toiled up the hill. Seconds later, down near the river flats, a battered green Renault flashed into sight between the trees.

'If I'm not mistaken that's Ol'man McCrossan's Renault,' said Max. 'Looks like they're both on their way up here.'

'Could be heading for the farm,' said Emlyn, standing on his pedals for a better look.

'I dinna think so somehow. An' if they're not, they'll be on us any minute.'

They'd drawn level with the gate that led to the spinney. Emlyn nodded at the concrete culvert beneath the entrance to the field, dropped his bike into the ditch and leapt down after it.

'Toss it here.'

Max lowered her bicycle, grimaced at her prized Doc Martens, and slid into the ditch. Dragging the bikes into the pipe, they squatted, listening for the sound of the Land Rover. Brown, silty run-off eddied lazily around their feet.

'You know they've only gotta look under here,' said Max, 'and we're history.'

* * *

Up on the road, the culvert vibrated as Lawrence McCrossan swung the Land Rover into the gateway. A pair of black Labradors stood eagerly in the back, their noses pressed against a partially open window. Shaking his head, McCrossan dropped from the cab, spat into the ditch and propped the gate open.

'What is it with that old bastard?' he said as he hauled himself into the cab and slammed the door. Unable to find first, he stabbed at the gears, gunning the engine. The tyres churned and slipped, spraying mud in an arc across the road, as the bulky vehicle slid sideways across the entrance with such ferocity that the rear wheel slithered over the edge of the culvert. He slapped it into four-wheel drive. But it was no use; the vehicle remained bogged on its springs, the wheel spinning over empty space.

'The self-righteous old … now look what he's made me go and do.' Sensing his agitation, the dogs started barking. 'Shut it,' he yelled, and they cowered on their blankets as McCrossan climbed down, swore and slammed the door so hard it bounced open again. 'Damn and blast! It's going to take the tractor to get this out.' Kicking the cab door shut, he strode away across the field towards Sleeper's Spinney.

* * *

Minutes later Emlyn and Max listened intently as tyres slithered to a halt on the dung-caked road above. A car door slammed and Ol'man McCrossan's reedy coughing echoed in the culvert. Max's breath was in Emlyn's ear. 'I hope it kills him,' she whispered.

63

'*Oi!*' yelled Ol'man McCrossan after his son. 'You've no bloody right, you hear.'

But his son, already across the first dyke and into the field beyond, paid no heed.

'Him and his bloody-minded, spur-of-the-moment decisions,' muttered Ol'man McCrossan, squeezing past the Land Rover. 'Going to be the end of us, they are.' He paused by the gate and sniffed the air. 'Perfume? I'm sure I can smell perfume.' He shook his head. 'Och, you daft bugger, you're imagining things.'

He hastened after his son. He was barely halfway to the first dyke when the Labradors started barking.

'What's got them going?' he wheezed, turning and scanning the road below. He glanced over his shoulder. Lawrence was almost to the spinney and seemed oblivious to the ruckus down on the road. 'Och, leave it,' he said, 'probably seen a hare.' And then he set off after his son.

* * *

Hunched next to their bikes, Max and Emlyn looked at one another.

'That ol' bastard's got a nose like a ferret,' whispered Max.

'We're going to have to leg it up to the spinney. Fast,' said Emlyn. 'Something's up with those two.'

He pointed along the ditch, and squeezing past the bikes, they splashed down the incline, their heads level with the roadway. A cacophony of barking broke out behind them and, in her fear that the dogs were loose and in pursuit, Max lurched forward, pulling Emlyn to his knees. One of the Labradors had its snout shoved through a partially open window, while the other whirled frantically in the back.

'Jeezus,' said Max. 'If they get out.'

Scrambling upright, their mud-covered jeans clinging to their shins, they hurried along to where the ditch became drier and stonier underfoot and finally disappeared beneath the road. Emlyn was up onto the verge and through the hedge in a flash. By the time Max pushed through the foliage he was already well up the wooded slope, moving further in between the trees where they wouldn't be seen.

'Wait up!' she wheezed, and, grimacing at her turn of phrase, raced after him.

64

Voices drifted through the trees. Ol'man McCrossan's agitation carried clearly to where Emlyn and Max lay hidden in the bracken.

'What … d'you reckon's … going on?' whispered Max between laboured breaths. She'd had trouble keeping up with Emlyn, who'd made only a token effort to wait for her.

'Argument,' mouthed Emlyn, passing her the field glasses. Max pulled focus and Ol'man McCrossan's face jumped at her.

'I see you'd no trouble climbing down in there this time,' said Ol'man McCrossan.

'Needs must when the devil drives,' said Lawrence McCrossan, his head and shoulders poking out of the entrance to the mound.

'The need didn'a seem to be so great Tuesday night. If it'd been you down in that hole, I reckon we'd've bagged ourselves more'n a dead dog fox.'

'You're forgetting the reason I'm none too partial to going in there,' said Lawrence. 'Or was shutting me in as a wee'un your idea of a joke? 'Cause I dinna hear any laughter – y'ken what I'm saying?'

'I'm warning you,' said Ol'man McCrossan, 'I'm not for moving 'em. I've a sense here, y'ken?'

'You're getting paranoid in your old age,' said Lawrence, clambering from the hole and heaving the slate into place.

'With one figure missing, you think I'm not justified?'

'I'm the keeper now ... remember.'

'Och, yeah, you're the keeper now right enough. But you're forgetting your history.'

'They've been moved before,' said Lawrence McCrossan.

'Aye, twice, an' look at the strife that caused. Oh yeah, you can smile, I know what you're think–'

'What, your theories about Flodden Field? If I've heard them once, I've heard them a thousand times.'

'I know what the history books say, but it wasn'a the Sassenachs that started the killing. Now, are you going to put them back in that damned hole or do I have to do it myself?'

'And what else?' said Lawrence. 'You gonna tell me we've faerie blood in our line? You've no' trotted that one out lately. I've not heard that one for a while.' Ol'man McCrossan continued to glare at his son. 'It's the twenty-first century, man, not the Dark Ages. You'll be asking me to walk three times widdershins around the spinney any minute. Why don't you make yourself useful an' fetch the tractor so we can pull the Land Rover out?'

'That's down to you,' said Ol'man McCrossan.

'Fair enough,' chuckled Lawrence McCrossan. 'But it was your bloody whining as got me riled.' He paused. 'Look, I'm no' doubting your feeling, your unease, y'ken, but that stems from the Fraser lassie and her feller. *There's* your disquiet. We're better off putting our energies into getting it back.'

'Oh, I'm doing that all right,' said Ol'man McCrossan. 'What about Hugh? He was seeing the Fraser girl, until we warned him off. Could he not do a bit of snooping?'

'Hugh's not a keeper of the stones – yet. You know the score there – us singing him an' all. Nah, it's way too complicated. This is for us to sort, not Hugh.'

'Are you soft, man, or what? We've a new keeper to train up, remember? What if something happened to you and me?'

'Nothing's going to happen.'

'Someone's to take over from you. Who's it to be if not the boy? No, Hugh'll do what he's told. And he can forget that apprenticeship.'

'Aye, and it'll be me doing the telling,' said Lawrence McCrossan. 'I've told you – I'll not let you bully him.'

'An' what if he doesn'a? It all ends here, is that it? Are you mad, man?'

'Mad, oh aye. I'll tell you about mad. There's mad for you, over at Huntleighbank Hall. And you're forgetting I'm keeper now.'

* * *

Emlyn grabbed the binoculars back from Max. He gripped them harder and refocused. Ol'man McCrossan was glowering at his son. 'They're moving them,' whispered Emlyn. 'That's what this is all about.'

Apart from the McCrossans, the breathless silence of the wood was like a smothering hand over his face, and the tin, secreted in his pocket, was like an itch he couldn't scratch. The desire to remove the wooden horseman was overwhelming.

* * *

Lawrence McCrossan lifted the last two turves and dropped them into position.

'An' this is how it's to be then?' said his father, treading an errant corner flush with its partner.

Lawrence McCrossan nodded.

'You'll put them away … safe, will you not?'

The two men stood facing one another.

'I've somewhere lined up already,' said Lawrence. 'I've a mind to do it as soon as we've the Land Rover back on the road, y'ken? Safe as houses, they'll be.'

'An' you'll do it right … everything as it should be?'

'Good God, man, I've been brainwashed with this since I were thirteen. You know your problem? You still think I'm that skinny kid you could bat from here to hell an' back.'

'My priority's what you've got tucked in your bag there.'

'Aye,' said Lawrence McCrossan. 'An' it's mine as well. Look, drive me back and you fetch the tractor up here … you can get everything set up ready to pull out the Land Rover. I'll take the Renault and get these stashed nice and safe. Everything as planned, see?'

'Aye, well, it's your plan not mine … an' I dinna like change.'

'But things change. An' we best change with 'em.'

'Aye, what do they say – change is a great teacher. Time we taught that Sylvesterson kid a lesson. I've a mind to fix his little game, you'll see. There's that wee animal of his.'

* * *

A choking sound rose in Emlyn's throat and he turned onto his back. Max clamped her hand over his mouth and folded her body frog-like over his, her eyes a silent plea to remain still.

65

The old man stalked towards the wall, muttering. Lawrence McCrossan followed at a distance, pausing twice, a distracted look on his face as if he were listening.

'They're going,' said Max.

'You heard him,' hissed Emlyn. 'He's got Digger.' Max still had him pinned to the ground. She was stronger than she looked. He could smell her hair, her perfume.

'Yeah, and jumping up, that'd be real bright, like. You've the thing on you. And we can still put it back. Like as not, he'll hand Digger back once he knows Dobbin's safe.'

Emlyn shook his head. 'You going to get off me or what?' he croaked.

Moving off him, Max pushed her head above the bracken. Through the trees she could just pick out the McCrossans as they crossed the second wall and headed towards the road. She stood, prodding Emlyn with her foot. He lay, gazing up through the branches.

'Come on, let's finish what we came for,' said Max. Emlyn climbed wearily to his feet and shook his head. 'Look,' she continued, 'it's our best chance. You know that. They know we took it but if they haven't seen us put it back, they canna prove nothing.'

'He's got Digger. You heard him.'

'We knew that. Well, guessed it.'

'Yeah. But I was thinking, maybe, that wasn't how it was, not really. Until just now. Now I know for sure the bastard's got my dog,' he jerked his thumb in the direction of the mound, 'fat chance I'm sticking their *wee man* back in there.'

'Jeezus, this whole mess, it's scrambling ma brains. All I know is, I've cranked that rusting excuse of a bike half across Scotland, been scared witless by bloody dogs and look at me, I'm covered in shite, and now – hey, surprise, surprise – you tell me we're keeping it.'

'He's *got* Digger, remember?' said Emlyn, rattling the tin. 'And they're not getting this until I've got him back.'

'I still think we should whack it back.'

'Bollocks to that! This is different, special. Taking risks ... that's what's needed here.'

'Special? Risks ... an' of course you'd know all about taking risks, being the middle-class twat that you are, like. Purely no chance. Playing it canny's the thing here, man.'

'What, you're gonna take it off me? Gonna sit on me again like just then? I don't friggin' think so, Max.'

'Okay, ok-aay, calm down. Let me think. Like I said, this is doin' ma head in.'

Separated by their thoughts, they stood side by side, looking out between the trees.

'He's got to have him stashed somewhere,' said Emlyn moodily.

'Hey ... maybe–'

'Maybe what? Tell me.'

'Well, it's a long shot an' ... we'd have to be drop dead lucky, like ... but Lawrence McCrossan's a caravan out on the Coffington road. He doesn'a use it much, so I've heard. Mebbe Ol'man McCrossan's stashed Digger out there? Anyway, you're right – a bargaining chip canna hurt.' Emlyn started towards the blind side of the spinney as if to leave. 'No, not the long way,' she said. 'Best we go straight for the bikes. They'll've gone to fetch the tractor.'

They reached the dyke and climbed over. As they crossed the fields, Emlyn looked back. 'It's no coincidence those two were up there. I think for the moment at least, I'm meant to have it.'

'Oh, Jeezus, he's gone all religious on me.'

'No. There's something I've got to do. I can't explain it. It's something to do with the dreams.' Max stared at him. 'Ever since I was little I've had this recurring dream – of drowning. But it's really weird. Like it's not myself, because, as I'm swallowing water, I'm reaching out to help at the same time.'

'Now you're really losing it, pal.'

'No! I tell you it's something to do with … with my dad.'

'I wondered when we were gonna get to that. Ol'man McCrossan said as much – the day I got given the push from the tea rooms.' It was Emlyn's turn to stare. 'He's up at Huntleighbank, right?'

'And I'm a screw loose as well. Go on, say it, if that's what you're thinking.'

'I never said that. A little paranoid, mebbe? But then this whole thing's dead bent, an' all.'

* * *

Down on the road they pulled their bikes from the culvert and stood listening to Ol'man McCrossan's Renault wind its way up into the hills.

'No panic,' said Max, 'Ol'man McCrossan'll be ages yet. That tractor of theirs is practically an antique, the tight bastard.'

Emlyn pulled his father's note from his shirt and held it out.

Max looked at it but did not take it from him. 'What is it?'

'Read it.'

She unfolded the paper, reading slowly. 'I'm having trouble with the handwriting.'

Ignoring her comment, Emlyn let her labour on, until she folded the note and handed it back.

'The boy – he was your dad?'

He nodded.

'And he's up at Huntleighbank?'

Emlyn nodded again.

'And what? He's a raving nutter?'

There was no edge to the way she said it. The words washed over him and he shrugged and looked away.

'The treasure thing, then? You think that's the horseman?'

He patted his pocket, rattling the tin again. 'The McCrossans want this back. There's something between Ol'man McCrossan and my father. I want to know what. And that bit about losing your way in the dark and not coming back – about dancing three times – what's that all about?'

'Dunno,' shrugged Max, turning her bike downhill and climbing on.

'No,' said Emlyn, 'not downhill. I don't care how old their tractor is, I've no intention of meeting them on their way up. We'll take the Earlholm road.'

'That's flamin' miles out of our way. And it's uphill.'

'It's a bit further.'

Max rolled her eyes and mumbled, 'Aye, by a bloody long way.'

Max grunted and turned her bike uphill. She wanted to say that the sickle man stuff in the note, that and the child's handwriting, seemed far-fetched. But she didn't. The line, about dancing three times, had gatecrashed Bridget's about the danse macabre – the dance of death, with the skeleton and the scythe – and was really creeping her out.

At the crest of the hill, they exchanged glances and stood on their pedals. As they cruised past the dykes and hedgerows, past isolated farms and conifer plantations, fears and questions thrummed along with the wind in Max's spokes, spinning her down into the valley.

* * *

The caravan sat wedged beneath the overhanging pine branches; to one side a fire track cut a grassy chasm between the trees. Emlyn stared at the flat tyres and the pitted and flaking body chocked up on blocks. The slim chance that they had missed something niggled at him, and he wandered down the track, calling for the terrier. Max waited nervously until he returned.

Emlyn nodded towards the caravan. 'What's he use it for?'

'Like I said, the word round town is that he doesn'a come here much. Come on, Em,' she said softly, 'Digger's not here. It was a long shot and Ol'man McCrossan's way too canny for that. Besides, ma arse has had enough of that bike to last it a lifetime.'

They picked their way between unkempt rose bushes, past a rusting water tank, and stood on the weed-choked area that had once been a lawn, staring at the smoke-blackened ruin. The roof had caved in and soot sprang shadow-like above the windows and the doorways. On three sides a sombre pine plantation crowded the plot of land.

'Look.' Emlyn pointed to some water-filled tyre tracks in the muddy ground. 'Someone's been here. Not long ago, either. The water's still draining back.'

'Could be anybody,' said Max.

'Nah, that's recent. Real recent! Sod it, Max, he's got to have Digger stowed somewhere.' Spinning around, he lashed out with his boot and kicked a hole in the rusty tank. A picture came. He was in the tunnel again. He didn't fight it. Lawrence McCrossan was there on his knees burying something beneath a dense carpet of pine needles.

Max grabbed his arm. 'You're doing the zombie thing again.' Her voice pulled him back.

'He's buried them around here.' She stared at him. 'The figures – he's hidden them near here, in this wood.'

Max grabbed his wrist and shook it. 'There's a few thousand acres of trees here. Where're you gonna start?'

She was right. Serried rows of trunks disappeared into the gloom. They could look for years and find nothing.

66

Emlyn had been tramping around Yeaveburgh for half the morning looking for Digger. Feeling despondent, he headed up to Mrs Fraser's in the hope that Max's offer to help hadn't evaporated, and turned the corner just as she pulled the front door to. A taxi was doubled parked outside the house.

'Whatever it is, laddie,' called Mrs Fraser, 'it'll have to wait.'

Max looked in his direction. Emlyn heard her say, 'Two minutes, okay?'

She stopped a short distance from him.

'I'm sorry. I know I said I'd help put up the posters and look for Digger, like, but–'

Emlyn shrugged.

'Where's your wheels?' said Max as an afterthought.

'Back tyre's finally carked it.' He nodded at the taxi. 'What's up?'

'We're away to Hawick – family stuff. Ma Uncle Mussy's in hospital.' Max glanced over her shoulder. 'Can you do us a favour, like? The Beezer's down at Hugh's work: the filling station. He's waiting for me to pick it up. Tell him to put it in the yard.'

'Me and him don't exactly see eye-to-eye,' said Emlyn.

'Two seconds is all. Go on, I'm busting to take it for a run. You can stick a poster up at the servo.'

'Yeah, sure.'

'You're purely belter, Emlyn, man.'

'Max-*ine*!' Mrs Fraser's head was out of the taxi window.

'Champion! I've got to go. In the yard, remember.'

Emlyn watched the taxi turn the corner and then headed off towards the Square.

* * *

Spanner in hand, Hugh McCrossan emerged from the gloom at the back of the workshop. 'What, and Maxie canna tell me herself – she has to send her wee man?'

'In the yard at the back of her place,' said Emlyn.

'That's all I know.' Hugh wiped his hands on an oily rag and stuffed it in the back pocket of his overalls.

Emlyn studied Hugh as he casually dismantled a suspension assembly. Hugh had to know something … surely? Had to know what was going on; he was one of them after all. If I can just get him talking, thought Emlyn, get him riled … maybe he'll stuff up, give the game away?

'Like messing about with engines – mechanical stuff?'

'It's something.' Hugh shrugged. 'Isn'a much in a place like this.'

'Keep you off the streets sort of thing.'

'Mebbe being on the street's a problem for you, but it's no' a problem for me. I'm ma own man. Y'ken?'

'Your grandfather doesn't seem to think so.'

Hugh took a step forward.

'Engineering? Seems your grandfather's not too keen on that particular avenue.'

'What would they know? They're farmers, gamies. Besides, who you been talking to?'

'Nah. No-one. Something I overheard, 's'all.'

'You should keep your nose out of other people's business.'

'He's made it my business.'

'Oh yeah, I forgot – your bloody dog. Well, he's no' got him. Anyway, the damn wee thing's been worrying the sheep.'

'Worrying sheep, eh! You wanna talk about sheep – look at you. They've got you bailed up like a ram in a pen and pretty soon they're gonna snip you good. Oh, yeah, that's got your attention. Yeah – they've something planned for you and it's not an engineering apprenticeship.'

Hugh stepped in front of Emlyn. 'You're talking shite,' he said. 'You've totally lost it, pal.'

'Yeah, well maybe you've lost *your* bottle.'

'Cobblers!'

'Cobblers, is it? You wanna see what this is all about, why he's taken my dog? What's in store for you? Wanna see why you cut your hand that day at Sleeper's Spinney?'

Hugh turned pale. 'How'd you know that? That's a family thing. Nobody in town even uses that name.'

'Oh, I know a lot about your family. Not just names either.' He went to turn away but Hugh grabbed him. 'You wanna see what this is all about?' shouted Emlyn. 'Do you? Then it's back at Bridge Cottage.'

Emlyn shook himself free and moved away.

'I think you're talking out yer arse – but, what the

heck. I've got to take Max's heap of scrap for a test run. I can run us down. It's nae bother for me, like.'

Hugh wheeled the bike into the lane at the rear of the filling station and attacked the kick-start. A cloud of blue smoke drifted between the buildings. He climbed on and stared at Emlyn, who was still standing inside the workshop. 'No helmets, but what the hell, eh.'

* * *

Hugh eased the machine into the driveway of Bridge Cottage, a tap on the shoulder indicating that he should pull up in front of the rusting pile of tin that doubled as a garage. Killing the engine, he watched intently from the saddle as Emlyn emerged holding a tin.

'You don't remember cutting yourself, do you?'

'Oh, not that again,' said Hugh.

Levered free by Emlyn, the lid clattered onto the gravel. Hugh looked about nervously. 'I feel weird,' he said, 'like déjà vu.'

Emlyn tipped the tin forward. 'Da-daahhnn!'

Hugh staggered from the bike, letting it crash onto the gravel, and vomited in the flowerbed. He was spinning away into his childhood: his father, his grandfather, the farm – everything was bright and hard and distant, and he felt small and alone. 'What the hell's that you got?' he said through his retching.

'I was hoping you might be able to tell me.'

Hugh coughed and spat and then straightened, wiping his mouth. 'Put it away, man.'

'This is why he's got my dog.'

Hugh went to pull the motorbike up but couldn't. He was shaking. 'It's like there's a singing in ma head. All mixed up with images. Images I dinna understand. Old stuff. Like out of history books, 'cept real: real and bloody.'

Why was he saying all this? The Sylvesterson kid was an out-of-towner, a Sassenach – an' us McCrossans, we're close, tight-lipped, speaking when there's something to say – why was he running off at the mouth to some Southerner?

He remembered the singing. It was all mixed up with the singing. He remembered being terrified as a little kid. Not because his old man used to hit him, or his grandad – you get used to that – but because there was always something out there and only the singing would keep it away. That was why they sung the old songs.

'That–' He pointed at the tin. 'That's like

everything I was ever scared of.'

Emlyn started to pull the carving free of the cotton wool. Hugh backed towards the shed, nearly tripping over the Beezer. At the head of the drive the horseman appeared.

'*Dinna* ... take it out!'

The figure sank back onto its bed and the rider faded.

Hugh was shaking. 'And the wee stones?'

Emlyn held one out, bottom up. 'They're like the wall.'

The sign leapt across the gap between them and Hugh stood transfixed. Time was the air around him. His breathing, the distant hills, Emlyn's face – all might shatter: a mirror, behind which the dark void sucked and eddied. He watched as the Sylvesterson kid replaced the stone. The mirror held; the gravel shifted under his boots.

'Will you put the lid on, man, that thing's – I dinna want to look at it, y'ken. It's like a dream. I can remember being up at the spinney fixing the wall with ma dad. But the memory, it's like an island. I canna remember it when I'm not there, not on the island.'

'I saw you. Your hand – you did that purposely.'

'Aye – to remember. I canna remember except

when I'm up there wi' them.'

'Your father was singing as he rebuilt the wall.'

'That's what they told me,' he said shakily. 'Learn the songs, sing them and you'll keep them away. I never understood what it was they meant.'

'Yeah, well.' Emlyn tapped the tin. 'It's to do with this.'

'Something's been getting up their nose, for sure. I thought it was because I told them I was off, leaving, as soon as I got ma act together.'

'Nope, it's what's in here.'

'Cobblers!' said Hugh. 'Your father's up at Huntleighbank and I reckon you're out of your tree an' all.'

'The horsemen hold some sort of power or–'

'Horse–*men*?'

'Twenty or so. Besides, if I'm out of my tree … you saw what happened when the lid came off.'

'What *was* that?' Hugh blanched. 'Nah, it was nothing. I didn'a see anything. It's you. You're crazy.'

'What, you think I'm messing with your head, making you imagine things? You're the one making the mistake, pal.'

'No way. An' I'm not your pal. An' now I'm outta here.'

Hugh glanced at the tin, reached for the handlebars

and, heaving the bike upright, wheeled it a short distance along the drive.

'Wait up,' said Emlyn. 'Do you know where he is?'

'Who? Grandad?'

Emlyn nodded.

'He's popping by to pick up the Renault.' Hugh looked nervously at his watch. 'Damn, he hates waiting on anyone.'

'Then the servo'll do fine. Me and him need to talk about Digger. You can drop me there.'

Hugh cranked the kick-start on the bike, but it wouldn't fire and he glanced anxiously up and down the driveway. 'I've to take this back to Max's. So, don't expect me to hang around.'

He attacked the kick-start again with vicious abandon.

Engrossed in getting the machine started, Hugh didn't see Emlyn move backwards into the shed, reach up casually among a mass of cobwebs and wedge the tin behind a roof truss. The bike fired, Hugh climbed on and Emlyn swung on behind. There was a spray of gravel as Hugh fishtailed the machine onto the road.

67

Emlyn stood in the workshop entrance, watching Hugh busy himself with the hoist, his eye half on Ol'man McCrossan. The hydraulics chirred and the Renault descended slowly.

'Still vexed about that dog of yours? Okay, is this plain enough for you?' said the old man, making a to-and-fro gesture. 'Horseman – dog. Dog – horseman.'

'You'd no right to take him. I could go to the police.'

He caught Emlyn with a cold eye. 'By all means pop along and see Sergeant Crozier.'

Raising his eyebrows, Hugh shook his head quickly. Emlyn took the hint, saying, 'Never mind the cops. Where's my dog?'

'Over at Hawick,' the old man continued, 'with a friend.' Emlyn registered Hugh's surprise as he straightened from his task. Jeezus, thought Emlyn, he really didn't know about Digger.

'Hawick – your friend – could all be a fairy story.'

'Aye, it could. If you want certainties, you're talking to the wrong man, y'ken?'

'Okay, what if I could get your pathetic wooden soldier? Today, say?'

'No time like the present. I'm away over to Hawick this afternoon. I could have your pup back here by ... five-ish?'

Emlyn nodded.

'Five o'clock then. Right?'

'Here?' said Emlyn.

'Riverside Park. You know it?' Emlyn nodded again. 'By the bandstand. But, no horseman – no dog. We clear on that?'

'And my father? There's something between you and him, and–'

The old man didn't let him finish. 'Your father's a few slates short of a roof,' he said and tapped his head. 'Short a few pieces of furniture up in the attic. Like father, like son, eh? Always nosing around, the two of youse. Just bring the wee thing to the park, as agreed.'

'Fine. But, when you've got it back, what you gonna do with it? Put it with the others?' Emlyn paused, watching Ol'man McCrossan's face intently. The tension in his legs, his arms, made him want to run, to get out of the old man's presence. 'Because you haven't got 'em, have you?' he continued. 'Not the rest of them. How many are there? What twenty, two dozen maybe? But they've been moved – someplace else – and you don't like that, do you, because you don't like it when people go against you?'

Emlyn saw the question settle on the retired gamekeeper's face, saw his knuckles whiten. He wouldn't think twice about lashing out. Hugh had moved away from the hoist towards the entrance and was standing behind his grandfather.

'Why don't you answer him?' Hugh's question came from nowhere.

The old man turned slowly but the blow came hard and fast. Gasping, Hugh doubled up, holding his stomach.

'Leave him alone,' said Emlyn.

'Or what? You want some too?' The old man paused, letting the words sink in. 'You dinna turn up,' he continued, pointing at Emlyn, 'well, I hate to think what might happen to that pup of yours.'

Emlyn backed away across the forecourt, while Hugh straightened slowly, his arms folded across his stomach.

'An' next time,' said Ol'man McCrossan, brushing past his grandson and walking to the office to collect his car keys, 'keep your trap shut. You can tell Ian to put the welding on the slate.'

68

With most of the day to kill before he had to be at Riverside Park, Emlyn's mind turned to his father. He needed the bulk, the comfort of his presence; hoped that it might erase the image of Ol'man McCrossan hitting his grandson. How could he do that? thought Emlyn. Dwelling on the McCrossans wasn't going to do him much good. No, he'd buy a paper and look at the cryptic. He was no use at them, but it'd pass the time and take his mind off Hugh's face. It had crumpled in surprise at the old man's swift aggression. He thought he'd seen tears but maybe not. After all, Hugh'd been winded. Yeah, a paper ... for his dad. Get that poxy family out of his head. Besides, the crossword was the only talking point they had.

Crossing the Square, he ducked into the newsagent's. The knot of women beside the magazine rack stopped chatting as Emlyn went in. He recognised one of them: Mrs Murcutt. She glared at him and started up a pointed conversation with the woman next to her. Emlyn caught fragments as he waited at the counter.

'The Fraser girl ... hang around together ... that's the one, her with the hair–'

'I've heard she's none too choosy, that one, y'ken,' said a thin woman with a headscarf.

'Been in trouble, 's'what I heard.'

'Runs in the family,' said Mrs Murcutt. 'Mind, the Fraser woman's no angel, believe me. Put herself about as a youngster, did that one. And later, after her husband died, poor man.'

They were staring at Emlyn. He looked back at Mrs Murcutt coldly until she looked away. The woman's a bitch, he thought, taking the newspaper and pocketing his change. And her son's no better. Pushing past them on his way out, he caught the last snatches of their conversation.

'– two abortions is what I heard –'

'– I heard that she had another one. Later. After she'd planted her *precious Douglas*.'

'– and that granddaughter of hers. Regular little

enchantress that one, with half the town's men with their tongues hanging out–'

Outside, Emlyn stood in the shop doorway.

Was that how everybody saw Max: an enchantress?

Something about the word niggled at him but he lost it. Max seemed like – well, *Max*. A bit pushy, and she had a mouth on her when she got going. For certain that'd get right up people's noses in a place like Yeaveburgh, he thought. She stood out. Caught the eye. No wonder Murcutt and her cronies called her an enchantress – probably worried their husbands would have a coronary. Threads of understanding materialised in the air around him and he punched his palm. He couldn't believe how slow he was. That was it. They'd called Max an enchantress. The librarian had called Merlin The Enchanter. En-*chant*-er! Chanting was what Lawrence McCrossan was doing up at the spinney that day – Hugh'd said as much back at the cottage – and in a language he couldn't understand. It'd been quite musical. And to be an enchanter, surely that had to mean that you called up spells, sung them or something. Wasn't that what magicians did, enchant people, chant words of power or something? What else could McCrossan's 'language' be but some sort of spell? And the markings on the stones – the whole lot designed to hold something inside the spinney. Maybe he could duck into the library; ask the librarian. She seemed pretty switched on about that Dark Ages stuff. He checked his watch. The bus would be here soon. Not enough time.

To Emlyn's surprise, his great-aunt, dressed in a tweed hat and a scruffy looking quilted waistcoat, came out of the shop and stood with him. 'Did you not see me over by the stationery?'

He shook his head. 'Sorry – school stuff.'

'School, mmm-nnn. It can be a bit of a distraction at your age.'

Wrestling with the idea of showing her his father's note, he said hesitantly, 'The silver frame, there was–' He stopped, uncertain as to whether he should continue, but there could be no going back with this, he decided.

'I don't want it back, if that's what you're about to ask.'

'Did my father ever mention … a horseman?'

'Good Lord! You know, I'd completely forgotten about the horseman incident.'

'Why do you call it the horseman incident?' said Emlyn.

'Your father had a series of recurrent nightmares. Went on for months. He'd wake the whole household, screaming at the top of his lungs. He seemed to think that a horseman was coming for him. My brother used it as a further excuse to curb his expeditions. An "overfed imagination" was the phrase. Not a good thing in a budding soldier. It came out that he had been caught by Lord Yeaveburgh's keeper.'

'Ol'man McCrossan?' queried Emlyn.

'The very same. He caught your dad up on the estate. I can see you're looking puzzled.'

'It's just that–' Emlyn paused: he had to be careful here. 'Well, Dad mentioned something about being caught up the valley and that's not estate land.'

'A lot of land was sold off when thc twelfth Marquess died: this was the days of death duties. McCrossan Senior bought it. Did very well out of it, thank you very much.' His great-aunt seemed deep in thought. 'The peculiar thing was your father never seemed to recall anything and denied all knowledge of the dreams, something that sent my brother apoplectic. But then Freud's notion of the unconscious wasn't high on his list of bedtime reading.'

'Huh?'

'My brother was a black-and-white man. The subtleties of the developing mind were lost on him.

From his perspective your father was simply lying. I'm sure Rory was merely working through some difficult episode, something that had frightened him perhaps. The sad part was, the more they rattled around up at Huntleighbank Hall, the more obsessed your father became with Arthur. By the time they moved in with me, it was all he would talk about. Of course, as he got older he didn'a let on the same way … but you know, even as an adult, I think he was haunted in some way by the Arthurian legends. He was a troubled man, your father.'

'Troubled?' said Emlyn.

'There, I've said too much. Old women should be seen and not heard.'

'*Troubled?* How do you mean? You can't just leave it hanging like that.'

'Your dad was fine once he left here and went off to university. He settled down at his work. Got on with things. Kept active, physically and mentally. He used to write to me. There were a couple of incidents before he met your mother but they were pretty short-lived. Then after they had you – I think you were about five or six – I got a couple of very strange letters from …' His great-aunt stared across the road, her words trailing off.

'Strange letters from who ... where?'

'Perhaps it's best if you speak to your mother.'

'You can't half tell me something. You've seen Dad, seen what he's like up at Huntleighbank.'

'Aye, he's suffering, poor man. Look, let's just say that this is perhaps not the first episode ... the letters were from some sort of hospital, sanatorium. He'd come back here for a short visit and there was a confrontation down at The Crown. I think that might've set him off once he got back home. I got the impression something happened between him and the McCrossans. He would never say, but, when he lived here, he went out of his way to avoid them.'

'Ol'man McCrossan,' said Emlyn, 'do people round here ever–' Emlyn chewed his lip as the old woman studied him cannily.

'Ever what?'

'Stand up to him?'

'Steer clear of that one, laddie, if you've a mind. I went to school with him. Even then, and we're talking fifty years, he was always turning up like a bad penny. Once he took over as head keeper to the Marquess, then it really went to his head.' His great-aunt stepped from the doorway. 'Well, I've a dental appointment that won't wait.'

Emlyn watched her disappear down Castle Wynd and then he crossed the road to the bus shelter. A trip out to Huntleighbank was definitely on the cards now; he needed to see his dad. He had some questions for him.

69

The day room was quiet. A television, the sound turned low, flickered in the corner. His father sat listlessly in a chair by the French windows, watching the trees move silently in the wind. Emlyn sat close by on the lounge, the newspaper on his knee, one eye on the remaining staff. He wanted to check out the upper levels of the house and was waiting for them to leave the room. Ol'man McCrossan's cruel throwaway line about his father being 'short a few pieces of furniture in the attic' had made him think about his father's childhood at Huntleighbank and his great-aunt's story about the loft. He had to get up there – check it out – but there were three nursing staff dealing with the inmates.

The cryptic crossword seemed to be seeking inspiration from the ceiling. So far he'd managed only two of the clues, both shorter words, and even those he wasn't sure of. He was trying to work up enough courage to ask about the note and what had happened all those years ago out at the spinney. And about the chanting. Yeah, the idea of the chanting was really bugging him. But his father's crumpled face, that look he always wore, held him back. Sitting in his coat like that, he looked like an overgrown kid waiting for an outing.

'Pity,' said Emlyn, lightly pencilling in another clue, 'that we can't sit outside today.'

No response.

One nursing aide remained. He stared at her and then at the clues.

'Come on, Dad, you got a couple of these last time. I'm hopeless. Here's one, nine down: "In the end, Interpol potentially seek war crimes fugitive." Oh, six letters.'

'Pol Pot.'

'I don't get it.'

'Last three letters of Interpol – "In the end", then the first three letters of potentially.'

'I don't think I'm ever going to get the hang of this,' said Emlyn, filling in the answer, one eye on the nurse as she retrieved a pile of magazines and strode from the day room.

'Be back in a minute, Dad.'

Emlyn stepped into the hall. A substantial part of the mansion was used by the administration. The area was designated Zone 2 and a swipe card was needed to access the upper part of the house. Frustrated, he cast around for a way up, but it seemed he was standing in front of the only door through to the second floor. He was about to walk back to the lounge when the door clicked and swung open, blocking any view of him. A man pushing a trolley barged through and without looking in Emlyn's direction lumbered off down the hallway. Emlyn grabbed the handle and shot through the doorway.

He was in the old part of the house, with its heavy wood panelling and ornate ceilings. The stairs were clear. He hesitated, one foot on the bottom tread, and then raced up. A keyboard clattered nearby and he could hear someone on a call, but the upstairs landing was empty. The walls were hung with nondescript paintings and everything had a subdued, institutional feel to it. A few of the doors had card readers, the rest were locked. He wandered down the hallway, looking up to see if there were any hatches or trapdoors in the ceiling – hadn't his great-aunt said something about ladders? – but no break showed in the neatly painted plaster.

This is stupid, he thought. What the hell are you doing sneaking about up here for? He paused at the end of the landing and peered through a window at the gravel driveway below. His enthusiasm outside the newsagent, when he had seized on the idea of the McCrossans as enchanters, had waned. It all sounded so implausible now. And he hadn't even asked his father any questions about his idea. He'd played it safe instead and got him interested in the crossword.

His reflection stared back from the glass. You're in a place for mad people, he thought. Maybe you should just stay; walk up to the charge-nurse and say, 'Give us a bed, I'm staying the night.' Looking past his reflection, he stared out of the window, his brow furrowed into a question. Sounds faded and the tunnel folded in around him. He was getting used to it now; knew when it was creeping up on him. Don't fight it, he heard himself saying, go with it. It's the sight – just something from the past. Not even your past.

The ringing silence pushed him out like a boat onto the still waters of another year.

He was looking down on the grounds again.

Things had changed. The lawns and flowerbeds had an unkempt, desolate air about them. Beneath the trees, patches of frost clung to the grass. A man was being restrained in the driveway. Some sort of argument was under way involving a limousine. The car was driven away and the man sat on the front steps, head in hands. From some great distance in his mind, Emlyn recognised the man as his grandfather.

The scene shifted. He was inside the house. A man's voice called angrily from somewhere downstairs. A small grimy window, overgrown with creeper, was set into the wall under the gable end of the attic. Sunlight chinked in beneath the slates and made bright spots on the dusty boards. Boxes sat piled against the walls and under the sloping roof. A rusting bicycle wheel and some inner tubes hung from hooks in the rafters. A dressmaking mannequin stood near the window, its shoulders soiled with bird droppings.

The boy sat cross-legged. A crude symbol had been scrawled thickly in crayon on the floor inches from his knees. The wax stub landed with a rattle in a dark corner. The boy had thrown it away. Hunched over now, he rocked to and fro.

Even from the remote outpost he had become, Emlyn knew these markings. They were the same signs scratched beneath the stones of Sleeper's Spinney.

He wanted to touch the child –

– his father –

– help him – but he knew he couldn't.

Different voices now, calling him back.

'You're not supposed to be up here.'

Down the corridor a woman stood watching in a doorway. Her mouth moved; it took an eternity to dismantle the words.

'You best go down or I'll have to buzz security.'

Emlyn nodded and she followed him downstairs, waiting until he was through the security door.

In the lounge, his father was still sitting hunched in his overcoat by the French windows. The newspaper and pen lay on the chair where Emlyn had left them.

He looked at his father. He just wanted to reach out and hug him but he couldn't; it wasn't that easy any more.

His unspoken questions hovered about them. He had to ask about the McCrossans, about their singing and whether it had anything to do with the idea he'd had in town of an enchanter, a singer of spells. Go on, do it, he thought. It's now or never, you bloody coward.

'The spinney, Dad? You remember the spinney?' His father's shoulders hunched. His massive neck settled further into his shirt collar. Emlyn knew he was taking a chance here. 'And the snow?'

His father seemed to take forever to turn his head. Emlyn grabbed the newspaper and scrawled the symbol he had seen. He went over it until the pen tore through the newsprint and then held it out for his father to see.

'You remember this, don't you? What is it? A rune? A magic symbol or something? What's it do?' Emlyn waited for a response but his father's face still held that blank, hurt look. He continued, adding: 'And the snow? Ol'man McCrossan? He used to be Lord Yeaveburgh's gamekeeper, and his son, his son Lawrence was there too. What happened, Dad? They sang something, didn't they? What was it? Was it some kind of spell?'

His father's face was coming slowly alive now; his eyes were more focused, sharper somehow.

'A wizard, an enchanter,' said Emlyn, pushing on, 'that would mean that they chant spells, wouldn't it? Sort of chant words of power?'

'The Lady, Merlin's witch, she was there. She's always there. Can you hear her singing, boyo? She's singing now. Her and her line: singing, singing.'

Emlyn's father clamped his hands over his ears. 'Plug your ears. Don't listen. She'll sing you. She sang me that day in the snow. Oh, yes!'

'Dad, what do you mean she sang you?'

'Can't go anywhere. Always following. On my back, he said. That's what Mr McCrossan said. On my back!' He tried to brush something from his shoulder.

'But … what's the chanting do?'

'Keeps them away.' His father swivelled in his chair, scanning the faces around the room. 'Keeps them inside: inside your head. And then the nightmares … come back, see. Come back and then–'

'Nightmares. What sort of nightmares? Drowning?'

'Aye, drowning. No! No! Not water. Never water. No. Blackness. Crushing dark. Suffocating.' His father turned a beady eye on him. 'What you doing, boy? Don't think I don't know what you're up to.'

'I'm not up to anything, Dad.'

'Nothing can stop them now. The wall's breached, boy. Only the raven girl can stop them.' He spun around, staring at an old woman sitting in an armchair on the far side of the day room. 'She's in it. They're all in it. And you now.'

His father stood.

'Who are they? And the signs,' said Emlyn, 'what do they do?'

'I want to sit under the tree now.' His father was rattling the handles of the French windows, trying to open them. 'I don't want to talk to you any more. I want to sit on the bench – under the tree.'

Some of the other residents were watching. Emlyn tried hard not to catch their eye. A skinny man with nicotine-stained fingers rolled moaning into a ball on the sofa. Somebody turned the volume up on the television. His father was crying. Tears welled and ran down his cheeks. The silent sobbing increased. The French windows rattled under the onslaught. A snot bubble ballooned from his father's nose.

Emlyn stood, not knowing what to do. 'Dad?'

A middle-aged woman he hadn't seen before appeared. 'You better run along,' said the nurse. Emlyn hesitated. 'Your father'll be fine.'

70

It was midafternoon by the time the bus dropped Emlyn in the Square. He hurried down through the town and out past the Marchbank. The front door to the cottage stood open; a police car was parked in the drive. The sergeant stood by the front window looking out. If he walked off, it would look suspicious.

'Is this about the burglary?' Emlyn asked from the lounge room doorway. His sister shook her head vehemently, while the officer looked between them quizzically.

'Burglary?' the officer asked.

'It's nothing, Sergeant. Really.'

'What's up then?' said Emlyn.

'What did you think you were playing at,' said Bridget, 'just visiting him out of the blue like that?'

'Will you tell me what's up?' said Emlyn.

The sergeant coughed, then turned his attention to Emlyn. 'I'm Sergeant Crozier. The nursing home called us out. Your father's gone missing. It seems he – that he became very confused shortly after you left. Did you talk about anything that might have upset him?'

'Nothing much,' said Emlyn. 'I took the paper so he could do the crossword if he wanted to. Will they find him?'

His sister folded her arms and turned away towards the fireplace.

'There are patrols out now looking for him. Likes crosswords, does he?' The sergeant seemed concerned to keep him on side.

Emlyn shrugged and looked at the carpet. 'He used to.'

The sergeant's radio crackled. 'Come in Tango-Bravo One.'

'Tango-Bravo One receiving. Go ahead, over.'

'The IC-one male we apprehended on the Edinburgh road. The one who refused to give a name, Sarge … we just handed him over to Huntleighbank. Over.'

'Copy that, Tango-Bravo Three. I'm with the relatives now, over.'

'He's calmed down. They've sedated him. He was raving about a wooden horseman. Some sort of model or toy soldier or something.'

'Tango-Bravo Three, I'll talk to you back at the station.' The sergeant clicked off his radio. 'Do you know anything about this wooden horseman?'

'You told me you'd taken it back.'

'Keep out of this, Bridget. You've no idea what this is about.'

'Look, we don't usually get involved in family matters but the staff said that your father looked extremely distressed before he went missing.' The sergeant waited, his eyes on Emlyn.

'I don't like him being in there. He shouldn't be in a place like that.'

'Fair enough.'

'He has trouble remembering what day it is sometimes. They give him … drugs.

'But he got upset?' said the sergeant.

'I thought,' continued Emlyn, 'that Dad might remember stuff from when he was a boy. He doesn't say much any more because–'

'Because of his condition?'

Emlyn nodded. The sergeant smiled and turned to Bridget. 'I'm sure it'll all come out in the wash.

There's a support team over at Huntleighbank if you need them.' The officer pulled his cap on.

'I'll see you out, Sergeant.' Then jabbing her finger in Emlyn's direction, she said, '*You* stay right where you are.'

Emlyn stared at the shelves of books. Outside the police car pulled onto the road and then Bridget appeared in the doorway holding his field glasses.

'You left them in the car.'

She tossed them at him and, slipping them into his coat, he pulled a large volume from a shelf. 'Archaeology,' he said, waving the book before pushing it back between its smaller cousins. 'That's all you two think about.'

'Your little wooden horseman – where is it?' said Bridget.

Emlyn slumped into the battered leather armchair.

'Emlyn, there was a policeman asking questions about this wooden horseman. I mean, did you tell Dad about it? What the hell's going on with you and–'

'Oh yeah, this is about horsemen all right.' Emlyn was on his feet. 'Not the little wooden figure you're so upset about. Oh, no. Real flesh and blood horsemen.'

'I *will not* be sidetracked on this. This carving you were carrying around – I want answers.'

'You really can't help yourself, can you?' said Emlyn. 'You and Mum think the whole bloody universe can be catalogued.'

'*Answers*!'

'What's the point? I can't talk to you. You wouldn't understand, not with your background. Not you. Not Mum – neither of you. Numbers: you crunch numbers – carbon dating this, thermoluminescence that – there's no way you're going to have a clue what I'm going on about.'

Bridget scrolled furiously on her phone and Emlyn pushed past her into the kitchen.

'Where do you think you're going?'

He flung open the back door and crunched across the gravel to the garage, where he pulled the tin down from its bed of cobwebs. They faced each other in the entrance.

'There is no antique dealer,' he said. 'Okay.'

'I bloody knew it. Right, so what's the deal then, eh?'

Emlyn felt tired, old, as if Bridget's questions could crush him, push him face down in the mud, stop up his nostrils, stop his breathing. He fiddled nervously with his scarf and thought about his great-great-grandfather drowning in the quagmire that had been Passchendaele. Momentarily, he toyed with telling her about the dreams before tossing the notion aside. He didn't want to scare her, not really; he just wanted it over. Wanted her to stop, to stop pushing. Everybody was pushing him – Max, Bridget, the McCrossans – and on top of that there was Digger's disappearance and his father's illness. His hands were trembling. He brandished the opened tin, with its figure. 'This is what it's about – these little wooden horsemen. Eighteen, twenty of them – I don't know.'

'There's more?'

'Yeah. A group of them.'

There was a scraping sound against the outside wall of the garage: the heavy weight of a horse being turned.

'It's stolen, isn't it?'

'Sorta – yeah,' he said, moving past her up the driveway.

Bridget's gaze shifted to the lawn where the rider's unseen hooves cut into turf. Emlyn could see him now even with the carving in its protective ring of stones. The horseman reined in and sat staring at him. Beneath him his mount snorted, trampling the grass.

'What was that?' His sister looked around nervously; her voice lacking its usual certainty. 'What's going on?' She was frowning at the gathering hoof-marks on the lawn.

'Like I told you, you wouldn't understand.'

'Stonewalling might work with Mum, but not me.'

'You can see the lawn; you work it out.'

'I'm phoning the police.'

A weary smile creased his face and he sighed. Hers was the same logic that he'd tried on Ol'man McCrossan up at the filling station. 'Phone away, Sis. Phantom horseman: deal with them every day, don't they?'

His sister continued to stare at the lawn. Several fresh impressions appeared as she spoke. 'What's going on, Emlyn? What are those marks on the grass?'

'If you can't explain them ...' he shrugged at the lawn, '... then how can I explain what's happening to me?'

'This is non-negotiable, Emlyn.'

Ignoring her, he started towards the road. Bridget took several quick strides and grabbed his wrist, pulling him up with a jerk. It was the hand holding the tin. The carving fell onto the gravel and Bridget screamed. She gaped in the direction of the rider for some moments before she turned to Emlyn with a pleading look.

'What is this, some kind of joke? I mean, you've some friends in one of those historical re-enactment societies or something?'

'You can see it, can't you?'

The horse whinnied and turned. Still clinging to his arm, Bridget quickly positioned Emlyn between her and the rider. He twisted free and his sister gasped.

'Where's it gone?'

Her voice was fractured, panicky. He could tell from her face that she could no longer see the rider; an idea came to Emlyn and he grabbed Bridget's hand. Still holding her, he squatted and retrieved the wooden horseman. His grip was firm and Bridget had no choice but to crouch alongside him, her upturned face towards the looming rider, her eyes wide and her mouth slack. He placed the carving between the stones, slid the lid into place and pushed it down with his knee.

'Da-daahhnn!'

Bridget moaned as the rider vanished again. 'You little ...' Spinning on her heel, she lashed out. The slap came out of nowhere and his cheek burnt.

They were both standing now.

It's touch, he thought. When she was touching him she'd seen it sure enough. Her face told all.

The voice again: so familiar, so like his father's. *Oh yes, her face tells all.* The voice a husky whisper in his head. *My eye is forced wide and I cannot look away.*

She moves among the dead. There is no pity in her voice. I grab her arm and see her plans laid bare. I see with her eyes and she with mine.

'With her eyes,' Emlyn repeated, 'and she with mine.'

'What?' Bridget croaked. 'Who are you talking to?'

'Myself, Bridge.' He smiled. 'Just myself.'

That was it. Before they'd touched she'd only been able to see the physical impression made by the rider. Yes, he could see it, but anyone else had to be touching him.

'You supercilious little – how'd you do that?' said Bridget, looking this way and that. 'Come on, I'm waiting for an answer.'

'Well, I could say smoke and mirrors, but I'd be lying.'

'Don't give me any of that airy-fairy rubbish. Where's your little mate from the pony club hiding?'

Lifting the lid, he removed the carving again, and took her hand. He could already see the horseman as he lifted the lid, but, as his fingers closed over hers, her shaking told him she could see it too. The rider lowered his lance and his horse took a few tentative steps towards them. Backing away, his sister collided with the cottage wall, and fell to her knees.

'Where is it?' she shrieked. 'Where … where's it gone?'

'He's still there. You just can't see him.' He stepped away from her. He felt sorry for his sister; as if he'd seen her clearly for the first time, realising it wasn't simply their half-heritage that separated them. They were different: lived in different worlds.

'I've got to go, Bridge. Sorry.'

'But … you can't just … not with him sitting–'

'No, I can't. It's probably best if you stay indoors. So here's what we'll do. You stay behind me and back around to the kitchen door. That's right.' Bridget followed his instructions to the letter. 'Open the door. That's it.' He turned and faced her. She was open-mouthed, glancing about wildly. 'Seriously, you best stay inside until I get back.'

'Emlyn–' Her voice was quivery.

'Best do as I say.'

Emlyn closed the door gently on her and turned down the drive. He caught a glimpse of his sister's face pressed against the kitchen window; her eyes darting, straining for a glimpse of what she knew could not be. No time for explanations right now, he thought. Not that her scientific outlook could encompass any explanation he was likely to provide.

He walked to the road and stopped. He wanted to be sure that his sister was too spooked to follow.

The horseman kicked his mount forward and followed. The rider didn't scare him so much this time. Whatever harm it could do seemed held in abeyance. The hair had still gone up on the back of his neck when it had appeared, but something told him it was all right.

Emlyn turned to face the rider. Looking down at him was a weather-beaten ox of a man in his fifties with grizzled hair and a spade of a beard, the wiry growth deep red. His right eye was bloodied and closing fast. He seemed cloaked in weariness and looked as if he'd led a harsh, tumultuous life. Emlyn sensed the man wanted his freedom; that to replace the lid condemned the rider to a waking sleep. He was close enough to touch the muddied britches. Instead, Emlyn reached out and touched the animal's withers.

No long slow tunnel this time. The sight fell upon him like a fist. The crushing gulf of time rang in his ears. A constantly trodden country: memories kept alive in the darkness.

A verse came into his mind unbidden:

Foreigners shall return among them
And breech the singing walls;
The long line dreads their coming.

A woman was bent low over the man, who reached out and grabbed her wrist, his eyes pleading knowledge of something. Of what, though? The sight spun him like a top. All about were the groans of wounded and dying men. Then it came: his Lord, thought Emlyn, he craves knowledge of his Lord's fate.

Arthur, I cry, what of Arthur? Laughing, she wrenches her wrist away and sings me down into the darkness. She turns then, holding the boy briefly with her eyes and he knows her.

Yes, Merlin's witch, the Lady – the Lady of the Lake.

The rider spoke to him out of the blackness.

You know, well enough, that it is my voice that fills your head. They fear you, boy. Our time is at hand and they fear your coming. You're the one spoken of in the verses. I've watched you on the bridge. Like Merlin before you, your mind runs with the water – runs in dreams and tellings.

I've a mind it's you and the raven girl the verses speak of.

Emlyn let his hand drop away. The voice, that had so agitated him earlier, had calmed him somehow. 'What is it you want?' he heard himself say. No answer came: only the man's eyes staring into his. 'Your time's coming, isn't it?' The dark eyes bored into him, willing him towards a hidden fate.

I'm shaking, thought Emlyn. Why is it I can see some things but not others, the important things? He needed to say something to still his fear, to somehow make the man in front of him – all that had happened – real. 'But you're not about to provide any answers on that front, are you?' His voice was croaky. 'All I can do is try and stop you hurting anyone. And the only way I'm going to do that is to keep a lid on you.' The unintentional pun, the irony of what he'd just said, somehow bedded down his decision to see Ol'man McCrossan. He squeezed the tin closed and started towards the Marchbank. It didn't matter that he didn't know how he felt. It didn't matter that a myriad of emotions were passing through him: fear; elation; responsibility; the heavy weight of a history he would never comprehend. He would hand over the figure. He would get Digger back.

Behind, he sensed the rider fall in and he smiled nervously. He rather liked the notion of an invisible military escort.

71

Emlyn was already halfway to The Diner, where he planned to wait on Ol'man McCrossan's return from Hawick, when his phone rang.

'Emlyn, it's Lindsay Fraser.'

'I thought you were in Hawick.'

'Back early.' There was a long pause. 'Can you come over?'

'I'm meeting someone.'

'In town?'

'Yes.'

'When?' she said.

'At five.'

'Then you've time enough. Come up for ten minutes, just for a cup of tea. Maxine's acting ... upset, like ... locked herself in her room. She's been saying … things. She willn'a come down. It's just that you two seem thick as thieves and I thought mebbe you could …' Mrs Fraser's voice tailed away into an awkward silence. Emlyn knew only too well that on no account could he afford to miss McCrossan. 'Please, son.'

It was the one word that might make him go. How did they know, adults? Did they have some script that was invisible to him? The one word: son. God, how he missed it from his father. With his mother it had always been Emlyn.

* * *

Emlyn stood on the landing outside Max's room, his knuckles poised inches from the door. He'd been gathering himself for several minutes. There was a tension, some unspoken wrong in the house. The stairs, the landing, the hall below were an airlock in which he was trapped, caught between Max and her grandmother, and in his cowardice he simply wanted to escape, to be jettisoned into the street.

'Max?'

Wood echoed under his knuckles.

'Your gran, she's upset. Max? You can't stay in there forever. I'll be downstairs.'

He took the stairs quickly and stood in the hall. Half-a-dozen paces away, beyond the bright rectangle of Mrs Fraser's letterbox, the street beckoned. He paused again, his hand resting this time on the polished brass handle of the kitchen door. Having agreed to come to the house, agreed to try and inveigle Max from her room, he'd now have to see this through. He opened the door and plunged into the warm smell of baking.

'I think she heard me,' he said, sitting at the table, where he watched Mrs Fraser's hands work the rolling pin back and forth. 'Maybe she'll be down … soon.'

'You're a good'un, son.' Pastry was cut into neat circles with a tumbler. 'Thank you.'

The clatter of trays and bowls continued unabated and Emlyn sensed that Mrs Fraser's activity was somehow linked to her granddaughter's refusal to come down. He was trying to think of something more to say, some way of excusing himself, when the door slammed open and the room filled with Max's anger. She sat; her chair tipped back, leaning against the wall, her arm on the table, a large bulging envelope in her hand.

'A pot of tea would be nice,' said Mrs Fraser, closing the oven door and looking up.

Max stared at her grandmother with ferocious intensity. Mrs Fraser's face was ashen as she stared at the handwritten address. 'Where did you get that?'

'From Mussy's place. From his sideboard. When we went back to clean up so he could come home. Aren't you gonna ask how I knew where to find it?'

Horrified, Mrs Fraser continued to scrutinise the envelope.

'What's McCrossan to us?' Max's question cut through the warmth of the kitchen. Emlyn knew he wasn't included in the 'us'.

'Did Mussy give you that?' The envelope no longer seemed to hold Mrs Fraser in its thrall. 'He had no right. No right.'

'Mussy?' said Emlyn.

Max looked through him. 'When we were away to Hawick in the taxi.' Her face was stony. A knot of emotion worked it like an unseen hand. 'Mussy's her brother: ma great-uncle, Musgrave.' She turned to her gran. 'Except he's not, is he?'

'It wasn'a his to give. He should never've–'

'He didn'a give them. He was in hospital, remember? What he did do, 'cause he thought he was on the way out, was drop a few hints when you went to the toilet. Now, what – is – McCrossan – to us?' She was almost shouting.

'I was worried about you, with that lad of his. He's no good, that one. They're all bad'uns in that family.'

'Crap!' Max slammed her fist down, startling Emlyn. 'So, what is it with McCrossan and you? What's your little secret?'

Emlyn sensed the fine, tight thread that bound them: it had cut into Mrs Fraser over the years, was still cutting; he could see the hurt as she struggled to form another lie.

'C'mon, tell us something that can make us change me mind, like. Not going to tell me? How about explaining this then?' Max pulled another smaller and more rumpled envelope from her hip pocket: the ink was faded; the stamp old fashioned; jagged paper teeth grinned where it had been opened in a hurry.

Mrs Fraser gasped. 'You've no right to my things.'

'Your things?' Max ripped a letter from the envelope and thrust it at Emlyn. 'Read it.' Emlyn stared at her. 'Go on! Read it – aloud!' Emlyn shook his head slowly. 'Okay then, I'll read it.'

'Maxine,' said Mrs Fraser, 'don't – *please.*'

'I always wondered what was in that old hat box. You used to let me look when I was little. Photos, is what I remember, lots of old family photos – and a big buff envelope.' She slammed her hand down on the larger envelope, where it lay on the table, and Emlyn registered the colour: pale buff. 'This envelope,' she continued, angrily. 'This one! But once I could read, then suddenly it disappeared, didn't it? I wonder what that was all about, eh?' Her voice straining for control, she flicked the letter open and began to read. '"Dearest Lindsay," blah, blah, "and how sorry" they are about "the terrible accident" and how "you must miss your Douglas terribly", and then we get to the main point. "What happened – happened. We can't undo that. It's the bairn we need to think on now. The child needs a home, needs to know where it came from. You're not the only one who's on your own."'

Max looked up.

Mrs Fraser's hand was clamped across her mouth. She mumbled through her fingers, 'I never wanted any of this–'

'It's signed "L". What's that "L" for, eh? Let me guess: lovely, lonely? And why are they so concerned with this "bairn", hummm? This baby due to be born – when? The envelope's postmarked about six months before I arrived. Were you starting to fill out a bit and had to leave?'

'Stop it,' said Mrs Fraser. 'You dinna understand.'

'I understand plenty. *They* did, too. Well, this *they* is a he, and the he has a name. Go on, say it. Say it!'

Mrs Fraser sunk onto a kitchen chair.

'L for Lawrence, eh? Lawrence *bloody* McCrossan. Who would've thought it, eh?' Max's eyes shone and her mouth was an ugly question mark as she slammed the letter onto the kitchen table, smoothing it with her hand. 'And my birth certificate, eh?' she rasped, tapping the buff envelope. 'Oh yeah, I've had a real good look through this lot. Always had some excuse whenever it was needed. But you had it all the time, didn't you – and why? Why would your grandmother need your birth certificate, eh? No wonder it was backwards and forwards to Newcastle all the time. You didn'a want your dirty little secret hung on the line to dry.'

'I just … couldn'a tell you, Maxine. I know it's hard for you to understand but–'

'Hard! *Hard!* No, I'll tell you what's hard. You – you're hard: hard work and hard-faced.' Max crumpled the birth certificate and threw it at her grandmother. 'An' I canna be doing with this any more, you hear?' She was shaking with rage. Emlyn thought she might strike Mrs Fraser but she stormed from the kitchen, knocking the chair over as she left.

Stiff-backed, Mrs Fraser collected the plates and placed them on the draining board. Emlyn's chair scraped the tiles as he rose and she turned to face him. Some minutes later a door slammed heavily and Mrs Fraser collapsed at the kitchen table, head in hands, and her shoulders heaving silently.

'I better go after her,' Emlyn said, righting Max's chair on his way out.

Outside, the street was empty. A motorbike engine echoed off the walls. Sprinting to the corner, Emlyn stood in the middle of the street and watched as the Beezer, its engine snarling, disappeared around a corner.

72

'Well,' muttered Max, 'at least bloody Hugh came good with the Beezer.'

Fierce with her anger and the roar of the engine, the back lane shot her into the street. She slammed her foot on the brake and slewed around, nearly hitting a lamppost, before she careered down the hill. Strapped behind her was a scruffy sportsbag with a change of clothes, her second pair of Doc Martens and a few photographs from Tyneside. The rest of it, the stuff in the wardrobe, could rot for all she cared. Hopelessness and rage washed through her.

How could her grandmother – no, not her *mother*; she couldn't say it, couldn't think it yet – have done that? And with *him*! How could someone lie to you and smile? Buy you presents at Christmas and on birthdays and not say? Say nothing.

Nothing!

She wanted to scream but her throat was choked. Her eyes leaked brittle tears. She wiped them away. How could she? All these years spent not knowing, hoodwinked by her mother, no, not her mother, but her soddin' sister – and dead now, like, these three years gone, and with no chance of putting it right. Hoodwinked by her – by that woman back there – back in that house. No, that wasn't her grandmother, that was someone she didn't know – didn't care about. Not any more. She'll never get me back there, in that house, she thought. No way. I'm never going back. *Never!* Not if my life depended on it.

Max spat, braked and threw the bike into another corner.

This was doing her head in – the whole friggin' deal: her gran; Emlyn and his psycho friggin' life; Hugh, Hugh's ratbag soddin' family. She wanted out from the lot. To get away – away from the shite-hole they called Yeaveburgh.

She spun the Beezer across one of the bridges and, passing the town sign, opened the throttle. Fuelled by her anger she flew on between the hedgerows, neither noticing nor caring where she was going.

Her fury rode pillion.

Recognising where she was, Max slowed down. She was on the Coffington road. Lawrence McCrossan's burnt-out cottage was just around the bend. L for bloody Lawrence, she thought, anger tightening and churning at her stomach. Yeah, well she knew all about him. No way was she about to turn around. Anyway, what were the chances of his being out there at this time of day? 'Nah, no way!' she growled, accelerating. The tyre spun and then bit and shot down the road.

Seconds later she was level with the abandoned cottage. The battered Land Rover stood parked on the feral lawn. Max had only a glimpse of a caravan door opening and Lawrence McCrossan tossing a garbage bag to the ground as she flashed past.

73

The Renault pulled up across from the park. Emlyn could see the small white and tan shape ducking back and forth along the top of the back seat. He fingered the tin in his pocket and started towards the car. The old man got out, motioned for him to stay put, and crossed the road.

'All in good time,' he called.

Ol'man McCrossan strode across and they were facing one another.

Emlyn went to hand the tin over, then pulled back. 'The sickle man – who's that? What's it mean?'

'My, we are into the technicalities.'

'So what is it?'

'Something beyond your ken, with your wee gadgets and your internet.'

Emlyn passed the tin across. Ol'man McCrossan opened it without a word and looked at him. Behind Emlyn there was the creak of harness and leather and the gentle snuffling of a horse. He didn't bother to turn; he knew what he would see. The lid was replaced and the noises faded.

'You're a smart lad, scratching the signs like that.' He started back towards the road. 'Not many would have worked that out.'

'Hey! My dog!'

'Dinna sweat, I'll fetch your wee mongrel.' A quick hand signal and somebody in the driver's seat leant over and swung the back door open. There was a squeal of tyres as a van braked hard to avoid Digger as he wandered aimlessly across the road towards the park.

'Digger,' Emlyn called. 'Here, boy, here.'

The terrier sniffed the rose bed near the park's edge and cocked his leg.

Emlyn whistled. 'Digger. Here, boy, here.'

Something was wrong. The dog stood listlessly, peering about. Emlyn snapped his fingers; that always did the trick. The terrier's ears pricked and then drooped as the Renault started up Berwick Street.

'You bastard,' Emlyn yelled, running over and scooping the dog into his arms. '*Bast-a-ard!*' He stood, helpless, beside the bandstand.

The pup wasn't Digger.

74

Never mind that arsehole, thought Max, he's nothing to you. She revved the throttle and the back wheel jinked under her, caught, and sent the bike crabwise towards the ditch. But what the hell was Lawrence McCrossan doing at the caravan at this time of day? She eased back, braked hard and swung the Beezer around, slowing to a crawl. Had he seen her as she rode past? The caravan door blocked any direct eye-line of the road and she was pretty sure his back had been turned.

She was stopped now, the Beezer chugging gently under her. Such a distinctive sound. But, she'd never been out on the bike, not before today, so there was no way he could link it to her. There was a forestry fire track a short way back. She'd dump the bike there and walk to the ruin. Whatever he was up to, she had to see for herself.

Resentment, mixed with curiosity, boiled up in her.

Did he know she was his daughter? He must. That'd explain all the crap between her … her *mother* and the McCrossans. Beneath the anger was a strange urge to see this man who was her father. She had to know what he was doing. She idled the bike back the way she'd come, turning over the reasons for her interest in her head. She had already eased the Beezer down the track and propped it out of sight against a fence post, when she remembered what Emlyn had said about the figures being buried somewhere in the plantation. That's what he was up to. Mebbe he's moving them, she thought, or checking on them? He, and that father of his, seemed pretty paranoid about their whereabouts. Yep, that had to be it.

Her mind was set now as she crept between the trees. Reaching the edge of the cottage grounds, she chose a spot near a stack of pine logs and lay down, hidden by bracken. The caravan door was shut. The Land Rover stood nearby. Was he still inside or had he already disappeared among the trees before she arrived? The caravan rocked briefly and was still.

I've got you now, thought Max, and you'll be going no place without me. If she could just find where he'd hidden the wooden figures, she'd have him by the short and curlies.

* * *

Out on the road it was late afternoon, but under the trees it was already dusk.

Max had been watching for nearly an hour and was beginning to think she'd imagined the caravan moving. She shifted her elbows in an effort to ease her position. Her stockinged feet ached with cold. She'd left her boots with the Beezer on the forestry track; she had no intention of letting McCrossan hear her follow him.

'C'mon, toerag, make your move,' she whispered. 'You've 'em hid around here someplace.'

Then, as if she had called him forth, there was a snick and the door slammed back against the body of the van. A match flared briefly and a cigarette glowed beneath the trees.

Max followed, feeling the ground with her toes. Twice she located dead branches before she put her weight on them. Ahead a torch flashed on and then out. What's the miserable shite up to, she thought.

Signalling someone? Nah, couldn't be. 'Not out here,' she muttered. 'Just you and me, pal … and acres of trees.'

The silence welled up around her and she waited. Had he heard her? Seen her? No, he'd moved off again. Max could barely hear his passage through the plantation. For such a big man, he was moving quickly and silently. She slowed, stopping every few paces to listen. Beneath the canopy it was difficult to judge distance. His torch flickered briefly in the gloom. She concentrated on the spot where she'd last seen movement, remembering the clicking sound of the dead torch up at the spinney.

Fear engulfed her for an instant. She wanted to run but forced her limbs into stillness, focusing on her anger, letting it well up and spread out around her like a cold pool. Oh, she was going to make the bastard pay, all right. He was there somewhere, standing beneath the trees, the same as she was. Her eyes made shapes out of nothing. The ache in her back and legs became a song.

The torch flicked on. Counting quickly, she reckoned off about fifteen or sixteen trunks between them, and then the beam went out. Had he seen her? A branch cracked. He was further away and in a completely different position than she'd suspected, heading back towards the caravan, a shadowy figure hidden by the trees. But she wasn't looking; her eyes were fixed on that last point, that last brief flash of light as it hit the earth.

Over at the ruin the Land Rover roared into life.

She waited until the faint echo dwindled to nothing down towards the river and then walked between the trees towards the spot she thought she had last seen the torch. A carpet of brown pine needles greeted her. Nothing: not even a boot mark. She began to search between the rows, looking for any disturbance and discolouration in the forest floor, and wondering if she'd become confused and miscounted. Although her eyes had adjusted to the gloom beneath the pines, it was still a struggle to pick anything out. Everything – the needles, the trunks, the seemingly endless canopy of boughs – had taken on the same dirty monotone. This has got to be roughly where he'd been, she thought. You canna have got it completely wrong, surely?

She stood, helpless, shivering, the damp cold rising through her calves.

It was no good. She'd never find them. Lawrence McCrossan had won; he'd had the last word. How could she pay him back now? How could she hurt him the way he'd hurt her? Disconsolate, she shoved her hands in her pockets and, as she turned to leave, her fingers closed over a book of matches, the one she'd taken with her the night Emlyn had closed the mound. They'd been in her pocket all this time. She'd slung the jacket on without thinking when she'd stormed out of her gran's.

Carefully, she struck one. Her hands were shaking. Anger and excitement welled within her in equal measure. Holding the flame before her, she crouched low and glanced about, uncertain what she was looking for. Nothing. She struck another and waddled sideways into the next row. There! A scrap of brilliant green wool snagged low on a trunk. He'd marked it, of course. She'd been so close; could have missed it so easily.

'Now I've got you, Mr bloody L.'

Sinking to her knees, she swept aside the carpet of needles and soil to reveal a ring of flat stones. She lifted one and turned it over. Her fingers were black.

'Well, if X doesn'a mark the friggin' spot, eh, McCrossan.'

She scraped at the soft loam. The severed tree roots told her someone had been there before her. Her fingers hit something hard. Wrapped in several plastic bags was a tin. She lifted it clear of the shallow hole and ripped the bags away. Squinting into the shadows, she lit another match. She could just make out a red-cheeked Santa Claus grinning back at her from a circle of holly.

'Season's greetings, McCrossan.'

Symbols had been scratched into the lid and in places bare metal gleamed pale. The marks had been gone over with something black. Max pulled the lid free. Jammed tight between sawdust were some twenty-odd wooden figures. Overwhelmed by an urge to lift them out one by one, she let her fingers brush the wooden forms.

A branch snapped behind her. She spun around. Something heavy turned and the pine branches shook. There was movement all around her but she could see nothing. A scream echoed between the trees and she realised it was hers. Jamming the lid on, she ran blindly between the rows towards the forestry track, boughs slapping at her in her panic. They were coming for her. She had stolen the figures and they were coming for her.

Emlyn had been right.

Why had she not listened to him?

75

Hugh heaved the broken gearbox casing to shoulder level and let it slam into the bottom of the bin at the side of the service station. He was fuming. The cheek of it, he thought. That bloody grandfather of his collaring him earlier, saying he wanted him to come with him down to Riverside Park – wanted him to hold the pup while he talked to Emlyn. Well, he'd told him to stick it. 'Go find one of your cronies over at The Crown to do your dirty work,' he'd said. His grandfather hadn't looked too pleased but seemed in a hurry and, grabbing one of his mates from across at the pub, he'd disappeared down Berwick Street in his Renault at a cracking pace.

Hugh looked across at the hills. Black clouds were massing at the head of the valley. Forget him, he thought, the old sod isn't worth the effort, and you'll be out of here soon enough. Sauntering back into the workshop, he spotted Emlyn trudging up the hill towards the Square. A small white and tan head was peeping out from his greatcoat.

'Well,' murmured Hugh, 'at least you've got him back.'

There was a peal of thunder and a rush of wind and a squall tore across the forecourt. Water cascaded from the filling station roof. The clouds swept in low and lights sprang on in every building as Hugh slid the workshop door across.

* * *

'The bastard! The frigging bastard.'

Emlyn's mumblings were ripped away in the wind. The rain was sudden in its horizontal ferocity, stinging his face. Across the Square was the bus shelter. He stumbled over to it. In one corner the wind seemed less ferocious and he slumped on the bench. The pup's nose peeped from his coat; the poor little tyke was trembling.

How could you have been so stupid, he thought, trusting a bastard like Ol'man McCrossan? Digger was gone. All the tricks he'd taught him; the way he'd leap into your arms if you gave him half a chance.

A ringing came from his pocket. Let it ring, he thought. Nothing mattered any more. Whoever it was rang out. Emlyn sat, his face crushed against the cold glass of the shelter, letting the water streaming down the opposite side of the pane wash him clean. His phone went again. He pulled it free and pressed it to his ear.

'Emlyn, man, this'll wind 'em up something wicked.' Max's voice was breathy and excited. 'Where are you?'

'Opposite The Crown.'

'I canna hear you. What's that noise in the background?'

'Rain,' he said above the roar. 'On the bus shelter.'

'What you doing there?'

'Nothing.'

'What's up?' said Max. 'Something's up. What's happened?'

'Nothing.'

'Dinna give me that bollocks. Something's happened.'

'Digger's gone.'

'We know he's gone. An' we're gonna get him back.'

'You don't understand,' said Emlyn, feeling his throat constrict. 'I wanted to get Digger back. I couldn't see the point any more, not after what you said at your gran's – sorry – you know what I mean. I arranged a meeting with Ol'man McCrossan to hand it over.'

'And get Digger back,' said Max.

'It's not Digger.'

'Then why hand the wee man over? Look, I'm not following this. I'm too hyped. Stay there. Ten minutes.'

The phone went dead.

76

Max's hair was plastered against her skull, her face white against her black clothes as the Beezer ploughed up the hill, sheets of water spraying from the front wheel. Blinded by the rain, she saw the shelter too late and braked hard. The bike skidded, cracking the back tyre against the kerb. She leapt onto the pavement as the machine keeled over, its engine silent. Scrambling to her feet, she grabbed the sports bag and dodged into the shelter.

'Emlyn, man, we've got the bastards.' She unzipped the sports bag and with a flourish pulled out the tin. 'Hey, no more messing about now, right? Mr Lawrence bloody McCrossan'll be singing a different tune when he finds out about these.'

Emlyn glanced across briefly and then turned his

face back to the glass. 'How'd you know where to find 'em?' he said.

'I was pretty wired, not exactly thinking straight, and I just took off on the bike and next thing I know, I'm sailing past the friggin' caravan and there he is. The rest was easy. I waited – followed him. You were right. They were there sure enough. Buried out in that plantation, a ring of his daft stones around them, and them exact same marks you were talking about chalked on the underside. An' all that supernatural bizzo ... it wasn'a shite. There was summat following me.'

'It was there when you kicked down the dyke. A horseman leapt through the breach you made. It's to do with Arthur.'

'Arthur who?'

'King Arthur.'

'Get away with you. You're having me on, right?'

Emlyn reached out. 'Give me your hand.'

'Hey, what is this, the back row at the flicks?'

'Your hand.' Her fingers slipped into his. 'The lid.'

Max stared at the tin; it was the first time she'd really looked at it properly. It had been too dark down in the plantation and then the ... She shivered. She didn't want to think about it. The Santa image had been heavily scored by something sharp and then traced over with a black marker.

'Take the lid off,' repeated Emlyn. 'But don't let go of my hand.'

Wedging the tin with her knee, Max revealed the wooden carvings snug in their sawdust bed. Squashed flat against the side was a ring of tiny stones. Had they been there down in the plantation? She couldn't remember seeing them.

There was a clatter of hooves and she looked up. A ring of horsemen stood in the Square, steam coming off the animals' flanks in the rain. The circle tightened around the bus shelter and she groaned in terror, pressing herself into the corner against Emlyn.

'Put the lid on.' His voice was strained. A rider had dismounted and was walking towards the entrance. Max couldn't move; her hands were paralysed. She couldn't believe what was happening.

77

'The lid! For God's sake, put it back on!'

But Max remained frozen as the warrior turned into the shelter. Reaching across, Emlyn fumbled, but the lid was tight and wouldn't push down. Max was pressed against the back of the shelter. The rider held a sword and its tip was at her throat. The lid hissed as Emlyn rammed it on with his fist and the riders disappeared.

'For crying out loud, Max, you got some sort of death wish or what?' He leant forward and looked into her face. 'Max?'

She sat, disconnected, staring at the rain, much as he had minutes earlier. He shook her gently and she leapt up, flailing at him.

'It had a sword,' shrieked Max. 'It was coming for us. Are you friggin' mad?'

Nursing the pup, he grabbed her wrist with his free hand and pulled her down on the bench.

'M-a-x, take it easy.'

'Purely no chance.' She glared at him defiantly. 'You bloody knew, you bastard, and you let me get these. You let me dig 'em up.'

'I sort of knew, yes. But I had no idea you were going to snatch them from under McCrossan's nose. I gave the other one back, remember?'

She stopped struggling and he let her go.

'You knew about them, though.'

'Yes,' Emlyn sighed.

'Knew those phantom horsemen would appear?'

'They're not phantoms,' said Emlyn. 'They're … they're real and they can hurt us.'

'Hurt us?'

'That's what they were talking about up at the spinney; they were worried about the horsemen getting loose. There's some power up there. You were right, down at the dig, about saying the signs were there to keep something in, something that the wall holds back. That night with the cars in your street, when you found me in the alley, there was this drunk and I think – he was stabbed and–'

'Malcolm McKlintock? He's still in hospital.'

'Like I told you outside the library, I heard the rider coming down the street as I got in the taxi.'

'Jeezus, man!' Max stood and walked to the entrance. Turning slowly, she said, 'So, what're we dealing with?'

'I don't understand how it works because other people can't see them – unless I touch them. It's sort of as if time has meshed somehow: they're in this time but not properly, and we're in theirs, but again not actually in it.'

'You can cut out that Doctor-Who-time-travel guff, for starters. You're doing ma head in with it.' She was sitting now, close up, staring at him. 'So what do we do?'

Emlyn shrugged. 'Give 'em back. It makes no difference. They're going to get them one way or another. I thought I could trade for Digger and look where it got me.' He opened his coat to reveal the terrier snuggled against his chest.

'That's not … he's too scrawny. They switch him, or what?'

Emlyn closed his eyes and leant his head against the shelter.

'Surely not? No, not even the McCrossans would … Emlyn, man … I'm … I don't know what to say.'

Max squeezed his arm and then leapt up. 'Right, then. They want to play dirty … I'll show 'em dirty. They can kiss this lot bye-bye, for starters.' Pulling Emlyn from the shelter, Max heaved the Beezer upright. 'Come on, the pub's open. Let's get in out of this. I need to think.'

Max wheeled the bike across the Square at a run and propped it in the alley next to The Crown. With Emlyn in tow, she ran for the entrance. The landlord was standing in the porch watching the heaving clouds.

'Your gran isn'a on tonight. Missus changed the roster last week.'

'Can we, like?' said Max, motioning to get past his bulk.

'Ach, go on then. No mention of this to your pals; I've ma reputation as a hard man to maintain.' He let them brush past. 'Will you look at that water? I'll be needing to light the fire if this lot keeps up.'

The pub was a gloomy cavern that smelt of yeast and stale cigarette smoke. A handful of regulars turned on their stools as they walked to a corner table.

'Gi's the pup,' said Max. 'I wanna hold him.' She pulled the Jack Russell from the folds of Emlyn's coat. 'He's cute.'

'He's not Digger though, is he?'

'No. Sorry. Why'd you hand the figure back then if it wasn't? You didn'a really explain.'

'He had him in the car,' said Emlyn. 'I thought it was Digger. In fact, I think that's the bloke – him with the grey hoody up at the bar – who Ol'man McCrossan had driving, the bloke who nearly pitched this little feller in front of a bread truck. I've half a mind to go and–'

'No, don't,' said Max, pulling him down. 'We've enough to worry about without you starting a ruckus. Mick, the landlord, he'll have us out on our ears.' She squeezed Emlyn's arm. 'Look, I'm real sorry about Digger. You don't think he's still got him?' she added after a moment.

Emlyn looked away and shook his head.

A few more regulars drifted in. The landlord came across with a box of kindling and knelt before the already made up fire. It wasn't long before he was cursing quietly. 'Can't seem to get it lit,' he said, grinning up at Max.

Dropping the pup back on Emlyn's lap, she said, 'Here, gi's a go.'

'I'm away to grab some firelighters. You can try, if you've a mind.'

The landlord disappeared behind the bar. Max crouched in front of the grate. One after the other, the matches failed.

'What are you doing?' said Emlyn, leaning over.

'I'm gonna burn 'em.' Emlyn stared at her. 'You heard me. He's lighting a fire and I've got something to throw on. Digger's gone and ma gran's not–' Max set her face and struck a match. Emlyn nodded, smiling weakly. He could see how fragile Max was; how close to losing it completely. But then he wasn't too far from that point himself. Sensing someone's gaze on him, he looked around. It was Ol'man McCrossan, immaculate in his tweed jacket and cap.

A wave of hatred engulfed Emlyn as he stood quickly to face him. How dare he just saunter in, fronting them after all that had happened? Emlyn wanted to yell, to scream that he was the lowest form of life: a treacherous, double-dealing dog killer. He said nothing. Something in the old man's cold gaze and the turned heads of the patrons said hold back. Max's caution about the landlord having them out on their ears echoed around the suddenly quiet bar. Sitting down slowly, he hooked the sports bag with his foot and slid it out of sight beneath the bench.

'Must be damp!' Max grunted, and threw the matchbox onto the pile of crumpled newspaper and kindling.

'Having trouble there, are we?' Max turned towards the voice as Ol'man McCrossan tossed her a disposable lighter. 'Try that.'

She stared at him briefly before holding the lighter flame to the paper. The edge darkened and charred, but wouldn't catch.

'Must be damp, like you say. What you need is some old dry timber.'

Max pushed past Ol'man McCrossan, and plonked down on the padded bench seat. Emlyn could see she was feeling for the bag with her feet. He nudged her leg. She picked up the signal and settled back.

Ol'man McCrossan looked from one to the other, studying them, and then leaning forward, his hands on their table, said in a low voice: 'Fifteen hundred years ma line's kept them wee men safe. Fifteen hundred years we've sung the signs and those carvings, sung the stones that surround them. You think I dinna know when something's awry.'

'Well, if they're so damn precious,' hissed Max, 'then that son of yours should have been more careful. I mean how smart was that, burying 'em out in a wood?' Emlyn knocked his leg against hers in an effort to get her to stop. 'No! Sod it, Emlyn. I'm sick of these two throwing their weight around. The whole flamin' town's scared of 'em, an' it's about time somebody whacked 'em back in their box.'

'An' you think you're it?' said Ol'man McCrossan. 'Just gi's 'em, eh? You don't know what you're on, either of you. Messing with things beyond your ken, you are. Anyway, I've seen your holdall there under the table. Now tell me why, my wee girlie, I couldn'a just take them off you now, if I've the mind.'

'Us *wee girlies*, we're top drawer in the screaming department.'

'You think you're clever, but you'll leave the pub soon enough.' He shifted his gaze between each of them for several seconds, and then moved off across the bar and sat down. There was a full pint on the table in front of him.

'We've done it now,' said Emlyn.

'Aye – sorry. I couldn'a help myself.'

They sat slumped and in silence, staring at the twitching pup asleep on Emlyn's chest. After a while he said, 'I think he gave him something.'

'What? I dinna follow.'

'Ol'man McCrossan, I reckon he gave the pup something, doped him, 'cause all he's done is sleep.'

Emlyn scratched the dog's ear but he didn't stir.

'Yeah,' said Max, 'he looks like me after a Saturday night out: comatose.'

'Wait on – Saturday evening,' he said, jerking upright. 'God, you're thick sometimes, Sylvesterson.' An image of the horseman in the cottage driveway had leapt into his head; how he'd fooled Bridget into thinking he had the figure in the tin when it had been safely hidden under his desk. Dropping the pup into Max's lap, he said, 'Wait here. I've an idea.'

'Hey, you're not leaving me here with that creep? He hasn'a taken his eyes off us since he sat down.'

Emlyn held up his hand, fingers splayed.

'You better not be any more than five minutes either.'

As he walked past Ol'man McCrossan's table he opened his coat, twirled like a catwalk model, and pushed through the double doors.

78

The grandfather clock in the foyer was chiming six. Upstairs, the chessboards looked as if no-one had touched them since Thursday night. The room was empty; nobody had arrived. Scots' weather – you could rely on it every time. Emlyn took a final look into the landing and then, dodging between the tables, he crossed to the cupboard. Unlocked. Brilliant! He pulled out a largish tin with tape on the lid. It was marked 'spare pieces'. He opened it and tipped the contents onto the bottom shelf. Shutting the cupboard, he walked to where the Lewis chess set sat on its low table. He stared at the pieces, trying to judge size and weight. He needed enough of them to fool that old bastard downstairs.

Quickly, he shot the pawns into the tin – the first few rattled horribly and he glanced over at the door – and then he selected four of the smaller court pieces. He shook the tin. Yep, they clunked, but not too loudly. The tin with the figures was packed tight with sawdust. Surely the old bastard wouldn't know that? He'd have to take the chance.

He grabbed the board and shot the remaining pieces onto the sofa, pushing them down behind the cushion. The board he slid out of sight beneath one of the armchairs before he slipped out to the landing where he leant gingerly over the balustrade. No-one was about and he headed downstairs, forcing himself not to hurry. At the bottom he paused, his hand on the swing door. No, the tin, it was too big – Ol'man McCrossan would see it. He'd have to blind-side him.

Something faltered inside him and he stood outside the doors for several minutes, terrified that someone would push through and the old man would see him. With trembling fingers, Emlyn positioned the tin against his hip, put his hand in his pocket to hold it in place, and then, as casually as he could, he pushed through the doors into the bar.

The place had filled up. With the sudden onslaught of the storm, businesses had closed for the evening. People were shaking coats off and talking about the weather. He slipped between them, careful not to bump into anyone, and pushed in alongside Max.

'Where the hell've you been?'

Emlyn glanced across at Ol'man McCrossan. A large group had come in and had halted, dithering near the door. The old man's view of them was momentarily blocked. Emlyn slipped his tin on the seat between them: 'See,' he said.

Max shook her head. 'Two tins: I dinna see what–?' He showed her the chessmen. 'Ah, a decoy. Now there's canny for you, man.'

'We can't stay in the pub forever. And you can't burn them here, not now, too many people. Besides, the fire's not lit. Come closing time, he'll have us for sure. So, we play by our rules, not his. Which means we leave, now. He's not expecting that. He'll follow, right? Make sure he sees you throw me the tin.'

'Champion. I like it.' Max nodded. 'We've a fifty-fifty chance.'

'Better. He's old school. He'll see this as blokes' business. I'll be surprised if he thinks you've got them.'

'Sexist tosser,' said Max, grinning. 'Him – not you.'

'Plus,' said Emlyn, ignoring her jokey tone, 'he's already cottoned to the fact that we've some way of protecting the figures, otherwise there'd be a dirty great phalanx of horsemen out in the Square. All twenty of 'em.'

Emlyn stuffed the tin into the sports bag and handed it to her. Scooping the pup under his arm, he squeezed out between the tables. He turned to her as they pushed their way out of the rapidly filling bar. 'Make sure you throw me the right tin, okay?'

Seated in his corner, Ol'man McCrossan watched the door hiss shut and tossed down his pint.

79

Outside, the rain had turned to flurries of snow. Under the sodium lights Emlyn could see that Max was trembling. As they crossed the Square, he put his hand on her shoulder for a moment. 'Look, I'm pretty wobbly on this myself.'

'Bollocks to wobbly,' said Max. 'I'm soaked from the ride an' it's brass monkeys all of a sudden. Look, the toerag'll be out any second. Best pick our spot, eh?'

'Let's stick close until he does.'

Emlyn and Max had reached the far side of the Square as Ol'man McCrossan emerged from The Crown.

'Now,' he whispered. 'The tin. Quick! And move away after, but not too far. Like you're watching. Scared to get too close.'

Emlyn took the tin, slid it beneath his coat and tried to quell his overwhelming desire to run.

'Well,' said Ol'man McCrossan, approaching across the cobbles, 'are the wee figures to find their way back to their rightful–'

Emlyn's breath plumed in the cold. 'Owners?'

'I was going to say "place". They're of this place, if not this time.'

Sensing Max backing away towards the shops, Emlyn said, 'I've no patience for your riddles, old man.'

'They're ancient,' said Ol'man McCrossan, 'and powerful beyond your ken. Do you no' see that?'

'Old are they? Well, not for long 'cause I'm planning on burning 'em.' Emlyn registered the flicker of panic before Ol'man McCrossan composed himself. 'Yeah, I thought that'd stop you dead in your tracks.'

'You'll have some of your own markings in there with them. The old signs hold them back but not entirely.' Ol'man McCrossan took a step forward, as if testing an invisible barrier. 'They've tasted freedom once too often today. Cold enough for you, is it? Arthur's last battle was fought at this time of year, on just such a day: bitter cold, so it's said.'

Something hard bumped the back of Emlyn's legs as he backed away and he glanced down. The heavy granite horse trough was at his knee. He edged around it, putting it between himself and his adversary. Something was wrong. An icicle hung from the lead piping; the surface of the trough was glazed with ice. Emlyn looked up. The old man was staring at him, his eyes hard under the brim of his cap.

'This isn'a normal weather. Something's leaking from your wee tin. It's not just the marks, see, it's the singing that holds them back.'

'I'll still give you a run for your money.'

'Lead on, then. These legs have seen their share of moorland.'

A low singing echoed off the shop fronts as the first flakes of snow began to fall.

'Max! He's trying to sing us, like he did me dad. Run, Max, run! Before he sends us mad.'

Max backed away, hesitating. 'The pup! Gi's the pup,' she said.

The terrier sailed through the air. Max caught him and took off towards the River Stairs. The old man advanced on Emlyn, a low drone on his lips.

'Your chanting doesn't seem to be working,' said Emlyn.

Ol'man McCrossan stopped his droning and a muffled silence filled the Square. No car's engine broke through the whirling snow; no footfall on the pavement; no movement. The whiteness settled on their shoulders and clung to their hair.

'I touched his horse, you know, and he said something, the rider. Well, not said – communicated. Something about me being the "one" – the one to end the long line.'

'I know the verse well enough. And what, you think you're the one? The one to end the long line, to make ma family, ma ancestors, to make nothing of fifteen hundred years of pain, of sacrifice, of tradition?'

Snow continued to carpet the ground.

'Aye, well, that bloody Lawrence had to move 'em – put 'em all *safe* in his hidey-hole. Wouldn'a listen, would he? Had to have it his way. Narrghh, you're nothing more than a prissy wee Southerner, with your smart ways and your mother, and sister, digging up what's best left lie in the ground. Same as all Sassenachs – you know nothing but what's staring you in the face.'

Emlyn strained his ears. The tinkling jangle of harnesses still rattled in his head. The fading hoof falls echoed eerily in dark enclosed spaces; they were following Max, he thought. And then another sound pricked at him: the low drone of a Land Rover climbing towards the Square.

'That'll be Lawrence now,' said Ol'man McCrossan, smirking. 'He'll not be pleased to have been outsmarted by a slip of a girl.'

Emlyn looked away to the Wynd and the old man lunged forward, knocking the tin from his grasp. As it turned in the air, Ol'man McCrossan's fingers grazed its edge, sending it spinning out of reach. Emlyn understood the strategy well enough. Ol'man McCrossan was hoping that when it hit, the lid would pop and the riders would be released.

80

Hugh locked the workshop and headed up Berwick Street towards the Square. He was shivering. Where the hell had this weather sprung from? He was going to have to walk. No way was he risking his precious bike in the snow. Too much invested in it already. Now if it had been Max's old crate … But even that old boneshaker wouldn'a have been safe in this lot. Man, it was really starting to come down.

On the corner of the Square he stopped in a shop doorway and dragged his jacket from his bag. Putting it on, he turned the collar up. He was about to head across to The Crown, see if his father was there, supping, see if he could scrounge a lift, when he spotted his grandfather and Emlyn over near the water trough. Another movement caught his eye:

Max, edging away along the shops and running off down Copersgate.

What the hell was going on?

Back by the horse trough, his grandad lunged at the Sylvesterson kid and they both went over. They were fighting over something. The old man caught him a beauty across the face. His father's Land Rover had pulled into the Square and was crawling towards the struggling figures. He hung back. The old man and his grandad would take care of Emlyn, but Max – her face, as she looked back before disappearing down Copersgate – told a different story.

81

They went down together in their struggle to reach their prize. Lashing out, Ol'man McCrossan caught Emlyn across the eye. A fizzing ball of colour exploded in his head.

'You youngsters never learn, do you?'

But despite his age, Ol'man McCrossan was already up, steadying himself on the slippery surface with one hand, the tin clutched to his chest. Emlyn swung his leg in an arc. The blow caught the old man just behind the knees and pitched him onto all fours with a grunt. Lunging forward, Emlyn wrenched the tin free and took off towards Castle Wynd as the Land Rover turned into the Square.

At the corner, he glanced back. Ol'man McCrossan was climbing in beside Lawrence. Emlyn plunged down the hill, his boots sledding on the treacherous surface. His cheek ached and his eye was starting to close over.

Without traffic or people, the sodium lights gave an eerie glow to the empty streets. Had the McCrossans sung the whole town to sleep? At the bottom of the Wynd he slipped and, holding the thought that at least they wouldn't be able to go much faster than him in these conditions, went down with a bone-jarring thump in the snow.

* * *

The snow fell thick now, making the white flanks of the Marchbank into an eerie, soundless tunnel. Headlights swept up behind Emlyn, casting his shadow across the earthworks. Glancing back, he shielded his eyes, and then plunged on, following the loop of the road until it came out onto the straight. Ahead in the whirling darkness somewhere, stood his mother's cottage and the bridge.

His phone rang and he yanked it out. The screen displayed his sister's number. Pocketing it, he moved on. His only thought now was running and evasion, but there was nowhere to go. Ahead, the bridge was a dark throat in the snow. He was being swallowed.

Something terrible was about to happen.

82

Careful not to make a sound, Max unlatched the gate into the laneway. The raucous squawk of her gran's favourite quiz show flooded into the yard. Opening the garage door, she switched on the light and slid the Father Christmas tin onto the bench.

The pup posed something of a problem; she needed both hands for the fire and he seemed determined to sleep. She was beginning to think Emlyn had been right about Ol'man McCrossan having given him something.

'Bastard,' she growled and looked about.

A crate full of clean rags stood next to the wall. Scooping out a hollow, she dropped him among the old towels and fabric offcuts, where he curled up and fell asleep. 'You'll be fine,' she said, scratching his ear, 'we're just gonna have a little bonfire – keep ourselves warm.'

She was shivering uncontrollably now.

'First things first,' she said, and grabbing her overalls from a hook, she slipped out of her wet things. The overalls were damp and greasy. She was trembling so hard she couldn't think straight, could hardly do up the poppers: she needed warmth. A decrepit wardrobe stood in the corner. Her gran kept rags and old clothes in it. She wrenched it open and pulled a moth-eaten coat from the pile. Dragging it on, she wrapped it about her and folded her arms, trying to stop her shivering by force of will. No buttons, damn. She rummaged through the pile, pulled free the cord from a dressing-gown and looped it around her waist. A hand-knitted beanie spilt from the pile and she jammed it on her head. 'Not my style,' she said, 'but what the heck.' Already she was warmer.

She grabbed the tin, placed it on the oil-stained concrete and fell to her knees. No, there was no going back now. Forget all that archaeological, historical crap. They're just wood, dead wood – and dead wood's for burning.

At the back of the garage, she found a battered fruit crate stuffed with newspaper and kindling. She scrunched some newsprint into balls, tipped the kindling on top and arranged a space into which she could tip the carvings. In a crab-like crouch she moved across to the pile of kindling and pulled Ol'man McCrossan's lighter from her pocket.

'Burning what's not yours to burn, eh?'

Max stifled a scream as the voice came from nowhere. A shadowy figure stood in the doorway, snow swirling around his shoulders.

'Rack off. You're a bloody useless waste of space, you know that.'

Snickering, Hugh said, 'You'll no' snag a new feller dressed like that.'

'What, an' it seems to you like I'm looking? Purely no chance.'

'You always talk to your ex-boyfriends like this? Anyway, I was watching from the other side of the Square – and I followed you.'

'Yeah, just like the rest of your tribe,' said Max with a scornful look. 'Always on the follow: you could get a job as a railway carriage.'

Hugh moved forward and picked up the tin. Max grimaced. She was powerless to stop him and screaming for her gran wasn't about to change anything. He was going to open it. Well, let the tosser go for it; whatever was coming was on its way.

Outside, something heavy shifted against the doors, rattling the lock.

'What's that?' said Hugh.

'Pull the lid off. You'll soon find out.'

'I already know what's in here – a wee wooden horseman.' He was still staring at the row of frosted glass panes at the top of the doors. 'Your new boyfriend showed me. Bigger tin, though. Christmas present for someone, is it?'

Sod you, pal, you're my half-brother: same blood, same skin and bone – in part at least. Confusion welled up in Max: she'd always wanted a sister, or a brother even, especially the times when she'd been dumped with her gran. Now she had one. Thank God they'd never...

She stuffed the thought down and lunged at him, snatching the tin. Well then, let's see if blood's thicker than water, like. He let go without any resistance and was left holding the lid.

Crouching, she tipped the wooden figures out. 'I'm burning them,' she said. Stones and sawdust spilt onto the floor. 'Either help, or sling your hook.'

'Burn away. There's enough oil soaked into that concrete to set the street alight.'

Max stared at Hugh. She'd misread him.

A dull clopping came from the laneway. A hoof crashed against the woodwork. They looked at one another. Another kick followed, splintering one of the panels.

'What the hell's that?' he said, leaping back. 'It's a horse, isn't it?'

'Aye, horses. An' we best keep ahead of 'em.' Max snatched at the figures with both hands, dumping them back in the tin. Grabbing several of the stones, she tossed them in on top. 'Have I missed any?'

Hugh stood transfixed as another panel stove in.

'*Hugh!* Is that it?' He looked down at the bed of kindling as if he'd woken from a deep sleep. 'Have I missed any?'

'There,' he said, pointing to one of the carvings that had slipped from the pile of kindling and lay hidden behind a ball of newspaper. Max grabbed it and shoved it in the tin. Scooping handfuls of sawdust and pebbles, she dropped them on top.

'Bring that crate, it's full of kindling.' Hugh seemed to be moving in slow motion. 'Hugh! C'mon – *the crate!* – and throw me the lid.'

Grabbing the crate, he tossed the lid across and she rammed it home.

The central panel of the door crashed in, the rotten timber scattering across the floor. Max snatched a wad of newspapers and jammed them into the crate Hugh held. Sweeping some oil-soaked rags from the bench, she stuffed them in his pockets. 'They'll burn well,' she said, as she yanked him through the side door and closed it. Crossing the yard, she eased open the back door and they slipped through the house. The television was still blaring from the kitchen as she pulled the front door closed with her key.

The spinney was calling her. She couldn't explain it, but what had started up on McCrossan land was to be finished there. 'C'mon,' she said, grabbing his wrist and dragging him up the street. 'Have you your wheels nearby?'

'You're kidding? In this snow? I followed you on foot.'

'Look, I've got to get to The Crown. The Beezer's up there. I need your help, Hugh. I canna do this on ma own.'

'Okay,' he said, ploughing after her, 'but tell me where you're going.'

'Where it all started – where we found them – the spinney.'

'The Beezer's a heap of junk. It'll never make it up there.'

'Hey, I canna be doin' with your attitude, me, not right at the moment.' Max ran on. 'The Beezer's our only chance.' She was shouting now. 'You want that lot to catch up, 'cause according to Emlyn they'll no' be messing about when they do. They'll stick us, no second thoughts. C'mon, we need to find some way of getting to the pub where those damn horses canna follow.'

Hugh said nothing, he simply grabbed her hand and dragged her down an alley, opened a side gate and clambered up onto a chicken coop. The birds cackled and fluttered. Nearby a dog barked inside a house. They dropped down the other side of the wall and took a right into a narrow passage between some houses.

Max looked back, straining her ears. The muffled thud of hooves was close by. She willed her legs to move faster. Choosing their route carefully – an enclosed stairway and a building site where they squeezed past the chain-link fencing – they reached the Square, tumbling and sliding into the alley by The Crown.

'Emlyn's some sort of decoy,' said Hugh. 'Am I right?'

'He's a chess set he nicked from somewhere.' Max pointed to the Beezer tucked in behind the bin. 'Now just get it started will yer.'

Hugh kicked the bike over. Smoke drifted over them but the engine didn't catch. Hooves clattered into the far side of the Square. 'Engine's too cold,' he said.

'For God's sake,' screamed Max.

Hugh flailed at the kick-start. At the mouth of the alley, invisible hooves compacted snow. The engine caught and Hugh leapt on.

'Get on!' he yelled.

Max was barely astride the bike before they fishtailed into the Square. The snow danced in powdery spurts around them. They collided side-on with an unseen object and a horse whinnied in pain. Hugh gasped; something sharp sliced through the lining of his jacket and slashed his arm. Steadying the bike, he eased it away from The Crown, gathering speed and confidence as he went. Max clung to him, looking over her shoulder and praying that he could keep them upright.

83

Emlyn stumbled onward.

The great soft flakes that earlier had drifted down out of the darkness had given way to mean flurries that whipped across the ground as if in search of someone or something. The hedgerows creaked and sighed under the constant battering, while in the wood across the river the bare fingers of the trees clawed the sky. McCrossan's Land Rover, its headlights dead now, crawled along behind him, shepherding him, never giving him a moment's respite. His calf muscles burnt with the effort of staying on his feet in the worsening conditions and a voice echoed in his head.

Our time is coming, boy. It is almost on us. Death follows us all and she'll drink where she will.

He knew he wasn't mad now; it was like a part of himself that he couldn't control, dogging him in both his waking hours and his dreams.

The Land Rover crawled closer, driving him on.

He was level with Bridge Cottage. His sister was only a few strides away but he could sense her fragile defences: the curtained windows leaking light from every room; a talkback radio show playing loudly from the kitchen; her car gathering its silent quilt of snow in the driveway. Home was no longer an option.

He ran on and he was up on the bridge, skidding down the far side, and over the stile at the end of the parapet wall. The embankment fell away to the river in a white curtain. His feet slipped and he was down the bank on his back, sledding, a tangle of arms and legs and a flurry of powdery snow, the chessmen rattling in their tin.

Up on the bridge, Lawrence McCrossan killed the engine.

Emlyn picked himself up and looked around. The riverbank stretched empty and white on either side. He moved down along the heavy stonework of the bridge towards the bank. A sheet of ice, thick enough that there was no sense of the water passing beneath it, had crept out along the masonry pier.

The black branches of a tree, uprooted by the spate and washed downstream, were wedged beneath the first arch, while the trunk, skewed against the bank by the power of the water, sat locked in the ice. He stamped his boot down: the ice held. How could it have frozen over so quickly? he wondered. The bitter cold, working its way beneath every fold, answered him.

He remembered his leap across the Edderton Water and stared out to where the river ran free of ice beneath the central arch. If he slipped here his greatcoat would pull him under. He peeled it off and threw it up the bank. Undecided what to do next, he fingered the end of his scarf. He should take it off; it could trip him or catch on something. But he couldn't abandon it. Out here, with the wild river running at his feet, it was his only connection to his family, to his father. He flicked one end over his shoulder and pulled the tin from the bag.

He wanted the threat of it going in the river.

Tentatively, he inched out alongside the tree. A dead branch presented itself. He reached for it, missed, and went down hard, still clutching the tin. He pulled himself up between two broken branches. Holding one, he balanced on the other. He was shaking, whether from the thought of what might happen or from the intense cold, he wasn't sure.

The ice had held: it was thicker than he'd thought.

84

'Cold enough for you, is it – *you stupid little scrote?*'

Ol'man McCrossan stood eyeing Emlyn from the bank. He pulled the butterscotch tin out and opened it. One by one he removed the small river stones Emlyn had placed around the figure. 'You think a few pebbles, a few markings'll save you?' he said, tossing them at Emlyn. The stones skittered across the ice and disappeared with a series of tiny splashes into the river.

Lawrence McCrossan slithered down the bank and stood behind his father. At their back stood the red-bearded rider, the animal's head bowed, its breath pluming in the air. Ol'man McCrossan said something in a language Emlyn didn't understand that sounded like a command. 'One word from me and he'll skewer you, no trouble.'

'Not out here he won't.'

'Oh my, we've all the answers, have we not? What happened between your father and me,' said the old man. 'That's what this is all about, eh?'

'You cursed him,' shouted Emlyn. 'You killed Digger.'

Ol'man McCrossan jerked his thumb at the rider. 'Cursed – sung – you think the like of this'n give a monkey's?' He replaced the carving in the tin and closed it; the rider remained.

'Ma father sung him, right enough,' said Lawrence McCrossan. 'But he wasn'a like all the other kids; he was different, a dreamer. It was just to sing away his memory, to frighten him.'

Impatient, Ol'man McCrossan stepped towards the riverbank. Emlyn grabbed at a branch to steady himself and scrabbled into a cleft on the tree trunk, his feet slipping on the snowy surface.

'Careful, or you'll have him and the tin in the water,' said Lawrence McCrossan, his hand on his father's arm. 'None of this makes any sense, I know, leastways, not from where you're standing. But, the horsemen, they've been contained time out of mind, generation after generation. The name McCrossan means "Son of the Rhymer". Each man, the first son–'

'This the full historical tour, then?' said Ol'man McCrossan.

'Each man,' continued Lawrence McCrossan, 'the first son, the son that survived, women too when there were no boys, was told their place, what they were to do: sing the stones and hold the horsemen back.'

'No,' Emlyn shouted. 'That bastard cursed him. Put the sickle man on his back. Said it'd follow my dad and that he'd journey in the dark and wouldn't come back. Why'd he say that to a kid? Ask him – *go on*!'

'Nah, you've got it wrong,' said Lawrence McCrossan, looking at his father.

'Oh, I said it right enough – an' I meant it. You've just forgotten, Lawrence. You've forgotten a lot of things. And I'd sing it again,' said Ol'man McCrossan, pointing at Emlyn and rattling the tin, 'but he canna be sung, not since he touched this'un's horse here. Like I said, boy, what's trapped in them carvings doesn'a give a monkey's what we think.'

'You had a choice,' said Emlyn. 'You didn't have to sing him. He was a kid: *a kid!*'

'Gi's them, eh. You canna stay there all night.'

Emlyn looked about him. There was nowhere to go. The cold seemed abnormal; sucking at him, shutting down his thinking. Wherever Max was, she would be trying to burn the figures. He remembered her struggling with McCrossan's lighter at the pub. She would need every minute he could give her.

'Tell me what happened,' said Emlyn, holding up the tin. 'Tell me why he needed to curse my dad or these go in the river.'

'Enough o' this.' Ol'man McCrossan cut his son off with a wave. 'Can you not see what's going on here? He's stalling for time.' He took a step forward onto the ice, only to be held back by his son.

'Wait!' said Lawrence McCrossan. 'He's no' got them.'

'Dinna talk daft, man? Like I said, the Fraser girl found where you'd buried 'em. Besides, you think this weather's just upped out of nowhere?'

Lawrence McCrossan shook his head. 'They may be gone, she may've lifted 'em from where I buried them, but I'm telling you they're no' with him. That's a different tin. It's bigger.'

'I knew it! I knew there was something wrong. I told you we should've split up.' Cursing, Ol'man McCrossan was onto the ice before his son could stop him. Emlyn and he went down together. The lid rolled under the bridge; the chess pieces went skittering towards the water. McCrossan Senior was on his knees, scrabbling for a hold as he tried to prise himself upright, his face inches from Emlyn's.

'Just a few chessmen,' said Emlyn.

'You cunning little shite. Pity about your dog, though.'

'What'yer do with him?' Emlyn grabbed the old man's wrist. 'Tell me, tell me what you did with Digger.'

The sight roared down into Emlyn like a wind from a great height. In his head he saw the weighted bag; the splash as Ol'man McCrossan flung it from the bridge into the night waters of the Yeave. He felt the panic of the struggling shape trapped inside.

Emlyn's punch grazed stubbly flesh as Ol'man McCrossan stepped to one side, slipped and went down on his knees, the butterscotch tin clattering from his pocket. Emlyn kicked at it, intending to send it into the river, but the ice gave no purchase and his foot only clipped it. The tin hit the dead tree and went skittering across to the bank near Lawrence McCrossan's feet. The gamekeeper reached down quickly, pocketed the tin and stood anxiously on the bank.

'You stupid little–' said the old man, grabbing one end of Emlyn's scarf and pulling him down. Emlyn ducked and the scarf slipped over his head.

Grabbing the broken stump of a branch, he wound the other end several times around the waterlogged timber and hung on grimly to the silk. The old man had taken his dog; he wasn't taking his scarf as well.

'You know your trouble,' said Ol'man McCrossan, struggling to his feet, 'you Sassenachs, you're too soft, too sentimental. You treat your animals as if they were–'

The sentence went unfinished. A deep groan echoed under them and Emlyn gasped as his foot pushed through into the icy water. The groan transformed into a creaking wail and, as if in slow motion, Ol'man McCrossan disappeared waist-deep into the water, where he clawed desperately at the silk, bellowing for his son. Seconds later, Emlyn felt his legs go into the river and he grabbed the tree trunk, locking his elbow around the broken stump. The silk tightened and the old man grimaced. Emlyn glanced towards the bank. On the opposite side of the tree, Lawrence McCrossan was inching his way towards them across the ice.

'I can't ...' Emlyn cried. 'I can't hold him.'

With a sliding jerk, Ol'man McCrossan sank up to his chest, splinters of ice skittering away across the frozen surface of the river. His face was contorted with effort as he pulled on the silk scarf and drew his hands level with his chest. Fear shone in his eyes. Emlyn knew the old man's dilemma: he couldn't let go, nor did he have the strength to pull hand-over-hand; the force of the water was too great. Emlyn reached out his arm. The old man lunged at his hand and missed. The ice shifted again and the scarf went slack, followed by a ripping sound as the silk tightened suddenly and then tore where the sharp edge of the stump had cut into it. Ol'man McCrossan's head disappeared below the surface just as his son's arm reached across Emlyn and plunged beneath the swirling blackness.

Lawrence McCrossan lay face down on the ice, his upper body balanced precariously across the dead tree. His face was knotted with the strain as he heaved the dripping head clear of the water; his hand a knotted mass of tendons as his fingers clung tenuously to the greasy untreated wool of the old man's pullover. The current swirled violently, turning the dead weight. A strangling noise came from the old man. The sodden neck of the pullover was cutting into his throat. His arm thrashed wildly against his son's and his burbling was cut short as his open mouth plunged beneath the water again.

'I canna hold him.'

Emlyn reached out but the old man had swung away from him when his son had grabbed him. Ol'man McCrossan was beyond his grasp.

'Help me!' cried Lawrence McCrossan. 'He canna swim.'

Lawrence McCrossan lurched forward, suddenly shifting his grip. The sleeve of the old man's tweed jacket broke the surface, the whiteness of the hand stark against the eddying current. For a moment the son clung to the cuff but slowly the sleeve peeled from the arm, the body rolled in the stream, and the empty jacket flattened out and floated to the surface.

'No-oooh,' hissed McCrossan, and cursing, dragged the sodden tweed up over the tree trunk and flung it across the ice. Rolling over, he fell back, spreadeagled on the ice, and stared blankly at the sky.

85

Hugh kept the motorbike away from the drifts that covered the hedges and gates. His fingers were numb and he was shivering. Max clung to his back, the box of kindling wedged between them. He could feel her trembling through his jacket.

'We should turn back,' he shouted.

The bike sledded on a corner and they nearly came off into a snowdrift.

'No! Keep going,' yelled Max, glancing over her shoulder for the pursuing horsemen. The whirling whiteness consumed everything around them. She knew they were out there somewhere. And that sooner, rather than later, they would find them.

86

'For chrissakes, *help me*!'

Lawrence McCrossan, belly-down now across the solid flatness of the ice, stared at the eddying water where his father had been seconds before. The river had taken the old man. The boy's voice fell into him from a great height. The boy. He must pull the boy from the river. He let the swirling water relinquish him, climbed to his feet and reached for the lad's hand.

'You won't let go ... will you?'

On the upstream side of the tree the ice was unbroken. Treading close to the trunk, he steadied himself. No need to lose another, he thought. With a grunt, he hauled the lad free of the water.

'Your father–' The boy was on his feet now.

'River took him,' said McCrossan grimly, and picking up the jacket from the ice, flung it onto the bank. 'I should've saved him, but–'

'The current, I could feel it dragging at my legs.'

'Aye, the soddin' river bloody Yeave. She's taken her share – but him? Why now, when I need him?'

The boy picked up his father's jacket from where it lay crumpled in the snow and held it out. He took it grudgingly, the sodden weight of it in his hand. Anger surged through him. He let it come. All this time, for what – the figures, the chanting and the dyke, always the dyke, with his childhood lying curled in him unused, and for what – so his father could slide away beneath the waters of the Yeave? He stared at the river, with its icy mantle. Gone … drowned …

'He's gone,' echoed the lad. 'Like my dog.'

'What?'

'Drowned … like he drowned Digger. He put him in a sack …'

The boy's voice faltered and he sank to his knees in the snow. His shoulders were shaking. He's crying, thought McCrossan, and I have no tears.

'Aye,' said Lawrence McCrossan, helping the lad to his feet. 'That'd be the measure of him. Come on, there's nothing to be done here.' As the lad reached for his greatcoat, once again his legs buckled under him on the slippery bank. McCrossan hauled him up, draped the greatcoat around his shoulders, took an arm and shoved him up the bank. 'I've some blankets in the Land Rover.'

Up by the road, the boy straddled the stile and looked at him. 'The horsemen,' said McCrossan, 'has the lass got them?'

'She's going to burn them.'

'Burn them?'

'The horsemen will be free. What's trapped in them will be free.'

'Free! Trapped! What is it you think is in those figures?'

'Arthur? I dunno. His men?'

'You see him,' said Lawrence McCrossan, pulling the butterscotch tin from his pocket and tossing it at the boy, 'sat on his horse down by the water.' The boy nodded. 'He'll not move till I give him the word. Go on, open it.'

The boy's chilled fingers freed the lid with difficulty.

'Pass me the carving.'

The boy tossed him the wooden horseman and breathing on it, McCrossan murmured a word not used in generations.

The rider turned his mount and took off across country at a gallop.

'Gone to join his brothers,' said McCrossan. He hurled the empty tin at the river, pocketed the carving and hustled the boy over the stile.

Up at the Land Rover, he pulled the blankets from the back. They smelt of dog, but the lad took them gratefully and wrapped them around himself.

'Oh, Arthur will be free all right.' He opened the driver's door. Nodding at the passenger side, he said, 'You best get in before you freeze to death.'

87

For the moment a bitter wind is in my face and I am free. It is a thing not tasted for an eternity. My horse is flagging and I spur him on up the wooded slope. They will be waiting for me – my comrades. I can see them in my mind's eye, much as they came that night to be sung in that ancient place – to be protected. What fools we were.

Yet they sit motionless, the horses with their heads bowed, the breath of man and beast pluming in the air, each man holding a torch. The flames blaze cold, untouched by the winds of this world now, but on that fateful night they brought warmth and comfort against the coming fight. Beyond sleeplessness and edgy with fear, one or two shift uneasily: soldiers who have a task to do and want an end to it. For some the end has already come. Human heads, leathery and shrunken from their long sojourn among the rafters above the fire, hang draped across saddles, the pale flaxen hair braided and knotted.

But the boy has come, as was prophesied by the Lady, curse her and all her line.

I laugh. The cursing has been done already. She did that long ago. Her first born, Merlin's blood, the son who she punished by bending his will to the keeping of the singing stones. It is his line that guards Arthur's guard.

Wolves call in the hills and I spur my horse forward in one last effort.

88

Emlyn slid in opposite Lawrence McCrossan. The gears crunched and they crawled off the bridge.

'That's no king, no warlord. That's the old gods – the forest itself. Twenty-three figures. All carved from different wood, different trees: rowan for magic, oak for strength and leadership. You want me to go on?'

'But I thought that–'

'You saw the rider take off. Did he follow you around before?'

'Yes.'

'Then best you listen hard because time's running out. Aye, the figures, they each represent one who fought alongside Arthur. They've their names too: Cei, Bedwyr, Gwalchmai. Warriors. Brigands. Freedom fighters. Fighters they were, whatever you want to call them. But Arthur, and the rider carved in his likeness, is different from the others. He had the seed of the old gods planted in him as a child and that was their undoing. He couldn'a be controlled. He became wild and cunning like an animal. What's trapped in that figure doesn'a see through our eyes. It's blind to pain, blind to the suffering of others. Now, tell me, where is she?'

'I'm not sure. Everything happened so quickly after I gave back the figure.' The cold pressed in around him and an image came into his mind: Max, shrinking from the riders. 'The spinney! Maybe she's there.'

'We best try it first. That's the direction the horseman took.'

With an awful delicacy, McCrossan drove up the valley.

'D-does … this th-hing … have a heater?'

Lawrence McCrossan pulled a couple of vents open and a blast of warm air rose around them.

'We couldn't light the fire in the pub,' said Emlyn. His teeth had begun to chatter uncontrollably. 'Not even … wi-with … with the lighter we were given.'

'They'll not take fire willingly but–' McCrossan glanced across at Emlyn. 'One of us could burn them. In the old stories it's always a woman as burns them. Just pray she hasn'a torched the one that matters.'

'The rider – wh-when I t-touched his horse – he said that I was the one, the one spoken of in the verses? But your – f-father didn't believe me.'

'Aye, the verses.'

'What are they?' said Emlyn.

'Old prophecies, they say.'

'What do they say – the verses?'

'Not much,' said Lawrence McCrossan. 'Riddles mostly. Nobody's ever made much sense of them, although plenty have tried.'

He began to recite.

'Foreigners shall return among them
And breech the singing walls;
The long line dreads their coming.'

The Land Rover crawled even slower up the hill. 'There's two more:

'Trapping time with his crystal eye
The cloaked one comes from the South.
His search is for one who is lost.

'The raven girl gathers all to her.
Black arms take the mighty to the flame
And their madness falls upon the earth.'

'I've heard that before,' said Emlyn. 'The first one, the "long line" bit–'

'That's impossible, laddie. Those verses are known only to the keepers.'

'I'm telling you, I've heard it. I just can't remember … Ye-es! When I touched the rider. In the driveway at Bridge Cottage, he was following me, and Bridget wouldn't let up. I touched his horse and his voice was in my head, that verse thingummy was in my head.'

'Aye, the riders can speak to us. That's true enough.'

'Max, she's always – d-dressed in black. My dad, he mentioned the raven girl.'

'You think that's Max?'

'It's gotta be Max. Surely?'

'Aye, I suppose–'

'What was the bit about trapping time?'

'Trapping time with his crystal eye, the cloaked one–'

'Crystal eye.' Emlyn's brow furrowed. 'I use binoculars … but to trap time, you'd need to take photos. My telephoto lens, don't you see: "His crystal eye". We're the ones – from the prophecies.'

'If you're right, then–'

But Lawrence McCrossan didn't finish. He was hunched over the wheel, his eyes narrowed, concentrating on every dip and turn. The snow was being driven straight off the great drifts piled against the hedgerows and onto the windscreen, hampering the wipers.

'They're tied to Arthur,' continued McCrossan. 'Swore oaths of allegiance. If she burns the others, his guard, their spirits will be free to pass into the west, aye, but–'

'Into the west?' said Emlyn.

'Aye, they believed that in death their spirits migrated to the west – to the Blessed Isles. Arthur's figure's a different matter. That's not just the soul of a dead warrior trapped in there – that's the Oak God. Burn him and we're in big trouble. The others, his guard, they'll be called back and–'

'And ... wh-what?'

'No-one knows for sure, as it's never happened, but we know the havoc they can wreak when they break their bonds.'

Coming around the bend, they nearly saw the animal too late; its shaggy brown fur and an awkward shambling gait were caught in the headlights.

'Is that ... wh-what ... I think it is?'

McCrossan nodded.

'How?' said Emlyn. 'What's happening?'

The bear shuffled down a wooded track. Watching the animal disappear into the whiteness, Emlyn swivelled in his seat, while McCrossan drove on with an intensity matched only by the silent snow-shrouded night.

89

'Burn them,' said Hugh.

'The damn lighter willn'a do anything in this wind.' Max glanced at the sky. The clouds were gone and the snow no longer falling. A distant baying drifted down from the hills. An answering howl came from the head of the valley. She could tell from Hugh's face that he was thinking the same thing as her. 'Tell me that's not what I think it is?'

Hugh knelt beside her. 'Gi's the lighter.' He shielded it with his hands. Flames caught the oily rags, licked at the kindling and black smoke spiralled into the night. The fire spat and hissed in its bed of snow. 'Now,' he said, 'before it dies down.'

Astride our mounts, we wait patiently in the snow. Arthur kicks his mare forward a few paces and the girl feels the point of his lance snag her clothing. She shudders and looks about wildly.

'Somebody just walked over my grave,' said Max, jumping up, the unopened tin clutched to her chest. 'They're here. The riders. I know it. We just can't see them.'

The wind died. The sparks flew towards the treetops and the drone of a diesel engine echoed across the snowy stillness.

'Your father, your grandfather,' said Max. 'They've found us.' She looked at Hugh, saw his bewilderment, and prised the lid free.

It is then, in her confusion and fear, she sees us, her eye alighting last upon our Lord.

Max knew him immediately: Arthur. And, although, in the way the mind works in moments of great fear, she registered every tiny detail – his dark, thinning hair, the stocky shortness of him, even the name of his horse, Llamrei – the man before her looked nothing like the images of the Hero-King she'd been fed as a bairn.

90

Arthur's mare shifted its weight and Max felt cold steel prick her shoulder. Blood trickled down inside her shirt.

'This canna be happening,' whimpered Hugh. 'The fire. Throw them on the fire.'

The girl's fingers close upon one of us. One of my companions will smell the sea and hear the waves crashing on that blessed shore.

'Don't burn them,' a voice called from the field.

'Emlyn?' whispered Max.

'For God's sake, don't burn them.'

'Emlyn, man?' she wailed and turned towards the voice. Confusion swallowed her. Lawrence McCrossan stood inside the ring of trees, a dark shadow in the firelight. She hated him. 'Where is he?' she screamed. 'What have you done to him?'

'Nothing, lassie, he's here. Have you burnt any of them?'

'I'll burn them all. Where is he?'

She threw another carving into the fire.

'Dinna do that,' said Lawrence McCrossan. 'You've no idea what you'll unleash.'

'As if I care.'

We are fewer in number now. Peredur is gone.

'Burn them and we're as good as dead.'

'He's right.' Emlyn stumbled into the clearing, stood a second beside McCrossan, and then sank to his knees near the fire. In a single bound Max had cleared the flames and Arthur's lance found only air where her throat had been. The tin fell from her hands, scattering the carvings at her feet.

'Keep him warm at all costs,' said McCrossan.

The girl kneels at the boy's side and takes his hand. She touches his cheek.

'We'll be okay,' said Max.

'Ol'man McCrossan,' chattered Emlyn. 'Th-through the i-ic-ce. G-g-gone.'

His words slapped her mouth open and she heard Hugh groan behind her.

McCrossan was on his hands and knees, murmuring. She thought he was praying and a hysterical laugh broke from her.

'I'm not strong enough by half, I need the old man,' she heard him say and the murmuring took on a new shape, changing to a low drone.

Max's laughter died and she watched, immobile, as the burly figure that was Arthur dismounted and held out his lance to the red-bearded rider. Stepping around the fire, he drew his sword. The bitter touch of it was beneath her jaw. The cold breath of iron rose in her nostrils. His eyes were on her and she knew his cold desire: for her to burn the figures. She looked away, pulled one from the snow and tossed it into the flames. The wood flared, burning quickly.

'D-don't. You don't know w-what you're doing,' said Emlyn.

'He wants me to burn them,' she said.

'The others, yes.' Lawrence McCrossan's voice came at her from a cold distance. 'Time, we need time,' he continued. 'The others can do nothing without him. But not his, y'ken? Not in the fire, or we're lost. You'll know when you've it in your hand. Be certain you dinna burn his.'

There are no certainties here. Only death. Whether for us, or one of them, remains to be seen. For in the end Arthur will do as he pleases. He will, on a whim, part the girl's head from her shoulders without blinking.

But he waits.

He is a sovereign lord and others do his bidding. It is for the girl to throw the figures into the fire. Fear is writ large upon her face. Her pace is measured and Arthur's impatience grows.

Max's fingers closed on another and she shuddered. The power long contained there held her: she could smell the forest, could sense the movement of the earth and the stars, no longer simply pinpricks of light but a high bright song. McCrossan's voice seemed to rise from the earth itself. Life coursed through her and death stalked the darkness between the trees.

She knew what to do. Her connection was to another world now.

She looked down at Emlyn's pale face and understood. His grip was weakening. How much time does McCrossan need? she wondered, wrenching her will away from Arthur and placing his figure on the ground beside her. Reaching forward, she chose another and pitched it into the flames. One by one she pulled them from the snow and watched them burn.

One by one we are gone.

As long as she is doing Arthur's bidding, the girl believes she is safe. It is Arthur's vanity that saves her, for the Oak God has left little room inside the man and what is left, the shreds of a Lord I once would follow without question, is but the vain pursuit of power and privilege. He sees it as fitting that we, his guard, should precede him into the flames. Sees it as his right, once his figure is burnt, to call us back across the bright water, call us back from our well-earned rest to ride with him.

It is then that I see that the Lady's web may catch us still.

And I remember what it is that I must do.

Beyond the dying fire was the last of Arthur's guard, a red-bearded ox of a man, his hair grizzled, his face lined and scarred, one eye closed and swollen. Max could not take her eyes off him.

There at the first and at the last, surely it is I, Arthur's faithful steward, whose betrayal will be remembered all these long years.

'Easy, girl, *easy,*' said McCrossan, breaking his chant momentarily. Resuming, he altered the pace, deepening the notes, rocking in time. Max felt a change but dared not shift her gaze from the red-bearded rider beyond the flames. Her whole being seemed concentrated on the blade resting against her neck.

Again Lawrence McCrossan paused. He turned to his son. 'Sing with me.'

'I canna,' said Hugh.

'I'll not hold him on my own, son. And we need time, y'ken?'

Here, among the Sleeping Stones, time spreads thin and wide like wine spilt upon flagstones. I must act soon. But hand and heart talk to each other not.

Max glanced up. Arthur's gaze bore down on her and held her. Whatever he was, this was no ghost, no phantom. The sinews in his forearm tightened as he shifted the weight of his blade.

He was real, she thought, flesh and blood and bone.

The stillness broke and the wind keened in over the fields, rushing between the trees. The flames flattened and crackled. Arthur shifted the sword tip from Max's throat to her ear and she heard the chanting falter in the icy blast.

'I c-can see them,' stammered Emlyn, grabbing her hand. 'The s-sickle man is coming for them.'

Small bright vignettes filled Max's vision. She could not believe that she was seeing what Emlyn saw. But see them she could: the peasants bent low, cutting the grain, their gleaming blades moving in unison; poor harvests and harsh winters; death moving from hut to hall; no-one safe. Her grandmother's – mother's – old saw: the wolf from the door, keep the wolf from the door.

Max shut her eyes. In her mind she could see the tensed muscles in Arthur's arm and sense the impending swing. It would be over now before it had even started. Hot liquid leaked between her thighs and steam rose from her calves. She wanted it to be over but there was only the vein in her neck beating beneath the steel edge and her hand clenching and unclenching in Emlyn's.

91

For Emlyn, the only contact now was Max's hand.

The pastel décor of Huntleighbank Hall filled his vision. The room was stifling. A lamp shone dimly on the bedside table. His father's cheek was pressed against the windowpane. Outside, snow flurries whirled about the Cedar of Lebanon, its branches creaking as it spoke to the night, the bench empty at its base.

Emlyn's father kept his face turned to the window, his voice no more than a whisper. Do you think they'd let me go and sit out under the big tree? I'd keep my coat on.

We need to stop him, Dad. You understand what I mean, don't you?

Stop him? said his father to the glass. You're in her world now, boyo. Standing on the threshold. Or perhaps she's here in our world, I don't know. Time means nothing here. Keep a hold on time is what you're supposed to do. What day is it? Tuesday? I like Tuesdays. We have sausages on Tuesdays.

Emlyn felt the numbing cold envelop him. It would be over soon.

She taunts me for stealing it, for taking the figure. It was Arthur's figure I stole that day, son. I touched it – held it. And they took it from me and put something on my back.

I know, Dad.

The cold took Emlyn, shaking him like a terrier shakes a rat. The teeth of the wind were wrenching him away from his father.

You can't stop him.

Emlyn made a last rally against the icy blast. Max mustn't burn them, he said. Don't you see?

I'm tired. I'm tired of walking the woods and no way out. I don't want to talk any more. Lost, you see.

The room was fading and his father's face remained turned to the window.

Then, quietly, as if talking to himself, Emlyn heard his father say: There's an oak, down by the bridge. Gave the biggest acorns. Merlin's Oak we called it. It's a gateway. A gateway for the gods.

He strained to hold his father but the distance unfolded into night and the cold spun him away, back to the spinney and the dying fire, back into his shivering body.

Arthur's sword was at Max's neck and he could do nothing but watch.

92

Emlyn turned his face towards the dying embers and Max's plight. He was powerless; he couldn't save her, couldn't save himself. For a moment the bitter wind stung his eyes and sucked the breath from his lungs before the sight drew his consciousness into the cold earth.

He was stumbling from the Marchbank towards the bridge. A memory? Or was he back there? Had everything else been a dream? The cold tunnel that was the bridge beckoned to him and he was wrenched away again, spinning into nothing.

I'm dying, he thought.

* * *

A grey, wintry light slanted down through the leaves. Dusk was settling on the snow-covered land like a shroud. This is a different time, he thought peacefully. Intuitively, he knew that this was where it had all begun.

Men on horseback waited among the trees at the edge of the wood. Below, where the marshy ground ran down to the river, a line of cavalry splashed across the shallows. Sensing battle, a horse snorted. The riders sat, their hair braided down the backs of their leather tunics, all with their thoughts, all with an eye on the ford and the approaching column.

Was each afraid of death? Each secretly hoping for life?

And me, thought Emlyn, is this my last vision? Will this be the last thing I see? His back was cold. Why was his back so cold?

Suddenly the voice was there, rich and calm and in his head.

We've moved beyond choices, you and I. Fate has us by the throat.

With effort, he asked, 'Who are you?'

You know well enough who I am, said the voice, *Cei, Arthur's sergeant-at-arms and companion.*

'Why am I here?' said Emlyn.

You are spun in the Lady's web and in my memories, grown so solid with the passing of time. You are both here, witnessing Arthur's last battle and my passing, and in your own time also. We stand in a gateway, you and I. That is the power placed in the wood by the Lady. We must do what we can and trust in providence now.

The girl – the others – I do not think they will fail you.

Spinning out across the fields that led to the fords, Emlyn was aware that he was both there looking back at the trees, at the cavalry edging forward from the wood, Arthur's guard at their head – and, somehow, simultaneously looking out through eyes of the red-bearded warrior at Arthur's side. He could feel the saddle shifting beneath him; a small stone that had worked its way into his boot; the tension around his chest; his fingers closing in readiness upon the sword hilt.

Remember, the gods go with us, says the Lady.

Arthur roars, lifts his lance, and, as the long shadows of the northern autumn creep across the earth, line upon line of horsemen break from the trees and gallop towards the ford.

Out in front with the guard, I do not see Vivienne whisper to her lover, Merlin, do not see her grab his reins and hold back his pony. No, she says. Better that we stay here amongst the trees. We must sing away his power. Not an easy thing, Master Merlin, when a sword is in your hand.

On the field of Camlann the two waves of horsemen mesh, a bloody warp and weft of shrieking men and women.

But Arthur stands, still, thought Emlyn, and will win through, surely. And yet he knows that cannot be, for somewhere he is stretched on the snowy mound, the dying fire at his shoulder and Max's hand in his.

Aye, would that had happened, boy. The prophecy would never have been foretold and you would not have been called by fate. None of us would.

All battles are savage but this – this frenzied willingness to die.

Warriors fall swiftly on either side. Numbers dwindle, leaving only the dead, between which pockets of tired, struggling men swing wildly at each other. It is here, sensing the last throw of the dice, that Modred calls his scattered household to him in twos and threes, and with a grievous cry wins through into the heart of Arthur's circle, driving his lance deep into his rival's side. Bellowing, I throw myself across Modred, and we disappear like drowning men. Trampled, pinned beneath a horse as a rider goes down, Modred's death is slow and painful, stealing over him the next morning as dawn creeps across the hills.

For others death comes fleet.

I fight on, my beard stiff with blood, one eye closing fast, only to fall to a woman's blade. Naked, apart from a breechclout and the blue-painted pattern that covers her body, her hair bound in a tight knot and pinned with gold, this Pictish woman has taken her fallen husband's blade. She comes from behind and I do not see her.

For forty years we pushed the Saxons back and held this country. Is this it? This bloody field; this place called Crooked Glen. How blind: how blind indeed.

The Lady stands among the slaughter. Those of Modred's who remain alive, even the Pictish folk, will not touch her and make the sign against the evil eye. Among the trees on the high ground, Merlin sits astride his pony. She smiles. All has come plain to him and he sees her deception. Climbing from his saddle, he draws back into the forest and his coming madness.

Vivienne's treachery bites deep. For Merlin had expected victory this day and it is Arthur's death that turns his mind. Even with the drawing forth of the Oak God from Arthur's body, he had played the odds, counted the cost, ever sure that Arthur would drive Modred back into his mountain fastness. Were not Arthur, his troops, his guard, seasoned campaigners? Was his arm not strong, his strategies cunning? But Merlin, his sight dulled by the scented laughter of Vivienne, could not see beyond her charms.

Vivienne moves among the dead. Of Arthur's guard, all carry the wooden figures. The amulets have served her purpose and she will have them back, placing each in her bag as the crows and ravens flap from her path. Those who are not dead she finishes with her knife. The horses too, for the men love their beasts more than their women and what are cavalry without their mounts.

There is one more figure she must collect. She comes to me last and kneels at my shoulder. Her face tells all. My eye is forced wide and I cannot look away.

Your time has come, sergeant-at-arms. There is no pity in her voice.

And Arthur? I croak.

She does not reply, but begins her song, knowing that he lies a short distance away, dead, for she has already sung him. I grab her arm, and in touching her I see her plans laid bare.

I look with her eyes.

I see the prophecies and her doubt.

I see the cloaked boy upon the bridge, watching the fish hang lazily above the gravel shoals as I had done as a lad. I see the raven girl as she burns the figures. I see the length of years before I am released.

I understand what will be done. I will wait, a still island of memories in that river we call time. I see what I must do and hate myself for it. For Arthur was betrayed not twice – by Vivienne and Merlin – but thrice.

My betrayal is yet to come.

93

Hugh felt hollow, empty, as his father's song gathered him up, his childhood fear of the dark forcing the chant from him. The old songs of protection rose in his throat, the alien words thick and strange.

'The tin, Hugh! The tin!' His father fell to his knees in the snow and made a sign in the air. 'I canna hold him much longer.'

Time collapsed around Hugh, seconds stretched to breaking point, as he dragged his gaze from the pale figure of Emlyn lying in the snow to Max, and then to the burly frame and the sword arm of the warrior who stood before her. Arthur's eye held his momentarily. Hugh's voice faltered. He was back amid childhood dreams, holding his terror at arm's length. Horses whinnied. He heard the cries of wounded men across the snowy landscape; men yelling in pain and fury.

Someone was shouting his name. It was his father.

Hugh blinked. A spear quivered in the ground at Arthur's feet and the red-bearded warrior dismounted.

'Hugh! The tin! The figure!'

Hugh leapt to Max's side and his hand closed over Arthur's carving, but it was rooted to the ground. He could feel the fibrous strength of it anchored in the earth, the shoots bursting beneath his hand; he could hear the tearing sound as he dragged it from the turf.

94

As Lawrence McCrossan bellowed at Hugh, Arthur twisted from the waist, drawing the sword high above his shoulder. Max watched, her eyes wide, her body shaking uncontrollably, unable to look away. A whimpering noise escaped her lips. Perhaps I'm praying, she thought, as something cut through the air. Thinking it was the blade, thinking that he had swung so fast she hadn't seen it, she called Emlyn's name weakly. There was a thud and a tremor at her feet: her head. Arthur had beheaded her and she hadn't felt a thing. There'd be a moment's pain and then she would be dead.

Something quivered in her field of vision.

Arthur's lance was embedded in the turf at his feet. He turned slowly to look at the last of his guard, the red-bearded horseman beyond the fire. Cei's sword was in his hand. I know his name, thought Max, the question as to how fading as she watched him release Arthur's mare and turn his mount so that he faced Arthur.

Cei's voice was gruff as he dismounted. The language was musical but one Max did not understand. He gestured with his free hand, tugging at his beard occasionally. She knew that he was insulting his Lord, challenging him. Arthur laughed, a deep woodland sound that chilled her, lowered his sword and turned its point towards his adversary.

Hugh was at her side then, almost knocking her over, and there was a sound, as if some great tree was being torn from the earth. As she pushed herself up from the snowy ground, she saw Arthur hesitate and turn, his face full of animal hatred. Again the blade swung back but this time she saw the stroke coming: saw the glimmering edge.

Excalibur flashed in the firelight and another lesser blade swung up and outward. Cei was between them, his parrying thrust deflecting the shimmering edge over her head as she ducked. She felt Hugh fumbling at her side, heard the hiss of the lid as the tin closed.

And Arthur was gone.

95

Emlyn lay with his head in Max's lap. Lawrence McCrossan crouched over the two of them.

'We need to get him to the Land Rover,' he said. Climbing wearily to his feet, he held out the tin. 'Take it, lassie. For the moment.'

Max stared at him. There were so many questions in her mind. He shook his head imperceptibly and she took the tin. Father and son took an arm each, and helping Emlyn up, they started down towards the spinney wall.

'I'm … I can manage,' said Emlyn. 'I saw the battle at the ford.'

'His last battle,' said McCrossan.

Max remained silent: the fire, Arthur's sword, the lance as it skewered the ground, all filled her head.

'My father ... my father was there. The oak by the bridge, he said it was "a gateway".'

McCrossan shuffled to a halt. He stared at Emlyn and then at his son.

'The trunk's split,' said Hugh. 'It was hit by lightning last week.'

'We – me and Max – we were there when it happened,' said Emlyn.

'I think,' McCrossan drew a long breath, 'your father means for us to put the figure in the tree.'

They were at the spinney wall. A short distance away, the Land Rover stood silhouetted against the snow, its engine still running.

'The tin, lassie,' said Lawrence McCrossan. 'It best not go beyond the wall until I've had time to prepare.' Max handed it back to him. 'Can you manage getting him over?'

'We'll be okay,' said Hugh.

They helped Emlyn over the wall into the field and across to the Land Rover, where he sank onto the back seat. A beeping came from the depths of his greatcoat. 'Your phone,' said Max.

'What?'

'It's okay.' She reached in his pocket. 'Text message, that's all.'

'What's it say?'

WHERE HELL R U.
WORRIED SICK
WITH WEATHER.
REPLY NOW. B

Emlyn slid across the seat to the far side and leant his head against the window. Max looked across at the huddled figure. 'I'll make something up.' Illuminated by the display, she composed her message –

STAYING NIGHT
MAX'S. C U
2MORROW. EM

– and pressed send.

Lawrence McCrossan stood inside the spinney wall, one hand deep in his jacket pocket, looking as if he were remembering something painful. He beckoned to Max and she trudged over.

'Will you come with me to the fire? Help me burn him?' Seeing her reaction, he added, 'No, not Arthur.' He pulled out the wooden horseman he had saved from the ice. 'Cei … the last warrior. He helped us at the end. You best climb over before you make up your mind.'

Max stared at the carving, the same one she and Emlyn had handled such a long time ago in her bedroom. She wanted to say no, but he'd handed her the figure before she could reply. As her fingers closed on the wood, she sensed Cei, no longer on foot but astride his mount, waiting up at the mound, the last rider, imprisoned once again now that the stones had been sung afresh.

As Lawrence McCrossan turned in among the trees, Max hopped over the dyke and followed him.

96

Cei, the man would say, there at the first and at the last. But it is I, Arthur's 'faithful' servant, who must betray my Lord, must watch the fire consume my brothers, my brothers-in-arms. I sit astride my horse, the last of his guard, awaiting my fate.

Arthur's fate – or the fate of that which dwelt in him – like Merlin's so long before, was set in train that day beside the pool so long ago. Merlin's figure, carved in secret by Vivienne's hand during those long winter nights, was ever destined for the great oak beside the river. And it is said that Merlin only sleeps. Always a conjurer of storms, the Green One's magic may work still across time and space. It is, perhaps, no accident that severs the lightning-riven bough from the river-oak.

The tapestry that is this tale is almost complete.

Only a few remaining threads need to be drawn tight, but this I must do, for the boy deserves no less.

* * *

As Arthur roared his name and I wrestled my horse to his aid, Merlin dismounted and walked in amid the snowy shelter of the trees. This was no longer the Merlin of legend, but an old man running from the realisation that the world is no longer his to command. A year and a day, until Vivienne's men found him, he would wander the forest, alone with his ravings, waiting for death.

For, although he knew the manner, the hour he could not see.

In her ambition Vivienne sought more powerful friends. Legend has it that it was shepherds, new converts to the faith, who drove Merlin to the river with their stones and their catcalls, but this I doubt. No, they were too well fed, these liegemen of her new husband.

And she too is there, amid the trees, invisible to his weary eye, singing his soul into the oaken figure. Her malice knows no bounds and she will have him bound in darkness.

The catcalls, the first stone – I see it plain as day. For all his powers, Merlin cannot save himself. He totters at the river's edge, heading for the shallower water of the ford so that he might escape his tormentors. It is a vision lived a thousand times: the rocks, the muddy bank, the fall towards the green sliding water; the brutal cry as the pointed stake of the fish trap pierces his flesh; the choking grip of his robe as it tightens about his neck. The green waters are a relief. The twisting eddies and currents speak the language of madness and dreams, for that is what he has become – a dream within a dream.

And here he remains – still – for Merlin was trapped in the great oak. Like me, his memories are all that is left to illuminate the darkness. It is the price paid for power; the price paid for blind love and an old man's desire.

With Merlin gone she turned her attention to us. All this I know because she released us thrice upon the world, calling us forth from behind the standing stones, not ghosts, but flesh and blood sung from the past. For had I not grasped her wrist as I took my dying breath? There was little at that moment she could hide from me. Through her cold eye and chill laughter, thinking she had us in her palm, I saw the cunning of her mind laid bare.

And she could not do with us what she planned.

Twice she tried, with partial success – raiding a neighbouring kingdom, breaking an alliance – but the effort to bend the Oak God to her will proved difficult and she put us away behind the standing stones with signs and words of power. Sometimes she would draw one of us forth to do her bidding.

She was an old woman when we were called upon again.

Her first husband was dead and she took a younger, more ambitious man as her consort. He proved to be her only love. And when, as must happen to all who rule, his kingdom was threatened, she brought us forth from the stones and sung us upon her husband's foes.

Released from our wooden prison, we ravaged their lines, and for a few brief hours she held success in her palm. But the power within Arthur was not so easily controlled, as Master Merlin knew well enough, and we turned upon her husband's men.

Vivienne's third foray went awry, crippling her one true heart.

Her wrath, her savage bitterness, knew no bounds and could not be washed away with wine or covered with fine silk. She cursed Merlin; she cursed Arthur and his line. The wooden figures in which she had placed so much faith had become a hindrance. One spring, with her death the following winter foreshadowing her every thought, she brought us forth for the last time. We were to be burnt.

She knew well enough what this meant. Arthur, caught upon the threshold of her magic, neither in her time nor his, would roam between worlds killing and maiming. And we, his faithful guard, would be trapped, doomed to follow where he led. But her estranged son, Merlin's seed, heard news of this and thwarted her scheme, taking the figures from her at the last moment. How she vowed his ruin.

Fearing another attempt, he had his mother placed in a priory. And there, behind its stout walls of stone, seven novices praying around her deathbed, with the little power she had left, she called down every foul curse she knew upon him and his line.

But as a Christian he knew his task well enough.

Sung afresh, we were placed, with great ritual, in the narrow tomb amid the broken stones, for the long line to watch over.

* * *

They stand quietly, the two of them, he of the long line and the raven girl, watching the flames gather round me.

A memory comes unbidden, forgotten before today, of the settlement lads running through the grass to the river and my sister chasing me because I have called her something foul. But she would not let go of my hand and I am old enough to do as the others do.

I plunge into the green water and strike out for the other bank. My sister cannot swim and must remain upon the shingle with her tiresome chiding. My friends' voices are clear on the summer air. I am being called. And, as the flames devour the wood, their cries turn to those of seabirds.

* * *

The voices of my comrades are calling from the west. I wade ashore, the coarse sand beneath my feet, the salt breeze at my back. The Blessed Isles, their wooded slopes rising from the seashore, stand before me … how long I have held to this dream.

97

'Toss him on,' said Lawrence McCrossan.

Max threw the carving onto the fire, and they watched as it sat amid the embers.

'He'll burn now, along with his comrades.' Something in his voice made Max glance up at the man she now knew to be her father. Tears welled in the corner of his eyes. She felt awkward, her head abuzz with questions.

'How do I know his name?'

'Do you, lassie?'

'Cei,' she said.

'Aye, Arthur's faithful steward and sergeant-at-arms.'

Flames licked at the wooden figure.

'It's caught,' she said.

'Aye, he's burning.'

On the other side of the fire the last rider sat patiently astride his mount. He was as still as stone, but smiling. He shimmered, raised his sword, and was gone.

'Best get the lad back,' said McCrossan. 'Get something warm into him.'

They walked to the dyke and climbed over. McCrossan looked up at the hurrying clouds that were blocking out the stars.

'Wind's backed to the southwest: rain.' As if on cue the first drops fell heavily on the Land Rover. 'Snow'll be gone by morning and the river'll rise.'

'Grandad – might he have survived?' Hugh stood, disconsolate, by the vehicle.

McCrossan shook his head and walked around to the driver's door. Another childhood verse haunted him as he climbed into the cab:

Yarrow said ta Yeave
Though ye run wi' speed
And I run slow
For every man ye kill
I kill twa.

SUNDAY

98

Emlyn leant against the rough stones of the bridge, watching the oak near the river. Two figures were high in its branches. One of them waved – Hugh – and Emlyn waved back. Lawrence McCrossan was threading a wire cable between the branches and looping it around a cut section of car tyre. Father and son were binding the split bough, tightening the cable.

That's how it had started, thought Emlyn, with him wedged in an oak tree. It would be hard to let go of everything that had happened. Part of him wanted to simply shut it all out; another part clung to the already fading images, sifting them, trying to work out which were his memories and which were Cei's. He knew his name now. Cei's voice was fading fast, although he could still hear an echo of it as he stood looking down into the water.

Memory is, at best, perhaps a trick of the light.

You stand there wondering whose voice it is you hear. You know now. There are so many voices: ours, our parents', brothers', sisters' – perhaps, if you are lucky enough, your children.

And there are the old voices.

The trick amongst the sparkling waters of this world is to tease from that riddle one's own song, one's own voice. Mine is fading. The gods have gone back to the earth whence they came and I am not needed any more.

99

Max leant on the parapet wall and stared out across the Marchbank. Her mother spoke, breaking her reverie. 'Your … your sister got herself pregnant the year the sea took her father. She was fast, that one. We were too pedestrian for her. She left for the big smoke.

'I was in the pub one night and I'd had too much to drink. Lawrence was there. We'd known each other since school.'

Max swivelled, watching her mother closely. The woman's eyes were bright and fixed on the distant hills.

'I took off. Newcastle. Your sister was in with some feckless bastard. She soon guessed what was up with me, the morning sickness was that bad. Gary, her son, my grandson, was a cot death. Three months. Wee thing – in a wee grave. She was never that stable, I know that now, but it really turned her. I didn'a see the turn at first. She hid it. She hid a lot o'things, that one. But inside she'd turned a corner and wasn'a coming back.

'I was going to have you adopted. She said why bother. I've lost my son, you dinna want this one. Give her to me. That's what she said, "Give her to me. I'll look after her."'

'This is doing ma head in. I want to call you Mum but it's just not right somehow.'

'Gran's fine for now.' Lindsay Fraser reached into her bag. 'I thought you might like to hand them back.' She was holding Emlyn's field glasses. 'He left them in the spare room.'

Max took the binoculars. There was a figure on the bridge down by Emlyn's cottage. She was close to crying again. She jammed the glasses harder against her eyes and Emlyn pushed himself up from the wall and waved. She swung the glasses across the fields. Two figures were in the branches of the oak. Hugh was waving back. Max lowered the field glasses and leant further onto the wall so that her mother couldn't see her face.

There had been a knock at the front door earlier

that morning. Her mother had answered it. The silence and the footfalls in the hallway had told Max who it was before the kitchen door opened and she had drawn a long breath as if it were her last.

* * *

Lawrence McCrossan took off his cap.

'You need to … I need to say this.'

Max folded her arms and he shifted his feet uneasily. 'The boy,' he said, 'Emlyn, is he …?

'He's asleep still,' said Mrs Fraser. 'I've no idea what you were up to last night,' she said, raising her hand to cut off McCrossan, 'an' I dinna want to know. But that lad's been through the mill. He'll be waking of his own accord, y'ken.'

He nodded and looked at Max. 'I don't know what your … what Lindsay's told you. You're my daughter. I'm your father. She's your mother–'

'You're not to blame,' said Lindsay Fraser.

'She's–' McCrossan bit his lip, searching for words. 'Your mother's trying to make – she's in shock. None of this fits properly for any of us. Please, I'll not be long saying this. What's happened has happened, we canna turn it back and I dinna just mean this – us – blood – I mean what's happened in the valley this past week. Anyway, what I'm trying to say is that this place is special. But to me it's special in a different way … there's a power in this valley.' He turned to Lindsay Fraser. 'There's something you should understand.'

'Lawrence, please–'

Max flinched: the name sounded strange. She was going to have to make some adjustments. They both were.

'No, I knew you were pregnant,' said McCrossan. 'We were drunk as lords that night. I wanted to come after you. But you shot through so quick. And I couldn'a leave.'

Max snorted. 'Hah!'

'This valley is a prison for me in the same way that those wooden figures were a prison for–'

Lindsay Fraser was staring at Lawrence McCrossan.

'You must've left,' said Max. 'Surely! Sometime?'

'Aye, a couple of times … but never far … before I took my father's place. I'm the keeper – I dinna mean ma job – keeping the horsemen behind the dyke, keeping them from hurting anyone. Our task, see – that what was inside the carvings never got loose in the valley. There's a price that comes with that. Like those before me, I canna leave. Aye, you can look at me. But I'm wedded to the ground we're stood on. It's like a curse. I took it willingly, so I'll no' complain. But I canna leave.'

'What,' said Max, 'you'll die or something?'

'Aye. Or worse. Not too many have tried it. I can go round about: into the next valley, downriver a ways, up into the hills. I always turn back. I always know. It sounds ridiculous, what with all our science and rockets and wee phones. Mebbe it'll change once we've dealt with the last of 'em – after we've done here, me and Hugh, well, we're putting it into the big oak by the river – an' I've a mind it might. But I have a mind I'll be testing the water – y'ken – before leaving the valley and rushing away down to Berwick.'

Max and Lindsay stared at him.

'I know you think what I did, to Emlyn and you, I did out of malice ... and you'd be partly right. But my family has sworn an oath time out of mind that the horsemen be contained at all cost.' He donned his cap and Mrs Fraser managed a lame grin. 'Anyhow, I've said ma piece.'

'Hugh's my brother then?'

Lawrence McCrossan's voice was thick and the words seemed to quiver in the air around them. 'Your half-brother, aye.'

'What about,' she couldn't say the name, 'Emlyn's dog?'

He pulled his cap off and crushed it between his hands.

'Aye, Hugh told me. Still, he's the pup, eh?'

'Digger's dead, like. Right?'

'Aye, I'd say so, lassie. My father was–' He faltered and looked away momentarily. 'Whatever I say … if I say he treated his own animals no better, y'ken?'

Max nodded.

Lawrence McCrossan paused by the door. 'Like I said, we're putting it to rest, putting the wee man back into Merlin's Oak later this morning.'

Max heard the words, the unspoken invitation, come at her from a great distance. She shook her head and McCrossan left, her mother on his tail. Standing there amid the clutter of small objects her mother had collected over her life, it seemed to Max that she had taken root.

100

'You say they're putting the carving into the oak tree by the bridge?' said her mother. 'Although, I'll not pretend I understand all that.'

'Here.' Max passed across the binoculars. Her mother raised them gingerly. 'You're to say nowt, to no-one – about the figure and what's happening down there.'

'As if I, of all people, canna keep a secret.'

'Aye. With secrets, you're top drawer.'

Lindsay Fraser lowered the field glasses and handed them back.

'Daughter, granddaughter,' she said, looking at Max directly for the first time that morning, 'you're still blood. Anyway, I'm away to do a spot of shopping. You look as if you've a mind to stay up here a wee bit longer.'

Lost in thought, Max nodded and then turned to speak to her mother. ‘He’s nice – Emlyn – in an odd sort of way, I mean. But he’s just, y’know – a boy, really.’

But her mother had already turned away down the narrow walkway. As she picked her way down the steps, she was muttering to herself. Max thought she caught the words before they were carried away on the breeze: ‘Aye, just a boy. Are they not always the source of a woman’s troubles.’

101

'Pay attention,' said Lawrence McCrossan, 'or you'll be out of the tree.'

Hugh ceased waving to Emlyn on the bridge, shifted his weight, and reached for the bamboo cane being pushed between the branches. Taped to its length was the steel cable that would pull together the split branches of the oak.

'Emlyn's over at the bridge.'

'Dinna fret, I see him well enough.' Hugh's father pointed to the heavy bough that had split away from the main trunk and was held only by another branch of even greater girth. 'Now, have you any ideas about how to get it around the outside there?'

'Climb out.'

Hugh squirmed between the branches until he could get his foot onto the huge bough. Pulling himself up, he inched his way out until he could pass the bamboo around the stricken branch. Once he had everything in position he let the rod dangle and, swinging it gently to-and-fro, arced it towards his father, who threaded the cable ends into a small hand winch. Slowly he cranked the lever and the belly disappeared from the wire. Hugh pulled a worn piece of car tyre from where he had it wedged in the fork of a branch.

'Slip it in behind the cable. Hold it 'til I've picked up the slack.'

Hugh threaded the tyre into place and watched as the cable took the strain. The heavy branch trembled and began to straighten. Father and son looked at one another across the gap of interlacing branches.

'It'll work,' said Hugh.

His father looked down at the base of the tree. Hugh followed his gaze. A battered case sat open on the grass. Inside sat a single wooden horseman surrounded by a circle of flat river slates. Each stone had a symbol chalked on its surface. A length of twine was tied around the figure and looped upwards to a branch near his father's elbow.

'I want it to work well enough, laddie. It's just that – all those years. All those lives: for what?'

Lawrence McCrossan looked at his son, shrugged and pulled the twine tight, making the wooden horseman spin. 'We've a few minutes' grace at best here, y'ken.'

The carving skidded and jiggled across the bottom of the suitcase and then swung clear in time to their chanting. Down at the river a horse splashed through the shallows, scattering birds from the reeds. The rider galloped towards the oak. McCrossan had the figure in his hand. Gently, he paid out the twine and lowered the rider into the gap, his other hand steadily cranking the winch.

Hugh watched as the split closed over the twine; heard the squeal of wood on wood. Glancing down, he looked for the rider, but it was gone. There was only the sound of birds, the breeze high in the oak branches, and the drone of a car crossing the bridge. High above them, a con-trail left its feathery signature across the sky.

102

'What you looking at?' said Hugh.

Emlyn was leaning out over the water. He had been listening to the voice as it faded.

'Sorry, what was that?' said Emlyn, shaking himself from the dream. 'Oh, yes, the grayling. They like the shallows here. The river'll be too high today.'

'And likely to stay that way for a while. I've a rod you could borrow,' said Lawrence McCrossan. 'If you've a mind. Once she's down.'

Emlyn shook his head and the three of them stood awkwardly on the bridge.

'Will that be the end of it?' Emlyn asked, looking at McCrossan.

'I canna feel him any more. Only time will tell if we've truly put him to rest.'

A vehicle shot from between the flanks of the Marchbank and came barrelling down the straight.

'Here we go,' sighed Emlyn.

Bridget screeched to a stop with the driver's door hard up against the hedge. Squeezing across the seat, she straightened her clothes, slammed the passenger door, and ignoring Hugh and his father, stalked onto the bridge.

'Whose clothes are those?'

'I had to borrow them. It's a long story.'

'Have you any idea how long I've been driving around town looking for you? Get in the car.'

'If I get in first you won't be able to get in,' said Emlyn.

'Hey, I've had it with your smart answers.'

'Where are we going?'

'Home.'

'We are home.' Emlyn gestured at the nearby cottage.

'For a drive,' said Bridget. 'We're going for a drive. During which you can bloody well explain what's been going on. I've already phoned Mum and she's really rattled about having to drive all the way up here.'

'This wouldn't be about a small wooden figure, would it, lassie?'

Bridget rounded on Lawrence McCrossan, fixing him with her gaze. Emlyn stared dumbfounded at the gamekeeper.

'What the hell's going on?'

'Dinna upset yourself,' said McCrossan. 'There's a perfectly rational explanation, I can assure you.'

'What, like his little mate on the horse? Have you any idea how much your little show upset me, Emlyn? Have you?'

McCrossan was already chanting.

'Oh, a cabaret performance: lovely. Emlyn, just do as I say and get in the–'

His sister seemed to lose her focus, twisting to face each of them in turn, as Hugh's voice joined in. The hairs prickled on Emlyn's neck. A long time ago the same words must have been used against his father. He watched Bridget's face, watched the anger and hostility dissipate and felt sorry for her. There was something here that she would never grasp, a world she and his mother had cut themselves off from long ago.

The singing ceased. His sister wore a vague expression.

'There was something I was going to ask you, Emlyn, but it's gone. Oh, Mr McCrossan, I didn't see you there. Would you tell your father that he can pick up the rent tomorrow?'

McCrossan nodded. Hugh looked at his shoes.

'Right,' said Bridget. 'I'm away to the dig.'

Back at the car she looked puzzled for a moment over its position before sliding across into the driver's seat.

'You can still sing her,' said Emlyn, 'even though the figures are gone?'

'Like I said to your friend Max, earlier, there's a power in this valley … it's like an echo chamber, carryin' and holdin' everything. Fifteen hundred years those songs have been sung. It'll no be washed away like the ice on the river, y'ken?'

'Will anything come back to her?' said Emlyn. 'Bridget, I mean.'

'No, laddie, it won't.'

'Can–' Emlyn paused, struggling to control his voice. 'Can you un-sing somebody?'

'Your father, you mean?'

Emlyn nodded.

'No.' Lawrence McCrossan registered the disappointment that clouded the boy's face. 'But I owe you some sort of explanation. My father was old school: a stand or fall, black-and-white man. When he sung your dad that day, when he made me sing with him, there was the weight of fifteen hundred years behind it. Like I said, this valley's an echo chamber.

'Nobody goes – went up to the Sleeper's Stones because they didn'a really register it, d'you ken what I'm saying? It might be on *the* map but it wasn'a on *their* map, their radar, if you like. For some reason it was different for your father and you.'

Emlyn nodded again. 'The place sort of spoke to me.' He didn't mention the voice.

'It's an old place, right enough,' said McCrossan. 'The standing stones, the tomb, who knows how old they'd be. Most of the stone ring was incorporated into the dyke when it was built.'

They walked off the bridge.

'Can we give you a lift?'

'I think I'll watch the water for a bit longer.'

Emlyn looked on as the McCrossans walked to the Land Rover: he wanted desperately to ask about Digger.

'Changed your mind?' said McCrossan, climbing in alongside his son.

Emlyn shook his head. 'Thanks all the same.' The words were broken bones in his chest; they needed to heal before he could speak them aloud. The pup was at Max's. He'd already decided to call him Digger.

103

Max pedalled furiously through the Marchbank and out onto the straight. The McCrossans drove past, waving and nodding, and were gone. She cranked the bike harder until she reached the bridge.

'What … no Beezer?' said Emlyn.

'I've to get ma licence before I touch it again.' They watched the water in silence. 'You anything planned?'

'Pop out to Huntleighbank. Tomorrow after school, maybe. See my dad.'

'Could I come, like? With what's happened, somehow I'd like to see him, just the once mebbe. Emlyn?'

He shrugged and nodded. 'You want to go for a walk?'

'Sure.'

Emlyn couldn't explain it but he wanted to be up high, somewhere above the everyday business that was Yeaveburgh. He was thinking of the hills, but he did not think Max would relish the suggestion, and he was loath to let her go just yet. 'The castle.'

Max didn't have the heart to say that she'd just come from there. She rattled her bike. 'I'll have to drop this off home.'

'Leave it by the barbican. It's hardly likely to get nicked.'

She laughed and they walked down off the bridge. They were almost to the Marchbank before they spoke.

'Wha'y'thinking?' said Max.

'All that stuff we're fed about Arthur being a king, even though he wasn't or anything–'

'All that guff about knights and round tables?'

'Yeah,' said Emlyn, 'well, in the end he was sort of crowned.'

'How'd'ya mean?'

'The dyke, around the spinney, and the standing stones, they're kind of like a crown.'

'Put a fair old dent in it, eh.' Max laughed. 'Never liked the royals, me. Even if I do want ma own coat of arms.'

'Try something different every week, eh.' Emlyn chuckled and then became serious. 'You really want to come out to Huntleighbank? You don't have to–'

'Is he–?'

'Mad?'

'Yeah, I suppose that's what I'm on about. You know, will he act strange or anything?'

'Mostly he just sits outdoors. There's a big tree out in the garden but it's getting a bit cold now.'

She winked at him and grinned. 'Aye, but just because I'm meeting your father doesn'a make us engaged or anything.'

104

Out on the Edinburgh road Emlyn coasted along beneath the trees. Winter had passed and the spring sunlight flickered across his face. The road was straight and clear of traffic. He aimed the bike and shut his eyes. The scintillation turned blood red under his eyelids. It seemed that he had ridden through that warm tunnel forever.

He opened his eyes. The bike had veered to the middle of the road. The broken white line disappeared beneath his front wheel. Huntleighbank Hall was around the next bend, but he was in no hurry to get there. His father would be sitting on his bench under the Cedar of Lebanon. They would take the crossword out and sit together: read the clues; fill in the blanks. He was getting better at solving them now.

SOURCES

The childhood verse that haunts Lawrence McCrossan as he climbs into the Land Rover after they've burnt the figures is a re-working of the traditional seventeenth century 'Two Rivers' taken from Arthur Quiller-Couch's *The Oxford Book of English Verse: 1250–1900*:

> SAYS Tweed to Till—
> *'What gars ye rin sae still?'*
> *Says Till to Tweed—*
> *'Though ye rin with speed*
> *And I rin slaw,*
> *For ae man that ye droon*
> *I droon twa.'*
>
> (ANONYMOUS)

For those readers interested in following up the notion of Arthur as a Dark Ages cavalry commander in the Scottish Borders, I recommend *Arthur and the Lost Kingdoms* by Alistair Moffat.

Acknowledgements

On the family side of things my thanks to Niki for encouraging me down this path and for her love, support and a constant belief; to my three sons, Alexis, Cei and Taliesin for grounding me; to Elishia and Adaya for bringing a new dimension to our family; to Graham, Tess, Greg, Aileen, Bert, Maria and John Crawford, and Sophia Koukouvas for their kindness and generosity whenever I go back to Europe; to Maria Vouis; and to Maida and Dick for my first introduction to Scotland.

In getting the novel on its feet I wish to thank Tom Shapcott for his insights and astonishing reading ability; the University of Adelaide Creative Writing program, the teaching and administrative staff in the Discipline of English, in particular the office staff: Shirley Ball, Bev Thomson, Michelle Lai, and Sue Mleczko; Gary Crew for his mentorship and shrewd insights into the genre; Sue Whiting, for her unstinting editorial expertise; Walker Books Australia for their unswerving support; my agents Mulcahy & Viney, and in particular Jonathan Conway for his enthusiasm and generous suggestions; Jane

Covernton for being brave enough to read one of the first drafts; Sue Williams, for her friendship and insights into the industry; Mark Caldicott for his back-to-back support, friendship and readiness to read drafts hot off the press; Kerrie Le Lievre for her knowledge of fantasy literature and for reading a later draft; Liam and Courtenay Hanson-Molam for test-driving the first few chapters; and the crew up at Flinders University, who started the ball rolling.

Special thanks are due to the people of the Borders, particularly Marjorie Blake for her help and hospitality; John Hawkins of the Trimontium Trust; Alistair Moffat for *Arthur and the Lost Kingdoms*; Inspector Kevin Murray and Constable John MacDougall; Jimmy and Prim Nairn; the Rector of Kelso High School, Charles Robertson, together with the School Band; Brian Wain; and Gillian Waite. Across the border I'd like to thank Matthew Johnson, Paul Mercias and John Tremelling.

A special thank you to Russell Beedles for being there at the beginning. And to the 'Exeter Brigade' – Patrick Allington, Anne Bartlett, Tony Bujega, Jan Harrow, Sabina Hopfer, Heather Johnson, and Christopher Lappas – in their metamorphosis from reading group to luncheon party to bar-flies.

Many thanks to the following people who have

been helpful in a myriad of ways: Angela Baker, Tully Barnett, Russell Bartlett, Phil Butterss, Ian Bone, Guy Carney, Kaye Cleave, Annabelle Collett, Jon Dale, Dallas Colley, Phillip Edmonds, Ruth Fazakerley, Liz Fotiadis, Zoë Gill, Kate Greenwood, Rob Hall, Julie Hanson, Zoia Harrison, Rosanne Hawke, Rachel Hennessy, Stephanie Hester, Sue and Rick Hosking, Alan Jenkins, Nicholas Jose, Maxine Joy, Sylvia Kelso, Heather Kerr, Mark Kimber, Mike Ladd, Elizabeth Lau, Marianne and Brian Lewis, Sandra Lyne, Alison Main, Denise and James Martin, Amy Matthews, Joy McEntee, Tony and Carol Moore, Vanna Morosini, Amanda Nettelbeck, Alison Newton, Simon O'Mallon, Sarah Minney, Paul Mitchell, Deborah Paauwe, Helen Payne, Michelle Phillipov, Lucy Potter, David Richards, Jim Roberts, Roy Roberts, Anne Robertson, Steve and Nola Routoulas, Ken Ruthven, Maggie Tonkin, Mandy Treagus, Ray Tyndale, Lee Salomone, Stephen Shortt, Greg Smith, Anna Solding, Rudi Soman, Catherine Wait, Rikki Wilde, Lesley Williams, Sean Williams, Tony Wilson, Farley Wright, Wendy Wright, Su-bo Xu, and John and Jenny Zammit.

Although dedicated to my parents, the novel is also in memory of Dorian Barnett, Antonios and Kalliope Koukouvas, Anne Murton, and Sue Williams, whose stories are indelibly interwoven with my own.

OUTLAW: THE LEGEND OF ROBIN HOOD - A GRAPHIC NOVEL

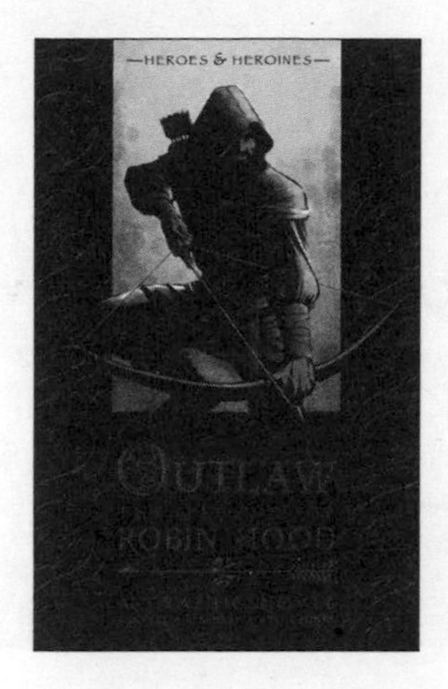

The year is 1192. The Sheriff and his men rule Nottingham with a savage fist of iron. In the haunted heart of Sherwood Forest, Robin devises a heroic plan. He will disguise himself and become an outlaw. He will see that justice is done for the people. But there are traitors in his camp, and it is not long before a hefty price is levied on Robin Hood's head...

Fast-paced graphic storytelling in a stunning full-colour, action-packed tale of the legendary hero.

Look out also for Beowulf as a graphic novel.

TONY LEE, SAM HART, ARTUR FUJITA

In the wild landscape of Dark Age Britain, Essa is abandoned by his father in a lonely marsh-village trapped between two warring kingdoms. Destined to become tangled in the bitter feud, Essa's part in it is more important than he ever dreamed. But how will Essa save those he loves and discover the secret of his true identity when he can trust no one?

"A rich, vivid historical fantasy and a tremendously assured first novel." *Philip Reeve.*

Follow the story of Essa's ancestors in Bloodline Rising...